CANDACE CAMP

A *Gentleman* ALWAYS REMEMBERS

POCKET **STAR** BOOKS

New York London Toronto Sydney

Pocket Star Books
A Division of Simon & Schuster, Inc.
1230 Avenue of the Americas
New York, NY 10020

This book is a work of fiction. Names, characters, places, and
incidents either are products of the author's imagination or are
used fictitiously. Any resemblance to actual events or locales or
persons, living or dead, is entirely coincidental.

First Pocket Star Books paperback edition June 2010

POCKET STAR BOOKS and colophon are registered trademarks
of Simon & Schuster, Inc.

For information about special discounts for bulk purchases, please
contact Simon & Schuster Special Sales at 1-866-506-1949 or
business@simonandschuster.com.

The Simon & Schuster Speakers Bureau can bring authors to your
live event. For more information or to book an event, contact the
Simon & Schuster Speakers Bureau at 1-866-248-3049 or visit
our website at www.simonspeakers.com.

Designed by Jill Putorti
Cover illustration by Alan Ayers
Hand lettering by Ronn Zinn

Manufactured in the United States of America

10 9 8 7 6 5 4 3 2 1

ISBN 978-1-4391-1798-9
ISBN 978-1-4391-5771-8 (ebook)

A Gentleman
ALWAYS
REMEMBERS

Chapter 1

In a few days she would be gone. Eve Hawthorne could almost taste freedom.

No more lectures from a stepmother only eight years older than herself. No more tight-lipped frowns at a remark deemed too frivolous. No more having to endure the heavy-handed attempts at matchmaking with whatever widower or bachelor her stepmother hoped might be willing to take Eve off their hands.

When Eve's husband died two years ago, he had left her, at twenty-six years of age, not only alone but nearly penniless. The Hawthornes had never been renowned for their ability to keep money in their pockets, and Bruce, the youngest son of a middle son of an earl, had had no income beyond his military commission, which had made it even more difficult for him to stay within his means. Eve used what little money Major Hawthorne had left her to pay off his debts, and even then she had been forced to sell their furniture and many of their belongings in order to satisfy his creditors. She had had no recourse but to return to her father's home to live.

After almost eight years of marriage and managing her own life and household, it would have been hard in any case to have once more become a dependent child, but since Eve's father had remarried several years earlier, Eve had found herself living not only on the Reverend Childe's charity but on that of her stepmother as well. It had not been a welcome situation for either woman.

Eve faced her stepmother now, determined to keep a pleasant smile on her face. Surely these last few days they could manage to get along without their usual subtle struggle.

"It is a beautiful day, Imogene," Eve observed. "Quite pleasant and warm for September. And Julian has finished all his lessons. Did he tell you how well he did in Latin?"

Eve realized as soon as she said it that her words had been a mistake. Much as Imogene Childe reveled in her son's intelligence and education, it was always a sore spot with her that she herself had not received the sort of classical education that Eve had had at the hands of the Reverend Childe. She did not like to be reminded that Eve helped her father teach Julian, whereas Imogene, his own mother, could not.

"I am aware of Julian's achievement in the subject," Imogene responded, her mouth pruning up. "But he has not made the progress he has by ignoring his studies and running off to play."

Eve knew better than to advance the argument that her half brother needed some time to play just as he did to study. Instead, she said, "But Julian will not be playing; we will be observing nature. The animals . . . the plants . . . the ways in which autumn is making changes in them. Besides, it is important for Julian to observe the beauty and wonder of the world that God has made for us, is it not?"

She smiled at Imogene sweetly, knowing that the pious woman would have more difficulty combating this argument.

But it was Julian himself who clinched it. "Please, Mother?" he asked, looking his most angelic. "Auntie Eve will be here only a few more days, and then she and I can't do this anymore."

The thought of her stepdaughter's imminent departure brightened Imogene's expression, and, with a sigh, she relented. "Very well, you may go with your aunt, Julian." She turned her gaze to Eve. "But pray, do not bring him home muddy again or with grass stains all over his clean shirt."

"We shall do our very best to stay clean," Eve promised her. She no longer tried to make her stepmother understand that one could not expect a young boy to remain perfectly tidy unless he did nothing but sit in a chair all day.

Mrs. Childe nodded, the tight corkscrew curls on either side of her face bouncing. "You had best remember, Eve, that the Earl of Stewkesbury is not looking for someone who will let his cousins run wild. The Talbots are one of the finest families in England. He wants a woman who is a model of decorum. Those girls' reputations will depend on what you do as their chaperone. It is a heavy responsibility, and I hope the earl will not regret entrusting it to someone as young and frivolous in attitude as you."

Eve managed to retain her smile, though it was more a grimace than an expression of humor or goodwill at this point. "I will keep that in mind, ma'am, I promise you."

After picking up her long-brimmed bonnet and tying it on, Eve followed her half brother out of the house and across the yard, cutting through the churchyard and cemetery to the beckoning field beyond. She smiled to herself as she watched Julian race ahead, then squat to observe some insect making its way through the grass.

The thought of leaving Julian behind was the only thing that tugged at her heart, marring somewhat the joy of leaving this house. Her half brother had made the past two years bearable, easing her grief over Bruce with his warm affection. Even his mother's rigid rules and sanctimonious airs had seemed less bothersome when Julian slipped his small hand in hers and smiled at her or tilted his head to the side like a curious sparrow as he asked her a question. Eve's marriage had been childless, which had long been a sorrow to her, but Julian's presence in her life had helped fill that hole in her heart.

It would pain her to leave him, but in only a couple of years Julian would be sent off to Eton as his father had been before him, and then Eve would be left in the house with only the company of her studious, abstracted father and her carping stepmother. It was a prospect to make one's blood run cold.

That was why Eve had jumped at the opportunity to chaperone Lord Stewkesbury's American cousins. Lady Vivian Carlyle, Eve's friend since childhood, was also close to the Talbot family, headed by the Earl of Stewkesbury. Lady Vivian had written Eve recently to say that the earl was in desperate need of a chaperone for his young cousins who had arrived in London from the United States. It seemed that the chaperone Stewkesbury had first hired to help the young women enter English society had proved entirely unsuitable. What was needed, Vivian had written, was a woman of good family who could act as an older sister or young aunt to the girls, taking them under her wing and instructing them—as much by example as teaching—in the things they would need to know to make their way successfully through a London Season. Vivian had thought immediately of Eve and wanted to know if she would be interested in traveling to Willowmere, the country seat of the Talbot family, to assume the position of chaperone.

Eve had written back to assure her friend that she would indeed welcome the opportunity to chaperone the American girls. In reply, she had received a letter from the earl himself, offering her a generous stipend for her troubles and stating

that he would send a carriage to bring her to Willowmere—
a gesture Eve found most gracious, though it was doubtless
inspired more by the fact that she was a friend of Lady Vivian than by any concern for Eve's own person.

The earl had given her two weeks in which to pack and
prepare for her journey, which meant that the carriage was
scheduled to arrive anytime in the next two or three days.
She had only these last few days to enjoy her half brother's
company, and she intended to take full advantage of them.
So she put all of her stepmother's injunctions out of her
mind and followed the boy through the field and down to
the brook.

They paused to watch the antics of a red squirrel and
later to investigate the remains of a bird nest that had fallen
from a tree. Julian had a healthy curiosity about all things
in nature, both flora and fauna, and Eve did her best to
read enough to keep up with his questions. She had never
thought to learn so much about butterflies, or pheasants
and robins, or birches, beeches, and oak trees as she had the
last two years, but she had enjoyed exploring such topics—
though she could not deny the little ache in her heart when
she thought of how it would have been if she had children
of her own with whom to share these wonders.

Before long they reached the brook that lay east of town
and followed it to a large rock perfectly arranged for sitting and watching the shallow stream as it burbled its way
over the rocks. Eve took off her bonnet and gloves and set
them aside, followed by her walking boots and stockings.
She kilted up her skirt and waded into the water after Julian,
bending down to look at the little fish arrowing past their
feet or chasing after a frog as it bounded from rock to rock.

Imogene's strictures were ignored as they laughed and
darted about. Julian had more than one streak of mud upon
his shirt, and the bottoms of his trousers had been liberally

splashed with water. His hands were grubby and his cheeks red, his eyes sparkling with pleasure. Eve, looking at him, wanted to grab him and squeeze him tight, but she was wise enough not to do so.

She was standing in the brook when she heard the sound of a horse's hooves, and realized that they must have drawn closer to the road than she had thought. She turned to climb up the bank, and a small snake brushed her foot as it slithered by her. Eve let out a shriek, forgetting all about the road and the horse, and Julian fell into a fit of laughter.

"Oh, hush, Jules!" she told him crossly, then had to chuckle herself. She was sure she must have presented quite a sight, jumping straight up into the air as if she had been shot. "'Twasn't funny."

"Yes, it was," the boy protested. "*You're* laughing."

"He has you there," a voice said from behind them.

Eve whirled around. There, on the small wooden bridge that crossed the stream, stood an elegant black stallion, and on its back was a man with hair as black as the steed's. They were both, man and horse, astoundingly handsome.

She felt as if the air had been punched out of her, and she could only stare at the man, bereft of words. The rider swept off his hat and bowed to her, and his hair glimmered as black as a raven's wing in the sunlight. His eyes were a bright, piercing blue and ringed by thick black lashes as straight and dark as the eyebrows that slashed across his face above them. Even on horseback, it was obvious that he was tall, his shoulders wide in his well-cut blue jacket. A dimple popped into his cheek as he grinned down at her, showing even white teeth. It was clear at a glance that he was the sort of man who was used to charming anyone he met.

"Hullo," Julian called pleasantly when Eve did not speak,

and he splashed out of the water and up the bank toward the man.

The stranger swung off his mount with a careless grace and led his horse off the bridge and down the embankment toward them. "I had not hoped to find a naiad on my travels today," he said to Eve, and his bright eyes swept appreciatively down her form.

Eve was suddenly, blushingly, aware of how she must look. Her dress was hiked up, exposing all of her legs below her knees, and her bonnet was off, her hair coming loose from its pins and straggling down in several places, her face flushed with exercise and heat.

"What's a naiad?" Julian asked.

"A water nymph," the man explained.

"And something *I* am not." Coloring furiously, Eve jerked her skirts down and shook them into place. There was little she could do about her bare feet or her hatless state, of course, for her shoes and bonnet lay several yards behind them on the rock. Her hands went to her hair, trying to tuck some of the stray strands into place.

"That is always what demigoddesses claim," the man went on easily, still smiling as he came up to them. "But even we poor mortal men can see their true beauty."

Up close, Eve could see the tiny lines that radiated from the corners of his eyes and the dark shadow of approaching beard along his jaw. If anything, such imperfections only served to make him even more handsome. Looking at him set up a jangling of nerves in Eve's stomach, and the afternoon seemed suddenly warmer and more airless than it had moments before.

"Don't be absurd." Eve tried for a tart tone, but she could not keep from smiling a little. There was simply something engaging about the man's grin, so easy and friendly.

"What else am I to think?" He arched a brow, his blue eyes dancing. "Coming upon such a lovely creature, the water running around her, the sun striking gold from her hair. Even the animals yearn to be close to you."

"Like the snake!" Julian giggled.

"Exactly." The stranger nodded at the boy gravely. He turned back to Eve. "There. Even a child can see it. Though, of course"—he tilted his head, considering—"one would think a nymph would be more at ease with the creatures of the fields and brooks than to scream at the sight of a snake."

"I did not scream," Eve protested. "And it wasn't the sight of it, it was the *feel*." She gave an expressive shudder, and both Julian and the stranger chuckled.

She should not be talking with such ease to a complete stranger, Eve knew, even if he was absurdly easy to talk to. She felt sure that Imogene would tell her that such charm was the hallmark of a rake. But Eve was not feeling cautious today. For the past two years she had done her best to live by her stepmother's rules, and soon she would have to be prim and proper, befitting the chaperone of young women. Surely she could steal this day, this moment, for herself. She could even flirt a little with an attractive stranger. After all, who was to know?

"It occurs to me that I should stay and guard you from such dangers," he said, and the dimple flashed again as his lips curved into a smile. "Who knows what sort of creature might need slaying? Indeed, I should probably escort you home."

"'Tis most kind of you, sir, but I cannot trouble you. You were clearly on your way somewhere."

He shrugged. "That can wait. It isn't every day that a man can rescue a nymph, or even a maiden."

Eve raised a skeptical brow. "I already have a champion." She glanced toward her brother, who had already tired of their conversation and was digging into the ground with a stick.

"I can see that." The stranger's eyes followed hers to Julian. "I can scarcely compete." He turned back to her. "But there may be other times when you are out without your champion. Times when some company might be welcome. I should be happy to offer you my services as an escort."

"I would not wish to delay you on your journey." Eve's eyes danced as she waited for his response.

"But I have arrived at my destination. It is my good fortune to be stopping in the village ahead."

"You are most kind," Eve responded demurely, casting a twinkling look up at him through her lashes. It had been a long time since she had flirted with a handsome man. Had she forgotten how pleasurable it was? Or was it this man who made it pleasurable? "Perhaps, if you are in the village for a time, we might chance to meet again."

"I can make sure that I am here for a time." For a moment the laughter was gone from his eyes, replaced by a warmth that Eve felt all the way down to her toes. "If you would but tell me where I might chance upon you taking a stroll?"

Eve let out a little laugh. "Ah, but that would make it far too easy, would it not?"

He moved closer, so that she had to tilt her head back to look up at him. "I do not think that you are making it at all easy for me."

He reached out, and Eve's breath caught in her throat, for she thought he was about to touch her cheek. But then he plucked a leaf from her hair and held it up to let the breeze take it.

Leaning in, his voice lowered, he said, "Surely a naiad should pay a token, should she not, for getting caught by a mortal?"

A frisson of excitement ran down her spine. "A token?"

"Yes. A price. A forfeit. They always do so in stories—grant a wish or give a present. . . ."

"But I have no gift to give you." Eve knew she should back up, should cease her flirting. But something held her; she could not look away from his bright eyes, could not stop the anticipation blossoming in her.

"Ah, that is where you are wrong, my nymph."

He bent and kissed her.

His lips were firm and warm, the kiss brief. And at the touch, Eve seemed to flame into life. She was suddenly, tinglingly, aware of everything—the sun on her back, the breeze that lifted the loose strands of her hair, the scent of the grass from the meadow, all mingling in a heady brew with the sensations, sudden and intense, spreading through her body.

He lifted his head, and for a long moment all she could do was stare up at him, her mouth slightly open in a soft O of astonishment, her eyes wide.

"I—I must leave." With an effort, Eve turned away. "Come, Jules, we'd best get back."

Her brother, still digging in the dirt, raised his head and turned. "Already?"

"There. You see? It has been too short a time. Pray do not leave when I have only just met you," the man protested.

"I fear we must." Eve backed up quickly, stretching her hand out toward Julian.

"At least tell me your name." He took a step after her.

"No—oh, no, I must not." She stopped and looked at him, still dazed by the swift tumble of emotions inside her.

"Then allow me to introduce myself." He swept her an elegant, formal bow. "I am Fitzhugh Talbot, at your service."

Eve stared at him, chilled. "Talbot?"

"Yes. I have business at the vicarage in the village, so you can see that I am perfectly respectable."

Talbot! The vicarage! Eve let out a little choked noise, and, grabbing Julian by the hand, she whirled and fled.

Eve ran along the bank of the stream, pulling Julian along after her. When she reached the rock, she picked up her things, not daring to glance back. She could only pray that Mr. Talbot would not take it into his head to follow her.

"Auntie Eve!" Julian did not have to be told to pick up his own shoes and stockings; he was clever enough to have caught on to the urgency of the situation. "What are we doing? Why are we running?" He turned his head and glanced back toward the road.

"He isn't following us, is he?" Eve asked.

"No. He's leading his horse back to the road." Julian paused. "Is he a bad man?"

"What? No. Oh, no. Pray do not think that." Eve paused to put her shoes back on and help Julian into his, then struck out across the field at as fast a pace as her brother could keep up. "I think he is the man who is coming to take me to Willowmere."

Talbot was the family name of the Earl of Stewkesbury. This man must be a relation of some sort whom the earl had sent to escort her. She dreaded what he would think when he realized that the "water nymph" he had seen cavorting in the brook, shoes and hat off, hair tumbling down, was the intended chaperone for the earl's cousins. That rather than a straitlaced widow, Mrs. Eve Hawthorne was the sort who romped about letting strangers kiss her!

"Then he *is* a bad man." Julian's lower lip thrust out.

Eve glanced down at him and forced a smile. "I am glad that you will miss me, Jules, but you mustn't think that Mr. Talbot is bad. He is simply . . . well, running an errand for the earl."

"But I don't understand." Julian panted as he trotted

along beside her. "If he is the man who's come to get you, why didn't you say who you were? Why didn't we walk back to the house with him?"

"If we hurry and take the back way, we can get to the vicarage before he does. I must change clothes before I see him."

"Oh."

"You know how your mother feels when you are messy and dirty? That's why we always tuck in your shirt and try to clean up before we return to the house. Well, I think that Mr. Talbot may feel as your mother does."

"But he was quite nice. He seemed to like you."

"That was when he didn't know who I was. It's all very well to like someone when you think she is just a . . . an ordinary person, but it changes when that person is supposed to be in charge of a group of young girls."

"I don't understand." He looked up at her, frowning.

"I know. It's something that makes more sense as you get older. I just need to make sure that when he sees me again, I look much more like a mature, responsible woman."

"And not a naiad?"

"Definitely not a naiad." Taking Julian's hand, she broke into a run.

Fitz stood still for a long moment after the woman ran away, staring after her in amazement. Sudden flight was not normally the feminine reaction to his name. At thirty-two years of age, Fitzhugh Talbot was one of the most eligible bachelors in England. He was the younger half brother of the Earl of Stewkesbury, and though his mother's family was not nearly as aristocratic as his father's, the money that she and her father had left Fitz more than made up for that minor flaw. These factors alone would have made him well liked by maidens and marriage-minded mothers alike, but he had also been blessed with an engaging personality, a wicked smile, and a face to make angels swoon.

Indeed, it would take a determined soul to find anyone who disliked Fitz Talbot. Though he was clearly not a dandy, his dress was impeccable, and whatever he wore was improved by hanging on his slender, broad-shouldered body. He was known to be one of the best shots in the country, and though he was not quite the rider his brother the earl was, he had excellent form. And though he was not a bruiser, no one would refuse his help in a mill. Such qualities made him popular with the males of the *ton,* but his skill on the dance floor and in conversation made him equally well liked by London hostesses.

There was, in short, only one thing that kept Fitz from being the perfect match: his complete and utter disinterest in marrying. However, that was not considered a serious impediment by most of the mothers in search of a husband for their daughters, all of whom were sure that their child would be the one girl who could make Fitzhugh Talbot drop his skittish attitude toward the married state. As a consequence, Fitz's name was usually greeted with smiles ranging from coy to calculating.

It was *not* met with a noise somewhere between a gasp and a shriek and taking to one's heels. Still, Fitz thought, he did like a challenge, especially one with a cloud of pale golden hair and eyes the gray-blue of a stormy sea.

When he reached the road, he swung up into the saddle and turned his stallion once again in the direction of the village. He did not urge the animal to hurry; Fitz was content to move at a slow place, lost in his thoughts. He had been willing enough when his brother Oliver asked him to fetch the new chaperone for their cousins. Fitz was often bored sitting about in the country, and the week or two until Mary Bascombe's wedding had stretched out before him, filled with the sort of plans that provided infinite entertainment for women and left him looking for the nearest door. So he had not minded the trip, especially since he had decided to ride Baxley's Heart, his newest acquisition from Tattersall's, in addition to taking the carriage. That way, he could escort the doubtlessly dull middle-aged widow back to Willowmere without having to actually spend all his time riding in the coach with her.

But suddenly the trip had acquired far more interest for him. His plan to return to Willowmere the following day now struck him as a poor choice. There was not, after all, any need for the girls' chaperone to be at Willowmere immediately. What with Cousin Charlotte as well as Lady Vivian overseeing the wedding preparations, there was more than adequate oversight of his cousins.

Fitz could put up at the inn for a few days and look around the village for his "water nymph." First he would pay a call at the vicarage to meet the widow and tell her that they would be leaving in a few days. He might have to pay another courtesy visit to the vicarage in a day or two, but other than that, he would be free to spend his time in a light flirtation—perhaps even more.

Fitz's avoidance of marriage did not indicate any desire to avoid women. Though he was too careful in his relationships to be called a rake, he was definitely a man who enjoyed the company of women. And after all, he had been immured in the country for a month without any female companionship . . . at least, of the sort he was wont to enjoy in London. But this naiad offered a wealth of possibilities.

He thought of the girl's slender white legs, exposed by the dress she had hiked up and tied out of the way . . . the pale pink of her lips and the answering flare of color in her cheeks . . . the soft mounds of her breasts swaying beneath her dress as she hopped from rock to rock . . . the glorious tumble of pale curls, glinting in the sun, that had pulled free from her upswept hair.

Yes, definitely, he wanted more than flirtation.

He considered how to go about finding her. He could, of course, describe her to someone like the local tavern keeper and come up with a name, but that would scarcely be discreet. And Fitz was always discreet.

He supposed that she could be a servant sent to tend the boy. However, her dress, speech, and manner were all those of a lady. On the other hand, one hardly expected to find a lady splashing about like that in a stream. And who was the child with her? Could the boy have been hers? There was, he thought, a certain resemblance. But surely she was too young to have a child of seven or eight, which was what he had judged the lad to be. Fitz would have thought that she was no more than in her early twenties. But perhaps she was older than she appeared. There were mothers who romped with their children; he had seen Charlotte doing so with her brood of rapscallions.

Perhaps she was the lad's governess—though in his experience governesses were rarely either so lovely or so light-hearted. Or maybe she was the personal maid of the boy's mother. Personal maids were more likely to have acquired the speech patterns of their mistresses than lower servants, and they also frequently wore their mistresses hand-me-downs.

None of these speculations, however, put him any closer to discovering the girl again. She had hinted that he might come across her walking through town, so perhaps she regularly took a stroll. Still, he could scarcely spend his entire day stalking up and down the streets of the village.

Lost in these musings, Fitz was on the edge of the village

almost before he knew it. Indeed, he had almost ridden past
the church before he realized where he was. Reining in his
horse, he looked at the squat old square-towered church. A
cemetery lay to one side of it; Fitz had gone past it without
a glance. On the other side of the church was a two-story
home, obviously much newer than the church but built of
the same gray stone. This, he felt sure, would be the vicarage.

It was a rather grim-looking place, and he could not help
but hope, for his cousins' sake, that the widow who resided
there was not of the same nature as the house. He thought
for a moment of riding past it, but a moment's thought put
that idea to rest. In a village this size, it would be bound to
get back to the residents of the vicarage that a stranger was
in town, and they would feel slighted that he had not come
first to meet them. Fitz knew that many deemed him an irresponsible sort, more interested in pursuing his own pleasure
than others' ideas of his duty, but it was never said that he
ignored the social niceties.

Besides, he thought, with a little lift of his spirits, as he
swung down off his horse, he would have an excellent reason to keep his visit short, since he needed to get his animal
stabled and find himself a room. Brushing off the dust of the
road, he strode up to the front door and knocked. The summons was quickly answered by a parlor maid, who goggled
at him as if she'd never seen a gentleman before, but when
he told her that he wished to speak to Mrs. Hawthorne and
handed her his card, the girl whisked him efficiently down
the hall into the parlor.

A moment later a woman of narrow face and form entered the room. Her dark brown hair fell in tight curls on
either side of her face, with the rest drawn back under a
white cap. Her face was etched with the sort of severe lines
of disapproval that made it difficult to guess her age, but the

paucity of gray streaks in her hair made him put her on the younger edge of middle age. She had on a gown of dark blue jaconet with a white muslin fichu worn over her shoulders and crossed to knot at her breasts.

Fitz's heart fell as he watched her walk toward him. Poor cousins! He had the feeling that the girls had merely traded one martinet for another, and it surprised him that the lively Lady Vivian would have recommended such a woman. However, he kept his face schooled to a pleasant expression and executed a bow.

"Mr. Fitzhugh Talbot, ma'am, at your service. Do I have the honor of addressing Mrs. Bruce Hawthorne?"

"I am Mrs. Childe," she told him. "Mrs. Hawthorne is my husband's daughter."

"A pleasure to meet you, madam." He took the hand she extended to him and smiled warmly down at her. "Clearly you must have married from the schoolroom. You are far too young to be anyone's stepmother."

The tight expression on her face eased, and color sprang into her cheeks. She smiled somewhat coyly. "'Tis most kind of you to say so, sir."

"I am the Earl of Stewkesbury's brother," he went on. "And I am here to escort Mrs. Hawthorne to Willowmere. I believe he wrote to her regarding the matter."

"Yes, of course. I have sent a servant to tell Mrs. Hawthorne that you have arrived."

She gestured toward the sofa, and Fitz sat down, relieved to learn that at least his American cousins had escaped living with this woman—and that he would not have to endure two days of traveling with her.

Mrs. Childe took a seat across from Fitz, her spine as straight as the chair back, which she did not touch, and inquired formally after his trip. They made polite small talk for a few moments before there was the sound of hurrying footsteps in the hallway. A moment later a tall, slender woman dressed in a gown as severe and dark as Mrs. Childe's, her blond hair pulled back and twisted into a tight knot at the crown of her head, stepped into the room.

Fitz shot to his feet, his customary aplomb for once deserting him. There was no mistaking the woman despite the complete change in her attire. The tightly restrained hair was the same pale ash-blond, the eyes the color of a stormy sea.

The middle-aged widow he had expected was, in fact, his water nymph.

Chapter 2

It was all Eve could do to keep her face calm as she advanced into the room. Inside she was quaking with fear that Mr. Talbot would denounce her as a frivolous flirt, utterly unsuitable to chaperone the earl's cousins. It would not matter that Talbot had flirted with her even more than she had flirted with him or that he had been the one to kiss her. Gentlemen, after all, were not condemned for such things. And a chaperone was held to a higher standard than an ordinary woman. She took a cautious glance at the man across the room. He had risen to his feet, a stunned expression on his face.

"Pray, allow me to introduce you to Mr. Fitzhugh Talbot," her stepmother said to Eve. "He is the Earl of Stewkesbury's brother, come to escort you to Willowmere. Is that not gracious of the earl?"

The earl's brother! Eve had hoped he was a distant and lowlier relative of the earl's—a second or third cousin, perhaps. Someone with little interest in the character of whomever the earl hired.

Eve's smile was tremulous as she extended her hand to Fitzhugh, saying, "Indeed, yes, most gracious. And quite generous of you, as well, Mr. Talbot."

"I assure you, it is my pleasure, Mrs. Hawthorne." Talbot had recovered from his surprise, and his expression was once again blandly polite, but there was a twinkle in his bright blue eyes that made Eve suspect his words could be taken in quite a different manner. "My great pleasure," he added, and a smile quirked at his lips.

Eve took a seat facing him, watching him warily. Was he toying with her? Making her suffer an agony of nerves while she waited for him to reveal her transgressions? Surely not . . . the amusement in his eyes seemed more conspiratorial than predatory.

"We had not expected you so early, Mr. Talbot," Eve began, searching for any topic that had nothing to do with her. It was only after she said it and saw her stepmother's frown that she realized her words might be construed as criticism. "Not, of course, that you are in any way too early," she added hastily. "I mean, well, really, of course, we did not expect you at all, but only the carriage. I just, that is . . ."

Imogene sent her a dagger glance, then offered Talbot as warm a smile as she was capable of. "I believe what Mrs. Hawthorne means is that you must have made good time on your journey here."

Again Fitz's blue eyes sent laughter dancing Eve's way before he turned toward Imogene. "Yes, I did. But I was riding, you see. I purchased a new horse recently, and I was eager to try him out. The carriage, I'm afraid, is still a bit behind me."

"He is a lovely animal," Eve offered. At Imogene's puzzled glance, she realized that she had made yet another misstep. "I saw him through the upstairs window," she hurried to explain.

Whatever was the matter with her? One would think she had never tiptoed through a delicate social conversation before. But she knew the answer to her question. It wasn't just Talbot's knowledge of her immature behavior that afternoon that unsettled her. It was the man himself, sitting there looking at her with those sky-blue eyes, filling up the space with his masculine presence, drawing her gaze to the handsome lines of his face.

"Thank you, Mrs. Hawthorne." Fitz stepped in to pull the conversation away from Eve's mistake. "Clearly you are a judge of horseflesh."

"My late husband was an avid horseman," Eve explained, feeling herself on firmer ground.

"Far too avid." Imogene's mouth drew up. "But then, one must not speak ill of the dead."

"No." Eve shot a hard look in her direction. "One must not."

Eve herself had often enough decried Bruce's obsession with horses. She had even burst into tears once when creditors were haunting their doorstep and Bruce had announced that he had bought another "prime bit of blood." It was as if by throwing himself into his neck-or-nothing riding, he could make all his other inadequacies disappear. However, Eve was not about to allow her stepmother to criticize the man. Whatever his faults, he had been Eve's husband and deserved her loyalty even beyond the grave.

Besides, Imogene's criticism had less to do with Major Hawthorne, whom she had barely known, than with the fact that his death in an impecunious state had forced Eve into the Childe household.

"I must say, Mrs. Hawthorne, that you are hardly what I was expecting in the way of a chaperone," Fitz said, steering the conversation onto a new path. "We had assumed that you were a woman of, ah, advanced years."

Eve glanced at him, fear clenching her stomach again.

Did he intend to use her age as an excuse not to take her back to Willowmere? "I-I am sorry, Mr. Talbot. But I assure you that I am quite capable, despite my appearance."

"I assure you, I am not offering a criticism. I am quite pleasantly surprised."

"Mrs. Hawthorne has been married and widowed for a number of years," Mrs. Childe offered. "She is much older than she seems."

Eve said nothing, merely gritted her teeth in a smile at her stepmother.

The conversation limped along for a few more minutes in this manner, and Eve began to relax. Surely if Mr. Talbot was going to expose her actions this afternoon, he would have done so by now. After a time, Imogene, obviously determined to be pleasant to the man who would be taking Eve away, asked Talbot to partake of supper with them.

"How very kind of you, ma'am." Fitz smiled, and Eve noticed that even her rigid stepmother did not seem to be immune to the effects of his smile. "But alas, I have a number of things to see to. The carriage should arrive this evening, and I need to make arrangements for our trip back." He turned toward Eve. "If it is not too difficult for you, Mrs. Hawthorne, I would like to leave tomorrow. What with the upcoming wedding, it is important that we return to Willowmere as soon as possible."

Eve could not hold back the joyful smile that spread across her lips. "No, it will not be difficult. I am quite prepared to leave tomorrow."

In truth, her bags had been packed for two days now. They could not leave too soon for her.

"Excellent. And now, if you will excuse me, I should be about my duties." Talbot rose, executing a graceful, punctiliously correct bow to the ladies, and politely took his leave.

Imogene watched his retreating back until he reached the

front door. "A most well-mannered gentleman. And such consideration from the earl. I hope, Eve, that you will remember to thank Stewkesbury properly."

Eve ground her teeth but replied evenly, "I will say all that is proper."

"It is a wonderful opportunity for you. An excellent family. You will be moving among the highest of the *ton*. Who knows, perhaps you will find another husband." Imogene allowed a thin smile at that thought.

"I am not looking for a husband."

"Every unmarried woman is looking for a husband. Of course, it will be difficult for a widow, given all the fresh young girls on the marriage market. Still, I am sure there must be a widower or older gentleman who needs a wife."

"I will be chaperoning the earl's cousins," Eve pointed out. "It is their interests that must be foremost in my mind."

"Of course, of course. But, as I am sure you are aware, this stint as their chaperone will last only a year or two, at best, before they marry. One must look to the future, after all."

"I will." Eve had found that it was simpler to go along with Imogene's statements than to argue. Speaking her mind inevitably led to an argument and hurt feelings, with Eve having to apologize in order to keep peace in the household.

Eve started out of the room, thinking that she could take refuge in packing the last of her things. However, Imogene strolled along with her. Eve was not sure if the woman was feeling friendlier toward her now that she would soon be gone or if she was simply eager to get in her last bits of carping.

"You will need to remember not to put yourself forward," Imogene told her. "A quiet, compliant nature is essential. No one wants a companion who puts herself forward or is loud or draws attention to herself. You smiled too broadly at Mr. Talbot this afternoon. I am sure he took note of it."

Eve forced herself to unclench her fists. "Few people dislike a smile."

"Too bold a smile indicates a forward woman, which is not what anyone looks for in a chaperone. It would be disastrous for you to engage in a flirtation with Mr. Talbot."

Startled, Eve turned to her. Could she possibly know? Surely not. "I did not flirt with Mr. Talbot."

"Perhaps not. But your smile was inviting. A man such as he is quick to take advantage of that."

"I thought you liked Mr. Talbot."

"Of course. He is the very model of a gentleman—so handsome, so charming, utterly genteel. But loath as I am to listen to rumors, I have heard things about Mr. Talbot."

Eve's curiosity sharpened. "What have you heard?"

Her stepmother pretended to abstain from gossip, but she was in constant correspondence with her cousin in London, who was one of the *ton*'s most notorious busybodies. As a result, Imogene often knew the scandals of the Season as thoroughly as anyone in the city.

"Well . . ." Imogene's eyes took on the glimmer reserved for reporting other's misdeeds. "It is said that Fitzhugh Talbot collects hearts like a miser hoards gold."

"He is a handsome man. I am sure he is a good catch."

"Of course. But he has no interest in marriage. He dances attendance on no eligible young female. It is said that he prefers a . . . woman of experience. His name has been linked to more than one widow and even to some married women. And of course, to women of a lower sort—though I suppose that is to be expected of most men."

"Are you saying that because I am a widow, Mr. Talbot will make improper advances to me?"

Her stepmother shrugged eloquently. "That is why you must be careful about offering any form of encouragement, even a smile."

"I did not smile at him in an inviting manner," Eve retorted hotly. "And we were speaking about leaving tomorrow, not anything illicit!"

"Goodness, no." The other woman let out a little titter. "As if I would suggest such a thing. Even though your upbringing was, perhaps, a little lax for the daughter of a man of the cloth, no one would accuse you of acting in a bold manner. However, Mr. Talbot does not know you as well as everyone around here does. He might misinterpret your . . . well, your rather indiscriminate friendliness. Your frequent lack of reserve."

"I shall give Mr. Talbot no reason to think badly of me," Eve said tightly.

"I am sure you will not. Just a word to the wise." She nodded at Eve as though they shared an understanding. "Mr. Talbot is far too handsome and charming not to be accustomed to having his way with women. One can hardly fault a man when women are constantly throwing themselves at him. And a woman who has been without a husband's affection for two years might find herself all too susceptible to his charms."

Eve pressed her lips together. If only her stepmother knew how little being a widow had changed her lack of husbandly affection!

"You might not realize it," Imogene went on. "And since your father is far too holy a man even to conceive of warning you about such a thing, it is incumbent upon me to do so. Have a care, Eve; you would not want to wind up as one of his string of conquests. That is all I have to say on the matter."

They had reached the door to Eve's room, and she turned to her stepmother, giving her a forced smile. "Thank you for your advice; I fully appreciate the spirit in which you give it. However, as you said, many people have false ideas about widows. An army officer's wife learns a thing or two about living above reproach, as well as about being alone. I am quite capable of rejecting Mr. Talbot's advances—or those of any other man." She gave Imogene a perfunctory nod. "Now, if you will excuse me, I must make certain that I am ready to depart when Mr. Talbot arrives tomorrow."

She slipped into her bedchamber and closed the door without giving Imogene a chance to utter a rejoinder. By tomorrow, her stepmother's recriminations would not matter. Eve leaned back against the door and allowed a smile to return to her face. Tomorrow she would be gone.

Eve opened the enameled blue watch pinned to her dress. It was seven forty-five, five minutes later than the last time she had checked it. With a sigh, she closed it again.

Normally she did not wear the timepiece. It had a rather old-fashioned look that did not suit today's styles. However, it had been her husband's last gift to her, found tucked away among his belongings after his death. It had been inscribed on the inner cover with the words "For my beloved wife," and she understood that Bruce must have bought it for her birthday, which followed only five days after his death. It was an expensive item, made of gold with fine blue enameling on the front and several small pearls framing a small oval painting of a bucolic scene. Normally she would have returned the watch for the money, as she had done many times before with the expensive gifts her improvident husband was wont to buy.

However, this time she could not bring herself to do so. It was Bruce's parting gift to her, her last link to him. Theirs had not been a normal marriage, it was true, but she had loved Bruce, and she believed that he had loved her, too. So she kept the watch, though it remained in her jewelry box most of the time.

Today, however, she had decided to wear it. It looked quite nice pinned to her dark blue carriage dress, with its high neck and faintly military buttons. It gave her, she thought, a rather efficient, professional air, which would be useful in countering the impression she had made on Fitzhugh Talbot the day before. In any case, it was practical on a day like this, when they would be on the road the entire day, away from clocks.

Very practical, she thought drily, if she was going to keep nervously checking on the time like this. With an inward sigh, she folded her hands in her lap and settled herself to wait with patience.

She sneaked a glance at Imogene. Her stepmother was reading her Bible, her back as rigid as ever. Eve had never seen the woman slump. It was unkind of her, she knew, to regard that as a fault, but somehow it never failed to irritate her. Her father sat beside his wife, his hands folded in quiet contemplation. There was, as always, an air about him of faint distraction, as though his mind were somewhere else. Eve smiled faintly. No doubt he was thinking of his Sunday sermon or contemplating some matter of theological significance. A kind and loving man, he was rarely completely *with* anyone, even his family. Her mother had been the glue of their family, and since her death, Eve and her father had not been close. He was content to let Imogene take the lead, even in dealing with his daughter.

Eve wished that Julian were there; she would have liked to spend an extra few minutes with him. But Imogene's rules were never to be broken, no matter what other circumstance might intrude—the boy's lessons began immediately after breakfast, at seven-thirty sharp. So Eve had popped into his room to say her farewells to him before she went down to breakfast. Thinking about it, she felt again the pang of loss that she had felt as she hugged him close to her.

The sound of a carriage outside broke into her sad thoughts, and Eve stood up, going to the window. An elegant black carriage stood outside, drawn by four well-matched bays. Behind it rode Fitzhugh Talbot on his sleek black stallion.

"He is here." Eve turned back and saw the expressive frown on Imogene's face. With an inward sigh, Eve resumed her seat, schooling her face into polite reserve.

Fitzhugh Talbot strode into the room a few moments later, smiling with his easy charm and executing a perfectly correct bow. Eve felt once again that catch in her throat as his bright blue eyes met hers, and she was glad that she had made an effort to keep her face calm and remote. Otherwise, she suspected, she would have grinned back, her eyes lighting up. One had to work, she thought, not to respond to the man. No doubt her stepmother was right about his string of conquests back in London.

"Ah, Mrs. Hawthorne," he said after greeting Reverend and Mrs. Childe politely. "I see that you are ready to leave. That is excellent. I fear we have rather a long journey ahead of us." He turned toward Imogene. "I do hope you will forgive us for not staying to chat."

"No, indeed. We quite understand, don't we, dear?" She turned toward her husband.

"What? Oh. Oh, yes. Long trip, perfectly right." The Reverend Childe favored them all with his vague smile. He turned to his daughter. "Good-bye, my dear. I shall miss you."

He hugged her, giving her back a little pat. Eve returned the embrace. She knew he meant the words. She also knew that within twenty minutes he would be back in his study, engrossed in his musings, scarcely aware that she was gone.

Her stepmother did not believe in physical demonstrations of affection, so Eve was spared an embrace with her.

A genteelly extended hand and an admonition to conduct herself properly were all that Mrs. Childe offered. Eve left on a wave of relief; she could feel her muscles relaxing as she walked from the house to the carriage. She knew that her life as a chaperone would be structured, of course. She would have to follow the rules of her employer, as well as enforce them upon her charges. She would be expected to be modest and quiet, to keep her thoughts to herself, in essence to fade into the background while still providing a constant presence.

But she would be making her own way, not living on the sufferance of her stepmother. She would not have to listen to Imogene lecture and scold. She would not be treated as if she were sixteen again. Most of all, she would be out in the world, not shut away in the country. There would be parties and plays and gaiety. And though she would be sitting on the edge of it, even that much seemed like an adventure.

A liveried servant sprang down to open the door and lower the step for her, but it was Mr. Talbot who offered his hand to help her up into the carriage.

"If you don't mind, I thought that I would ride with you for the first leg of the journey and let the groom follow with my horse," he told her.

Eve's stomach clenched. Was he going to lecture her on her behavior of the day before? Or was he going to try to seduce her, as her stepmother had warned?

Something of what she felt must have shown on her face, for he smiled faintly and said, "I assure you I shall not intrude upon your privacy for the entire trip. I simply thought it might serve us well to spend a little while getting acquainted."

"Yes, of course." Eve's cheeks flared pink now with embarrassment, and she hurriedly entered the carriage and sat down. As Talbot got in after her and closed the door, she

turned toward him. "I was simply a little surprised. I did
not mean any disapproval or—that is, I would not have expected to ride by myself. It is, after all, your carriage."

His grin widened at her blushing confusion. "Well, actually, it is my brother's. So neither of us has rights to it."

Eve could not resist his smile. "No, I suppose not."

The vehicle in which they sat was as luxurious as any in
which Eve had ever ridden. The seat was upholstered in soft
leather, well padded, and the squab behind her back was
equally soft. A pocket beside her held a rolled-up lap robe
should she grow cool, and the leather curtains were rolled
up partway to let in air and light. It was quite roomy, with
ample space between her seat and Mr. Talbot's across from
her. But despite all this, she could not feel quite comfortable.

For one thing, she was all too aware of Fitzhugh Talbot.
The foot or so that lay between their knees seemed hardly
any distance. He was too handsome, too masculine. His
mere presence seemed to fill the carriage. Eve was not accustomed to traveling alone in a carriage with a man; the only
times she had done so had been with her husband or her
father. With a stranger, it was altogether different. Such a
small space seemed intimate, connected. Or perhaps it only
felt that way because the man she was traveling with was this
particular man. There was something about him that made
a woman feel . . . well, she was not sure what. Uncertain,
perhaps, and very, very aware of him.

She had heard of him, of course. Though at first his name
had meant nothing to her other than that he was related to
the earl, after her stepmother's revelation of his preference
for "experienced" women, she had begun to remember bits
and pieces that she had heard over the years. Eve had not
lived in London or been a part of the *ton*, after her marriage, for they resided wherever Bruce's regiment had been

quartered, but she had retained many friends among the *ton* and had corresponded with them regularly. So she had heard tales of the young men about the city, including Stewkesbury's brother—wealthy, aristocratic, and bored, they lived a life of ease and, all too often, dissipation. Talbot was, at best, a flirt. And if Imogene's gossip was correct, he was firmly settled into a promiscuous life, with no intention of marrying. He was, in short, the sort of man who flirted with everyone and seduced widows and married women, leaving a trail of broken hearts behind him.

Eve, however, was certain that she could handle him. She had learned long ago how to turn aside unwelcome advances. Obviously she had not made a good start yesterday by behaving the way she had. It would be no wonder if Talbot thought the worst of her. Just recalling it made her cringe. What had she been thinking? Well, obviously she had not been. She had been too happy, too filled with anticipation at the thought of leaving the vicarage.

More important, of course, was what was he thinking? He might consider her a possible dalliance, someone who could be easily persuaded to provide him with a few nights' entertainment. On the other hand, he could just as easily be appalled at the thought of her chaperoning his cousins. He might have ridden in the carriage with her so that he could voice that opinion. Or maybe he would tell his brother how poorly she measured up as a guardian of impressionable young girls. How humiliating it would be if she traveled all the way to Willowmere only to have the earl dismiss her and send her scuttling back to her father's house!

Whatever his intentions regarding her, Eve knew that the best approach was to ward him off. She squared her shoulders and laced her fingers in her lap. Holding herself as tall and straight as Imogene, she looked at him.

"Mr. Talbot, I want you to know that the way I acted yesterday is *not* my customary behavior. When I am with my brother, I tend to be more . . . carefree, shall we say, than I normally am. I would never behave in such a manner around my charges. Nor would I allow them to indulge in such behavior."

"Would you not? That is too bad. I found the way you behaved yesterday most enjoyable. Indeed, I had hoped that you and I could explore the streams around Willowmere in such a manner." His eyes lit with amusement.

Eve resisted the appeal of his twinkling eyes and replied primly, "*That* is not possible. As your cousins' chaperone, I have no intention of indulging in flirtation."

"I am stricken." He grinned, belying his words. "But I am willing to give up the flirtation. I had something rather more . . . pleasurable in mind." Though he still smiled, there was now in his eyes and tone a certain warmth that was unmistakable.

Eve flushed. She glanced away, all too aware that the heat spreading through her was not simply that of embarrassment. There was something undeniably arousing in the suggestive tone of his voice. There had been times in her marriage when Eve had wondered if she was not perhaps, well, too *low* in her desires, too easily aroused, too physical. Surely a true lady would be repelled by his bold words, not secretly tingling all over.

"Mr. Talbot, you go too far," she said in a choked voice.

"Oh, I am certain I could go much farther."

A gurgle of laughter rose in Eve, but she firmly pressed it down. She suspected that she should not find Fitzhugh Talbot amusing; she was certain she should not let on that she did. Clearing her throat, she presented him with her stoniest gaze. "I fear that we are straying far from the topic."

"Are we? I'm sorry—what *was* our topic? I thought we were contemplating our behavior at Willowmere."

Goaded, Eve snapped back, "I wish you would cease these . . . these innuendos and games. Please tell me plainly—do you mean to tell the earl that I acted unsuitably yesterday?"

"Good Gad, no." His brows rose lazily.

Eve relaxed. No doubt there were many things she had to worry about where Mr. Talbot was concerned, but at least that was not one of them.

"Oliver would be certain I had lost my mind if I ever uttered an opinion that insipid," he explained, and Eve had to smile. "For another, Oliver wouldn't care a snap what I thought. He is the one who makes the decisions. I simply . . ." He made a vague wave of his hand. ". . . enjoy life."

"I should think everyone tries to do that."

"Not with the sort of dedication I devote to the subject. Indeed, there are many who do their utmost *not* to enjoy life." He cocked an eyebrow. "Pray, do not be offended, but do you think that Mrs. Childe tries to enjoy life?"

A gurgle of laughter escaped Eve's lips. "Imogene? No. I think one can safely say that she tries very hard not to enjoy it."

"There. You see my point. My brother, on the other hand, does not try *not* to enjoy life. He simply has so many things he believes he has to do that he has little time for enjoying anything. Of course," he added judiciously, "he would probably tell you that there is pleasure to be had in doing one's duty. Personally I have always found that one's duty invariably crops up at the exact moment when you are about to go out on the town with friends or attend a race, and instead you wind up visiting deaf Uncle Gerald or going to your godmother's musicale."

"Or escorting chaperones."

"Oh, no, my dear Mrs. Hawthorne, you will get no such statement from me. I find escorting chaperones the most delightful of tasks." His mouth curved sensuously, and his voice was almost a caress. "Especially when the chaperones are as lovely as you."

"I should have known better than to try to engage a flirt in an exchange of wits," Eve said.

"A flirt? You wound me."

"You are not a flirt?" Eve tossed back. "Then what would you call yourself?"

"An admirer of all things beautiful."

There was a warmth in his voice that turned her insides to molten wax. Eve was suddenly aware that despite her best intentions, she had once again found herself in precisely the sort of flirtation she had been determined to avoid.

Eve strove for a quelling tone. "Pretty words, sir, but I suspect they have been used many times before."

"Never with such truth." His gaze dropped from her eyes to her mouth, and his own mouth softened.

He wants to kiss me, Eve thought, and she realized, shocked, that she wished he would. He shifted and reached toward her. Eve's heart slammed in her chest, and she tensed, heat surging up inside her, waiting breathlessly as if she teetered at the edge of a cliff.

Chapter 3

Eve's eyes half closed in anticipation as his fingers went to the tie of her bonnet, pulling the bow apart with a single tug. He lifted the hat from her head and set it beside her on the seat.

"There, that's better. Now I can see your face."

Eve blinked, startled. Her cheek tingled where his fingers had grazed her cheek as he took off the bonnet, and her gloved hand went unconsciously to that cheek. Had he wanted to kiss her, or had that been only her imagination? She gazed out the window, forcibly gathering the threads of her composure.

"Tell me about my charges," she said after a moment, turning back to Fitzhugh Talbot, schooling her features to be once more polite and distant.

"There are only two of them now. I mean, there are four sisters, but one of them has married and left Willowmere, and the other is about to be married, so you will have only two under your care. They are our cousins, who grew up in America."

"Who is getting married, and who will remain in my charge?" Eve asked.

"Rose, the second oldest, married an American, and they

have already gone back to that country. The eldest sister, Mary—Marigold is her full name; their mother had a fondness for flowers—is to marry Sir Royce Winslow. He is my half-brother on our mother's side but no relation to our cousins or any of the other Talbots."

"It sounds complicated."

His mouth quirked up. "Things often seem to be that way where the Bascombes are concerned. But I think you will like them. I hope you enjoy riding. The girls adore it, especially Camellia."

"Yes, I do, though I have not ridden in some time."

"Don't worry, you'll soon be back to form. We go riding almost every day."

"We?" Eve's pulse quickened. "You accompany the girls?"

"Almost always. With Royce getting married, I will be their only instructor now."

"I see. Then you . . . expect to remain at Willowmere?"

Eve had assumed that he would not stay, that he would depart for London as soon as he brought her to the estate. Surely a man such as Fitz Talbot would not be content cooling his heels in the country. He would want London, with its lure of cards and clubs and sophisticated beauties.

His eyes went to hers, and he gave her a long, slow smile, the deep dimple springing into his cheek. "Yes. I expect to be at Willowmere for quite some time."

"Oh." Eve felt caught in his gaze, faintly breathless. "I—I would have thought that you would wish to return to the excitement of London."

"Don't worry." His eyes did not leave hers, and his voice was rich with meaning. "I shall not be bored. I expect to occupy myself quite satisfactorily at Willowmere."

Eve looked back at him, unable to summon a reply. All an impoverished widow had to recommend herself was her reputation, and she could not allow even a breath of scandal to tarnish it. She could *not* let herself be led into a flirtation—or something more—no matter how handsome or charming Fitz Talbot might be.

Eve pulled her eyes away from his, staring for a long moment at her hands clasped in her lap. When she looked up at him, her face was schooled into a polite mask, her voice colorless. "How nice. I am sure that your cousins will be most happy to have you at Willowmere."

His blue eyes twinkled with amusement, but he inclined his head gravely as if in acknowledgment. "I am glad you think so. Shall I tell you about Willowmere?"

Pleased that he had accepted her rebuff, Eve listened as he launched into a description of the family estate. He told her a few interesting tidbits of the Talbot family history and also folded in points of interest in the town and surrounding countryside. He was a master of conversation, at once effortless, impersonal, and entertaining. It was easy to talk to him, and before long Eve found herself relaxing and chatting with him, the moments of tension gone.

Before long they rolled into the courtyard of an inn to rest and water the horses, and when they resumed their journey he chose to ride outside the carriage.

Left to her own devices, Eve gazed out the window, looking at the scenery and thinking about what lay ahead of her. It was not long, however, before she realized that it was actually Fitzhugh Talbot riding beside them that caught her eye far more than the scenery. He cut an elegant figure on horseback that was impossible to ignore. Tall and slender, with wide-set shoulders and narrow hips, he was both powerful and graceful. She could not help but notice his hands as they tightened on the reins or his muscular thighs as they gripped the sides of his mount.

Making an exasperated sound, Eve reached up and released the leather curtain, letting it roll down to block her view. She was acting like a ninny, she told herself, as if she had never seen a handsome man on horseback before. Bruce had been a major in the Hussars, and she had seen many a superb horseman. None of them had had a face to make an angel swoon, but still . . . she should be immune to the romance of a man astride a beautiful stallion.

She settled into the corner of the carriage seat, gazing across the carriage and out the window in the opposite direction. The night before had been a restless one, and it was not long before her eyes fluttered closed.

She awoke when they stopped for lunch. It was a welcome respite, and after they ate, Eve was glad when Fitzhugh suggested a short walk before they returned to the carriage. As he had that morning, Fitz rode in the carriage for part of the afternoon and spent the rest of the time on his horse. It was, Eve thought, most considerate of him to give her the time by herself, but frankly, she found the ride deadly dull when he was not with her.

The inn where they stopped for the night was pleasant and spacious, with polished oaken floors. The aroma drifting from the kitchen piqued Eve's appetite. The innkeeper grinned from ear to ear when he saw Fitz and quickly led them up to their rooms, chatting all the way.

Eve washed up quickly and changed into a clean dress before hurrying back downstairs to dine. She found Fitz in the dining room, and she noticed that he, too, had changed into a fresh shirt and neckcloth, this one knotted in a basic arrangement.

"Ah, Mrs. Hawthorne." He came forward to meet her. "What a vision you are. One would scarcely believe that you have spent the entire day on the road."

"I might say the same about you," Eve replied, her eyes twinkling.

"I did my best, though my valet would be happy to tell you that it was an inferior effort. He is always certain that I will bring disgrace on him when I travel alone. It is a wonder to him when I manage to return relatively intact."

They sat down to a hearty meal and began to eat. "It looks as though Stiles has outdone himself tonight," Fitz commented. "He must have been spurred by your presence."

"It's delicious." Eve glanced at him. "He seems to know you well. You must have stopped here often over the years."

He nodded. "Indeed, since I was a lad. My mother and I traveled this way when she went to visit her family in Leeds. And later, after she passed away, my grandfather sent me every summer with my valet."

"The same one who is certain you cannot dress yourself?"

"Oh, no. This one was more keeper than valet, really. He was one of the more disagreeable footmen, large enough to keep me in line and dour enough not to be inveigled into letting me get into some mischief or other. If there was one thing upon which my two grandfathers agreed, it was the necessity of exercising control over my adolescent person-age."

"And were they correct?"

"Naturally. I was an imp of Satan. Fortunately I developed this dimple at an early age." He touched his cheek. "It saved me from many a well-deserved beating."

"I cannot believe you were such a scamp."

"I had a tendency to kick over the traces," Fitz admitted, smiling a little. "But when one has an older brother like Oliver, there is little else one can do."

"He was a paragon?" Eve asked shrewdly, taking a last bite and shoving her plate aside. She settled back in her chair, taking a sip of her wine.

"Exactly." Fitz nodded, pleased at her understanding. "It

would have been impossible to be as sober, steady, and intelligent as Oliver. Instead I turned my sights on being feckless. Fortunately I found that well within my reach."

A gurgle of mirth escaped Eve. "I think, sir, that you exaggerate. After all, you did perform the duty of escorting the new chaperone to Willowmere."

"My dear Mrs. Hawthorne, I can assure you that escorting a beautiful woman such as yourself is not an onerous duty."

"Ah, but as I remember, you were expecting the chaperone to be a woman 'of advanced years.' So your impulse could not have been so selfish."

He grinned. "'Tis true. I thought you would be middle-aged. Indeed, I cannot remember her specific words, but I believe that Lady Vivian gave us a rather misleading expectation of your age."

"Oh, dear." Eve's stomach fell. "Will the earl be terribly displeased when he meets me?"

"He will not hold it against you. My brother is a very fair man." Fitz's grin grew. "Don't you remember? He is a—"

"Paragon," Eve finished with him and smiled. "I sincerely hope he does not hold my age against me. I would hate to return to my father's house."

"I should think so," Fitz agreed candidly. "I hope it will not offend you when I say that I was there only a few minutes and I had no desire to remain." He glanced at her mischievously. "There was not really any need for us to hurry back for the wedding. It is a week away."

"I, for one, am glad you said there was. But I should not speak ill of my father's wife. It is difficult for two grown women to live in the same house, especially when they are as different as Imogene and I."

"I am sure I should not speak ill of her either, but I suspect it would be the end of one or the other of us if I had to live there."

"Sometimes I think it will be the same with us, as well."
Eve looked at him, her eyes dancing. "I am not usually so
blunt. You are a very bad influence, I think."

"So I have been told."

"You look completely unrepentant."

He smiled at her, the aforementioned dimple creasing
his cheek. "Sadly, I am that as well." He leaned toward her,
lowering his voice confidentially. "What sane man would
not want to be a bad influence on such a beautiful woman
as you?"

His eyes looked straight into hers, the humor replaced
by warmth. The look sent a thrill through Eve, and she felt
suddenly breathless and exposed, as if he had looked deep
into her and seen the hidden heat that lay there, untapped,
unwanted.

"I should go to bed now," she said abruptly, then blushed.
A lady said she was "about to retire"; she did not mention
the word *bed* lest it inspire suggestive thoughts.

Hastily she pushed back her chair and rose. Fitz stood
with her. "Let me escort you to your room."

"No. I will be fine. You stay and finish your wine."

"There is no reason for the females to retire," he told her
lightly. "I have no need to drink a glass of port, and I'd far
rather be with you."

Eve looked up at him, then wished that she had not, for
it was hard to look away again. Fitz's eyes were deep pools of
blue, pulling her in as his face loomed closer. He was going to
kiss her, she thought, and she knew that she should pull away.

But she did not.

His lips were soft and warm, pressing gently at first, then
moving against hers, supple and insistent. Eve shivered. It
had been so long since she had felt a man's mouth on hers.
After a time, Bruce had avoided even that. She had almost
forgotten how it felt—or had it ever felt like this?

Fitz's kiss was warm and sweet, like honey in the sun. His tongue traced the line where her lips came together, sending tingles running through her. Eve's lips opened to him, and his tongue slid in to taste and explore. Heat poured through her, startling in its intensity. She wanted to melt into him, to wrap her arms around him and press her body against his. For an instant she wavered, stunned by the pleasure rushing through her.

But in the next instant she came to her senses and stepped back. "No."

Her hand came up to cover her mouth. Her lips were soft and moist, still tingling from the pressure of his mouth. She could not look at him as she struggled to pull her unruly senses back into order.

"Eve . . ." He took a step toward her.

"No." Eve raised her head. "However I may have appeared to you yesterday, I am not 'easy.' "

He smiled faintly. "I do not think you are easy at all. Indeed, I think you will be quite difficult." He paused, then added, "But well worth the effort."

Eve was appalled at how much she wanted him. Surely after all these years she should be well past feeling this way. She was no longer an impressionable girl to be swept away by a handsome face and form.

Well, at least she had learned enough not to let her feelings show. She lifted her chin, ruthlessly keeping her voice cold and stern. "I am surprised, Mr. Talbot. I would not have taken you for the sort of man who would take advantage of a woman under your brother's care."

He gave a short, sharp shake of his head. "I have no intention of taking advantage of you. I have never bedded a woman who did not want me."

Eve felt sure that was true. Fitz Talbot would not have

to force a woman; no doubt they fell into his hands like so much ripe fruit.

"I would never press you to do anything you do not want to do."

He reached out to take her hand. Eve knew that she should pull her hand away, but she did not. She simply watched, her eyes caught and held by his as he raised her hand and pressed a soft kiss upon the tip of her finger. Her mouth went dry, and her breath caught in her throat as he worked his way down the line of her fingers, gently, slowly kissing each fingertip.

"Are you truly repelled by my touch?" His voice was low and seductive.

Eve's tongue seemed stuck to the roof of her mouth. She trembled, and she knew that he must feel it in her fingers. With a great effort of will, she pulled her hand from his and walked away.

"Perhaps you think widows are fair game." Eve swung back to face him, her head high. "That they are loose and immoral. But I assure you, sir, I am not."

"What I think about widows . . ." Fitz came to her, his steps slow and steady, his eyes boring into hers. ". . . is that they are infinitely more desirable than other women." He stopped, his eyes still locked to hers. "And you, my dear Eve, are the most desirable of them all."

He was only inches away. She could feel the heat radiating from his body, smell his scent. Hunger blossomed deep in her abdomen, warm and insistent. Everything within her seemed to soften, yearning toward him. Unconsciously she leaned forward.

His arms went around her, crushing her to him, and his mouth came down on hers. He kissed her long and hard, his arms like iron around her, imprinting her soft flesh with his body. Eve held back for an instant, then her arms went around him, clinging to him with all her strength. She kissed him back, her mouth pliant and hungry, luxuriating in the taste, the scent, the feel of him. He filled her senses, and she could feel her body opening to him, her breasts swelling gently.

Fitz broke their kiss, his breath rasping harshly in his throat, and stared for a moment into her eyes, his own eyes only inches away, deep, fathomless pools of blue. Then he tilted his head the other way, changing the angle of their kiss, and took her mouth again. Their lips clung and separated and clung again. She could feel the ridge of his hardened maleness pushing against her, and her core tightened in response. She wanted to feel . . . she wanted to know . . .

With a soft cry, Eve broke away from him. His arms opened, freeing her, then fell to his sides. He stood, his face stamped with passion, and his look of hunger almost sent Eve flying back into his embrace.

She wrapped her arms tightly around herself, as though to keep from doing just that, and took another step backward. Drawing a deep breath, she rattled out, "Please . . . please do not do this. I cannot, I will not, come to your bed. If you have the slightest regard for me, please . . . stay away from me."

Eve whirled and hurried from the room. He did not follow.

She dreaded facing Fitz the following morning at breakfast. However, he was as polite and charming as ever, and no word was spoken about the evening before or the way it had ended. When it came time to leave, Fitz handed Eve into the carriage, then mounted his horse to ride outside. Eve could not help but feel a pang of disappointment.

Of course, that was what she had asked him to do—to

stay away from her. Her life would be much easier if he was annoyed and kept his distance. It was his closeness that was tempting, his friendship that was all too likely to trip her up.

Even sitting alone in the carriage, Eve could feel a blush rise in her cheeks at the memory of her response to Fitz the night before. No doubt she had confirmed all the rumors about widows—ripe for the plucking, they would fall easily into one's arms. Unlike a maiden, a widow would know the pleasures of the marital bed and be eager to experience them again.

She let out a little snort, crossing her arms. The pleasures of the marital bed had never been part of her life. She leaned her head back against the seat and closed her eyes. It was all too easy to remember the details of her wedding night—the nerves, the anticipation mingling with fear, the first few moments of kisses and caresses, followed finally by frustrated curses and Bruce rolling away from her.

She had not understood it at the time. She had been too innocent, too inexperienced. When they had entered their bridal chamber, Bruce had gone into the dressing room to change clothes, courteously leaving her the bedchamber in which to undress. Eve had changed into her virginal white nightgown, with its rows of carefully embroidered ruffles, brushed out her hair so that it hung long and loose about her shoulders like a golden cloud. Then she had climbed into bed and waited for him. It had seemed odd that it had taken him even longer to undress and come to bed than it had her, but she supposed he was simply giving her plenty of time to get ready. It had been even more peculiar that Bruce seemed as nervous as she when he had gotten into bed beside her. But then he had put his arm around her, and she had snuggled against him, and they had talked. Gradually she had begun to relax. He had begun to kiss her, and something had stirred deep inside her, a tingling, teasing, intriguing feeling. He had caressed her, too, his hand roaming over her, and she had been aware of a desire to feel his hand beneath her nightgown, against her bare skin. Nerves had subsided, chased away by her eagerness to follow those tantalizing new sensations.

But they had led to nothing else. His kisses had become harder, almost frantic, and he had balled up her nightgown in his fists, clutching it almost desperately. She had sensed something was wrong even before he began to fumble at his own body beneath his nightclothes. Red-faced, sweating, he had pulled back. Letting out a string of curses, he had jumped out of their bed and picked up the nearest thing handy, some little knickknack on the bedside table, and sent it sailing across the room to crash into the fireplace.

Eve had begun to cry, certain that she had somehow spoiled everything. But Bruce, for all his faults, had not been the sort of man to blame others. He had turned to her, his face rigid with self-disgust, and said, "No, it's not you. It's me. It's always me."

Then tears had started in his eyes, and he had sat down on the edge of the bed, pressing the heels of his hands to his eyes, struggling not to break down. Eve, not knowing what to do or even what was really wrong, had wrapped her arms around him from behind and whispered endearments to him, assuring him that things would be all right, that they would try again, that everything would be different.

"No," her husband had said, his voice raw. "I hoped it would be. I thought because you were a lady, a good woman, that it wouldn't happen the same way. I thought because I loved you, it would change. I would change. That I would be able to——" He broke off, then ended in a whisper, "I fear I have done you a grave disservice, Evie. I'm sorry."

A sigh escaped Eve at the memory, and she raised her head, blinking and turning to look out the window. *Poor*

Bruce. His inability to perform had haunted him all his life. Oh, he had not given up completely that night. He had tried again and again, but always with the same results—Bruce frustrated and angry at himself and Eve warm, tingling, and unsatisfied. Or, at least, at first she had been. After a time she had grown to dread the increasingly rare occasions when Bruce would take her in his arms. Later she had come to feel nothing but disinterest, or even a vague resentment, knowing that it would come to nothing, as always.

Eventually he had stopped trying altogether, and in the last few years of their marriage they had lived together like a brother and sister, fond, even loving, but with no physical bond. She saw that all the things Bruce did—his extravagance, his evenings of drinking and gambling with his fellow officers, his neck-or-nothing riding—were expressions of his anger at his own sexual failure. He embraced any activity that proved his manhood, fearlessly throwing himself into things a more prudent man would avoid. He had always regretted being too young to fight in the Peninsular campaign, buying his first commission barely in time to defeat Napoleon. He had chafed at a military life without war. And when he died, thrown from his horse as he took a fence in his soaring style, Eve had grieved for him, but she had felt some hope, too, that at last he had found peace.

As for herself, Eve had found that there lived within her more sensuality than she would ever have guessed. She had known the stirrings of desire and been surprised; she had felt the teasing touch of pleasure and wished for more. It would have been easy enough to find satisfaction if she wished. But Eve would never have betrayed her husband that way. Even if she had been the sort to take on a lover, it would spell ruin for her hopes of making her own way in the world by becoming a chaperone or companion. No one would accept her for such a position with less than a perfect reputation.

Eve glanced out the window, her eyes going to Fitz. She leaned her head against the frame of the window, admiring the way he sat on his horse, the breadth of his shoulders, his profile as he turned to look at something. It was easy to watch him. Easy to like him. Eve was going to have to make an effort not to be ensnared by his charm.

She hoped he would not stay long at Willowmere after the wedding. He would grow bored and return to London. Likeable though Fitz was, Eve had no illusions about the life he lived—he was part of that set of aristocratic young bachelors who idled away their time in London, always seeking some new pleasure, whether an opera dancer, a boxing match, or a new gaming club. Fitz might be interested in pursuing her right now, but that would fade when she did not give in to his advances, and then he would go back to London, seeking something more interesting.

The thought did not lighten her spirits.

The inn had packed a luncheon for them, and they stopped at midday to eat it, looking out over one of the magnificent vistas of the Lake District. Hills rolled away in the distance, and below them glittered a dark tarn. But their stay was brief, for both were eager to press on. Willowmere, Fitz explained, was not too far now, only another hour.

Both tension and anticipation rose in Eve as they drew nearer. She could feel the horses picking up speed as the road grew more familiar to them. They passed through a small village, and before long the vehicle turned onto a lane. Eve sat up straighter, leaning close to the window. They emerged from a line of yew trees onto a wide, grassy area. To the right lay a view of a small dark tarn with a summerhouse and a quaint little bridge crossing the pond.

But Eve spared only a glance for the picturesque scene. Her attention was fixed on the house that lay in front of her.

It was large and rambling, with no particular architectural style. It seemed rather to have simply grown up over the years, wings added on as the need or whim arose, so that it sprawled out, sometimes three stories, sometimes only two or even one. Though most of the house was stone of a honeyed hue, the shade varied somewhat, the stones darkened here and there by time and wear, and a small part was built of brick. One wall was almost entirely covered with a blanket of ivy. The overall effect was, oddly enough, not discordant but homey and warm, like a cottage that had somehow grown enormous, an atmosphere enhanced by the shrubs softening the foundation and the gardens that stretched out on either side of the house. Willowmere managed to be both imposing and charming, and she liked it immediately.

When the carriage rolled to a stop, Fitz dismounted, tossing the reins of his horse to a groom, and came over to open the carriage door. Affection and pride were evident on his face as he said, "Welcome to Willowmere. How do you like it?"

Eve took his hand and stepped down, then took a long, encompassing look at the house. "It's lovely," she replied honestly, smiling at Fitz. "Just beautiful. Is this where you grew up?"

He nodded. "Yes. Lived here for seventeen years, except for occasional trips to London." He pivoted to look at the house again. "I have to confess, I always love to see the place. Come inside. I want to introduce you to Stewkesbury and my cousins."

Eve took the arm he offered, and they walked from the drive through the small and tidy front lawn to the door. It opened a moment before they reached it, and a smiling footman bowed to them.

"Welcome home, Mr. Talbot."

"Thank you, Paul. Is my brother about?"

"They are both here, sir. His lordship is in his study, and I believe that Sir Royce is with him. I sent word to his lordship as soon as we saw the carriage approaching."

"This is Mrs. Hawthorne," Fitz told the footman as he handed him his hat and gloves. "She will be staying with us for some time."

"Ma'am." The footman bowed and took Eve's bonnet and gloves as well.

She turned as two men strode into view. One of them was clearly Fitz's brother, for his coloring and build were much the same. Slightly shorter than Fitz and a trifle broader through the chest and shoulders, he had very dark brown hair and gray eyes, and his features were similar to Fitz's, though not blessed with the same perfection. The other man was also tall, but his hair was a dark blond, his eyes green, and his face, though handsome, was different from Fitz's and the other man's.

Both men, however, were smiling as they strode forward. "Fitz!"

"Stewkesbury. Royce." Fitz stepped forward to shake hands with the men, then turned toward Eve. "Allow me to introduce you to Mrs. Hawthorne. Mrs. Hawthorne, these are my brothers, Lord Stewkesbury and Sir Royce Winslow."

The earl was staring at her in some surprise, but he recovered quickly and stepped forward to bow to Eve. "Mrs. Hawthorne, welcome to Willowmere. I trust you had a good journey?"

"Yes, it was very nice, thank you." Eve smiled, though her nerves tightened. Obviously the earl was as surprised as Fitz had been about her appearance. She wondered exactly what Vivian had told them.

"Mrs. Hawthorne." Sir Royce bowed to her. If he was surprised, he covered it more quickly or more efficiently than his stepbrother, for there was nothing on his face but pleasant interest.

"My cousins will be so pleased to meet you," the earl began. "I will send for—"

At that moment there was an ear-piercing shriek from upstairs.

Chapter 4

The scream was followed by a shout of "Pirate!"

In the next instant a dog came flying down the steps, followed by several young women. The dog was small and seemed equipped with springs, for he bounded down the stairs then across the entryway in great leaps. His hair was short and white, with black splotches scattered here and there and one black spot around one eye. The black patch, Eve presumed, had given him the name Pirate—that and the way a scar curved from his lip across his muzzle, lifting his lip in a permanent sneer.

He carried in his mouth a circlet of white silk flowers, and from it flowed a swath of white lace and ribbons. It was this prize that apparently engendered the shouts and frantic pursuit of the women behind him. Spotting visitors, the dog charged at them, jumping up at Fitz, then merrily whirling and darting around Sir Royce's legs. Sir Royce grabbed at the animal but missed, and Pirate headed toward Eve. Eve clapped her hands and leaned forward, curving her arms, and the dog jumped straight into them. She tightened one arm around him, reaching up with that hand to grasp the circlet, and with the other hand she reached down and began to scratch his stomach.

Pirate's eyes closed, and his mouth opened, tongue lolling out in an expression of pure ecstasy. In doing so, he released the veil into Eve's grasp, and she quickly pulled it away.

"Oh, thank you!" One of the girls sprang forward to take the veil, smiling with relief.

"Well." The earl raised one eyebrow. "All doubts are resolved. Clearly, Mrs. Hawthorne, you are the woman for the job."

"True," Sir Royce added, grinning. "If you are able to control Pirate, the Bascombe sisters should be an easy task."

"Thank you," the girl who had spoken earlier repeated. She was pretty, with lively gray-green eyes and a strawberries-and-cream complexion. Her hair was light brown, with a few sun-kissed golden streaks running through it.

She bore enough resemblance to the dark-haired woman behind her for Eve to deduce that they were sisters, and since Fitz had said that there were three of the Bascombes still in residence, Eve presumed that the slender girl with the dark golden blond hair and gray eyes must be one of the remaining sisters.

"Mrs. Hawthorne, allow me to introduce you to my cousins." The earl ended her inner musings by stepping forward. "Miss Bascombe."

He indicated the woman with chocolate brown hair and eyes a mixture of blue and green. This must be the eldest of the sisters, Mary, who was getting married in a week. She had strong, though handsome, features in a heart-shaped face.

"Miss Camellia Bascombe." The earl nodded to the girl who looked the least like the others, the gray-eyed blonde. "And lastly, this child is Miss Lily Bascombe." Though he kept his face impassive, the twinkle in his eyes indicated that he knew exactly how this appellation would affect the girl who had taken the veil from Eve.

"Cousin Oliver!" she cried in protest. "I am not a child. I'll be nineteen in only a few more months."

"I apologize. You are right. You are nearly in your dotage."

Lily Bascombe made a face at the earl before she turned to Eve. "I was trimming the veil, and Pirate came out of nowhere and pounced on it. Mary would have killed me if he'd torn it. It was very clever of you not to try to pull it away from him but to get him to drop it."

"He looked precisely the sort to enjoy a tug-of-war," Eve responded, smiling. "So I thought a distraction might be the answer."

"I must thank you, too." Mary Bascombe stepped forward to shake Eve's hand. She spoke in a clear, no-nonsense voice and had a firm handshake. "Since it is my veil you saved."

"I am happy to be of service." Eve smiled at her, then turned to the other sister. Camellia's grip was as firm as Mary's and her gaze as straightforward.

"And I believe you know me," came a voice from behind them on the stairs.

"Vivian!" Eve whirled to see her friend standing at the landing.

The red-haired beauty laughed and came down the last set of steps in a rush, holding out her arms to Eve. Eve hurried forward to give her a hug.

"Oh, Viv," she murmured. "It's so good to see you. Thank you."

Vivian smiled as she released her friend. "You may not thank me long. We are in the midst of a wedding whirlwind here, and you will doubtless be caught up in it."

"She already is," Mary Bascombe remarked, holding up the veil. "Mrs. Hawthorne managed to capture Pirate and take away my veil. I'm afraid he drooled on some of the flowers, but that can be remedied."

"I told you she would be perfect," Vivian replied.

"Yes, you did." The earl stepped forward now, casting a wry look at Lady Vivian. "'Tis odd, but I seem to have gotten the impression that Mrs. Hawthorne was a much . . . more mature woman."

"Did you?" Vivian's large green eyes widened innocently. "I cannot imagine how that happened."

"Can you not?" Stewkesbury murmured drily.

Vivian gazed back at him, a challenging light in her eyes. "I do believe I said she was a friend of mine." Her voice turned brisk as she linked her arm through Eve's, moving them both closer to the earl. "In any case, it scarcely matters, does it? What counts is that Mrs. Hawthorne is precisely the person to help you. Being nearer in age will make it much easier for the girls to rely on her when they need help. Won't it?" She turned toward the group of sisters.

"Oh, yes." Lily and Camellia were quick to chorus their agreement.

"She's much better than Miss Dalrymple," Mary added, her eyes lighting mischievously.

The earl released a huge sigh. "Yes, I know, and I am well aware that *I* am the one who made that error in judgment. No doubt you are right, Lady Vivian."

"I am shocked to hear such words from your lips." Her eyes danced merrily.

After another meaningful glance at Vivian, the earl bowed slightly in Eve's direction. "I am sure that Mrs. Hawthorne will do an excellent job."

"Mrs. Hawthorne must be tired after our journey." Fitz spoke up. "She would probably welcome an opportunity to rest for a while."

"Of course. You are right." The earl nodded. "We should not hold you here any longer."

The Bascombe sisters clustered around Eve and Vivian,

offering to show her to her room. But at that moment there was a knock on the front door, and they all turned as the footman opened the door.

A slender woman dressed in a sprigged muslin dress and blue spencer stood on the doorstep. An ornate bonnet sat on her head, the blue lining of it matching the color of her short jacket and reflecting the blue of her large, limpid eyes. Golden blond curls framed her delicate oval face beneath the hat, and the wide blue ribbon was tied in a charming bow beneath her chin. She was, in short, lovely.

Her eyes went first to Fitz, who was standing closest to the door. "Why, Fitz! It is good to see you back! It has been quite dull around here with you gone."

She smiled dazzlingly at Fitz, Eve noted with a spurt of irritation.

"Lady Sabrina." Fitz's greeting and bow were perfunctory.

"I am sure all the girls in the village have missed you sorely." Lady Sabrina reached out to touch his sleeve lightly. "You will have to tell me all about your journey."

"I fear there is little to tell."

It was difficult to make much conversation of this response, so the lady's eyes moved on to Sir Royce. She merely gave him a cool nod before approaching the earl. "Hallo, Stewkesbury. I was returning from my little shopping excursion, and I thought I would offer Lady Vivian a ride home."

Her gaze swept on to Vivian, then fell to Eve standing beside her. "Oh."

The lovely face changed subtly, becoming suddenly harder and colder. The ice-blue eyes dropped from Eve's face down her form, taking in everything about her from her blond hair to the two-year-old dress Eve wore.

"Lady Sabrina, please allow me to introduce you to Mrs. Hawthorne. Mrs. Hawthorne, this is Lady Sabrina Carlyle." Stewkesbury performed the introductions.

"I see." Lady Sabrina's tone was contemptuous. "You must be the new hired companion."

Beside her, Vivian stiffened. "Mrs. Hawthorne is a particular friend of mine and has been for years."

"Mrs. Hawthorne has kindly agreed to be our guest for a time," the earl inserted smoothly. "We are all most grateful, as I am sure that my cousins will be lonely after their sister's wedding."

Eve smiled at Lady Sabrina with all the sweetness she could muster. "It is a pleasure to make your acquaintance, my lady. I have long wanted to meet Lady Vivian's aunt."

Beside Eve, Vivian choked back a gurgle of laughter, and Lady Sabrina's gaze turned glacial. Quickly, Vivian jumped into the silence, saying, "Thank you, Sabrina. 'Twas most kind of you to stop to give me a ride, but there is still much here to do, and I would like to visit with my friend. The earl kindly offered to send me home in his carriage, so you need not trouble yourself."

"Of course. Well . . . then I will take my leave of you."

Eve noticed that no one, even the earl, made any effort to persuade Lady Sabrina to stay to visit or have a cup of tea. She watched, a trifle puzzled, as the woman swept back out the front door.

An awkward silence fell over the group after Lady Sabrina's departure. The earl cleared his throat and said, "Well, cousins, if you will show Mrs. Hawthorne to her room . . ." He bowed toward Eve. "Again, welcome to our home, Mrs. Hawthorne."

"Thank you, my lord."

He turned to the other two men. "How about a drink to wash away the dust of the road? I received a letter from your business agent, Fitz. He has some rather important financial matters he needs you to answer."

The men started off down the hall, Fitz saying lightly,

"No amount of drink could make that conversation palatable. Cannot you just reply to the chap, Oliver?"

Vivian took Eve's arm. "Come. I think you'll be quite pleased with your accommodations." They started up the stairs, the Bascombe sisters falling behind them. Vivian leaned in closer to Eve. "Well, my dear, barely here fifteen minutes, and already you've won over your charges, impressed the earl, and made an enemy for life."

"I did not mean to," Eve protested. "Well, at least the part about making an enemy. I do hope the girls like me, and the earl will not dismiss me out of hand."

"Have no fear of that. I know you, Eve. Soon he'll be telling himself that sending for you was the best idea he ever had."

"I don't know. Everyone seemed awfully surprised at my age. What did you tell them?"

"I never mentioned your age. I simply told them how wise and mature you were, how well you would be able to deal with two lively girls. Isn't that right?" Vivian turned to the Bascombe sisters for agreement.

Mary laughed. "That's true. Cousin Oliver never asked directly how old Mrs. Hawthorne was."

Vivian nodded. "There, you see? The picture he formed in his head is entirely of his own making. Had he asked me, I would have told him that you were only a few months older than I."

"You're very good at avoiding the direct question," Lily added. "I wish I could do that. I always sound as if I'm being weasely."

"That's because you *are* being weasely," Camellia told her.

"Now, girls," Mary said in a tone that suggested that she was long accustomed to mediating between her younger sisters. "You don't want to drive Mrs. Hawthorne away when she's barely arrived."

"I think it will take more than a little squabbling to drive me away," Eve told her.

"That's good." Mary grinned impishly. "Because what no one has told you is that, while there will be only two sisters left to deal with, it is the two who are the hardest to control."

This remark naturally brought hot denials from Lily and Camellia, and the three girls were soon embroiled in a laughing, good-natured argument which ended as soon as they reached Eve's room. Lily swung open the door with a flourish and ushered Eve inside. The others followed, all waiting for Eve's reaction.

Eve looked around her, astonished. The room was much larger and better furnished than she had expected; indeed, it was much grander than her own room at home. A bed with a high tester in forest green stood between two windows, both of which looked out over the gardens at the side of the house. A comfortable-looking wingback chair stood near the window, and the dresser, highboy, and wardrobe offered more space than Eve had clothes. A small secretary and a vanity with mirror completed the furnishings, along with a comfortable-looking hassock placed close to the fireplace. It would be a favorite spot, Eve thought, on a cold winter evening.

"It's beautiful," she told them honestly.

"It was our sister Rose's bedchamber before she got married and went back to America." Lily offered. "Lady Vivian told Cousin Oliver that you must have a nice room and not be stuck off in the nursery or somewhere."

"And Cousin Oliver said that since it was of such great concern to Lady Vivian, perhaps *she* should choose the room," Camellia went on.

"Which I did," Vivian concluded. "Of course, Stewkesbury was just being sardonic." She chuckled. "That will teach him to make such an offer to me."

"Well, it's a lovely room, and I appreciate it. All of you."
Eve looked around at the ring of smiling faces. "I hardly
know you, but I have the feeling that we are going to be
great friends."

Lily let out a little squeal of delight and hugged Eve. "I
think we are, too. Cousin Oliver was right—it really will
be easier when Mary leaves if you are here. Won't it, Cam?"

Camellia nodded. She was not as dramatic or emotional
as her younger sister, but Eve could read the goodwill in
her face, and she was unexpectedly touched. Without even
knowing her, these girls seemed to hold her in more affection than Imogene ever had.

"All right, girls," Mary began briskly, putting an arm
around Lily's waist and tugging her away. "I think it's time
we gave poor Mrs. Hawthorne a chance to chat with Vivian.
Besides, we have to repair my veil, remember?"

She smiled at Eve, and the sisters trailed out of the room.
Eve let out a sigh and sank into the chair, feeling suddenly
weary. "Oh, my, what a day."

"But worth it to be away from Mrs. Childe." Vivian
pulled out the stool from the vanity table and sat down on
it, turning to face Eve. "Please tell me that."

"Goodness, yes!"

While Eve washed her face and hands, Vivian rang for
tea. A few minutes later, Eve was settled comfortably in the
wingback chair, clad in her dressing gown and brushing out
her hair, while Vivian had taken a seat beside her on the
hassock.

"Thank you, Viv, for all of this." Eve made an encompassing sweep with her arm. "It means more to me than you
could ever guess."

Vivian colored a little, looking vaguely uncomfortable.
"Come, now, it was not much, truly. You were the perfect

choice. I did nothing but present Stewkesbury with the idea. You know I would like to do much more."

"I know."

"Why won't you stay with me?" Vivian went on. "I rattle around in that great house."

"I cannot ask that of you. It would be too much."

"It's not, truly."

"I cannot allow you to support me. What would that mean for our friendship? There would be duty and obligation and gratitude. It wouldn't any longer just be two schoolmates from Miss Coverbrooks' Academy for Young Ladies."

Vivian chuckled. "Perhaps not. But I hate to think of you having to live with your stepmother. You could at least come visit me for longer than a month at a time."

"Perhaps I will, when I am between employment."

Vivian heaved a sigh. "All right. I can see that it is useless to argue with you."

Eve grinned at her friend. "When has that ever stopped you?"

There was a knock on the door, and a maid brought in a tray containing not only a pot of tea and two cups but a plate of warm scones.

"I have never known a chaperone to be treated so royally," Eve said as she poured their tea.

Vivian shrugged. "The girls are well liked by the staff. And the last chaperone was not. A high-handed, disagreeable woman. I would have urged Stewkesbury to cut her loose, but that would only have made him dig in his heels."

"Really? Usually gentlemen jump to do your bidding."

"His cousin Charlotte and I used to play tricks on him when we were young. Charlotte and I were great friends, you know, and in the summers I would visit my uncle and aunt. Their home is quite close by. Oliver is seven or eight years older than we are, and he was always such a sober, responsible sort."

"A prig?"

"No, I wouldn't call him that. Even then, he had a sense of humor. But he was at Oxford and older and thought himself far too lofty for us. I was completely smitten with him, which made me even more horrid in my pranks."

"Really?" Eve looked at her friend with interest. "You never told me that!"

"I never told anyone. Well, I could barely admit it to myself. I knew it was absurd, even then. Seven years is a vast difference at that age. He thought I was a scruffy hoyden—which I was," she admitted fairly. "And I knew he was a rigid stickler, no matter how handsome he was."

"And what about now?"

Vivian glanced at her friend in surprise. "Oliver? And me?" She let out a little laugh. "No, that is still absurd. We are utter opposites and always will be. He is, I admit, a handsome man, but I can hardly be in a room with him for five minutes without setting up his bristles, and he mine. I'd hardly been around him in years—he spends little time in London—yet the moment I saw him again we were once more at odds." She shrugged. "I suppose I am fond of him in that way you are of people you've known since you were a child, no matter what they're like. And of course, he is the sort of man one could turn to if one were in a bad spot. But a romantic interest?" She shook her head, chuckling. "Definitely not."

Eve abandoned the topic and picked up a scone. "Well, then, tell me all the latest *on-dits*. You know, it is your letters that have made the past two years bearable."

Vivian smiled, and the two women settled down for a cozy chat.

* * *

Finally, Eve brushed the crumbs from her hands and rose to her feet. "This has been wonderful. But I was not hired, after all, to sip tea and gossip with you. I think I need to get back to my charges."

As Eve donned her dress, Vivian rose, too, and they left the room. It was easy enough to find the Bascombes, for chatter and laughter spilled out of the bedchamber next door. The three women in the room turned as Vivian and Eve paused at the door.

"Mrs. Hawthorne! Lady Vivian!" Lily greeted them with a flashing smile and came forward, holding out the veil. "Look! I repaired it, and you can't even see where Pirate drooled on it anymore."

She proudly held out the headgear, and Eve examined it. "My, yes, it's very well done."

Mary, too, came forward. "Have you rested enough, Mrs. Hawthorne? I am certain Cousin Oliver would not expect you to watch over the girls all the time."

"Thank you, I feel fine," Eve assured her. "I was eager to hear about the wedding plans."

Camellia rolled her eyes. "Oh, no, here we go again."

"Hush," Lily told her sister. "Everyone else enjoys hearing about the wedding. Show her your dress, Mary."

The dress in question was hauled out of the wardrobe and appropriately oohed and aahed over. Then followed a lengthy discussion of the flowers and decorations necessary for the church and for the celebration following the ceremony.

"Will there be a large number of people?" Eve asked.

"Not too many," Vivian volunteered.

"It's more than enough for me," Mary retorted. "I scarcely know any of them."

"A few of Royce's relations. My friend Charlotte Ludley— she's the Bascombes' cousin, you know—and her mother,

Lady Cynthia." Vivian began ticking off guests on her fingers. "Lord and Lady Kent."

"But not Aunt Euphronia, thank goodness," Camellia stuck in. "Although she *was* gracious enough to write a letter to Mary telling her how grateful she should be that Sir Royce was willing to marry her."

Eve's eyes widened. "Did she really?"

"Yes." Mary's gray eyes turned stormy. "She praised Royce for the 'sacrifice' he was making for the family."

"Mm. She probably did not dare show her face after that," Eve surmised.

"Too true. I'd have given her a piece of my mind." Mary looked at Eve. "Do you know Aunt Euphronia?"

"Lady Harrington?" Eve gave a little smile. "Indeed. If one has had a Season, one knows Lady Harrington."

"She criticizes everything," Vivian said. "But she has to be invited, because if you don't, she carps even more. She cannot be ignored."

"Oh, dear." Lily drooped. "Will she be there criticizing us?"

"Doubtless." Vivian nodded. "But don't worry; she will complain about all the other girls as well."

"Did she complain about you?" Camellia looked skeptical.

Vivian laughed. "She still does."

"But you are a duke's daughter. I would have thought she considered you above reproach," Mary put in.

Both Eve and Vivian laughed. "No one is above reproach in Lady Euphronia's eyes," Eve assured them. "Except, I suppose, herself."

"She allowed that my family lineage was at least long," Vivian told them wryly. "My father wasn't some vulgar mushroom, which is, I believe, how she referred to Lord Kelton, whose ancestors have held their title for only two hundred years. But the Carlyles were a bit too 'wild' for her taste—an opinion, I must warn you, that is held by some others in the *ton*. And of course, the color of my hair was apparently an affront to her good taste."

Camellia let out a crack of laughter. "That's rich! What about you, Mrs. Hawthorne? What did she say about you?"

"Let's see . . . that I put on airs above myself, for my father was only a vicar, and even if his cousin is an earl, well, one must draw the line somewhere. And oh, yes—" Her eyes kindled as she recalled another memory. "She said that I must have washed my hair in lemon juice and stood out in the sun to make it so pale, which I have *never* done."

"Does that work?" Lily asked.

Eve had to chuckle. "I don't know; I never tried it."

"Aunt Euphronia is a wicked old crone." Camellia set her jaw pugnaciously. "And you better not let her bully you, Lily."

"I won't—at least, not if you are there with me."

"I shall be, though I'm sure the balls and soirees and all that will be deadly dull."

"I suspect you will find them interesting enough when all the young men cluster about you," Eve told her.

"Me? No, that will be Lily."

"It will be both of you," Eve corrected her firmly. "Trust me on this. You are very attractive; you are the earl's cousins; and you have a romantic history. Both of you will be the center of attention. That's why the earl wants you to have a chaperone. He doesn't want you thrown into all that without adequate preparation."

"I thought he just wanted to torture us." Camellia's half-smile indicated that she was at least partially joking.

"No, silly, he doesn't want us to embarrass him," Lily put in.

"To be fair to the man, I think he does not want you to embarrass yourselves," Vivian told her. "The earl doesn't really move that much in society or care about it. If someone tried to embarrass him with your behavior, he would simply curl his lip and ignore the man. I truly think he is trying to help you."

"Yes, just think how mortifying it would have been if you had had to go to some grand dinner back when we didn't know which fork to use for the fish," Mary pointed out.

"That's it," Eve agreed. "They always say one should learn from his mistakes, but I find it's much better to figure it out beforehand, don't you?"

"Well, I still say I'd rather stay here and ride and shoot," Camellia put in flatly. "Which reminds me, it's time for our shooting lesson, Vivian."

"Shooting?" Eve's eyes widened. "You and Vivian are learning how to shoot a gun?"

Camellia laughed, and Vivian explained, "No, Cam is teaching me how to shoot. She's terribly clever that way. She can use a knife, too."

Startled, Eve looked at her new charge.

Camellia sighed. "I know. I know. A proper lady shouldn't know such things."

Eve chuckled. "You might not want to admit it to the ladies of the *ton*. But I am most impressed. It must make you feel quite . . . confident, even on your own."

"Exactly." Vivian jumped to her feet. "That is why I want to learn it myself. I've improved a good deal, haven't I, Camellia?" She turned toward Eve. "Come join us, why don't you?"

"Yes, let's all go," Lily agreed.

"Just let me get my bonnet," Eve said. She smiled to herself as she went back to her room. She would not have to worry here that her life would become too dull.

Chapter 5

Fitz and Sir Royce strolled out of the earl's office, leaving Stewkesbury settling down behind his desk to read a stack of papers. Sir Royce cast an amused glance at his half-brother and said, "Neatly played. I never thought you would manage to pass your agent's letter off on Oliver."

Fitz chuckled. "You doubted me? Really, Royce, I am hurt."

"You know, it might behoove you to spend a little time on your business affairs yourself."

Fitz raised his brows. "Why? When there are so many things I would prefer to do? Oliver enjoys that sort of thing; you know he does. He likes to look pained and tell me I should pay more attention, but I know he expects to do it in the end. And he's far better at it."

"Still . . . how can you be sure that no one's cheating you?"

"Oliver? Are you mad?"

"No, of course not Oliver."

"Well, he looks over all my businessman's reports, and he will catch it if the chap's bamboozling me. And our uncle runs the business, so all I have to do there is accept the money, just as you do. Surely you don't think Uncle Avery is cheating us."

"God, no." Royce frowned. "But . . . well, wouldn't you like to know what you have?"

"I like to know that I have enough to buy a team of horses if I choose or a new jacket or whatever takes my fancy." He shrugged. "And I know there's plenty for that. If there were not, I would have heard about it endlessly from Crabbe and my uncle and Oliver." He smiled. "I'm not like you. You had your father's estate to inherit—a house, land. Grandfather raised you and Oliver to manage those things. I, on the other hand, inherited only money. You know how our mother's father was—he wanted us to be gentlemen and never stain our hands with the actual business."

"But surely someday you'll have a house. Land. When you marry."

Fitz sent him a wry look. "What is it about proposing to a woman that makes a man assume every other man is going to take the plunge?"

Royce looked a trifle sheepish but retorted, "Perhaps because we've found out how quickly one's convictions change when one meets the right woman."

"I have met many 'right' women," Fitz shot back. "Indeed, few of them, I find, are 'wrong.'"

"You know what I mean—the one who is right for you. Who makes you wonder why you ever thought you wanted to remain a bachelor."

Fitz smiled fondly at his brother. "I am very glad that you have found Mary. And I wish you both the happiest of lives. You know that. But I don't think wedded bliss is in my future."

They had strolled out of the house as they talked, and after a brief pause for Royce to light his cigar, they continued around the terrace to the side of the house. They paused at the sight of the Bascombe sisters, along with Lady Vivian and Mrs. Hawthorne, standing in the yard beyond the garden. A target butt had been set up there, and twenty paces from it Vivian and Camellia were taking turns aiming and firing at it. A footman stood nearby, holding the case of dueling pistols, and one of the gamekeeper's men stood beside him, reloading after every attempt.

"Ah. Target practice." Royce smiled, watching the women—or, more accurately, watching Mary as she talked to the others.

"Care to join them?" Fitz asked.

"I'm enjoying watching," Royce replied with a grin.

"They are a sight," Fitz agreed. "Too bad I'm related to most of them."

"Not Vivian."

"Mm. Lovely, true, but I prefer a subtler beauty. There's something about hair the color of spun gold . . ."

"Have you taken a fancy to Mrs. Hawthorne?" Royce looked at him with interest. "Oliver will have your hide if you cause a scandal with our cousins' chaperone."

Fitz grimaced. "Please. When have I ever caused a scandal?" When Royce opened his mouth to reply, Fitz added quickly, "In recent years, I mean, not when I was a callow youth."

"You are generally discreet."

"I am always discreet," Fitz corrected him.

"Still . . ." Royce shrugged. "Rather close to home."

"I have no intention of taking advantage of her."

"Of course not. It's just, well, carrying off trysts right in your own home, with no one finding out? It's a trifle risky."

"But dear chap, what would be the fun if it were *safe*?" Fitz tossed him a grin and started down the stairs to join the women. With a sigh and a shake of his head, Royce followed him.

*   *   *

Over the next few days Eve found it almost absurdly easy to establish a relationship with her new charges. The Bascombe sisters were friendly and open, easily accepting her as one of them. Eve fell in with the wedding preparations, helping them sew and pin and write out place cards, going with Mary to visit the vicar's wife, and even helping her discuss the arrangements for the wedding feast with the earl's cook.

Mary, brave and outspoken in so many ways, was less assured when it came to taking on her new role as a gentleman's wife. "No one at home would believe it," she told Eve confidentially. "They all, quite frankly, consider me rather bossy. But when I face the earl's servants, I know they are all thinking that I don't belong."

"Nonsense. Of course you belong. I have never dealt with the number of servants that the earl has, but the principle is the same. You cannot let them see that you're scared. You must present an air of confidence; you must remember that you are in command."

"It would be easier if I knew what I was doing." Mary gave her a wry smile.

"I believe that bluffing is the key."

The days remaining before the wedding flew by, each one bringing some new crisis or other that had to be managed. The earl's aunt Cynthia arrived with her daughter Charlotte, Lady Ludley. They were accompanied by Lord Ludley, Charlotte's husband, and their rambunctious brood of boys. Fortunately for everyone, Camellia took it upon herself to keep the boys entertained outdoors on some adventure or other. Lady Cynthia and the Ludleys were not a problem. Unfortunately the same could not be said of Lord and Lady Kent, who were highly aware of their own importance. Though Charlotte and her mother treated Eve as a friend of Vivian's, the Kents were inclined to treat her as a sort of higher-class servant, and they brought most of their complaints to her.

Late in the afternoon before the wedding an unexpected visitor arrived at Willowmere, strolling into the house and greeting the footman with the air of one familiar with the place.

"Hallo, John." He handed his hat and gloves to the footman just as Eve and Lily came down the hall, carrying rolls of wide ribbon to be used in decorating the grand ballroom. "What the devil's going on here? There must be five gardeners out front, clipping and raking."

"Who is that?" Lily breathed to Eve. She came to a dead stop, staring at him, her eyes starry.

The man was, Eve had to agree, something to behold. Though not as handsome as Fitz—a high measure to be judged against, Eve had to admit—he was nonetheless striking. His face was highlighted by broad, soaring cheekbones, and his eyes were an unusual golden brown, almost the same shade as his caramel-colored hair. He was dressed for traveling in a lightweight drab coat decorated by several shoulder capes, which he removed now and handed to the footman. Beneath he wore buckskin breeches, an olive green coat of kerseymere, and gleaming top boots.

"It's the wedding, sir."

"Wedding! Good Gad, don't tell me Stewkesbury's getting himself leg-shackled. I would think Fitz would've slipped me the word."

"No, sir, it's Miss Bascombe, his lordship's cousin."

"Oh." The visitor seemed to lose interest at this. "One of that buffle-headed Gordon's sisters? Devil take it, I've stepped into a right mess, then, haven't I? Perhaps I should just nip out before—"

He cast a glance around the foyer, and his eyes fell on the two women who had just entered. His brows shot up. Then a slow smile spread across his face, and he swept them a deep bow. "Ladies, your servant. Pray, ease my mind and tell me that neither of you is the imminent bride. I should hate to know that such visions of loveliness are about to be removed from the ranks of the unmarried."

Lily giggled, blushing, and dipped a little curtsey in return. "No, sir, it is my sister Mary."

"Ah, you have relieved me. But I cannot believe that Fitz has never told me that he had cousins such as you and . . ." He looked a little questioningly at Eve.

"I am not a cousin. I am their chaperone," Eve told him in her most quelling tone.

"A chaperone? Never!" He placed a hand theatrically on his heart. "You make me doubt my senses."

There was the clatter of footsteps on the stairs, and a moment later Fitz burst into view. "Neville!" A wide grin split his face as he trotted down the last few steps. "I *thought* that was your curricle I saw. What the devil are you doing here? Never tell me you came for the wedding." Fitz reached him and shook his hand, clapping the other hand to Neville's shoulder.

"How could I? I was unaware it was happening. Am I in your family's black books now?"

"I never dreamed you would want to attend," Fitz retorted.

"Well, and so I wouldn't," their visitor agreed cheerfully. "Or at least I would not unless I had seen the beauty of your guests. Never tell me this lovely young lady is Gordon's sister."

"Good Lord, no." Fitz turned toward Eve and Lily. "I am sorry. Mrs. Hawthorne, Cousin Lily, allow me to introduce you. This chap who's been rattling away is my friend, Mr. Neville Carr. Carr, please meet Mrs. Hawthorne and Miss

Lily Bascombe. Miss Lily is one of our American cousins. I told you about them."

"No doubt you did, but you know I so rarely listen. You should have told me that Miss Lily was enchanting."

Lily dimpled and blushed, her eyes sparkling. Eve took her firmly by the arm. "A pleasure to meet you, Mr. Carr, but I am afraid that we must go now. We have an urgent task awaiting us."

Lily reluctantly let Eve pull her away, though she murmured in an injured tone, "They don't need the ribbon *that* badly."

"Mm." Eve kept her tone light and noncommittal. "It's only polite to allow your cousin a bit of time alone with his friend. Besides, it's always to one's advantage to appear indifferent."

"Oh." Lily fell silent, considering this.

Behind them Eve heard Neville Carr say, "Sorry to barge in on you like this, Fitz. I had the urge to get away for a bit. Thought of you whiling away the time up here, and I imagined you'd welcome the company. Bit awkward, though. I'll nip down to the village and get a room at the inn. Head back to London tomorrow."

"Nonsense. There's no need for that," Fitz protested. "The wedding's tomorrow, and almost everyone's leaving the day after that. Stay. Royce will be happy for you to attend the wedding."

"It's Royce who's getting married?" Neville's voice rose. "Devil a bit! Of course I'll stay. Never thought I'd see this day."

The men turned and walked off in the other direction, and Eve could no longer hear their words. Apparently Lily had been listening to their conversation as well, for she turned now to Eve, her eyes sparkling.

"Wasn't Mr. Carr handsome? How long do you think he will stay?"

From the look on Lily's face, Eve could only hope that it was not long.

The next day dawned bright and clear, with just a nip of autumn in the air to remind everyone that it was, after all, September. It was a perfect day for a wedding, and a beaming Mary clearly thought so, too.

Eve, thinking to give the sisters a chance to bid good-bye alone, went downstairs to check on the arrangements in the ballroom. Everything seemed to be in place, lacking only the flowers that the gardeners were to cut that morning.

"Everything in order?"

Eve turned to see Sir Royce standing just inside the doorway. He advanced into the room, adding somewhat doubtfully, "I'm not bringing down some horrible curse on our heads by being here, am I? I've been warned away from so many rooms in the past week I'm beginning to feel I should have retreated to Iverley Hall."

Eve smiled. She had come to like Mary's future husband. More lighthearted than the earl and less carefree than Fitz, he was, she thought, perfectly suited for the headstrong, engaging Mary Bascombe. He would be able to hold his own, Eve thought, when it came to battles of will, but he seemed at ease with Mary's strong personality, even proud of it, and was more apt to laugh about her "American ways" than to try to change them. Eve could only hope the other girls found men as well suited to them.

"I think you are safe from dreadful curses here," Eve told him. "'Tis only the bride and the dress that are banned from your sight." She gestured toward the room. "How does it look?"

"Beautiful." He made a turn, taking it all in. "Of course,

I'm so nervous right now I'm surprised I can even see it. No one ever told me the wedding day turned one's knees to jelly."

"Don't worry. You'll pull through." Eve chuckled. "I remember my husband told me afterward he'd rather have jumped an untried hunter over a four-foot fence than face his wedding day."

"I sympathize. It's silly, of course. I'd rather marry Miss Bascombe than anything in the world, but the thought of standing up in front of a churchful of people to do so gives me the shivers."

He began to stroll idly through the room, and Eve paced alongside him, feeling he needed a friendly ear.

"It's not just that, though," he went on thoughtfully. "It's knowing that now you are responsible for another human being, that the heart and happiness and well-being of the one you love most in the world are in your hands." Royce turned to her, his brows drawing together. "It's all so fragile. What if I make a mistake? What if I disappoint her? Fail her? What if she is unhappy at Iverley Hall? Or with me?"

Eve reached out and laid a hand on his forearm. "Sir Royce, I have not known either you or Mary long, but I can tell by your words that you have a good heart. Even if you stumble, even if you err, as everyone does, I can tell you this: Mary Bascombe is not a fragile flower to wilt at the first disappointment. She is a strong woman; she won't break. Nor will she suffer in silence, I dare say. If she disagrees with you, if you hurt her, she will say so."

He chuckled. "You can rest assured of that."

"Then she will not let things go far astray before she tries to rectify them. She won't let you let her down. And neither will you. You love each other, I know. Do you trust each other?"

He nodded. "I'd trust Mary with my life, and she'd say the same for me."

"Then whatever bumps come along, they will not overset you."

He looked at her for a long moment, then smiled. "Your husband was a lucky man to have a wife such as you, Mrs. Hawthorne. Thank you." Royce patted her hand. "You have returned me to the land of reason."

Eve laughed, letting her hand drop again to her side and turning to walk with him out of the ballroom. "Sir Royce, I do not think you had a long journey to make."

Eve parted from Royce near the stairs. She stood for a moment, pondering whether she should go upstairs and check on the Bascombes or go to the kitchen to make sure that all was in order there. She glanced over at the long table in the hallway, where the butler set the mail each day, separated out for each person. As usual, there were a few letters for the earl, but a square white envelope sat apart from that pile, and Eve saw with some surprise that it was addressed to her.

She picked it up, noting that her name was printed in clumsy letters. It must be from Jules, she thought, smiling as she thought of her half-brother. He had not yet mastered the art of cursive handwriting. She broke the seal of red wax and opened the letter. In bold, block letters that seemed to jump off the page, she read:

**YOU DON'T BELONG HERE
LEAVE**

Eve stood for a long moment, simply staring at the paper. Quickly she closed it and glanced around her almost guiltily. *Who could have done this? Why?*

She opened the note and read it again, letting the words sink in. They were written in broad strokes, straight up and down, like the hand of an uneducated person or a child. But surely no child would do such a thing.

She looked at the front of the letter. Aside from the address beneath her name, there was nothing to indicate that it had been mailed—no stamp, not even any wear and tear. She had assumed it had come in the mail because it had been on the table, but it could have been placed there anytime that morning. Someone local must have done it—and after all, why would a person from somewhere else tell her to leave?

There was no threat, but the thick black letters, and the obvious malevolence that lay behind them, frightened her a little. She felt suddenly vulnerable, exposed. At first she wondered if it could be from one of the servants. But she could not remember doing anything that might have offended any of them. It was far more likely, she realized, that the writer had simply disguised his handwriting.

Could it be from someone here in the house? Eve's heart twisted at the thought. The girls had been more than kind to her, and even the earl seemed friendly enough. Her lips twitched into a smile at the notion of the elegant earl scrawling out this missive, then sneaking in to lay it on the table.

No. There was only one person who disliked her: Lady Sabrina. Eve could envision Sabrina penning a nasty little note. Still . . . it seemed absurd that she could have taken such an antipathy to Eve after meeting her only one brief time.

Perhaps one of the girls had done it in jest. There was a definite sense of mischief about Lily and Camellia. It was possible they might think it great fun to scare the new chaperone even if they liked her. The note seemed a bit excessive, but Eve could not help but remember the sort of books Lily enjoyed reading, with imperiled heroines and ghosts and clanking chains.

Eve wondered what she should do. She quailed at the thought of taking the note to the earl. Really, when she thought about it, it was such a trifling thing. It would be embarrassing even to show it to Stewkesbury. Fitz, of course, was approachable, but she did not want to go running to him for help. He might take it the wrong way, think she was trying to throw out lures to him. Her cheeks pinkened at the thought.

Besides, if she had offended one of the servants, it would only make them resent her more if she involved Fitz or the earl. Nor did she want to get Lily and Camellia into trouble. If they had done it, it could have been nothing but a jest. And if it was Lady Sabrina, however absurd that seemed, she had done it out of spite; there wasn't really any danger to Eve in the note.

The best thing, she decided, was to pretend that nothing untoward had happened. Whoever was behind it, the only reason could have been to cause Eve distress. If she remained cool and unconcerned, it would spoil all their fun. The more she thought about it, the clearer it became. Not even mentioning the note was the way to ruin their trick.

At that moment, there was a knock on the front door, and Eve jumped involuntarily. She turned toward the door, but Paul was there before her, coming from the drawing room.

Vivian swept in, followed by her maid, who carried in her arms a long bundle, wrapped around with a sheet. Vivian handed the footman her bonnet and gloves as she looked across the entryway toward her friend. "Eve, there you are. Just who I wanted to see. How is everything proceeding?"

"I checked the ballroom. I was trying to decide whether to check in the kitchens." Eve hastily stuffed the folded note into the pocket of her skirt.

Vivian nodded. "I'll do that. You show Pauline to your room. I'll join you there in a moment."

Without wasting another word, Vivian headed off down

the hall toward the kitchens. With a shrug, Eve turned and led the maid up the stairs to her room. She eyed with some curiosity the bundle the woman carried, but she said nothing. Inside her bedchamber Pauline laid the bundle down on the bed and folded back the sheet covering it. Inside lay an elegant gown of Nile green silk and pale gold tissue. Carefully, the maid picked it up and laid it aside on the bed, revealing another dress beneath it. The bottom dress was a confection of pale blue satin and white lace, with a square neckline and short puffed sleeves.

"How lovely." Eve reached over and smoothed out a wrinkle on the bodice, straightening the sleeves. "But why did Vivian bring her dresses here?"

"She says she's planning on dressing here, ma'am. On account of her helping you arrange the flowers and seeing to things."

"I see."

"That's why she brought me, so I could help her dress and do her hair." Pauline cast a considering glance at Eve. "I could do your hair, too, if you'd like. Her ladyship said you might need help, what with all the maids here busy with the party."

"Mm." Eve suspected that it was to facilitate this last offer that Vivian had decided to dress for the wedding here. "And why did Lady Vivian bring two dresses? Is she planning to change after the wedding?"

"Oh, no, ma'am. I wouldn't think so."

"It seems odd that she would bring two gowns, don't you think?"

"I wouldn't know about that, ma'am." The maid was suddenly quite busy shaking out the dresses and smoothing the wrinkles. "Her ladyship does as she pleases."

"Always."

Eve turned away, knowing that she would get nothing further from the maid. Pauline had been with Vivian for years and was utterly loyal.

So Eve waited until Vivian came into the room a few minutes later and asked, "Why did you bring two dresses, Vivian?"

Vivian turned her vivid green eyes on her friend. "Why, the blue one is for you. I realized that you must have been wearing mourning the last year or two and that you might not have an up-to-date gown that would be suitable for the celebration."

"What I have will be fine, I am sure."

Vivian sighed. "Honestly, Eve, must you be so painfully proud? I would like to think that if I had been stuck in the country and hadn't bought a dress in London for two years and you offered me one of your gowns in the latest fashion, I would be pleased to accept it."

"Easy enough for you to say since you will never be in such a situation," Eve retorted.

"I cannot see why it is such a terrible thing to offer a friend a gown that one bought and instantly regretted. It is too pale a blue for me, and I doubt I shall ever wear it. The only other person I know whom it would suit is Sabrina, and I refuse to give her one of my gowns—not that she would accept it, for she would never admit that I had purchased something attractive. I do hope you are not telling me the same thing."

Eve rolled her eyes. "Of course not. It is a gorgeous dress, and you know it."

"Yes, I do, and it would look perfect on you. But if you prefer to let it rot at the back of my closet because you are too proud to accept a gift from a friend, then at least let me lend it to you for this one occasion."

"I have a dress."

Vivian wrinkled her nose. "Not one that isn't gray or brown or dark blue, if what I have seen this week is any indication."

"Vivian . . . I am a chaperone. I am supposed to be unnoticed."

"I don't see why. No doubt you should not outshine your charges, but both Lily and Camellia are pretty girls. They can withstand the competition. And they are quite goodhearted; they will not mind if you look pretty."

"I know that. They have already offered me the use of their sister Rose's clothes. They told me she left a whole trunk of dresses here because she had too much to take them all back to America." Eve made a face. "Do I look like such a ragamuffin that everyone is offering me clothes?"

"Of course not. The Bascombes are doubtless sensitive about such things because of the state of their clothes when they arrived. What few frocks they had were years out of style. Charlotte and I had to outfit them completely. Being kind and generous girls, no doubt they want to help others."

"I do not mean to thwart their generosity, and there are a few of the day dresses that I might wear, but most of Rose's gowns are too young for a woman of my age and position."

"Your age!" Vivian's brows soared upward. "My dear girl, you are only six months older than I. Are you saying that I dress in a style too young for my advanced years?"

"Don't be absurd." Eve grimaced. "I had forgotten how very accomplished you are at twisting one's words to suit your purpose. Vivian . . . my dearest, sweetest friend . . ." She went to Vivian and took both her hands in hers. "There is a world of difference in how the world looks at you and me. You are the daughter of a duke, a leading light of the *ton,* and still one of the most eligible women in all Britain. Whatever you wear or do or say is instantly fashionable, and everyone tries to imitate it. I, on the other hand, am a vicar's daughter, a widow, and a chaperone. If I tried to dress as you do, I would be censured."

"You are the one who is being absurd. You are still young, and you have served two years of mourning. That should be more than enough for even the highest stickler. And you are not some chaperone who has been hired to sit in the background and provide a nominal presence to satisfy the requirements of society. You are doing a friend a favor. You are helping me sponsor these girls in their Season. I need to make sure they are ready for their debuts, or else my own social credit will be damaged."

"Oh, really, Viv . . ."

"And—" Vivian rolled on inexorably. "The earl needs the same sort of person for his cousins' sake. He needs someone who can participate in the social scene with them, not sit against the wall. You must help guide their conversations and gloss over whatever missteps they take. Turn Camellia's offer of shooting lessons, for instance, into a merry little tale concerning all of us participating in it at a house party here. You understand what I mean."

"Yes, of course."

"Well, to do that, you cannot be sitting behind everyone else, wearing gray and pretending not to exist. You must be yourself."

"And to do that, I must wear your dress?" Eve cocked an amused eyebrow. She could feel herself slipping, and she knew that Vivian would sense it as well. It was no doubt terribly weak of her, but she could not help picturing herself in that vision of ice-blue satin and white lace.

"Let me ask you this: Do you really expect the girls to take fashion advice from a dowd?"

Eve's eyes widened. "A dowd!"

"Well, you seem to be trying to make yourself into one. Where is the dress you had planned to wear today?"

Eve pulled the gown from her wardrobe, somewhat cha-
grined that it was indeed gray with long sleeves, and its only
decorations were narrow ruffles at the sleeves, hem, and
neckline.

"Honestly, Eve, have you become a Quaker?" Vivian took
the dress from her and laid it beside the blue one on the bed.
She turned back to her friend, crossing her arms over her
chest. "Now, tell me, which of these would you rather wear
tonight?"

Eve looked at the gowns and knew she was lost. Without
a word, she picked up the gray gown and thrust it back into
the wardrobe.

Chapter 6

The wedding went off without incident. Mary was radiant in a gown that had been rush-ordered for her from Madame Arceneaux in London, her blue-green eyes glowing as she walked down the aisle to join Sir Royce at the altar. Sir Royce, Eve was pleased to note, looked proud and happy, his earlier unease apparently gone. Lily made no attempt to keep the tears from streaming down her cheeks, while even Camellia let out a sniffle or two. Eve herself had to swallow a lump in her throat as she looked at the couple, gazing at each other with such love in their eyes.

Later, back at Willowmere, the new bride and groom greeted their guests, flanked by the earl as the head of the family. Eve was tense about seeing Lord Stewkesbury. Would he care that she had not dressed appropriately for a chaperone? He seemed like a man who was punctilious about such details. To her relief, he merely bowed and offered her a pleasantry. She could detect no tone of censure in his voice. Perhaps Vivian was right.

Eve moved on to congratulate the new couple. Somewhat to her surprise, Mary hugged Eve.

"I'm so glad you are here to take care of my sisters," she told Eve. "I don't feel as much that I'm deserting them."

"Of course you are not deserting them," Eve assured her. "I am sure they will miss you, but I shall do my best to keep them happy and occupied. And once you return from your honeymoon, well, Iverley Hall is not so far away, is it?"

For the wedding supper the servants had opened up not only the everyday dining room but also the grand dining room, which boasted a table long enough to seat twice as many as the one in the smaller room. The seating arrangements had been one of Vivian's most exacting tasks. Mary and her sisters were of no help, regarding her with blank stares as she tried to explain the order of precedence that came into play, as well as the wounded feelings that were likely to occur if mistakes were made.

Eve was seated among those of lesser note, barely above the squire and his wife, but she was frankly happy to be far away from Lady Sabrina, who gazed at her with icy condescension each time their eyes met. Perhaps Lady Sabrina *had* sent the note. Yet, as soon as Eve thought that, she tried to imagine Sabrina sneaking into Willowmere, risking being seen by a servant or one of the occupants of the house. It was ludicrous, especially with no more motive than to upset a woman she barely knew.

Vivian had told Eve that Sabrina could not stand for anyone to challenge her reputation as the most beautiful woman in the county. Looking at Sabrina tonight, Eve could well believe it. She had dressed in a manner that indicated she intended to outshine everyone at the celebration, even the bride. Sabrina had, Eve thought, gone a little too far, for her dress seemed almost suited for court attire. It was of pale silver lamé over blue satin, with silver Van Dyke trimming across the bodice and around the sleeves as well as a wide border of large embroidered blue satin roses around the hem. Diamond and sapphire jewelry glittered at her ears, neck, and wrists.

"If only she were wearing ostrich plumes in her hair," Vivian had murmured sardonically when she saw Sabrina, referring to the usual headgear worn when being presented to the queen.

Unfortunately, Eve thought, Lady Sabrina did not seem to understand that no elegant garments or expensive jewels could compete with the radiance in Mary's face today.

Eve kept an eye on Lily and Camellia throughout dinner even as she carried on a conversation with the squire's wife. She was determined to tend to her duties as chaperone—even if she had let Vivian talk her into wearing this unchaperone-like dress. The girls were enjoying themselves. Neville Carr had been placed between the two sisters, and every time Eve glanced at Lily and Camellia, they were smiling or chatting animatedly—especially Lily. Eve felt a small tug of concern. Mr. Carr was charming, and Lily was both romantically inclined and naïve. Lily might take seriously what a more sophisticated girl would realize was meaningless flirtation.

Despite her firm intentions of watching only her charges, Eve could not keep her eyes from straying now and then to where Fitz sat. Ensconced between a plain young woman and an older lady of haughty mien, he managed not only to keep both of them smiling but also to flirt with the young matron across the table. Eve could not help but remember the way she had warmed to Fitz's smile, how the twinkle in his eyes had seemed meant for her alone. But clearly he practiced his flirtations on every woman he met—and just as clearly, they all responded with the same flattered warmth. She worried about Lily not understanding the lack of meaning in a flirtation, and here she was guilty of the same naïveté!

It was good, she told herself, to be reminded that Fitz Talbot was simply a man who could not keep from charming any woman around him. And any woman who let herself take him seriously was quite foolish.

Eve was pleased to see that once the dancing began, neither Lily nor Camellia wanted for partners. A quick check of their dance cards showed her that they had not agreed to dance more times than was correct with the same man, and they had sprinkled several older, stodgy gentlemen in among the younger ones.

"You are very popular girls," she said, smiling. "But you're quite right to save a dance each for your cousins, Sir Royce, and Lord Humphrey." She did not add that she was equally pleased to see that Mr. Carr's name was entered for only one dance on Lily's card. The less said about that, the better.

First Mary and Sir Royce danced alone, and everyone watched, smiling. When the orchestra struck up the second tune, however, a number of others took to the floor. Eve watched Lily and Camellia join in the country dance. The earl was partnering the new bride, while Sir Royce danced with Vivian. Lord Humphrey, stately and faintly old-fashioned in his formal black knee breeches and coat, led out Lady Sabrina. She glanced around and spotted Fitz forming a set with his aunt, Lady Kent, on his arm.

After that, he took to the floor with one lady after another. Eve found her eyes coming back to him time and again, even though she knew it was foolish to do so. He was an excellent dancer, and every woman who danced with him was soon smiling and laughing, even the stiffest of matrons. Eve watched the way he bent his head closer, as if his partner's words were too precious to be lost, the way his smile lit his face. She could not help but wonder if one or another of these women had indulged in something more than flirtation with Talbot.

Somewhat to her surprise, the squire came up and jovially asked Eve to dance. Had it been one of the younger men, she probably would have refused, for she feared it was not a chaperone's place to be dancing. However, she could scarcely turn down an aging gentleman such as the squire, so she took his arm and spent the next few minutes in a lively country dance. They formed part of the set with Fitz and his cousin Charlotte, and as the dance ended, Eve and her partner happened to stroll off the floor beside Fitz and Charlotte.

"May I have the honor of the next dance, Mrs. Hawthorne?" Fitz asked when the squire bowed to them and moved back to join his wife.

Eve's heart sped up, and she glanced down, afraid that it might show in her face exactly how much she would like to accept his invitation. "I'm not really here to dance but to look after Lily and Camellia."

She glanced around, searching for the two girls, and found them chatting with the earl and Mary. Fitz followed her gaze and grinned.

"I think they are taken care of."

"Goodness, yes," Charlotte agreed. "They've enough relatives here tonight to keep even them out of trouble. You should dance, Eve; it's a celebration."

Fitz held out his hand, his blue eyes twinkling at her in that way that could make the iciest woman smile. Eve hesitated, her chest tightening with anticipation and yearning. Charlotte gave her an encouraging wave forward. Eve turned and put her hand into Fitz's, walking with him onto the dance floor. As the couples gathered on the floor, Eve realized belatedly that the next dance was to be a waltz. She cast a glance toward the side of the ballroom, but Fitz, correctly interpreting her look, tightened his hand on hers.

"Oh, no, you can't change your mind and leave me standing here on the floor," he told her, his dimple deepening in his cheek. "Imagine what people would say."

"Did you know this was a waltz?" Eve shot him an accusing look.

"Is it?" He glanced around as if surprised. "Ow!" He turned back to her, laughing. "Did you pinch my hand?"

"I did indeed." Eve lifted her chin pugnaciously. "For putting that innocent look on your face. Really, Mr. Talbot, you are a . . . a . . ."

"Bang-up cove?" He offered helpfully. "An out-and-outer?"

Eve swallowed a giggle. "No. I would say something more along the lines of a deceiver."

"You have the oddest opinion of me. One can only wonder why you agreed to waltz with me."

"I didn't. I mean, I didn't know it was a waltz when I agreed."

The music began, and Fitz took her hand, his other hand going to her waist. It was nothing, Eve told herself; she had waltzed with other men many times. A major's wife did not lack for dancing partners among the junior officers. Other men had put their hands upon her waist to guide her around the floor, and it had never caused her pulse to speed up or her insides to melt. There was no reason she should feel that way now.

Yet she did.

"Your reputation will not crumble," Fitz assured Eve as his hand tightened fractionally on her waist, and they started around the floor.

Fitz was an excellent dancer, which came as no surprise to Eve. Still, she was not prepared for how very light and effervescent she felt as he swept her around the floor, how her heart seemed to lift within her. She could not keep from smiling up at him, and she remembered how Mary had sim-

ply glowed as she had danced with Royce, gazing up into
his eyes. But no, she thought, she could not look like that.
Mary's glow had come from love; what she felt was just . . .
bedazzlement.

The difference, of course, was that being dazzled didn't
last, no matter how fresh or glorious it might feel. Still, for
the moment it was wonderful. So Eve gave herself up to the
pleasure of the waltz, letting the music fill her and the look
in Fitz's eyes warm her.

Her mood lowered somewhat when she glanced to her
right as they turned and saw Lily dancing with Neville Carr.
Lily's face was bright, her eyes sparkling, and Eve's heart
sank. Exactly what she had feared was happening. As Eve
was well aware, dancing with a handsome, charming man
was a powerful thing emotionally. While Eve herself might
be old enough and experienced enough to know how fleet-
ing the feeling was, she was certain that Lily was not.

After that, Eve kept an eye on the couple. When Lily
and Carr left the dance floor, she would have to join them,
she thought. A third person's presence was the surest deter-
rent to romantic flirtation. But when the dance ended, Fitz
tucked her hand in his arm and began walking toward the
open terrace doors.

Eve tried to tug her hand away, and Fitz glanced at her
in surprise. "It's a lovely evening. A stroll along the terrace
would be refreshing."

"No, I can't. I should get back to Lily and Camellia."

"You can spare a few minutes away from them. I am
sure they will be kept quite busy on the dance floor. And, as
Cousin Charlotte said, there are plenty of assorted relatives
about to keep an eye on them."

Eve looked around and spotted Lily chatting with Mary
and Royce. Neville was by her side, but as Eve watched,

he bowed and moved away. Eve glanced back at Fitz. She wanted to go with him, and he was right—for the moment, at least, Lily was being watched over by other relatives. There was no need to hover.

She gave in, and they started once again through the door. There were several other couples on the terrace, escaping the stuffy ballroom. Eve and Fitz strolled along, looking out over the garden. Torches burned along the main path down into the garden, illuminating the fountain and the curved stone benches that surrounded it.

A little to Eve's surprise, Fitz did not suggest they go down into the garden but simply continued along the terrace. The sounds of the party faded as they drifted farther away.

"You look uncommonly beautiful tonight," Fitz told her.

Eve shrugged it off with a laugh. "'Tis the gown. Vivian insisted I borrow one of hers."

He cast a sideways glance at her. "Believe me, it is not the gown. If the elegance of the gown was the only consideration, Lady Sabrina would be the loveliest woman here, and we both know that is not the case."

Eve smiled. No doubt it was wicked of her to enjoy his dismissal of Lady Sabrina, but she could not help it. Every time the woman had looked at Eve tonight, Eve had felt as if Sabrina was measuring where to stick in the knife.

"Be that as it may, I fear that the gown must be the reason for the change in my appearance."

One side of his mouth curved up. "I admit that the color suits you better than brown or gray. But I think the fact that you are letting yourself enjoy the festivities has something to do with the alteration. You spend too much of your time doing things for other people and not tending to yourself."

"Now you sound like Vivian. I was, I must remind you, hired to look after Lily and Camellia."

He cocked one eyebrow. "That included arranging the flowers? Writing out the place cards? Helping Mary negotiate with the cook and butler?"

"There was a great deal to do. I could hardly stand by and watch everyone else work. I will remind you that Vivian helped as well."

"I know. And from what I know about you, it is exactly what I would expect you to do. But you do not always have to be working. You can have fun sometimes as well."

"I do. I am." They had reached the end of the terrace, where another set of stairs led down into the side garden of the house. Eve turned to face Fitz, her back to the railing. "I thank you for your concern about my . . . happiness. I think perhaps I have forgotten, a little, how to have fun."

"From what I saw of Mrs. Childe, I imagine it is difficult to have fun in that house."

"It is. Poor Julian." Eve sighed. "My little brother—he is the child you saw me playing with."

"At least he has a good sister."

"Yes, but now I have left him."

"And your tender heart feels bad about that, I imagine."

"Yes, of course. I cannot help but feel that I deserted him."

"You have your own life to consider. And he is, after all, Mrs. Childe's son."

"Yes. And he will be leaving next year for school."

"Ah. Then he will make his escape as well."

"Yes. Though I have been told that school is a miserable place for many boys."

"I wasn't miserable there."

Eve chuckled. "I am sure you were not."

He shrugged. "I know. I have been told that I am disgustingly lacking in sensibility."

"No, not that. You're just . . . you're the sort of person

who makes friends even if he doesn't know anyone. Who takes boring situations and makes them fun."

"Well, one has to, doesn't one? Otherwise you'd be left with only boredom."

She smiled up at him. "True."

It would be so easy to get lost in his eyes, Eve thought. So easy to remember the way it had felt to be in his arms, to have his lips against hers. She had told herself she would not think about that evening at the inn, but here, alone with Fitz in the dim light of the moon, it was hard to keep that promise.

She knew he wanted to kiss her. She had known it when he invited her out onto the terrace. If she turned away now, he would accept it. He would not hold her against her will. But deep inside, Eve also knew that she did not really want to leave. She wanted him to kiss her, to hold her, to bring up in her again all of those wonderful, powerful sensations.

A breeze skimmed across her, lifting the loose wisps of hair around her face and brushing her bare arms. Eve shivered.

"Here." Fitz took her hand and led her toward the stairs going down into the side garden. "I know where it's warmer."

There was enough light from the moon to see the path that led through the low bushes and plants to a walled enclosure against the side of the house. Fitz opened the iron gate, and they slipped into a small garden.

The wall around them was about four feet high, so that there would be sunlight during the day, but the plants inside were protected from the wind and cold. Fitz led Eve to a low bench that sat against the house, facing west. As they walked past the rows of plants, sharp, distinctive scents rose from them, mingling in the air. Eve thought she detected . . . was it sage? Rosemary?

"An herb garden!" she said with some delight. "We must be in an herb garden."

He smiled. "You have a good nose. The garden is dear to Cook's heart. In the dead of winter she will accept dried herbs, but most of the year her seasonings come from here. Wait." He reached out and stopped Eve as she started to sit, then pulled off his jacket and laid it on the bench. "There. I cannot have you ruining your dress."

"Now you are ruining your coat."

He shrugged. "Ah, but I don't look as lovely in this coat as you do in that dress."

Eve had to laugh as she sat down. "Do you have an answer for every argument?"

"I try to," Fitz admitted agreeably as he sat down beside her.

It was warmer there, for the wall cut off the breeze, and the air was pleasantly redolent of the herbs. Eve drew in a breath. "It smells delightful."

"I'm glad you like it. It was one of my favorite spots when I was a boy—perfect for being a medieval city or a fortress. A castle."

"I can well imagine." Eve thought of a black-haired, blue-eyed boy playing there, fending off attacks with his wooden sword, and a soft smile touched her lips.

"It was built centuries ago as a winter garden for one of the ladies of the house. When I was young, it held the last-blooming flowers of the fall, the less hardy shrubs. But when the present cook came here ten years ago, she wanted it for her herb garden. Since she cooks divinely and is willing to live in the hinterlands, a garden seemed a small price to pay."

Fitz pulled off his gloves and took Eve's hand, pushing down the long, elegant glove that ran up almost to her elbow. She glanced at him, startled. "Fitz!"

"Eve." He looked at her, eyes twinkling wickedly, then returned to the task of pulling off her glove, fingertip by fingertip.

"Whatever are you doing?" she asked a trifle breathlessly. "'Tis most improper."

"'Tis not the *most* improper thing I could do." He stroked his thumb and forefinger along each of her digits, shoving the thin kidskin down, and each slide of his fingers sent a sizzle of heat straight through her.

She should jerk her hand away, Eve thought. She should jump up and leave. But still she sat, her hand in his, watching him strip away her glove. And as she watched, the heat in her abdomen coiled and grew. His fingers were slow and sensual, all of his attention focused on baring her hand, as if it—as if she—were the most important thing in the world to him. She could not help but think of his hands stripping away other pieces of her clothing with that same care and attention.

When he was done, he laid her hand in his palm and traced his forefinger down the back, following the delicate bones out to each of her fingertips.

"You have elegant hands," he told her, and raised her hand to his lips, pressing a soft kiss upon her palm.

"Fitz . . ." Even to her own ears, her voice sounded weak.

"So slender and white and soft."

Eve looked down at her hand, resting in his much larger one. He had placed her hand so that it aligned with his, finger upon finger, pale and delicate against his slightly darker and rougher skin.

"Have you ever realized how enticing evening gloves are, so soft and supple, like a second skin? They cover half your arm, the tops easing down in gentle folds, as if they might slip off, and yet they stay there, revealing only that strip of skin between them and your sleeves. It makes a man's mind stray. I have been thinking all evening of slipping that glove from your hand."

Heat rose up her throat, though the dark hid her blushes.

It seemed absurd that his words alone, the barest touch of his hand, could spark desire in her like this. Yet she could not deny that she trembled inside.

Fitz kissed her hand again, then touched his mouth to each finger. His lips were velvety and warm upon her flesh, and she did not protest when he turned her hand over and pressed his mouth to her palm, then to each fingertip. By the time he finished, her breath was fast in her throat, her pulse pounding. As if he knew the state of her pulse, his lips moved to the tender skin of her inner wrist, kissing the narrow blue vein.

A soft sigh escaped Eve's lips, and her eyelids fluttered closed. Slowly he kissed his way up her arm, pausing to trace a design with the tip of his tongue on the inner surface of her elbow. Lost in pleasure, she did not pull away when his mouth left her arm and moved to the bare skin along her collarbone but only tilted her head to the side to allow him better access.

His mouth teased and tasted her, moving along the hard ridge of bone beneath the soft skin, coming at last to Eve's throat. She felt the flush of heat that lit his face, heard the rasp of his breath, and she could not help but feel a flash of delight to think that he was as affected by this moment as she was.

"Eve," he murmured against her throat. "Sweet, sweet Eve."

She felt herself bending, yielding, melting. He lifted his head, his hand going to her cheek, and Eve turned her face to meet his kiss. They kissed slowly, lingeringly, savoring every facet of their pleasure. The sharp odor of the herbs mingled with the scent of him. The cool evening air brushed her overheated skin. The dark, encompassing night wrapped around them, hiding them from the rest of the world.

Eve was no longer thinking about what she should be

doing or whether this was right or wrong. Her world was narrowed down to this—this moment, this kiss, this way she felt. Hunger and eagerness rose in her and was matched by him. Their kiss deepened, their mouths melding. Fitz pulled her up and onto his lap, breaking their kiss only long enough to reposition her. He curled one arm behind her back to brace her as his lips once more sank into hers.

Wrapping her arms around his neck, Eve clung to him. His free hand came up to rest at her waist, his fingers digging in a little, and as their kisses became longer and more passionate, his hand slid up, moving over her stomach, caressing her, and finally coming to curve around her breast. Eve twitched a little in surprise. It wasn't that Bruce had never touched her there—he had, usually with a kind of desperation—but his touch had never made her feel like this.

When Fitz's long fingers cupped her breast, light and sure, her whole body flooded with heat. Her abdomen was heavy and molten, eager for his touch, her nipples pointing like tight little buds. He caressed her, his thumb moving over her nipple, coaxing it into even greater hardness. Then his hand moved, delving beneath the top of her dress, and suddenly she felt his skin upon hers, his fingers gliding down over the soft orb of her breast. Eve shivered at the pure pleasure of it, the faint friction that aroused and absorbed her. His fingertips found the taut button of her nipple, and she let out a soft noise at the sensation. Heat snaked through her, spreading through her abdomen and opening her, flooding her with moisture.

There was an ache there now, a yearning, and instinctively Eve moved her hips. He tightened in response, releasing a low groan, and his head snapped up. Fitz gazed at her for a long moment, his face almost harsh with arousal, his eyes glittering in the dim light as he stared down at her.

"Eve . . . Eve . . . we go too far. God, how you tempt me,

but we can't. Not here, not now. There is too much chance of discovery."

The same old sense of resentment and hurt flashed through Eve for an instant—once again she had been set aside. In the next moment it was followed by a saving sense of anger. Eve pushed out of his arms and onto her feet. He started to rise, but she whirled, her eyes flashing, her hand flying out in a warding-off gesture.

"No!" she cried in a low, harsh whisper. "No!"

She turned and fled the walled garden.

Chapter 7

Eve dashed up the stairs to the terrace, then paused to catch her breath. She glanced behind her. Though she had heard Fitz let out a low curse and an urgent command to wait, he had not followed her. She wasn't sure whether that pleased or angered her. She wasn't sure, in fact, how she felt about much of anything at the moment, other than that she knew she had been foolish beyond words to go with Fitz to the garden. He had been right—though it was galling that he had been the one cool-headed enough to think of that and stop what they were doing.

It was absurd. What had she been thinking? She had let the evening—the waltz, Fitz, the romance of the wedding—all go to her head. She had not thought about the rest of her life, only about the here and now. No doubt Fitz could offer her a great deal of immediate pleasure, and he would be happy to do so. But it was not his life that would be ruined, it was hers. She had been lucky tonight, but it could have ended disastrously. From now on, she had to make it clear to Fitz that there could be nothing between them, not even romantic walks in the garden.

Eve shook out her skirts and drew a deep breath, then moved along the wall of the house and peered cautiously around the corner. There were still several people on the terrace, but she could see that all of them had moved to the opposite end and were looking out across the side yard that led toward the stables. So Eve was able to slip around the corner and along the terrace to mingle unobtrusively with the other guests.

They were watching, she saw, a small drama being played out just beyond the hedge on the east side of the house. At some distance away in the outer yard, tables had been set up with refreshments for the villagers and estate people who had come to join in the wedding celebration. The area was lively and a little boisterous, with the sound of laughter and talk and music. A number of people were dancing. But it was not the gaiety that held the spectators' interest. It was the sight of two of the earl's servants wrestling with a short, wiry man as he tried to climb over the low hedge into the garden. The man was struggling and cursing, but the servants paid no attention, inexorably pulling him away.

"Who is that?" Eve asked.

A man in front and to the side of her turned, saying, "Some chap who tried to sneak into the wedding feast, apparently. Says he wants to see the bride."

"Why does this sort of thing always happen whenever the Bascombe sisters are involved?" A woman half-turned toward the man who had spoken to Eve and smiled at him, plying her fan playfully.

It was Sabrina.

Eve could not keep from saying, "I would not think, Lady Sabrina, that the earl's cousins have aught to do with intruders jumping the hedges."

Sabrina's eyes narrowed as she noticed Eve. "You were not here, so you would not know, but at the ball only four weeks ago, the Talbots dragged off another man who had invaded the gardens."

"Really?" One of the men standing nearby said. "How odd!"

Eve had sensed another woman come up behind her, and now she heard Vivian speak in her coolest tone, "Why, Lady Sabrina, as I remember, that was *your* party, was it not? And here you are again. Perhaps it is you, not the Bascombes, who is the catalyst for these strange men bursting in."

Eve smothered a laugh as she glanced at her friend. Vivian was watching Sabrina, the faintest of smiles curving her lips.

"And I thought the country was boring," another woman commented in amusement as the people around them turned to look at Sabrina and Vivian, their interest in the intruder waning at the prospect of watching two aristocratic ladies verbally spar.

Sabrina's brows snapped together, and Eve could almost feel the effort of will it took for Sabrina to swallow a hot retort. "My goodness, Lady Vivian, how you do like to spin a tale! If you aren't careful, one of these days someone will take you seriously." She looked at Eve. "And Mrs. Hawthorne. How are your charges this evening? I hope the children are enjoying the dance, but I am a little surprised to find that you have left them unchaperoned."

"They were quite well chaperoned when I came out to get a breath of fresh air," Eve replied honestly.

"Indeed. Such lovely girls, but a bit of a handful, I expect. You will have your work cut out for you." Sabrina's eyes dropped to Eve's hands, then widened. "Why, Mrs. Hawthorne! I believe you are missing a glove."

Eve froze. She had completely forgotten about the glove Fitz had removed from her hand. When she jumped up and ran out of the garden, it must have fallen to the ground. She flushed now, remembering, and she could only hope that the darkness would hide her guilty blushes.

"Oh. Yes, I am," she began weakly, frantically scrambling to come up with a reasonable explanation to counter the knowing look in the other woman's eyes. Eve would not be surprised, frankly, if Sabrina could hazard a guess about the man responsible for the loss of that glove.

"However could that have happened, I wonder," Sabrina went on, her pale eyes dancing. "Perhaps we should help you look for it."

Eve stared at her numbly, but Vivian came to her rescue. "Why, Sabrina, how absurd. Of course Eve did not lose her glove. How could one mislay an evening glove? She spilled punch on it a few minutes ago and gave it to a maid so the stain would not set. We were just about to go up and get a new pair from your room, weren't we, dear, when we saw this commotion outside." She shrugged and gestured vaguely toward the refreshment tables in the far yard. "But of course, then it turned out only to be some villager who'd indulged too much in the punch."

"Yes. I—I had better go now," Eve agreed quickly. "It does look quite foolish, doesn't it? Pray excuse me, my lady." She nodded toward Sabrina and walked away.

Vivian went with Eve as she hurried into the ballroom and across it to the hallway beyond. As they climbed the stairs, Eve whisked off her other glove.

Not looking at her friend, she said, "Thank you for coming to my aid."

"Of course. What else would I do?" Vivian replied. "That horrid woman. Trust Sabrina to spot whatever might be amiss and grind away at it. I should have asked her what she was doing out on the terrace without my uncle."

Vivian cast a glance at Eve, but when Eve made no reply, she was quiet. She watched, frowning a little, as Eve searched the drawers for her second pair of long gloves.

"Eve . . ." Vivian began as Eve pulled on the gloves. "I saw you dancing with Fitz Talbot earlier."

"Why, yes," Eve replied lightly. "A marvelous dancer, isn't he?"

"Yes, and a charming man as well. If you have a question about a social nicety or a problem involving attire or horse-flesh or a persistent suitor, Fitz is the man I would go to for advice." Vivian paused.

Eve sighed and turned to face Vivian. "All right. Yes. I went into the garden this evening with Fitz. That is where I lost my glove. I know; you don't have to tell me. I was horribly reckless and foolish."

"No, I am sure you were not. Fitz is a wonderful man— the perfect escort. He's witty, handsome, always amusing. But everyone knows that he is an inveterate bachelor. He is thirty-two years old and has never indicated the slightest interest in any young woman. He is not marriage-minded. He doesn't take advantage of women; I would never suggest that. But everyone knows that he partakes only in discreet affairs with mature, sophisticated women."

"Like widows."

"Yes, like widows. They offer fewer entanglements. Sometimes he sets up an actress or opera dancer as his mistress. But he does not marry." Vivian's brow furrowed with concern, and she took a step toward Eve, reaching out a hand to touch her arm. "I am sorry, dear, I do not mean to hurt you. But I cannot bear to see you hurt by him, either. I fear it would be far more long-lasting."

"Don't be silly, Viv." Eve managed a little laugh. She hoped it did not sound as hollow as it felt. "I'm not still wet behind the ears. I have taken Mr. Talbot's measure. I am well aware that he has no interest in marriage. Indeed, I have none, either. I intend to do quite well, living on my own."

"Yes, I know. I'm not a prude. I would never say a word against you carrying on a discreet affair with Fitz if that would make you happy. But I fear you are far too likely to give him your heart rather than indulge in a bit of fun."

"I am determined to do neither of those things," Eve assured her. "I intend to be a sober, responsible woman. One with no interest whatsoever in men or frivolity. In short, a proper chaperone."

"Oh, Eve, no!" Vivian looked horrified. "I could not bear it if you turned into such a creature."

Eve chuckled at her friend's expression. "Most people would not find such an ambition appalling."

"But they do not know you as I do. You are my dearest friend. You were always so sparkling, brimming with laughter and fun. It has pained me to see you become . . . subdued over the years. I hate the way life has worn at you. To think of you planning to do away with your vivacity—well, it makes me quite ill."

Eve smiled faintly. "I am sure I will not completely attain my goal. One doesn't usually, does one?"

"But to resign yourself to a life without love . . . to spend all the rest of your days running errands for crotchety old women or herding silly young girls around, well, it just won't do. You are a beautiful woman and still young. You will fall in love again and marry."

Eve shook her head, smiling in a bittersweet way that pierced her friend's heart. "No, I think not. Fitz Talbot is not the only man whose interest lies in bedding widows, not marrying them. Unless her husband died leaving her a grand estate, a widow is not sought after as a mate. Men prefer someone young and new."

"Oh, tish-tosh. You cannot tar all men with that brush."

"Really?" Eve raised her brow. "This insistence that I marry seems a bit odd, coming from you. You are as unmarried as I, and I have yet to see an indication that any gentleman has caught your eye."

"My eye, perhaps. Not my heart." Vivian shrugged. "But we are not talking about me. I will be quite happy without marriage. I find Miss Wollstonecraft's arguments quite persuasive. But you—you are a woman who was born to be a wife and mother. You are as natural at love as I am not." She dropped her lightly sardonic tone and went on earnestly, "Oh, I wish you would come and live with me for just a few months, at least. Then you would be able to meet men in some other capacity than chaperoning other women about. You would be able to find the man for you."

"You forget, I already did. I have no interest in marrying again."

Vivian sighed. "You are the most stubborn creature. Ah, well, I will concede . . . for the moment. Let us go back to the party."

"I think that I shall stay here for a bit longer. I am somewhat tired."

"Curse my tongue. Now I have made you sad. I'm sorry. I am such a fool. I should not have said anything."

"Don't be silly. You would not be Vivian Carlyle if you held your tongue. And you did not make me sad. I merely want a moment or two to rest." She smiled teasingly. "I promise I won't stay in my room, feeling sorry for myself. I'll be back down in a few minutes."

"Well, all right." Vivian hesitated for another instant, then stepped forward impulsively and gave her friend a hug. "You are the best of women. Don't let any of us wear you down. Including me."

Vivian turned and left the room, and Eve sat down on the edge of her bed with a sigh. She knew that she would have to return to the party. For one thing, she was supposed to be watching Lily and Camellia. But more than that, she refused to hide in her room. She would not give Sabrina—or Fitz—the satisfaction of seeing that they had affected her. She might have slipped this evening, but she would recover. She would set her sights on what she wanted, and she would not be distracted again. From now on she would treat Fitz with the sort of polite reserve that was appropriate for the brother of her employer, nothing more.

But right now, just for this little moment, she thought as she leaned her head against the bedpost and closed her eyes, right now, she would remember those breathtaking minutes in the garden and contemplate what might have been.

Fitz stepped through the ballroom door, searching the room for Eve. He did not see her anywhere, but the place was crowded, so he moved slowly through the throng of people. By the time he reached the door, he was sure that she was not there. He thought of going farther afield in search of her, but he had enough experience with women to know that it was a foolish impulse. If she did not want to see him, he would only make matters worse by tracking her down.

He spotted his brother Oliver walking down the hallway, and Fitz went after him, gliding into place beside the earl and murmuring, "Sneaking a visit to the smoking room alone?"

Stewkesbury glanced at him, amusement in his eyes. "Well, it looks as if alone is out of the question now."

"Yes, I believe so." Fitz grinned unrepentantly. "But at least you've escaped Kent and Jessop."

"God, yes. They had me cornered between the orchestra and the potted palm. I began to fear I'd never get away. Thank heaven Bostwick rescued me."

"He's handy that way."

"There's always some problem or other that requires my attention at an affair this size. Which reminds me—it's just as well you caught me. I've a few things I need to discuss with you."

Fitz made a wry face. "Oh dear."

Oliver smiled faintly as he opened the door to the smoking room and they stepped inside. "Nothing horrible. It's just that I need to return to London." He crossed to the liquor cabinet and poured both a drink from one of the decanters there. "Business—I had to leave early when I came here, and what with staying for the weddings, it's becoming rather urgent that I take care of a few matters." Oliver cut his eyes toward his brother and added, "And yes, I will stop in to talk to your man of business for you."

Fitz reached out to take the glass from his brother, smothering a smile. "I knew you couldn't resist."

"Will you remain on the estate while I'm gone?"

"Of course. You needn't ask."

"Good. Thank you. Higgins is quite capable of managing the estate on his own—though he'll probably want to report to you for form's sake. And should he have some major decision to make, no doubt he would prefer someone of higher authority to make it. But you should not have any trouble there. The thing is, I prefer not to leave our cousins here with only Mrs. Hawthorne, however excellent she may be. There was an incident tonight—"

"An incident?" Fitz straightened, his eyes narrowing. "What sort of incident?"

Oliver sank into the chair across from his brother, moving his hand as though to wave the problem away. "Nothing, I'm sure. Some chap tried to climb over the hedge into the east garden."

Fitz's brows soared upward. "Who? Why?"

The earl shook his head. "I have no idea, on both counts. Unfortunately, the grooms hustled him away and tossed him off the estate before anyone thought to tell me about it."

"One of the locals in his cups, I imagine."

"Yes, well . . . that is the part that worries me a little. They did not recognize the man."

Fitz stared. "It wasn't someone from the estate? Or the village?"

The earl shrugged. "I talked to Jem and Bertie myself. They've lived here all their lives. And they swore to me that they did not recognize him. A slight man, dressed in workingman's clothes, an ordinary sort—except for his insistence on seeing the bride."

"That's what he said? That he wanted to see Cousin Mary?"

"As best they could remember. But he was bosky, they said, and talking a lot of nonsense. Unfortunately they can't recall his exact words."

"The devil." Fitz frowned. "Do you think it's something to do with the Bascombes?"

"I sincerely hope not. As far as I know, all the miscreants have been taken care of. Mrs. Dalrymple, the chap who tried to kidnap Rose and Mary, his accomplice. Surely there isn't another one lurking around."

"I suspect it was just someone who was passing through town and heard about the celebration and decided to partake of the free food and drink."

"And when he was drunk, he decided he should go inside and see the bride. No doubt you're right. But still, given everything that happened last month, I'd rather not leave the girls unattended except for their chaperone."

"No, of course not. You needn't worry. I'll keep an eye out for strangers or any unusual happenings. And Neville's here."

"How long is he planning to stay?"

Fitz shrugged. "I get the impression he's avoiding his father. Could be a week . . . or three . . . or six. You know how Neville is."

"Mm. Next to him, you are a pattern card of responsibility."

Fitz ignored the jab, saying, "I'm sure he would stay longer if I needed him. And you have to admit, he's a good man in a fight."

"Gad, I hope it doesn't come to that. And don't tell the girls. Camellia will decide to arm herself to the teeth."

Fitz chuckled. "No doubt. Vivian, too, now that Cam's been training her."

"That's all we need—Vivian Carlyle, armed. As if she isn't dangerous enough without a pistol."

Fitz studied his brother for a long moment but said only, "Don't worry. I shall take care nothing happens to any of them."

"Thank you." Oliver glanced at Fitz and smiled. "It is good of you to stay here so long. I know that ruralizing bores you."

"Oh, I don't know," Fitz said, his mouth twitching up in a grin. "I'm beginning to find that the country offers far more entertainment than I'd ever imagined."

Chapter 8

Over the course of the next few days life settled into a pleasant routine at Willowmere. The new bride and groom departed, along with the wedding guests, and only a day after that the earl returned to London as well, leaving them a much-depleted party, with only Fitz and his friend Neville to keep Eve and the two remaining Bascombe sisters company.

As the days passed Eve thought now and then of the ominous letter she had received, but she still could not identify anyone who might have sent it. None of the servants ever looked at her with animosity or guilt, and if Lily and Camellia had sent the note, they were indeed tremendous actresses. Eve glanced at the table in the entryway whenever she passed it, wondering if another note might appear there, but none did. Finally, she decided that the matter must have been merely a freakish occurrence.

Life settled into a pleasant routine. Lessons were no longer the onerous occasions they had been in the past. While Eve continued to instruct Lily and Camellia in deportment, she did so by recounting various stories she had heard and events she had witnessed during her own come-out ten years earlier.

"You may think that things have changed since then," she told them playfully, "but let me assure you, except for the fashions and the hairstyles, they have not."

She told her stories well, and since she was open to any questions Lily or Camellia had, their discussions wound up ranging far and wide, covering topics that doubtless would have astounded the earl. The result, however, was that the girls absorbed far more than they ever had with the infamous Miss Dalrymple.

Their mornings were largely spent in the informal upstairs sitting room, where they had a view of the lovely side gardens leading down to the small tarn and summerhouse. They talked, sometimes working on the finer sewing skills as they did so, and Eve demonstrated the proper ways to walk, stand, sit, and curtsey, as well as such things as how to use a fan to best advantage when flirting. Needless to say, Lily found such bits of knowledge far more useful than Camellia did, but even Cam was intrigued when Eve described the time she used her folded fan to provide a sharp poke into the belly of an importunate suitor.

"Now, *that* is useful," she said, picking up her fan and examining it with more interest. "I imagine there are several places where it could do some damage."

Eve chuckled. "What a bloodthirsty girl you are, to be sure."

"Not bloodthirsty," Camellia protested. "I just like to be able to protect myself. And my sisters. I don't understand why everyone finds that odd."

Eve tilted her head to the side, considering her statement. "I think it is the manner in which you protect yourself, not the intent, that is unfamiliar to us. You see, in the *ton,* all of the ladies you will meet are intent on protecting their own as well. It is simply that they use gossip and fashion and rules of behavior to do it."

"Rules!" Camellia's tone was scornful. "How can you use rules to fight with?"

"Don't be such a clunch, Cam," Lily told her. "Of course rules can protect one. If a girl is never alone with a man, there can be no question attached to her good name. And if her reputation is unsullied, she is much more likely to attract a man of substance. Isn't that right, Eve?"

"Exactly. Marrying her daughter to a man of wealth and standing is the best way a mother can ensure her daughter will have shelter, food, clothes, and safety the rest of her life."

"I would think you would rail against that, Lily," Camellia told her sister. "What happened to marrying for love?"

"I didn't say that was what *I* would do," Lily retorted. "People marry for love so they can be happy. Happiness is an entirely different thing from safety." She turned toward Eve. "Isn't that right?"

"There are those who hold that it is a trifle hard to be happy without some degree of security."

"Well, yes," Lily agreed. "One would not wish to starve. But if you aren't willing to take a chance, you'll miss the grand adventures, won't you? And *I* intend to have grand adventures."

Eve smiled at the girl, aware suddenly of longing piercing her chest. "Then the rest of us will have to make sure that you are protected." Though Eve said the words lightly, she was in earnest. Her concern over Lily's attraction to Neville Carr had not diminished.

The gentlemen generally spent some time in the afternoons chatting with them in the drawing room, and every afternoon included a dancing or riding lesson, sometimes both. Since Fitz and his friend were invariably with them for these lessons, the result was that Lily and Camellia spent a great deal of time with Mr. Carr. Eve did not worry about

Camellia, who treated Carr much as she did Fitz (though without the same respect for his shooting skills, which she found negligible).

Lily, however, showed unmistakable signs of being smitten by Carr's charm. To make matters worse, Eve was beginning to suspect that Neville was interested in Lily. A girlish infatuation was one thing; should Neville reciprocate the emotion, it could spell disaster.

Eve sprinkled her conversations with the girls with casual references to the dangers of giving one's heart too soon, the tendency of some gentlemen to flirt without having a serious intent, and the importance of not showing a preference for one gentleman. "It never does to let a man know you care; he's apt to become complacent and sure of himself. Besides, you open yourself up to gossips, who will say that you are setting your cap for him. Or worse. Then, if he does not make you an offer, you will be embarrassed in front of all the *ton*."

Still, she could not dwell on the matter too much without it sounding like a lecture, and Eve was well aware of how little Lily or her sister was inclined to listen to lectures. Any attempts to specifically warn the girl away from Mr. Carr would, she suspected, have the opposite effect.

Eve made sure that the two of them were never left alone together, knowing that it was far more difficult to flirt when there was another person present—and even harder to develop a grand passion. In this endeavor Eve had an unwitting ally in Camellia, for the two sisters were rarely apart. But Eve could not be with the girls every minute of the day, and there was always the possibility that Lily might run into Neville.

One evening, as Eve played the piano and Lily and Camellia joined in song, Eve saw that Lily's eyes kept returning to Mr. Carr. He was watching Lily with a faint smile on his lips, and there was a certain light in his eyes that reminded Eve forcibly of the look she had seen more than once on Fitz's face when he gazed at her. It was a look that, from Fitz, would set her heart to beating faster. She suspected that Lily had much the same reaction to Neville.

Eve realized that she would have to speak to Fitz about the situation. She would have done it earlier, no doubt, if she had not been so studiously avoiding being alone with Fitz. Even though they were thrown together at meals and every evening, as well as the riding and dancing lessons, there was no possibility of any romantic entanglement—or even talk of romance—as long as there were other people around. Fortunately, her plan of sticking to Lily's side had served Eve well in regard to Fitz, too. Eve had taken no strolls around the garden on her own, and she was careful not to go down to a meal until she heard Lily's and Camellia's voices in the hall. Once or twice she had crossed paths with Fitz in a corridor or on the stairs, but Eve had given him only a polite smile and word of greeting before she hurried on her way. The hardest part, she knew, had been fighting her own inclination to linger with him. Still, she had grimly hung on to her resolution and stayed away from him.

However, the next afternoon, when they were out riding, Eve purposely dropped behind the others, hoping that Fitz would seize the opportunity to talk to her and fall back as well. She could not deny a small measure of satisfaction when he did so.

"Well, Mrs. Hawthorne," he said, smiling. "'Tis a rare occasion indeed when I get a chance to speak with you alone."

"I wanted to talk to you about Lily," Eve said briskly, determined to make their conversation impersonal.

He raised his eyebrows slightly. "Indeed? And what about Lily?"

"I fear that she may be forming an attachment to your friend Mr. Carr."

"Neville?" Fitz shrugged. "He is always popular with the ladies. But he is never serious."

"Lily doesn't know that. She is young and inexperienced. She does not know that he is an accomplished flirt. She believes him when he pays her compliments. It's not the same as it would be meeting him during the Season—there she would have many young men vying for her attention, all of them flirting with her. She would see Mr. Carr flirting with other ladies, and she would realize that it means no more when he does it with her. But here, she is thrown together with him for a great deal of time, and she sees only how charming he is to her. I have tried to explain to her how things are, but talk does little to combat what one feels. I fear she will tumble head over heels in love with the man."

Fitz gazed at her thoughtfully. "Why do you dislike Neville?"

"I hardly know the man."

"I know, yet still I sense that you do not approve of him."

Eve hesitated for a moment, then shrugged. "It is true that what I have heard of him does not recommend him to me."

"The stories about Carr are highly exaggerated. For that matter, the stories about me are exaggerated. There are more than a few who would tell you that I am a rake as well." He caught the glance she sent him and chuckled. "Oh dear. Now you are going to tell me that I *am* a rake."

"I did not say that." Eve shook her head, a little flustered by his too accurate assessment of her thoughts. "Besides, we are talking about Mr. Carr. Is it not true that he once seduced a young officer's wife on a bet?"

Fitz stared at her blankly. "What? I don't recall—"

"Her name was Fanny Bertram. She was Lieutenant Harry Bertram's wife. Her husband served under mine six or seven years ago, so I knew her. There were . . . rumors. They followed her wherever he was stationed. Finally, one day, in a storm of tears, she told me the whole story. Harry and Fanny kept rather fast company when they were first married. There were bets placed at Watiers as to who would be the first man to seduce the new bride. Neville Carr was the man who won the bet." Eve looked at Fitz. "Do you remember now?"

"Vaguely." He shrugged. "It was a long time ago, and we were both foolish young men, just out of Oxford and on our own for the first time. Young men are apt to do a number of thoughtless things."

"Did you—" Eve's breath caught, and she had to swallow before she could continue. "Did you participate in the bet as well?" It surprised her how much it hurt to think that he had.

"I? Good Gad, no. I mean, I may have placed some money on it one way or another—I don't remember—but I never tried to seduce Fanny. That isn't my sort of sport."

"Oh, yes, I forgot. You don't pursue married women; you prefer widows. Fewer entanglements." The words came out more bitter than she had expected, and Eve tried for a lighter, amused tone as she went on. "You know, Vivian warned me that you were well known for seducing widows. I didn't tell her that I already had firsthand knowledge of that."

"I didn't kiss you because you are a widow!" Fitz retorted indignantly.

Eve arched an expressive eyebrow. "No? As I remember, you told me widows were more desirable than other women. Did you not?"

"Well, yes, but that was a compliment. I was flirting with you."

"Is it not true that you have had a number of affairs with widows?"

His jaw clenched. "Yes, I have. But it isn't as if I go about accosting widows. Nor do I set out to seduce every widow I meet."

"So it is simply that a widow is the sort of woman you prefer."

"None of that has anything to do with you." Frustration tinged his voice. "You cannot think that I pursued you only because you are a widow."

"No. Not *only*." Eve shook her head. "In any case, it does not matter. We are not talking about you but about Mr. Carr."

Fitz looked as though he wanted to pursue the matter, but then he sighed and said, "Yes. We are talking about a foolish incident that took place many years ago. Was it really so wicked? Fanny was a forward sort; it was only a matter of time before she cuckolded her husband. She bedded Neville quite willingly. It isn't as if he destroyed a good woman's virtue."

"If that isn't just like a man to say something like that!" Eve glared at him. "You cannot possibly know what would have happened if your friends had not played with that couple's lives for their own amusement. Perhaps Fanny would have betrayed her marital vows, but it would not necessarily have happened with such rapidity. And it certainly would not have happened in such a publicly humiliating way. The rumors followed them everywhere they went for years afterward. It was quite damaging to Lieutenant Bertram's career. He finally had to request to be sent to India."

"The devil take it! I did nothing to ruin their marriage."

"You may not have participated in Fanny's seduction, but you aided in the fatal wounding of that marriage—all of you wealthy, indolent young men who have nothing better to

do than to sit about making bets on nonsensical things and
drinking and gambling, with no care for anyone else in the
world. You don't care what happens to a woman when her
reputation is ruined or how the world will judge her, so long
as you can have your fun!"

Fitz stiffened, color washing the high line of his cheekbones. He reached out and grasped her hand on her reins,
pulling her to a halt beside him. "Do not!" His voice was
low and harsh, the very quietness of it seeming to increase
its intensity. "Do not dare to assume that anything I feel
for you has aught to do with what happened to Fanny Bertram. Or with any other woman I have known. I have lived
for thirty-two years, so, yes, I have had other women, some
of them widows. I have done foolish and oft times selfish
things. But I have never purposely hurt a woman. And I do
not want you in my bed because you are a widow and offer
'fewer entanglements.' I want you because you . . . are you."

For an instant heat shimmered between them. Fitz's eyes
were bright blue, piercing in the sunlight, and it seemed to
Eve that they pinned her to the spot. Then a laugh from in
front of them drifted back, and the stillness was broken. Fitz
dropped his hand from hers, looking ahead at the others.

"That may be so, but it is still true that your desire for me
does not include any 'entanglements.'"

He was silent for a moment. "I have no interest in marriage, no. I am talking about mutual pleasure and a free relationship on both sides."

"I fear such a relationship has far more freedom for the
man than the woman," Eve pointed out tartly.

"Then marriage is your goal?" Fitz asked.

"I am done with marriage. That does not mean I am willing to trade my good name for a night's romp in your bed."

He smiled sensuously. "Oh, 'twould be much more than
that, I assure you."

"The only difference is time." She turned her head away. "And we have drifted far afield again. The subject was Mr. Carr and his influence on Lily."

"That incident was many years ago, Eve."

"Still, he is a dangerous man to have around impressionable young girls."

"Neville would not try to seduce Lily!" Fitz's tone was shocked. "Perhaps he is a bit of a rake. Certainly he is a flirt. But he is my friend. He would never besmirch my cousin's reputation."

"Perhaps not. But what about Lily's heart? What is fun and flirtation to a sophisticated man like Mr. Carr seems like love to a romantic young woman like Lily. You know how she is, the books she reads. She thinks that life should be full of 'grand adventures' and great passions. While he is amusing himself, she is all too likely to fall in love. He may for your sake refrain from hurting Lily's reputation, but she could still end up with a broken heart."

"How do you know he will break her heart? What is to say that he might not fall in love as well? There is nothing wrong with Neville as a match for Lily. He is the oldest son, Lord Carr's heir, and their estate is substantial. Yes, he is a little older, but many men are older than their spouses."

Eve looked at him, her head tilted to one side inquiringly. "Is he not engaged? Vivian told me he was."

"Vivian talks entirely too much."

"Is it not true?"

"He isn't formally engaged. Or at least he was not the last I heard. But it has been an understood thing for years that he would offer for Priscilla Symington. Not, of course, that they will suit," he added darkly. "But Lord Carr thinks marriage will settle Neville down."

"One might think that Lady Priscilla would have some say in the matter."

Fitz snorted. "Frankly, I've never seen that Lady Priscilla cares much whom she marries." He sighed. "Very well. I will keep an eye on Neville. I doubt he will stay long anyway. He rarely does; he's easily bored, and the country offers little to distract him."

They rode on for a moment in silence. The heat of their argument had largely dissipated, and for the first time Eve reflected on what she had said to Fitz. She realized that she had overstepped her bounds, taking the brother of her employer to task in this manner. She had been doing well, she thought, at maintaining a professional distance from Fitz, but somehow as soon as she started talking to him, her personal feelings had come tumbling out. It seemed as though her good intentions always crumbled into dust whenever she was with Fitz.

"I am sorry," she began stiffly. "I should not have said what I did. It was not my place. I did not know you or Mr. Carr then, and it is none of my business. I fear I let my concern for Lily overwhelm my manners."

He turned to look at her. Eve kept her eyes fixed on her horse's head.

"Eve, look at me."

Reluctantly she turned toward him. His face was serious, his blue eyes for once not alight with laughter or warmth. "I do not want or need your apology. You said only what you thought. There is no reason for you to watch your words with me. I am not a man who desires fear or obligation— either in your speech or in what you do. I would never . . . force you or take advantage of you."

"I realize that. It—it is not *your* desires I fear." Eve kicked her horse into a trot and rode forward to join the others, leaving Fitz looking after her, surprised.

When they returned home from their ride, they found the

house in an uproar. The butler, Bostwick, fairly bristling with outrage, was snapping orders at the footmen, while Mrs. Merriwether, the housekeeper, and several of the maids were clustered about one of the upstairs maids, who sat, pale-faced, on a bench in the entryway. As Eve and the others came in the front door, everyone in the entryway jumped and whirled toward the door. When they saw who it was, the maid on the bench burst into wails, and the butler strode forward.

"Mr. Talbot, sir."

"Good heavens, Bostwick, what is going on?" Fitz glanced around at the cluster of servants.

"The house, sir, has been invaded." Bostwick's plummy voice rolled out the words.

Fitz stared. "I beg your pardon."

"Jenny came upon an intruder in the hallway outside the bedchambers." He gestured toward the girl on the bench.

"It was horrible!" The maid paused in her tears to look up at Fitz. "I was never so scared in my life!"

"Someone was in the house?" Fitz's face darkened, his brows rushing together. "What the devil is the meaning of this? Who was it?"

The girl shook her head. "I don't know, sir, and that's the truth." She cast a baleful glance at the butler with this remark, which Eve took to mean that Bostwick had not readily believed Jenny.

"She says she'd never seen the man before," Bostwick admitted. He added with a touch of asperity, "Nor could Paul identify him. Apparently when Jenny came upon him and started screaming, the fellow fled down the stairs and out the side door. Paul saw him run through the hall downstairs."

"No one recognized him?" Fitz, too, looked skeptical.

Eve understood his disbelief. It was surprising that no one knew the intruder. The village was small, and most of the people in the area were known to everyone else, at least by sight.

"Did he take anything?" Fitz looked from the butler to the maid and back. "Hurt anyone?"

"Neither Jenny nor Paul remembers him carrying anything, and we could not find anything stolen, at least upon a cursory glance," Bostwick answered. "Apart from a fright, I cannot tell that anyone was hurt, either."

"Then what the devil was he doing here?" Neville asked.

"Presumably he was frightened away before he got whatever he wanted." Fitz directed his piercing gaze at the butler. "What did he look like?"

Bostwick's mouth curved down, which passed for a grimace with the stone-faced butler. "I have not been able to elicit a clear picture."

"He had brown hair," Paul offered.

"No, he didn't!" Jenny raised her head and glared at the man. "I tell you it was sandy-colored! And he was balding at the front but it was longish on the sides. And—and he was a small man."

"More like medium. As tall as me, I'd say," came Paul's response.

"He was little." Jenny set her jaw stubbornly.

Fitz quirked an eyebrow. "Can you agree on the clothes?"

"Dark."

Jenny nodded. "Brown coat and trousers."

"What sorts of clothes?" At the puzzled looks, Fitz went on. "I mean, was he dressed like a gentleman? Or in rougher attire?"

"Oh." Jenny's brow cleared, and she let out a little giggle. "He wasn't no gentleman, sir. He was dressed like a gardener or a gamekeeper or such. Ordinary."

"So . . . work clothes. Small or medium, sandy hair or

brown . . ." Fitz summed up their reports. "Jenny, where did you see this chap exactly?"

"In the hall upstairs, sir. I was carrying the sheets to put on Miss Camellia's bed, and then I saw him. He was walking right toward me."

"So he was outside Miss Camellia's room?"

"Well, right before that, where the break 'tween the rooms are."

"Ah, in front of the windows, then." At Jenny's nod, he asked, "How far were you from the culprit?"

When she stared at him blankly, Camellia added helpfully, "He means the stranger, Jenny."

"Oh. Sorry, sir. 'Bout as far as from me to Mr. Bostwick."

"Then fifteen feet."

"I guess. And then when I screamed, he ran right past me and down the stairs."

"The back stairs?"

"Yes, sir."

"Where did you see him, Paul?"

It took only a few questions to establish that the footman had heard the screams and had run toward the back of the house, only to see the intruder running down the back hallway, a narrower passage used primarily by the servants, and out the side door that led to the stable yard. It was soon clear that he had seen the man at a distance and from the back and in dimmer light. Fitz, nodding, dismissed everyone, including Paul and the butler, leaving only Jenny and one of the other maids, who held Jenny's hand, which seemed to calm her.

"Now, then, Jenny, let's talk about the man." Fitz squatted down so that he was at eye level with the girl and smiled at her. "Bostwick and Mrs. Merriwether are not here. I won't get angry if you tell me you were not telling us everything before. I simply want to know the truth. Are you quite sure that you had never seen this man before?"

The maid could resist Fitz's smile no more than most women. She blushed a little as she smiled shyly back at him. "Oh, no, Mr. Talbot, sir, I wasn't shamming. I swear. I'd never seen him."

"Then he is not local?"

This had apparently not occurred to the girl, for she tilted her head to the side, looking a little surprised, before she said, "No, I guess he must not be."

"Did he say anything to you at all?"

She wrinkled her brow. "He said something under his breath, like, but I couldn't tell what it was. I think, though, from the way he looked, that maybe it was a curse. 'Cause I'd come upon him, see, and spoiled it."

"Very likely. What can you remember about his face?"

Again she frowned in thought. "He was small, and like I said, he was losing his hair—in front, you know, so he had a really tall forehead."

"You said his hair was sandy. On the light side or the dark side?"

"Lighter, I think. He—there were strands that were lighter—maybe he was going gray. I think maybe that's what it was. And he looked older, too, you know—lines on his face and all."

"As old as Mr. Bostwick?"

"Maybe. Maybe more. He was different-looking from Mr. Bostwick, darker, like he'd been in the sun more. But not as dark as Stedley." She named the head gardener, a man nearing seventy years, whose face was as brown and wrinkled as a dried apple.

"Did you see his eyes?"

"They were light. Sort of ordinary."

"Blue?"

"Not like yours, sir." She blushed and ducked her head. "Maybe gray."

"What were his features like? Big? Small? Was his face narrow? His jaw large?"

"Smallish. His eyes were small, too, and his eyebrows were light like his hair. His mouth was a tight little line. He looked—like a rat, you know?"

"It sounds a lot like the man they found trying to sneak into the wedding supper the other night," Eve said.

Fitz looked at her sharply. "You know about that?"

Eve nodded. "I was out on the terrace." Color stole into her cheeks, and she turned her eyes away from Fitz, remembering why she had been on the terrace at that time.

"We didn't know about it!" Camellia protested. "Why didn't anyone say anything?"

"Oliver kept rather quiet about it, not wanting to disturb Mary's and Sir Royce's celebration," Fitz explained smoothly.

His cousins cast him doubtful looks. "That doesn't explain why he said nothing after they had gone," Lily pointed out.

"Oh, you know Cousin Oliver," Camellia retorted. "He was being 'protective' again. He thinks we're too delicate to know the truth."

Fitz chuckled. "I think you disabused him of that notion some time ago. It was more, I think, that he hoped to avoid your going about with a pistol in your pocket."

"Well, what sense does that make?" Camellia pointed out practically. "If there's someone lurking about, we ought to be prepared."

"That is precisely what I intend to do," Fitz assured her. "Oliver and I assumed the incident at the wedding feast was a one-time thing . . . that it was someone passing through, who decided to partake of the refreshments and wound up in his cups. But if the chap is still about . . ." He turned to

Eve. "You say the man at the wedding looked like Jenny's intruder?"

Eve shrugged. "I didn't get a very good look at him because it was dark and there wasn't much light, but he was small and dressed in those sorts of clothes. And his hair was light and long, his features small. I don't know that it is the same man."

Fitz nodded. "Seems an unlikely coincidence." He turned toward Neville. "Why don't you and I check about the house, see if we can find any evidence of this fellow's breaking in?" He swung back to the women. "Jenny, you and Tilda get back to the servants' hall. I'm sure Cook will give you a nice cup of tea to settle your nerves."

When the maids were gone, Fitz looked at Eve and his cousins. "I think, ladies, that given this new information, we shall have to be more careful around here. No riding unless Neville or I are along. In fact, it would be best if you did not stray far from the house."

"Not again!" Lily groaned.

"Really, Fitz," Camellia agreed. "I'll carry my gun. Why isn't that enough?"

"I am sorry. I know that you are an excellent shot. But Oliver left me in charge of your safety, and I have no intention of letting anything happen to you. Any of you," he added, casting a significant look at Eve. "I trust, Mrs. Hawthorne, that you will have the good sense not to let your charges go out alone or to do so yourself."

"We cannot even walk in the garden?" Eve asked, dismayed. "Surely the gardens are safe."

"Not alone. If you'll remember, this fellow came all the way into the house today. He could easily come upon you somewhere in the garden. I don't intend to let anything happen to you. To any of you," he added.

"It's like being in prison," Camellia grumbled.

"A pleasant prison, I hope," Fitz replied, then sighed. "Very well. As long as you go about in pairs, I suppose it's all right. I will put some men patrolling in the gardens, as well as set up a guard at night. But if anything else untoward happens, I shall have to insist on your going no farther than the terrace."

Lily sighed, and Camellia rolled her eyes, but they did not push the matter. Fitz, apparently satisfied that they had acquiesced to his edict, went on, "Now, if you ladies will check your rooms to see if anything is missing from them, I would appreciate it. Neville? Shall we take a turn around the house?" He cast a questioning glance at his friend, who nodded, and the two men bowed and departed.

Eve followed her charges up the stairs. She was somewhat surprised by Fitz's reaction to the news of the intruder. It was worrisome, of course, but she wouldn't have expected him to be quite this protective. She was not as accustomed to doing things on her own as Lily and Camellia were, but Fitz's edicts had even set her back up a little. It wasn't as if any of them had been threatened—indeed, the intruder had not done anything, really, either time. It seemed rather excessive for Fitz to threaten to confine them to the house.

They parted and went into their own bedrooms. Eve crossed to her dresser, where a small jewelry box sat. She had only one item of value, after all. She opened the box. In the center lay the small enameled pocket watch Bruce had given her. She picked it up, smoothing her fingers over the cool surface.

It was of little value, of course, compared with the hundreds of expensive items that lay around Willowmere. She doubted that the intruder would have bothered to take her bits of jewelry, even the watch. Nor was there likely to be another thief sneaking into the house. Still, it made no sense to leave her one valuable item lying in the box on top of the dresser, where anyone might see it. Perhaps she should start wearing it every day. But it was a trifle cumbersome and tended to pull at the delicate muslins and cambric of her day dresses, unlike the sturdier fabric of her carriage dress. Besides, she did not really need it in this house, where there was a clock in nearly every room.

Opening her top drawer, she pulled out a nightgown and wrapped the watch in it so that the end result was a tight ball of white cotton nightgown. She put it back in the drawer beneath the other clothes. As she did so her fingers brushed against a piece of paper. It was the note she had received before the wedding, which she had stuffed down below her nightclothes.

Drawing it out, Eve opened the piece of paper and looked at it again. Uneasiness stirred in her. Perhaps she should show the note to Fitz after all. But even as she thought that, she hesitated. If Fitz saw this, he might make good on his threat to restrict the women to the house. Lily and Camellia would never forgive her. Nor did she relish the idea of being so constricted.

And surely there was no connection between the note and the intruder today. How could there be? The note must have been sent by someone who knew her, and Eve was certain that she had never seen the man who had tried to interrupt Mary's wedding party. There was a possibility that the two intruders were different people, but given Jenny's description of the man, that seemed unlikely. No, she told herself, the note had to be unrelated to the intruder. There was no need to show it to Fitz. And it was better all around to keep Fitz out of her personal life.

Chapter 9

Fitz sat in the chair behind his brother's desk, idly twirling an ornate letter opener. He was troubled, not a state in which he spent much time, nor one that he enjoyed. The first matter that disturbed his thoughts was the intruder who had entered the house the day before. In all his life, no one had ever broken into Willowmere. Fitzhugh Talbot was not a man who feared much, so the idea of a slight man breaking into his home did not arouse any sense of danger. However, it both astonished and offended him. Willowmere was the fortress of his youth, strong and inviolate. No one should be able to invade it or tarnish its sanctity.

A fierce protectiveness arose in him for Eve and his cousins, who must have been frightened by the thought of an intruder. Well, he amended mentally, being an honest man, it had probably frightened Eve. He was not sure exactly what it would take to frighten the Bascombes, but he was sure that it would be far more than a maid's tale of a thief in the house. However, he found that the thought of Eve being scared was enough to make him clench his fist, imagining it closing about the fellow's throat. She could have been in the house when the man entered; she could have come face to face with him.

It galled him that this happened while Eve and his cousins were under his protection. What was even more infuriating was the fact that he had absolutely no idea who the intruder had been, what he had been doing there, or where he had gone afterward.

He and Neville had tromped around the outside of the house after hearing Jenny's account, but they had found nothing to indicate that the man had entered in any other manner than the way he had left. There were a few shoe prints in the dirt outside the side entry, but as several servants had run out that way after the man, there was no hope of distinguishing which prints belonged to the intruder. Certainly there was no indication of which way he had gone. He could have ducked into the garden or sprinted down past the stable yard to the river or in the opposite direction to the trees and the road beyond.

None of the servants had heard or seen the intruder until Jenny and then Paul started shouting, and none had gotten a good look at him except the maid. The gardeners had seen nothing, and neither had any of the grooms in the stable yard, which had so annoyed Fitz that he had roundly cursed them for being witless fools, a rarity for a man of Fitz's usually equable temperament. But it did not, of course, change the fact that in the end he was left with nothing. He sent one of his men into the village to seek out information about any strangers in town and ordered everyone to be on guard in the future.

But it troubled him to have no course of action to pursue, and he spent much of his morning trying to think of some way that he could discover the identity of the intruder. Those were not his only thoughts, of course, for he found himself returning frequently to his conversation with Eve the day before and the accusations she had hurled at him.

Her words still rankled. She thought him indolent and

idle, as feckless and uncaring as the youths who had bet on Fanny Bertram's virtue. He could not deny that he had known about the bet, even laughed over it with his friends, but that had been many years ago, when he was young and foolish, and he was no longer the same man. He was not the sort who uncaringly played with other people's lives for his own amusement.

That was what had really stung—that she had implied that he did not care what happened to her or her reputation as long as he could get her into his bed. Did she really think that he was just playing with her life for his own pleasure?

He would not deny that he was thinking of his own pleasure. Every moment he spent around Eve made him want her more. He was charmed by her laugh, her smile, the light that lit her face when she was happy. Even the sound of her voice in the hallway or another room had the power to make his spirits lift a little and set him to seeking a reason to join her. She was exquisite, enchanting . . . and thoroughly desirable.

He found himself sitting and watching her—at the dinner table, in the drawing room, indeed anywhere he saw her—and thinking of having her in his bed. He imagined her slender, willowy form naked beneath him, her shining pale hair spilling like a waterfall over his pillow. He remembered the scent of her, the taste, the feel, and his need for her grew more urgent daily. Being around her like this and not having her was enough to drive a man wild.

Surely there was nothing unusual in his wanting and pursuing her. She was a beautiful woman. But it was not as if he wanted a quick tumble. He wanted to make love to her, spend time with her, be with her. This thought struck him with some surprise, for he had not really considered before what he wanted with Eve beyond the simple fact of his desire. But he knew that he wanted more than a few days or even a few weeks. It would, he thought, take months to explore the possibilities that awaited him with Eve.

Nor was he thinking only of his own pleasure. He wanted to give her pleasure as well, to make her happy as she made him happy. And while he was sensible that the consequences for her could be far graver than those for him, he had no intention of letting it get out that they were having an affair. They would be discreet; he would never reveal that they were lovers. He would not expose her to scandal.

With an exasperated sigh, Fitz slapped his palm down on the letter opener, stopping it in mid-turn. He was being, at best, disingenuous. Of course he would not reveal anything, but he knew well enough that things tended to come out no matter how one tried to cover them up. Servants talked; others saw the looks that passed between lovers, and they gossiped. Even if there was no real knowledge, there were always rumors. And rumors, he knew, could be as damaging to a woman in Eve's situation as any truth.

She would not only face the disapproval of society, she would be barred from the only sort of employment a woman like her could seek. No one would hire a chaperone who was rumored to be having an affair. And he knew the fact that she was having an affair with him would only make it worse. He was too sought after in the marriage mart, too well known for any affair with him to pass quietly.

Fitz frowned and shoved back his chair, getting up to pace the room. Was he being selfish? Was he ignoring Eve's best interests in the pursuit of his own desires? He had, he admitted, started pursuing her without any thought to what would happen to her. Not trying to harm her was not the same thing as actually protecting her.

The only way he could ensure that, he knew, was by not having an affair with her. Which was, of course, the last thing he wanted to do. Fitz stopped in his pacing, scowling fiercely.

"Has that globe offended you?" An amused male voice came from the doorway of the study. "Shall I act as your second?"

Fitz turned. Neville Carr was lounging in the doorway, one shoulder propped against the doorway, idly swinging the silver quizzing glass that hung from his lapel.

"What?" Fitz looked blank.

The other man pointed toward the globe on the stand before Fitz, and Fitz realized that he had been staring down sightlessly at the object as he frowned in thought. He smiled faintly.

"No. I was thinking of other things."

"The chap who broke in here yesterday?"

"What? Oh, yes. It's rather frustrating; I've no idea how to get hold of the fellow. Come in, sit down. Tea? Coffee?"

Carr shook his head. "Hibbits brought my coffee upstairs."

As Fitz well knew, Carr was not in the habit of arising at what he considered a barbaric hour to participate in a meal he could not stomach. Instead he was given to sleeping till ten and drinking a stiff cup of black coffee brought to his room by his valet, Hibbits, before dressing and finally sallying forth to face the world a little before noon.

"It's puzzling," Neville conceded as he took a seat in one of the two wingback chairs in front of the desk.

Fitz sat down across from him. He put aside his other worries for the moment and turned his mind to the other problem that had disturbed his rest the night before—his young cousin and his good friend. After Eve's warning he had watched Lily and Neville carefully throughout dinner and the evening. He had been forced to acknowledge the truth of Eve's words. Lily and Neville seemed to enjoy each other's company a great deal. Lily's pretty gray-green eyes rarely left Carr's face, and Fitz lost count of the number of times the two of them had glanced at each other and smiled.

The attraction was clearly not on Lily's side alone. Neville talked and even flirted a little with Camellia and Eve as well—Fitz was not sure if Neville was capable of addressing a woman without flirting—but he did not speak to them as often or look at them in the same way he did Lily. It was no wonder he talked to Lily, of course, given the way her face fairly glowed whenever he turned her way.

Idly picking a piece of lint off his sleeve, Fitz said, "How is Lady Priscilla? Have you seen her lately?"

The corner of Neville's mouth tightened. "Far too much of her."

Fitz's brows lifted. "Hardly the words of a suitor."

"Bah." Neville waved his hands dismissively. "It's not Priscilla. Actually, I haven't seen her an inordinate amount, and when I do, she is invariably pleasant. It's her mother who is everywhere I turn. That's why I fled. First I left London. The next thing I knew, she had followed me to Malverley, dragging poor Priss along with her. I realized, of course, what a mistake I had made by seeking refuge at home. Lady Symington and Father joined forces to hound me night and day. They want to make the announcement. 'What are you waiting for? Priscilla is nearing twenty-five. People are beginning to talk.' I tell you, I was beginning to see them in my sleep. Finally I bolted. I thought even Lady S. would not pursue me all the way to the Lake District."

"I wouldn't be too sure. When Lady Symington gets the bit between her teeth, she's the devil to stop."

"No need to tell me," Neville replied with some bitterness. "That's the worst of it, the thought of being tied to that woman the rest of my life."

"Priscilla?"

"No. Priscilla's all right. She's a quiet thing. Doesn't seem to care what I say or do that I can tell. It's her mother I can't bear being shackled to."

Fitz smiled faintly. "Well, surely you can avoid her."

"I don't know how. Can hardly run from your wife's mother, can you?"

"Perhaps Priscilla would enjoy escaping her as well."

"One would bloody well think so."

"I thought you were reconciled to proposing to Lady Priscilla."

"I am. I was. The morning before I left I made up my mind that I would do it. Get the hounds off me. But then I went down to the sitting room, and there was Priscilla. I knew this was the moment. But I sat there. And she sat there. And all I could think about was being stuck the rest of my life at Malverley with Priss. Lord and Lady Carr. A brood of children running about. I tell you, it was enough to make my blood run cold. So I told her I was leaving and had come to bid her farewell. Then I threw together my things and ran. Thank God for Hibbits, or I'd never gotten it done in time to miss my father and Lady Symington."

"Then you don't mean to marry Priscilla?"

Neville sighed. "No. I can't cry off. Everyone's been expecting me to propose to her for years now. Father's right in that; if I don't come up to the mark, she'll be shamed in front of the entire *ton*. She's expecting it. Everyone's expecting it. And there's my infernal duty—I have to marry and produce heirs." He shrugged. "Priss will do as well as any other woman. Better than most, really. At least she won't care what I do or where I go."

"Doesn't sound like any woman I know."

"Nor me." Neville tilted his head, considering. "Priscilla is a different sort. Never know what she's thinking. But I can't see any partiality toward me. She's polite, even kind; sometimes I swear I see her looking at me with sympathy in her eyes. I'm inclined to think she's no more eager to marry than I am." He paused. "Which is damned odd, if you ask me. Most women I meet are interested in nothing but marrying and having children. But Priscilla is curiously unmaternal. My sister was there with her newest infant, and I didn't see Priscilla cooing over it once. No reason to, of course; it was red and squalling and looked just like poor Medford."

"God help him," Fitz responded feelingly.

"No, it's worse—the babe's a girl."

Fitz laughed. "Even a mother might have trouble cooing then, I would guess."

Neville sighed. "I'll have to go back there. Ask her to marry me. It's not going to get any easier."

"Maybe you shouldn't propose. It doesn't sound to me as if either of you wants to do it."

"Not really. But, well, can't get out of it now. And Priscilla will suit me well enough, I'm sure. Some clinging, loving wife would doubtless be worse. Anyway, there's the scandal. Father would cut me off. Lady S. would probably skewer me with her hat pin."

"A messy end," Fitz commiserated. "If I were you, I'd go back to London."

"No you wouldn't. You would never have gotten yourself into this mess."

"Ah, yes. I am so responsible."

Neville lifted one elegant shoulder. "No need to be responsible; you've got Stewkesbury for that. But you don't let people squeeze you into things. You'd do the right thing, or you'd have told them long ago to mind their own business."

"You think me a very brave chap if you think I would say that to Lady Symington."

"Perhaps that *is* going too far."

They were silent for a moment, then Fitz said, "The girls will be sorry to see you go, I know." He paused. "Particularly Lily."

He glanced toward Neville as he said the words, and Neville straightened, narrowing his eyes. "Is that what all this is about? Lily?" Neville let out a crack of laughter.

"You have been paying a good deal of attention to her," Fitz responded mildly.

"Are you going to ask me next what my intentions are?" Carr's eyes danced. "Honorable, I assure you. I would never try to seduce Miss Lily. She is a delightful young lady, and, well, really, Fitz, she is your cousin, after all."

"I am aware that you would not set out to harm her. Otherwise we would be having a far different conversation." Neville's eyebrows soared upward at Fitz's words, but Fitz plowed ahead, his face serious. "But surely it must have occurred to you that Lily may not see your attentions in quite the same way as you do. She's only eighteen and rather unsophisticated. She is not accustomed to flirtation and compliments. Where you intend mere badinage, she may see declarations of affection. I watched her last night and saw how she looks at you."

"What inspired this sudden bout of cousinly care?" Neville asked, the amused look still lurking in his eyes. "Ah. I think I can guess. The lovely Mrs. Hawthorne." When Fitz did not speak, he nodded, his guess confirmed. "I have not been able to charm Mrs. Hawthorne, I fear. I am aware that she is suspicious of me."

"She is here to watch over my cousins. She is not likely to overlook Lily's budding affections."

"And I am a rake, am I not, in her eyes?"

Fitz paused, then said carefully, "Her husband was a major. She knew Fanny Bertram."

Neville stared at him without comprehension for a long moment. "Who the dev—oh." His face cleared. "Good Gad, that must have been ten years ago."

"Fanny confided in her sometime after the matter. You were, I gather, the villain of the piece."

"No doubt I was. Well, I need not wonder at the dismal lack of success I've had charming her." He paused, then added, "Fanny was a willing participant."

"I know. I told her. But Eve—Mrs. Hawthorne—saw only the aftermath . . . and through Fanny's telling. Regrets are easier borne if one has someone to blame for one's mistakes."

"Well, the beauteous Mrs. Hawthorne can rest easy. And you as well." Neville grinned as he stood up. "I have no interest in harming Miss Lily. If my charms are too great, I shall have to moderate them. I assure you, I will be very careful with your cousin." He chuckled as he sauntered to the door and turned back to Fitz. "Who would have guessed that Fitzhugh Talbot would turn into such a staid sort? I might almost think it is Stewkesbury in front of me."

Fitz scowled at his friend, and with a flourish of a bow, Neville left the room. Fitz stood up and glanced around the room. There was really nothing to do there; he didn't know why he had taken to coming into the study every morning since his brother left. It wasn't as if he was going to actually do any estate business. He knew that Oliver did not expect him to. Higgins, the estate manager, would handle nearly everything, and if a problem exceeded Higgins's authority or ability, he would shelve the matter until Oliver returned home.

He turned and walked to the door. Just as he stepped into the hall, however, he saw Higgins walking toward him, hat in one hand and an accounts book in the other.

"Mr. Talbot." Higgins nodded deferentially. "I usually report to Lord Stewkesbury every Friday if he doesn't come by the estate office earlier."

Fitz recalled that his brother normally dropped by the estate manager's office almost every day to check on things. "Ah, I've been shirking my duty, haven't I?"

"No, sir. I did not mean to imply that. I just thought I could bring you up to date on, um, what I've done this week. If you wish. Or I can wait until Lord Stewkesbury comes home, if you'd rather."

The man's request was, Fitz knew, mere courtesy. Fitz had never displayed the slightest interest in the running of the estate on the few occasions when he had been at Willowmere during Oliver's absence. Higgins no doubt expected Fitz to wave away the report. The man probably assumed Fitz was indolent and selfish, as Eve had accused him of being. Too lazy and disinterested to care about his brother's concerns or the problems of his tenants.

"No need to wait. Let's go over it now." Fitz regretted the words almost as soon as they were out of his mouth. But, he reflected, as he led Higgins into the study, at least he had the satisfaction of seeing that he had astonished the estate manager almost as much as he had himself.

Eve was in the drawing room with Lily and Camellia when the butler announced the arrival of Lady Vivian and Lady Sabrina. Eve looked up, surprised, and had to smother a smile as the two women walked into the room. Sabrina's smile was as brittle as glass, and Vivian's face reminded Eve forcibly of a sulky five-year-old.

Sabrina greeted the Bascombe sisters with seeming delight and tossed a brief 'Good day' to Eve, scarcely glancing at her. "It's been an age since I have seen you," she went on, addressing Lily and Camellia. "I was so pleased when I learned Vivian planned to pay you a visit this afternoon."

She dimpled prettily and threw a teasing glance at Vivian. "I am afraid I quite forced myself upon poor Vivian. But I told her I cannot allow her to keep the Bascombes to herself."

"You had all week to visit them," Vivian pointed out, "while Uncle Humphrey and I were away."

"Oh? You have been gone?" Eve asked.

"We wondered why we had not seen you," Lily added. "Cam and I were thinking we would have to call at Halstead House." She stopped, perhaps realizing her wording was not entirely gracious, given the presence of the mistress of Halstead House, and cast a guilty look toward Eve. "That is, I mean, not that we would not want to call at Halstead House."

"Did you travel far?" Eve put in quickly to smooth over the moment.

"Only to Cousin Peck's. Well, he is my grandfather's cousin, so I am not entirely sure what he is to me." Vivian paused, then added with an impish grin, "Other than a family obligation."

"Now, Vivian dear, you should not be so hardhearted toward Cousin Peck. He cannot help that he is deaf," Sabrina offered with a sweet, forgiving smile.

Vivian responded with the same sweetness, "Since you are so fond of him, I cannot but wonder that you cried off going with us."

"I would, of course, have accompanied Lord Humphrey to his cousin's, but I was quite laid up with one of my horrid megrims."

"Of course." Vivian turned back to the other women. "In any case, it's not his deafness that I find difficult. It is the fact that he lives in a great drafty pile and is so cheeseparing that he will not allow a fire in any room before November, so that one has to go about bundled up in spencers and shawls, even at the dinner table. His conversation consists of nothing but the great cost of everything from coal to cabbage, and all the while everyone knows that he's full of juice."

"Really, Vivian." Sabrina's mouth pinched. "Must you use such vulgar cant?"

"It describes him perfectly," Vivian retorted. "And we are among friends. I don't think Camellia and Lily will mind."

"Of course not," the two girls chorused.

Sabrina smiled thinly. "Still, it will scarcely help poor Mrs. Hawthorne's efforts to teach them how to converse in the drawing rooms of the *ton,* will it?"

"I think Miss Bascombe and Miss Lily understand the difference between speech among family and friends and that with mere acquaintances," Eve responded. "It is very kind of you, though, Lady Sabrina, to be concerned about them."

"Besides," Vivian added, "they will also have your conduct as an example to counter mine."

Sabrina narrowed her eyes at the other woman but apparently could find nothing at which to take offense, so she kept silent. A small silence fell upon them. Lady Sabrina's unaccustomed presence added an awkwardness to the usually talkative group.

"We are going to have a dinner party," Lily offered after a moment, with an air of relief at having found a topic. "Eve—I mean, Mrs. Hawthorne—said she thought we were ready."

"Indeed?" Sabrina looked amazed but followed it with a quick smile. "But how wonderful. Your chaperone is quite right. 'Tis a perfect opportunity for you to exercise your social skills without having to worry about any mistakes you will make."

It was all Eve could do not to grind her teeth. She was beginning to understand what Vivian had been talking about when she described Sabrina's way of wounding with compliments.

"Yes, isn't it?" Camellia agreed cheerfully. "I'm sure it's just like shooting or riding; you have to practice to get really good at it."

Eve had to look down to hide a smile. Trust barbs to bounce off Camellia like arrows off armor. The Bascombes' confidence, she was finding, was likely to carry them through any situation, social or otherwise.

Lily went on happily describing their plans for the party, politely asking Lady Sabrina for her opinion of the dishes they should have, even though Eve knew that they had already made their decisions regarding the menu. Lily, Eve had noticed, was growing more adept at the art of conversation, despite her slip-up a few moments ago, regarding it as a sort of game, a concept that, Eve thought, would stand her in as good a stead as Camellia's general indifference to other people's opinion.

As she talked, Vivian said to Eve, "Pray, may I borrow that, um, book we discussed last week?"

"Of course." Eve smiled. "Ladies, if you will excuse us . . ."

Eve dared not look at her charges as she and Vivian slipped out the door. Vivian shared the same sentiment as she looped her arm through Eve's, murmuring, "I know I should not have abandoned Lily and Camellia to Sabrina like that, but I did not think I could bear another minute in that woman's company. Really, we have been back only a day, and already Cousin Peck's drafty castle seems more and more appealing."

Eve chuckled. "Was it really as bad as that?"

"Worse. Everyone dreads visiting him, but Uncle Humphrey feels guilty if he does not do so regularly since he lives only a half-day's ride away. I'm glad I went, for it seemed to make my uncle happy. It was nice to talk all the way there and back." She sighed. "Though I think perhaps he doesn't feel entirely well. Or perhaps he's merely sad. He talks a great deal about Aunt Amabel, which of course infuriates Sabrina."

"I can understand that it would annoy a second wife."

Vivian shrugged. "No doubt. But do not expect me to feel sorry for her. She should not have married a man who was still mourning his wife if she did not want to have to live with the woman's ghost."

Eve smiled. "I would not expect you to feel any differently. That is one of the most endearing things about you—your utter and unqualified loyalty to those you love."

Vivian smiled. "I am glad you think so. I have heard it called less flattering things . . . like being bloody-minded."

"I presume you must plan to return home soon, then, to get away from Lady Sabrina."

"I told Uncle I would stay another week. It will give me a chance to visit with you, and he was loath for me to leave. I think he has realized what a mistake he made in marrying Sabrina. That's the problem, of course, in marrying. If you make a mistake, you are burdened with it for the rest of your life. As my parents were—I know that is why Father has never remarried." She gave a little shiver. "I could not bear that. Anyway, I can endure Sabrina one more week, I think, as long as I can slip away from her to visit you now and then. Next time I shan't tell her I'm coming and order the carriage. I'll just go out for a ride. Besides, I imagine this afternoon's trip will be quite enough for Sabrina as well. We argued all the way over."

Eve smiled. "Really? I would never have guessed."

Vivian chuckled. "No need for sarcasm. I realize I must have looked thunderous when we arrived. After hearing myself criticized for twenty minutes for everything from my hairstyle to my too free manner, I am surprised we were both still alive when we got to your door."

They had reached Eve's room, and Eve glanced around. "What book should you like? I'm not sure I have anything you haven't read, probably many times."

"That doesn't matter. I'll say we couldn't find it. Or perhaps I'll take one of Lily's. She won't mind as long as she isn't reading it. Come here. Sit down with me and tell me what has been happening. What has transpired between you and Fitz?"

"Why, nothing. Why should there be anything?"

Vivian rolled her eyes as she perched on Eve's bed and patted the space beside her. "This is me you are speaking to, remember? I hope you don't expect me to believe that you and Fitz have had nothing to do with each other for the past week."

"Well, we have not. At least, not alone." Eve sat down on the bed, turning to face her friend and curling her legs up under her. "We have been together in company many times—every day, in fact. But except for once when we talked about his cousins, I have been quite careful not to be alone with Mr. Talbot." At her friend's frown, Eve raised her brows. "What? It was you who warned me against him."

"I didn't mean for you to barricade yourself away or start wearing your hair in that spinsterish knot."

Eve chuckled, her hand going automatically to the bun at the nape of her neck. "I am not barricading myself away. And I don't see that it's a problem if I choose to wear my hair in a sensible manner. As you can see, I have given in and am wearing the clothes Rose left behind, so it isn't as if I am being dowdy—which is not, in any case, a cardinal sin."

Vivian smiled. "No, 'tis but a venial one, I believe." She

reached out and placed a hand on her friend's arm. "I have been thinking and thinking. I'm not sure I should have said what I did about Fitz. I like him; truly I do. There is nothing to say that he might not change. Nor is there any reason why you should not enjoy yourself if you choose to. No one will know; I am quite certain Fitz is utterly discreet."

"No, you were right. I am not the sort of person for a casual affair. Nor am I going to deceive myself into thinking that Fitz will suddenly change. My mind is quite made up." Eve was unaware of the wistful expression that crossed her features as she said the words.

Vivian drew in her breath sharply. "But you wish it were not so."

Eve glanced at her, surprised, and opened her mouth to deny her friend's words. Then she sighed and nodded. "I do."

"Do you care for him? Have you already given your heart?"

"No. I mean, I do like him. There is little not to like about Fitz. I do not love him. But . . ." She leaned forward, her voice lowering as she said, "Oh, Viv, the way I feel when he kisses me!"

Vivian's eyes widened in a way that made Eve suspect her friend was not quite as sophisticated as her manner indicated. "You mean you have—has he—"

Eve shook her head. "We have kissed, that's all." She ignored the other liberties he had taken; there was no need to tell Vivian *everything*. "But I have never felt that way before."

"Oh my." Vivian paused. "Even with Major Hawthorne?"

Eve blushed. She had never told anyone, even Vivian, about the problems of her marriage. It had always seemed a betrayal of Bruce, and, empty as their marriage had been in that respect, she had loved him too much to expose him. Besides, it was altogether too embarrassing to talk about, even with her closest friend. So she had allowed Vivian to assume that theirs had been a normal marriage, and she could hardly explain to Vivian now that she was as lacking in experience as Vivian herself.

"No," Eve said in a lowered voice, looking away. "Not even then. It is—I feel—so tempted." She raised her head to look at Vivian. "Have you ever felt that way?"

"Sadly, no."

"That night of the wedding, when you found me on the terrace, I had been in the herb garden with Fitz. I was—Vivian, I was lost not only to propriety but to all good sense. If anyone had stumbled upon us, I would have been ruined. But it was Fitz who stopped."

"That is a good sign. I mean, that he would be discreet and careful, not expose you to gossip."

"Even discretion cannot guarantee that, and you know it. But the point is not that *he* was careful but that *I* was not. I am not myself when I am with him. Or maybe I am a me I should not be. It doesn't matter. What matters is that Fitzhugh Talbot is dangerous. I have to stay away from him."

"That may prove rather difficult. Willowmere is large, but . . ."

"I know." Eve frowned. "I tell myself that I have been doing quite well, but the truth is, I have been sorely tested. When Fitz is not around the day is duller. When he comes into a room the whole place is suddenly brighter."

"Mm. I've noticed that . . . when Sabrina leaves."

Eve smiled at her friend's remark. "Yes. It is like that. Only bigger." She sighed. "I never expected this problem when I agreed to come here. I can only hope that when the earl returns, Fitz will have grown bored and decide to return to London." She did not look particularly happy at the prospect.

"Why do I think that is not what you really hope?"

"Because you know me too well." Eve gave her a rueful glance. "Why is it that we want what isn't good for us?"

"I don't know." Vivian's face turned wistful now. "But isn't it odd how the Talbot men fall into that category?" With those words she hopped off the bed. "We'd best get back to the others. It is a trifle hard to justify looking for a book this long."

Stifling the curiosity Vivian's words had aroused, Eve followed the other woman out the door.

Chapter 10

When they returned to the sitting room downstairs, Vivian and Eve found that the Bascombe sisters had been joined by Fitz and Neville. Lady Sabrina was flirting madly with Neville while Lily sat across the room glaring at the woman.

Neville, Eve noticed, was not flirting in return. Indeed, when she and Vivian entered the room, he sprang to his feet with alacrity and bowed. "Mrs. Hawthorne. Lady Vivian. Please, sit down." He gestured toward the chair where he had been sitting, which stood at right angles to Sabrina's.

Eve, her eyes twinkling, obligingly sat down in the spot he indicated, while Neville shot over to the hearth to join Fitz. Fitz gave him a sardonic look before he bowed to Eve and Vivian.

"Ladies. So good of you to join us. Lady Sabrina was describing the beauties of the gardens at Halstead House."

"Yes, I was telling Mr. Carr he must come and view them sometime. But of course, it would be difficult to best the gardens of Willowmere. I am sure Mr. Carr is well occupied here."

"Indeed, we go riding every day," Lily responded. "As well as taking walks in the gardens."

Sabrina cast the gentleman in question a glance from beneath her lashes, an impressive maneuver given the fact that he was standing several feet away and somewhat behind her. "Perhaps you will be so good as to show me the gardens here, then, Mr. Carr, given that their beauty is unequaled."

"An excellent idea." Lily popped up from her seat. "Why don't we visit the garden right now? I am sure that we can show you some lovely sights, Lady Sabrina, even if the flowers are all but gone."

Eve smothered a smile. Apparently Lily was not as unprepared to deal with the social warfare of the Season as Eve had assumed. Eve cast a look at Fitz, and the glinting laughter in his eyes was almost enough to make her spill over into giggles.

Everyone, it seemed, was eager to view the gardens. The American girls did not wear their bonnets, as was often the case, and today the other ladies joined them, for the pale autumn sun offered a welcome warmth on their faces. Even Sabrina abandoned her hat, perhaps realizing that her shaded face offered little competition for the way Lily's features glowed in the sunlight.

Eve was content to stroll behind the others, letting the distance between them lengthen. She had few worries about Lily spending time alone with Neville as long as Sabrina was around. Fitz, she noticed, also lagged behind, matching his long strides to hers.

He glanced toward the others, now well ahead of them, and said, "I spoke to Neville this morning."

"Oh?" Eve glanced up at him. He was gazing straight ahead, and she could not see his expression.

"He has promised to be most circumspect in his conversations with Lily. He told me that he has no intention of providing the slightest harm to her reputation." As Eve started to speak, he went on quickly, "I reminded him that her heart was in question also, and he assured me that he would be careful with her feelings as well. I think he likes the child, but he knows that it can go no farther than that. He has not yet proposed to Lady Priscilla, but it is his intention to do so in the future. He considers himself committed to it."

"I see."

"I believe him. He is my friend, and as I said, he likes Lily. He would not wish to hurt her."

"Thank you. I know that it must have been difficult for you."

"I felt a bit of a fool, questioning him about his intentions." He cast a grin at her. "And no doubt I shall have to endure some jests about my newly acquired stodginess."

"It was good of you."

"I felt so filled with righteousness that after that I talked to Stewkesbury's estate manager."

"My goodness." Eve pulled a face. "Such courage in the face of danger."

"Yes, well, you may laugh. But it was dicey, I assure you. I was in danger of expiring from boredom within minutes after he started."

Eve let out a laugh.

"I have never heard so many facts about things I am not even slightly interested in. It was a wonder I didn't start to scream and pull my hair like a lunatic." He shrugged. "I fear I must be the lightweight you named me after all."

Eve looked at him with some dismay. "No, please, do not take what I said to heart. I spoke in anger. I know that you are not an uncaring or thoughtless person. There's nothing wrong with disliking to listen to reports. Not everyone enjoys numbers and business arrangements. That does not mean that you are not good at a number of other things."

"Well, there is dancing. And gossip. I'm rather good at them. Not to mention introductions; I rarely get a name or title wrong."

"Those are not insignificant skills. I am sure you are the savior of many a hostess."

"Mm. No doubt. And if I were in the wilds of Lily's and Camellia's country, no doubt my shooting abilities would come in handy . . . though I do not think I would care for the lack of amenities."

"Nor would I. But still, your handiness with your pistols did make me feel safer after that fellow broke into the house."

"I knew we could hit on something useful if we kept at it." Fitz grinned. "I found out a number of important things from the estate manager."

"Indeed?"

"Indeed. Will Blankinship's daughter is ill. The widow Carter's hens are laying poorly."

"Oh my."

"Yes. Someone's barn roof needs to be rethatched, but alas, my poor brain, I cannot remember whose it was. Most important, Tim Whitfield's wife has borne him a new son."

"Ah. That is important."

"Yes. I am sure I ought to do something. Oliver would, but I'm not sure what it is I ought to do. I think the estate manager expected me to know, so I dared not ask. I must congratulate the father; I am certain of that much. But am I supposed to go look at it? It seems an intrusion somehow."

"You must congratulate the father, but I think visiting the wife and child is more the sort of thing the lady of the house does. She takes a basket of foodstuffs, of course, and no doubt something for the child, and oohs and ahs over the infant. I suppose that Lily and Camellia are the closest thing here to ladies of the house." Eve brightened. "This would be a good experience for them. It is the sort of thing they will have to do in the future, after they are married. We can get all we need from Cook and the housekeeper."

"Excellent. I will escort you three there and congratulate Whitfield while you admire the baby."

Eve smiled at him. It occurred to her that she was far too happy at the thought of spending an afternoon with Fitz, even if they would not be alone. She could only hope that it did not show on her face.

She glanced ahead of them. "Oh dear. They've left us behind."

"What? Oh." Fitz followed her gaze. He shrugged. "I do not think you have to worry. Lady Sabrina will be more than an adequate chaperone for our Romeo and Juliet."

"Do not call them so. Lily would be lost to all reason if she thought that."

"Come." Fitz took Eve by the hand and whisked her onto another path. "I want to show you something."

Curious, she let him lead her along the colonnaded arbor. After a few twists and turns they slipped between two high hedges, and Eve found herself in a corridor of green. The hedges on either side were a good foot taller than even Fitz, so that she could see nothing but the hedges and the sky overhead. Passing offshoots of corridors, Fitz turned confidently right at one, then left at the next.

"A maze!" Eve exclaimed. "This must be quite old."

"A century at least. It was allowed to fall into disrepair some years ago. When Oliver and Royce and I were children, it was overgrown, but we found it a wonderful place to play. Oliver had it trimmed up when he came into the estate so it looks much as it did originally. He improved the center, too; you'll see."

Another turn and a coiling curve, and they were in the heart of the maze.

"Oh!" Eve let out a gasp of delight. "You're right. It's lovely!"

She turned around, taking in the small circular area. Green hedges grew high all around, enclosing them from the outside world, so that they seemed to be standing in a small verdant room. Stone benches stood on either side of a small pond in which two large goldfish swam, making lazy ripples in the water.

"It's wonderfully peaceful."

He nodded, looking down at her. Eve realized that he had not let go of her hand as they navigated the maze. His thumb was slowly circling her palm, sending pleasant shivers up her arm. She should tell him to stop it, should snatch her hand away. Indeed, she should have done that some time earlier.

"I have thought about what you said." His voice was low and serious, for once without amusement or charm. "I would not harm you for the world. This morning I made up my mind that I would not seek you out again, that I would not try to entice or persuade you into my bed, no matter how much I wanted you there. But now, looking at you . . . I find I cannot remember any of those excellent reasons we should stay apart."

Eve's first thought was that neither could she, though some lurking influence of reason kept her from saying the words.

Fitz reached up and stroked his knuckles slowly down her cheek. "Your skin is like satin. Sometimes when I'm sitting there, watching you across the drawing room, I think about how it felt beneath my fingers, how smooth and soft."

"Fitz . . ." Eve's voice was shaky. "We should not."

"I know. I know." He cupped her face in his hands. "I

want to be wise. But when I am with you all I can think about is kissing you. Tell me you don't feel the same."

She opened her mouth, but the words would not come out. "I can't. You know I want—"

Whatever else she was about to say was cut off by his mouth as it clamped down on hers. And, as it had every time he kissed her, desire flooded Eve. Her body warmed, her abdomen turning heavy and achy, echoing the changes in her breasts. Whenever she was apart from Fitz, she told herself she was exaggerating the way she reacted to his touch, but as soon as he kissed her, she knew that her memories, if anything, paled in comparison with the reality. Heat blossomed between her legs, and she wanted to press herself against Fitz, to feel his hard muscle and bone digging into her flesh.

His hands had dropped to her hips, pulling her up against him. She put her hands on his arms and slid them upward, exploring the hard curves of his muscles beneath his coat. She wondered what it would feel like to let her hands roam over his bare skin, to see and touch him naked. What would it be like to give in to her desires? To sink to the ground with him and let herself go?

No. It would be madness.

Eve pulled herself away, half turning from him. "No. Please, Fitz, I must not." Her hand went to her mouth. Her lips were soft and damp, faintly swollen and tender from his kisses.

"I know. Of course. You're right." He swung away and stood, staring intently down at the pond.

"Did you . . . did you really decide not to . . . do this?" she asked after a moment, her voice light and a little wondering.

"Yes, of course. I thought about what you said—your reputation and how if any scandal were linked to your name it would be disastrous for you. I considered how, no matter how discreet we were, some word might leak out. Or how rumors could spread even if no one knew for sure." He turned back to her. "I would not hurt you for the world, Eve, you must know that. I am not so concerned for my own pleasure that I would take advantage of you in any way."

She looked back at him, her blue-gray eyes lambent. "I am glad that you have . . . such concern for me."

"Of course I do." He moved quickly back to her, taking her hands in his. "I can promise you that no man would dare say a word against you. They'd not want to face me at twenty paces." His blue eyes glinted in a way that Eve had never seen before.

A faint smile curved her lips. "But you could hardly shoot them all."

He returned a cocky grin. "They wouldn't test me." The amusement dropped from his face. "But I could hardly call the women out. Or stop their gossip."

"I know. And I—I appreciate your seeing that." Eve paused. "Still . . . we are far from London."

His eyes narrowed. "Eve, what are you saying?"

"Just fustian." She shook her head. "I'm talking nonsense. We shouldn't even consider it."

"Absolutely not."

They stood for a long moment, gazing at each other. And then they were in each other's arms again, their bodies straining together, their lips meeting in hunger. She was mad, Eve thought as she wrapped her arms around his neck, going up on tiptoe to kiss him. Completely mad.

A girl's laugh wafted through the air. Eve and Fitz froze. A moment later they heard the low rumble of a male voice. They broke apart, and Eve whirled to walk a few steps away. Her nerves were clamoring, and she was sure her face must be flushed.

"How could we have forgotten?" she moaned softly. Her fingers went to her hair.

Fitz moved closer, reaching out to tuck a stray strand of hair back behind her ear. She could not suppress the shiver that ran through her at his touch.

"You look beautiful," he assured her in a low voice.

She pulled out a pin and repinned the hair he had just touched. "Do I look—? I feel—" How could she describe the jangling of her nerves, the excited, heated rush of pleasure that still pumped throughout her body? "I am afraid they will know what we were doing the instant they look at me."

"Don't worry. It won't be that soon." His voice was barely above a whisper. "Even Neville doesn't know the maze. Let them stumble about a bit."

"What about Vivian?"

"The devil!" He scowled. "She knew it well enough when she used to visit Charlotte. But it's been years. I don't know how well she would remember it."

"It's never wise to underestimate Vivian."

He nodded. "Too true. You sit down and observe the tranquil pond. I shall sally forth to find them."

They heard Lily's laughter again, much nearer, followed by Neville's voice, "Another dead end! Miss Bascombe, I fear that you are a terrible scout."

These words were followed by a softer female voice, the words unclear. Fitz nodded toward Eve, and she sat down quickly on one of the benches, gazing at the fish swimming about the pond and trying to still her own tumultuous thoughts. Fitz strolled away.

A moment later she heard him laugh. "Lady Vivian! Cousin Camellia. What took you so long? Mrs. Hawthorne and I have been waiting for you an age."

"It's been twelve years since I've been here," Vivian

pointed out. "But you'd best go find the others. Lady Sabrina was quite certain Cam and I were headed the wrong way, so the three of them blazed their own trail."

A moment later Vivian and Camellia entered the heart of the maze, joining Eve on the benches. Vivian cast an appraising eye over Eve but said nothing other than a comment on the beauty of the pond. Camellia launched into a description of Lady Sabrina's attempts to divert Neville onto a path alone with her and Lily's determined thwarting of her every attempt. By the time Fitz led the others to the pond, the three women were deep in conversation.

Lily's color was high, and there was a decided sparkle in her eyes. However, the light in Sabrina's eyes was not as pleasant, and she had a difficult time maintaining her usual sweet tone. At least, Eve thought gratefully, Sabrina was so irritated with Lily that she did not spare a glance for Eve or make a comment on the fact that Eve and Fitz had separated from the others.

After a brief interlude admiring the pond and its surroundings the party started back, Fitz leading the way out. Once again Lily and Sabrina jockeyed for position beside Neville. Cam rolled her eyes and dropped back to stroll with Vivian and Eve. Eve was glad that the two of them kept up most of the conversation, for her thoughts kept running back to how foolish she had been and how close she could have come to ruining her reputation. It made her blood chill to think of what would have been the consequence if Lady Sabrina had come upon her and Fitz locked in a passionate embrace. She could not continue to give in to her desires like that. She had to hold herself aloof from Fitz. She had to make it clear to him that she would not have an affair with him. If she did not, she could easily lose her reputation and all hope of future employment.

And quite frankly, she had more to lose, even, than that.

It would be all too easy to lose her heart to Fitz, to let the passion he could bring up in her lead her into falling in love with him. She had given her heart before to a man who loved her but could not meet her passion. She was not about to give it again to a man who could satisfy her desires but would never love her.

When they reached the house Lady Sabrina and Vivian departed in their carriage, and the rest of them split up. The Bascombes and Mr. Carr headed toward the game room, but Eve noticed that Fitz started down the hall toward his brother's study. She hesitated, her gaze going to the game-room door. Surely Camellia's company would be enough chaperonage for a few minutes, Eve thought.

She turned and lightly hurried down the corridor after Fitz.

He was just sitting down behind the desk when Eve entered the room, and he bounced back up when he saw her.

"Eve." He smiled. "Come in. You have saved me from the account books the estate manager brought me. Please, sit down."

"No, thank you. I will not take up much of your time." Eve clasped her hands in front of her and came to stand in front of the desk across from him. She had to be firm. "I wanted to say that what happened earlier was my fault. I should not have said or done what I did."

"There was no harm. No one saw or heard anything."

"This time. But next time we might not be so lucky."

"Don't worry." He walked around the desk and took her hands in his, his eyes warm as he looked down into her face. "We shall be more careful. No one will know."

Eve pulled her hands from his. "That is not all that matters. Just because no one will know doesn't make it a good thing to do. I am not interested in a casual affair. But that is all you *are* interested in. Isn't that right?"

"I would not call it casual," he said, but his face had lost its warmth, and he took a step backward. "Are you saying that you want more than that? Marriage?"

"No." Eve's eyes flashed. His actions had betrayed his feelings for her . . . or rather his lack of them. Obviously he was in no danger of losing his heart to her. "I don't want marriage, either. What I am saying is that all you care about is your pleasure. Your desire."

"The pleasure would be mutual. I promise you that."

"I refuse to risk my entire future on the hope of pleasure," Eve shot back. "I intend to establish a life for myself. I want to be a good chaperone to Lily and Camellia and get more such employment in the future. I don't want to be dependent upon my father or indeed any man. And I don't want to provide a few weeks' entertainment for you."

Fitz's mouth thinned, and there was a flash of something like steel in his blue eyes. Then he nodded briefly. "Of course. If that is what you wish."

It was not what she wished, Eve knew. But she was even more certain now that it was the only thing she could do. With a short nod she turned and walked out of the room.

Her head was pounding, she realized as she walked down the hall, and she could not bear the thought of joining Neville and the girls in what was bound to be a lively and noisy game. There was, after all, no other kind where the Bascombes were involved. Somewhat guiltily she turned toward the stairs, promising herself that if she could just lie down for a few moments with a cool cloth on her forehead, she would be fit thereafter to oversee the group again. Cam, after all, would be with the other two, and Neville had promised Fitz not to pursue Lily.

As she neared the stairs her gaze went automatically toward the hall table. She had been checking the place every day since she had gotten the note. There had not been another message for her, much to her relief, but she continued to check.

Today, however, there was a white square sitting alone on the table. She stopped, her heart pounding. There was no reason to think that the piece of mail was for her, she told herself. It was far more likely that Mary or Rose had written their sisters or that the earl had sent some missive to Fitz. For that matter, most of the time the mail was addressed to the earl. Still, Eve could not subdue the sick feeling in the pit of her stomach. She forced herself to walk over to the table.

Eve's name was written across the front of the white square—not this time in the same blocky print but in a dark, forceful masculine hand. Her fingers trembled slightly as she picked it up and turned back to the staircase. She did not dare look at the letter there where someone might walk in at any moment. She carried it up the stairs to her room, trying to convince herself that the letter would turn out to be perfectly innocent. The problem was she could not think of any man who would have written her besides her father, and this was not his ornate, rather spidery hand. Friends of her husband, of course, had sent her letters of condolence, but his death had been two years ago, and those were long since received, even from the officers who had been sent to serve in India.

Inside her room she shut the door and examined the letter closely. Unlike the other note, this one had been sent through the mail; it was clearly stamped. The wax seal on the back was stamped with a different design, though it, too, was an anonymous, general sort of seal rather than initials or a crest or some more distinctive symbol.

She was putting off reading it, she realized. Eve slid her

finger beneath the flap and broke the seal. Opening it, she read:

> "Mrs. Hawthorne,
> The watch is dangerous. Destroy it. Throw it away.
> Otherwise the Truth will come out, and you will suffer
> for it. Your husband's Reputation will be ruined.
> He was not the man you think. The watch carries the
> taint of Scandal, and it will stain you as surely as it
> would have stained the Major.
>   Signed,
>   Your Friend

Eve stared at the letter, her mind reeling. What could this mean? Bruce, involved in a scandal? His reputation ruined? It was absurd. Whatever faults Bruce might have had, he had been an honorable man. Duty had been his byword. Yes, he had had his secrets, chief among them his inability to perform as a husband. But that was a private matter, affecting no one but herself. Bruce would never have knowingly entered into anything scandalous.

Almost as ludicrous was the idea that his final gift to her could somehow be proof of this scandal. She tossed the letter onto the bed and went to the drawer where she had hidden the watch. She pulled it out and sat down to examine it more thoroughly. She ran her fingers over the elegant enameled front decorated with pearls and the ornately engraved back. She opened it to read the inscription on the inside of the cover: "For my beloved wife." She even placed her thumbnail beneath the plate that covered the watch works and pried it open, thinking that perhaps something had been hidden inside. There was nothing but the usual wheels and cogs.

Closing the watch again, she sat, thinking. The two notes

were very unalike, even in their messages. The first had only told her to leave. This one advised her to get rid of her watch and impugned her late husband. But despite the differences, they must have been written by the same person. It was too absurd to think that two different people were writing her anonymous notes.

It made no sense. Eve closed her eyes. She thought briefly about snatching up the watch and the notes and running downstairs to Fitz. But she knew she could not do that, not after she had just crowed about her desire not to depend on any man. Not after she had told him she wanted him to stay out of her life.

Besides, he was the earl's brother. And she certainly did not want news of this letter getting back to the Earl of Stewkesbury. He would not want her chaperoning his cousins if she was somehow involved in a scandal—or even if there was a possibility that she could be involved in a scandal. The fact that she did not know what the scandal was did not change the fact that it could explode right in her face at the worst possible moment. The earl would not be willing to risk that, not when his cousins' all-important introduction to the *ton* was at stake.

Carefully she wrapped the watch back up in her nightgown and returned it to the drawer, sliding the second note under the first one she had received and covering both with the nightgown. She walked over to the window and stood, staring out over the landscape.

Someone out there had written to her. She could not imagine who had done it or why. She was not even sure whether that person was someone who wanted to harm her in some way or someone who was trying to save her from harm. A friend surely would have told her directly if he knew of a problem about her watch. Unless, of course, the sender did not want her to know that he knew about the scandal.

Perhaps he was even involved in it. In that case, it was likely that he was as interested (no, probably even more so!) in saving his own reputation as in preserving Bruce's.

Or maybe he just wanted the watch and had come up with an elaborate scheme to get it from her. But that idea, she admitted, seemed far too unlikely. Better simply to steal it . . . which brought her back, of course, to the man who had broken into Willowmere the other day. It seemed more likely to her now that the events were connected.

The question, of course, was why? And who? Most important, how was she going to deal with it on her own?

Chapter 11

The next day Eve accompanied Lily and Camellia on their visit to the farmer's wife who had been newly delivered of a baby. Lily was eager to see the new baby; Camellia was less enthusiastic about the child but welcomed any opportunity to get out of the house and onto a horse. They were escorted by Fitz, who went to congratulate the father, one of Oliver's tenants, and Neville, who declared that with everyone else gone there was nothing to keep him at Willowmere.

Eve was keenly aware of Fitz's presence. He treated her politely, but there was a reserve to his manner that had been missing before. He did not ride beside Eve, gradually dropping back so that the two of them were riding behind the others, as he usually did when the group went riding. Instead he rode beside Camellia at one end, while Neville rode beside Lily at the other end, with Eve sandwiched in the middle. Though she was not excluded from the conversations, neither was she an integral part in either of them, and she realized with some dismay that for the first time she felt like a chaperone, in the group and yet not of it.

She could not keep from glancing Fitz's way from time to time. The bright blue eyes, the classic profile, the elegant way he sat on his horse all stirred her viscerally. It seemed the height of irony that now that he had acquiesced in her demands not to pursue her, she found him even more desirable. She realized suddenly that she was sitting there gazing at him like a moonstruck fool, and she jerked her eyes away. It was clear that he had no trouble treating her like an acquaintance; she told herself that she could do the same.

The visit to the new mother and child went off smoothly. Lily showered the baby with compliments and even asked to hold him, pleasing the new mother, and both girls were so unaffected and naturally friendly that when they left both Mrs. Whitfield and her mother agreed that they were true ladies even if they were Americans.

They rode home along a track that skirted the fields. As they cut through a meadow, involved in a lively conversation, suddenly Camellia pulled her horse to a stop, pointing up above the trees in front of them.

"Look!"

They all obediently lifted their eyes. There, wafting gracefully toward them, was a large, brightly colored balloon, a basket dangling below it.

"Oh!" Lily gasped, her eyes shining like stars. "I have never seen one, only drawings."

As they watched, hands shading their eyes against the sun, the bright blue balloon grew lower and lower as it sailed toward them. They could see a figure on board now, scurrying from one side to the other, and as he worked at the basket, things dropped from it.

"What's he doing?" Camellia asked.

"Tossing off ballast, I'd guess," Fitz said. "I've seen them before. He's losing altitude, so he's getting rid of the weights, trying to give the balloon more lift. He's worried, I imagine, about running into the trees."

"With reason," Neville put in, as the basket swept across the top branches of a tree.

Unconsciously Eve edged her mount closer to Fitz as they waited tensely, watching the basket skimming the treetops. The figure had apparently given up tossing off the ballast and was now pulling on some ropes. Eve's horse danced nervously as the large object grew closer, as did the other animals, and she tightened her grip, murmuring calming words to the mare.

The balloonist managed to clear the woods, but he could not avoid the lone tree that lay a few yards past the others. The gondola crashed into the oak's branches and was dragged further into the tree by the force of the balloon. The basket turned and bumped down through a few more branches. The man inside it came spilling out and tumbled the rest of the way through the tree to the ground.

Lily let out a shriek as Neville muffled a curse. Fitz spurred his horse forward toward the balloon, and the others followed suit. The wicker basket was wedged in the tree, tilting precariously, one side crushed. Some ropes dangled free; others were still attached to the huge silk balloon, now deflating on the grass beyond the tree.

Fitz jumped off his horse and ran to the figure lying on the ground. The man was quite still, his eyes closed, and one leg was bent awkwardly beneath him. Eve held her breath as Fitz knelt beside him.

"He's breathing," Fitz reported.

"Thank heavens." Eve slid off her horse, as did the rest of them, and hurried over to Fitz and the balloonist.

"He's unconscious and bleeding from this wound," Fitz said, looking up at her. "And unless I'm mistaken, that leg is broken."

Eve pulled her handkerchief out of her pocket and handed it to Fitz as she sank onto the grass beside him. Fitz folded the cloth into a pad and pressed it against the bleeding wound. They all stared down at the injured man. His skin was tanned, and dark stubble dotted his square jaw and chin. His hair was a mass of wild black curls. He let out an inarticulate groan and moved his head. All of them leaned forward. His eyes popped open, eyes almost as dark as his hair, and he stared at them blankly for a moment.

"Mon dieu," he said softly, and closed his eyes again.

"He's French?" Camellia asked as she, too, dropped to her knees.

The stranger opened his eyes again and started to sit up, clapping a hand to his head and letting out another groan. Then he began to talk, spewing out French.

"What's he saying?" Camellia asked.

Eve looked at Fitz. Her schoolroom French had mostly vanished through lack of use. The best she could do was recognize the language.

Fitz looked back at her and shrugged. "French was never my best subject. I think he's asking about someone."

They all looked up at the basket hanging above them, clearly empty.

"Was there someone else?" Eve asked. "What happened to him?"

It was Neville who said, "I think he's talking about his balloon. He keeps calling it 'his beauty,' but I don't think it's a woman. He asked if it's ruined."

Neville began to speak in French to the man, his words halting. The man responded with another torrent of impassioned verbiage as he struggled to sit up. Neville looked blank, the flood of French obviously too much for his abilities.

"Excitable sort," Neville commented.

Fitz put a hand on the Frenchman's chest, firmly pressing him back to the ground. "Yes, that's all very well, but you need to lie down. You've been injured. You're going to hurt yourself further."

With a groan, the man stopped talking, sinking back and closing his eyes. Neville began his halting French again, but the man shook his head.

"No, no. Please. Enough." The balloonist raised his hand to his head. "I need—how you say—give me a moment. My head, it is—" He made a soft but explosive noise, pulling his hands apart dramatically.

"Your head hurts," Camellia offered pragmatically.

"*Oui. Merci.* How is she? How is my balloon?"

They all turned to look at the huge collapsed bag of silk.

"Um. Well, it's deflated, I'm afraid," Fitz began.

"Good. That's good. It won't go—" He made a floating motion with his hands.

"No. That's right. Monsieur . . ."

"Leveque. Barthelemy Leveque." He tried to push himself up onto his elbows again. "I must get up. I must see—"

"No. I'm afraid you cannot. Besides this rather nasty cut on your head, which I don't advise reopening, I am very much afraid that you have hurt your leg."

"No. No. I must—my gondola—" Again he pushed up on his elbows, and this time Fitz relaxed the pressure of his hand. Leveque came halfway up before he paled and sank back down. "Yes. Well. Perhaps I rest . . . a little."

Fitz stood up and turned to Neville. "Ride to the house and bring back some servants and a wagon. Tell them we'll need planks or a door to put him on."

"I'll go with you," Lily volunteered. "And get some bandages."

Eve started to protest but held her peace. It would not help to bring it to Lily's attention that Eve did her best to keep Lily and Neville from being alone together. It would, she suspected, only make the girl start figuring out ways to evade her chaperonage. And there was little likelihood that there would be any loverlike exchanges on a fast ride back to the house for help. To suggest that Eve accompany them would seem odd; Lily scarcely needed help to get the man bandages.

So she said only, "Tell Mrs. Merriwether to prepare a bedroom for Monsieur Leveque."

Lily and Neville rode off, and the other three settled down to wait with the injured Frenchman. He was restless, craning his head and frequently muttering to himself in French. Fitz stripped off his jacket and laid it over Leveque, who shivered a little and offered Fitz a faint smile.

"*Merci.* I am a little cool." The Frenchman sounded rather surprised by the fact.

Eve leaned in closer to Fitz, murmuring softly, "Will he be all right, do you think?"

He turned to her, his brows knitting. "I'm not—" He stopped abruptly, and something flared in his eyes, then was quickly tamped down.

Eve realized suddenly how close her face was to his, and she stiffened, her cheeks flooding with color. "I—excuse me."

She stood up and moved back. Fitz rose lithely and followed her. But his manner and tone were stiff as he went on in a low voice, "I cannot know for sure. If a broken leg and that cut are the worst of it, I think he'll be fine. But who knows what damage has been done inside him?"

"Of course." Awkward with Fitz now, Eve fell silent and looked back to where Camellia sat beside the Frenchman.

"Did you come all the way from France in your balloon?" Cam asked.

The stranger nodded. "*Oui,* from Paris. You know Paris, *mademoiselle?*"

"No. I'm from the United States."

"Ah. I go there one day."

Fitz shifted, then moved back to stand beside the Frenchman. Eve remained where she was, very aware of the distance between them. She wondered if it would always be like this now. Firmly she tried to suppress the little pang in her heart that the thought caused.

"You mean, you're going to the United States in a balloon?" Cam asked in an awestruck voice.

"But yes! It has been done. Now I am traveling across the English Channel and up to Scotland." His face fell. "Or I was."

"It looks terribly exciting," Camellia went on. "I've always wanted to go up in a hot-air balloon."

"No. No." Leveque looked distressed. "Is not hot air. That is old. Mine is gas balloon. Hydrogen. Much better. More control."

"Camellia, perhaps we shouldn't question Monsieur Leveque," Eve began.

"No, no!" Leveque protested, waving one hand around dramatically. "It helps to talk. It take my mind off the, um—"

"The pain?" Eve asked sympathetically.

"What? No, no." The Frenchman shrugged off his apparently broken leg. "It is *ma belle*—my balloon. Does it have, what you call them, rips?" He twisted his head.

"I shouldn't think so," Cam told him cheerfully. "It didn't catch on the branches. When the basket caught, the balloon deflated. It's spread out on the field."

"Good. That is good." He turned to look at Fitz. "You must be very careful when you fold it up."

"Must I?" Fitz raised an eyebrow.

"*Oui*. Is very important. It is silk coated with rubber."

"Don't worry," Cam hastily assured him. "I'll oversee the work myself. We can put it and the basket in a barn. Right, Cousin Fitz?"

Fitz sighed. "Yes, I suppose we will. We cannot leave the thing lying in the field." He turned a quizzical eye up to the tree. "Though I'm not so sure about the basket."

"*Sacré!* It is ruined?" Leveque groaned, twisting to try to see up in the tree.

Things continued in this manner as they waited for Neville to return with the rescue party. Camellia was surprisingly good at calming down the Frenchman, responding to his instructions about the welfare of his equipment with assurances that all would be followed to the letter, then distracting him with more questions about ballooning.

Before long Neville and Lily returned, having ridden back faster than the wagon and servants. Lily had brought bandages and water, and they started to clean his wounds.

Neville pulled out a surprise of his own from the canvas sack they had brought and held it aloft. "I thought you could use a bit of medicinal brandy to get you through the process."

Leveque's dark eyes lit up. "Ah! *Merci, monsieur.*" He took the bottle and drank from it.

Eve began to bandage Leveque's scrapes and cuts, and Fitz moved quickly to help her. She cast a grateful glance at him, and he smiled back, and for that moment, at least, things were as easy between them as they had always been.

Leveque continued to medicate himself liberally, holding out the bottle in invitation to Neville. Neville dropped down beside him and took a swig from the proffered bottle, offering it to Fitz.

Fitz rolled his eyes as he declined. "Perhaps one of us should still be sober while we get him into the wagon."

Neville and Leveque had no such worries, and by the time the wagon arrived they were companionably singing songs in French—at which Neville apparently was more proficient at than speaking.

Lily and Camellia, watching Neville conduct an imaginary choir as they roared out the unintelligible words, giggled, and even Eve could not help but smile, though she added with a small sigh, "I cannot believe that this is what Lord Stewkesbury was envisioning for his cousins' outings."

"Oh, Cousin Oliver's not really so stuffy," Lily told her. "He can be quite nice when he unbends."

"Better for Leveque to be foxed when they lift him into that wagon," Fitz put in. "Just be glad that the girls don't understand French."

Eve smiled faintly. "I am aware of the use of alcohol to dim the pain; it's a practice favored by military men. I am only surprised that you are not joining them in the medicating."

"I am quite taken aback by it myself." Fitz grinned. "I think I must be becoming a dull fellow. One hopes that Oliver will return soon, before I slide irredeemably into a life of responsibility."

The head groom, a man accustomed to broken bones, directed the footmen and grooms as they picked up the Frenchman and laid him out on the door they had brought along. Despite their care, Leveque paled beneath his tan, and his eyes rolled back in his head.

"Better that way," Neville commented, standing up and straightening his cuffs.

He did not, Eve noticed, appear nearly as inebriated as he had moments earlier when he sang with Leveque. His eyes twinkled a little as he smiled at her. "One has to keep up the patients' spirits, doesn't one? I'm sure Fitz will tell you that I have the hardest head in Christendom."

The party rode back to the house, where the butler supervised carrying the wounded man up the stairs and into a room at the end of the hall. Leveque had awakened during the ride back to the house, and from the ashen color of his skin and the drops of sweat that dotted his forehead, Eve suspected that he wished he could have passed out again.

The doctor arrived and inspected the patient, then announced that, as they had suspected, Leveque's leg was broken, though, he added cheerfully, at least it was his lower leg, not his thigh, and only one of the bones.

"Much better. Much better. Easier to keep the leg from shortening." Then he shooed the women out of the room, keeping Fitz and Neville to pull the leg back into place.

"Well!" Camellia looked disgruntled as they left the room and walked toward their own rooms. "As if we couldn't stomach seeing a leg set."

"Thank you very much, my dear, but I think I would prefer not to see a leg set," Eve replied.

As if to punctuate her words, there was a loud cry behind the closed door, followed by a string of French words that could only be curses.

"Me too," Lily agreed with a shiver.

Even Camellia looked paler. "Still . . . I resent him assuming I couldn't stand it."

Eve chuckled as she stopped at her bedroom door. "I am sure you do."

A few minutes later, after she had washed and changed into one of the muslin dresses she had inherited from Rose, Eve emerged from her room to find Fitz coming down the hall.

"How is our patient?" she asked.

"Asleep. The doctor left him a draught for the pain, so at least Carr won't have to drink him under the table again tonight. Dr. Adams assured me it would be at least six to eight weeks before the man's leg heals. He'll be laid up in bed the whole time so the splints can keep his bone in place, else they'll knit wrong. I hate to think what Stewkesbury will say to having a French houseguest for the next two months."

"Mm. Well, there was no way you could avoid his crashing here."

"I suppose not. Though somehow I cannot help but think that if Oliver had been here it would not have happened."

"He causes the wind to blow?" Eve asked lightly.

Fitz cast her a sideways grin. "Sometimes I think he might. Things run more smoothly when Oliver is around." He brightened a little as he added, "Although I must say that since the Bascombes arrived he's had his challenges."

"Camellia has volunteered to keep Monsieur Leveque entertained, so that should help. She seems rather fascinated by balloon travel."

"Camellia is fascinated by anything that involves movement or danger. Best, I assume, is both of them together, so that should make ballooning a favorite." He turned toward her. "Do you think it's likely Cam is going to start suffering the pangs of love, too?"

Eve shrugged. "I have not seen her pay such attention to any other man."

Fitz let out a small groan. "Now I shall have to investigate him, won't I? Make sure he's not married or a lunatic—well, I mean, more of a lunatic than any other balloonist. Oliver really will have my head if I let Cam develop a *tendre* for some lowborn French madman."

"Surely he cannot be all three."

"Ha! If Camellia is attracted to him, I'll probably discover he's something even worse."

Over the course of the next few days Eve herself began to wonder if Fitz's joking comments might be true—at least the part about Cam's attraction to the Frenchman. As Camellia had promised, she rode out with servants and oversaw the rolling up and carrying off of the large balloon as well as the retrieval of the broken basket from the tree. She spent a good deal of each day reading to Leveque or patiently answering his questions about the disposition of his balloon and equipment, peppering him in between with questions of her own.

Eve had to commend Camellia's generosity and her willingness to help, but as the days passed she could not help but wish that the girl would leave Leveque to the servants' less entertaining care. Eve had not realized just how much she had come to rely on Cam as an extra chaperone for Lily and Neville. With Camellia so often in the sickroom Eve had also had to cut her lessons with the girls short, which left Lily with more time on her hands. And while in the past Lily could be counted on to curl up with a book when she had nothing to do, now she was less likely to read than to talk to Neville Carr.

Eve urged Lily and Neville to join Cam in Leveque's room for games or conversation, but she could never count on them remaining there for long, for neither Lily nor Neville could endure a great deal of conversation about the mechanics of lighter-than-air flight. Quite frankly Eve could see their point. She, too, tended to grow heavy-lidded when Leveque got started on the finer points of ballooning. Still, it was most frustrating to think that she had Lily and Carr safely in the company of others only to find thirty minutes later that the two of them had gone for a stroll.

She hated having to track them down and thrust herself into their *tête à tête* as an unwelcome third. But since even Fitz seemed to be occupying himself elsewhere these days, the duty fell to her. She was certain that he was avoiding her. Whereas once he had seemed to pop up wherever she was, now he disappeared when she was near. It was what she had told him she wanted, of course. And at least it saved them from the awkwardness that seemed to befall them whenever they were together.

The problem, unfortunately, was that she hated not being with him. She wanted to talk to him, to look at him. She wanted, quite frankly, for him to kiss her again. Even worse, she was finding that his absence did not make her stop wanting him. She thought about Fitz all the time, even dreamed about him at night. And whether she was awake or asleep, her body heated every time he came into her mind. It was galling to think that he apparently did not have the same problem. *He*, it seemed, could spend any amount of time away without missing her in the slightest.

At least there was the dinner party with the Carlyles to give Eve something to keep Lily—and herself—distracted. On the day of the party they received a note from Sabrina saying that Lord Humphrey had had an unexpected guest and requesting permission to bring the person with them. It was no problem, really, as the guest was a man, and that would make their numbers even. But the coy way Sabrina had avoided naming the guest was rather irritating. Eve, note in hand, went upstairs to tell the girls, but she found only Camellia, who was, oddly enough, lying down in her room.

"Are you all right, my dear?" Eve asked, coming farther into the room. "Are you ill?"

"No. Only a little tired," Camellia answered. "I have been reading to Barthelemy, and it made me a trifle sleepy." She rose on her elbows, grinning. "Him, too, apparently, for he fell asleep. So I thought I would lie down."

When Eve told her about Sabrina's request to bring a guest, Camellia frowned. "Why won't she say who it is?"

"I don't know. She loves being the center of attention, even in a small way." Eve paused, then asked casually, "Where is your sister? I had thought she was with you."

"She was. She read for a while, but then she decided to go for a walk in the gardens." Cam wrinkled her nose. "I think she's not happy with me for spending time with Barthelemy."

"You, um, seem to like Monsieur Leveque a good bit."

Camellia shrugged. "He's interesting. When he recovers he says he will take me up in his balloon. I'd love to do that. Wouldn't you?"

Eve smiled. "I believe I would prefer to keep my feet on the ground."

"I think it would be wonderful to go floating over the trees. Though," Camellia added with her usual pragmatism, "it does seem a bit uncomfortable, with the cold and all and being blown off course. Still, I think it would be great fun, at least once. Besides, I enjoy learning how things work. Have you ever seen a steam engine? I should like to see a steam engine, too." She sighed. "There are lots and lots of things that I would like to see."

"Perhaps you shall."

"I don't know. Sometimes I wonder. First I was too young, and then we came here."

"Do you not like it here?" Eve asked, surprised.

"No, it's not that. I do like it here, actually. It's just . . ." She frowned a little. "It sounds silly, I guess, but everyone keeps leaving. First Rose, then Mary. I always knew they would marry; they were bound to fall in love. Now Lily is all moon-eyed over Mr. Carr, and I can't help but think that she is going to marry, too."

"She wants to marry Mr. Carr?" Eve's stomach tightened. It had gotten even more serious than she had feared.

"No. She hasn't said that. But she's always talking about him. Neville did this, and Neville said that. But even if it isn't Mr. Carr, she'll marry someone someday. She's bound to.

Lily's just the sort of girl who will marry. Don't you think?"

"Probably." Eve nodded. "I imagine that you will marry, too."

"Maybe. I don't know. I don't ever feel all mushy the way she does."

"Not everyone feels 'mushy,' I imagine."

"Not as much as Lily, at least." Camellia grinned, but her smile fell away quickly. "Sometimes I think I'm going to wind up being here all by myself, just me and Lord Stewkesbury. Which I do not think will make him happy, either. I know he will say I shouldn't do any of the things I'd like to do or go places I'd like to see. I shall have to defy him to do them. Of course, I don't really mind that, but . . . it's funny. I never realized it before, I guess because I always had my sisters. People think I'm brave, but when I think about being alone, it scares me."

"Of course it does." Eve leaned over and hugged Camellia. "Nobody likes to be alone. But I don't think it will be so bleak. Lord Stewkesbury doesn't seem unreasonable, and you will still see your sisters. There's Vivian. And I shall be here."

"Will you?"

Eve smiled. "Of course. You will need a chaperone until you get married."

"You think I will marry?"

Eve nodded. "You are very pretty, you know, and easy to like. I understand that you had no lack of partners at Lady Sabrina's dance."

"Dancing's fun. But that doesn't mean I'll get married. All the men I met at the dance were boring."

"Well, there are many more men out there. And you, I think, are feeling a little under the weather. Why don't you take a nap and see if you don't feel more optimistic later?"

"All right." Camellia smiled at her and obediently turned

over on her side as Eve reached down and took the light cover from the foot of the bed and spread it over her.

Eve left her room and started down the hall, thinking to check on the Frenchman. A flash of white caught her eye as she passed the windows halfway down the hall, and she paused to look out.

There in the little herb garden below she saw Lily and Neville Carr. They were standing very close, and he was bending over her. Both of her hands lay in his. They were not kissing or even embracing, only looking at each other. But there was a world of meaning in their posture.

Eve's heart plummeted. Her fears, she thought, had come to pass. Lily and Neville Carr were in love.

Chapter 12

Eve started to run down to the herb garden but thought better of it. She did not want to charge in on Lily like a stern matriarch, tearing the couple apart. Whirling, she hurried back to her own room to grab her bonnet, gloves, and spencer. From her small sewing kit she took her scissors. Pulling on her outdoor garments as she went, Eve rushed down the back staircase to the terrace and around to the side stairs. There she slowed to a casual stroll and, humming a tune, strolled along the path toward the herb garden. The noise of her approach would, she hoped, give Neville and Lily ample time to separate and take up more innocent poses.

Singing a line of the song, she strolled through the open gate, then stopped in apparent surprise. "Lily! Mr. Carr. I'm sorry. I didn't expect to see you here."

Lily was seated on the bench where Eve herself had sat with Fitz—best not to think about that!—while Neville stood two feet away from her, his hands clasped in front of him. Both were turned toward Eve. Lily's eyes were too wide and innocent, and she was blushing furiously.

"Mrs. Hawthorne." Neville bowed.

Lily jumped up. "Hello. Mr. Carr was just showing me the herb garden."

"Isn't it lovely?" Eve asked. "I quite enjoy it, too. I came to see if there was any lavender. Poor Camellia is lying down; I think she has a bit of a headache. I hoped lavender might help."

"Oh!" Lily stared. "Cam's sick?"

"She said she was only tired. But it's so unlike Camellia, don't you think? I suspect she must have had trouble sleeping or a headache or some such thing." Eve glanced around. "Now, let's see, where is the lavender?"

"If you ladies will excuse me . . ." Mr. Carr nodded to them politely. "I think I'll just pop up and check on our Frenchman."

"That's very thoughtful of you." Eve smiled at him and gave him a good-bye nod. As he walked off, she turned back to Lily, whom she found eyeing her warily. "I think that is lavender against the far wall, don't you? But alas, I fear there are no blossoms left."

She started toward the plants, Lily trailing along after her. As she had said, there were no blooms left on the plants.

"Ah, well, perhaps the housekeeper has some lavender water. Normally I do, but I was quite out."

"Is that really why you came out here?" Lily asked.

Eve raised her brows. "Whatever do you mean?"

Lily lifted her chin a little. "I thought you might have been looking for Neville and me. Because we were alone out here."

"I see. Well, I am sure that you and Mr. Carr were acting in a perfectly proper manner, were you not? Although you are right—once we are in London for the Season, you will have to be more careful about being alone with a man for any reason. People, I'm afraid, are eager to gossip."

"It's so stupid! I hate all these rules."

"They are rather strict for young unmarried women, I'm afraid. I chafed under them, too. However, that is the world we live in, and I can promise you that you do not want to be viewed as scandalous. You don't want to be excluded from Almack's."

"Neville says it's deadly dull."

"It is. But still, everyone wants to be there." She paused. "Mr. Carr is a charming man."

"Oh yes." Lily's unguarded face took on a brighter glow. "He says you do not like him, but I told him I was sure that wasn't the case."

"I don't know him well; I have heard of him, of course."

Lily looked at her suspiciously. "Now you are going to say something bad about him, aren't you?"

"Bad? No, not bad. Indeed most people find it something to congratulate one on. Mr. Carr is said to be on the verge of proposing to Lady Priscilla Symington. The word is that they have been expected to marry for years."

"Yes." Lily's pretty face clouded. "He told me. He said that he could not be less than honest with me. Don't you think that shows what a fine character he has?" Her eyes shone. "He could have pretended otherwise; I would not have known. It is so sad—being obliged to marry someone you do not love. And just because your father demands it!"

"It does seem terribly unfair."

"I knew you would understand."

"I do. I think it is most unfair of parents to put such expectations upon their children. Nor can I think that such a situation would make for a very happy marriage."

"He does not love her at all. I know he does not."

"But as a gentleman he is duty-bound to follow through. She has been waiting for him for years; it would make her an object of ridicule if he backed out now."

Lily looked away. "I know." Her voice came out a little hoarse, and Eve thought she saw the flash of tears in her eyes. "It's so tragic."

"Of course your sympathies are engaged." Eve picked her words carefully. "It is a sad situation, not just for Mr. Carr but for Lady Priscilla as well, I should imagine."

Lily's eyes widened. "But she is to marry Mr. Carr."

"We do not know that she cares for him any more than he cares for her. And if she does love him, how sad it must be to marry someone knowing that he does not love you."

"Then why can't she set him free?" Temper flashed a little in Lily's voice. "If she knows he does not love her, why would she want to marry him?"

"Few woman look forward to being labeled a spinster," Eve pointed out drily. "But it would be more scandalous than that. She would be considered jilted, or the nearest thing to it, even though they are not actually yet engaged. It would be a scandal, and while he might be held more to blame, she would suffer a great deal from the rumors. It is hard to be the object of pity, just as it is to be the object of scorn."

"I suppose so, but it seems very poor-hearted to me."

"It is not, I am sure, the sort of thing that you or one of your sisters would do. But many young women are much less . . ."

"Shocking?" Lily suggested a little roguishly.

"I was going to say independent." Eve reached out and linked her arm through the girl's affectionately. "I know it is a hard situation for Mr. Carr and Lady Priscilla, but it is you I am concerned with. I do not wish to see you hurt. I am afraid your hopes might rest on his not marrying the lady, and I do not think that will come to pass."

"No, I know it won't. Neville—I mean, Mr. Carr—and I are nothing more than friends." She let out an unconscious little sigh. "How could we be anything else?"

Eve went down to the dinner party that evening with some trepidation. While it would be good for Lily and Camellia to get some experience as hostesses, she wished that their guests did not include Lady Sabrina. Eve felt sure that Sabrina would snipe at Lily's and Camellia's efforts at putting on a dinner party. Neither of the Bascombes was at her best. Lily's spirits had drooped noticeably after her talk with Eve, and Camellia had been unaccustomedly listless and cranky. Any of Sabrina's poisonous "compliments" would deflate the girls even further.

When Eve walked into the small anteroom where they gathered before dinner, she was relieved to see that both sisters were already there and seemingly in good spirits. Camellia's cheeks were high with color, and her eyes sparkled, and Lily seemed to have returned to her usual merry self.

Eve's eyes went involuntarily to Fitz, who rose and bowed when she entered but made no move to come talk to her. A trifle stung, she started toward Camellia and Lily, but before she reached them the butler announced the arrival of the Carlyle family. Eve braced herself, turning to face the group of people entering the room. Her mouth dropped open, and she stared in astonishment.

Behind Lord Humphrey and his wife, walking with Vivian, was a man with arrow-straight bearing and brown hair, gray at the temples. He had a hawk nose and a square chin, and his quick glance around the room seemed to take in everything at once. His eyes lit on Eve, and he smiled.

Lord Humphrey was at that moment introducing him. "My old friend Colonel Willingham," he said to Fitz, and the colonel turned to bow to Fitz. "The colonel happened to stop by on his way to Lancaster the other day, and I was able to persuade him to stay with us."

"I hope I'm not an intrusion," the colonel said in a crisp voice.

"No, sir, not at all. We always are eager for guests here in the country. Pray, allow me to introduce you to my cousins."

Fitz began with Camellia and Lily, and the colonel bowed to them. But when Fitz moved on to Eve, the colonel smiled and walked over to her. "No need to introduce me to this lovely young woman. Mrs. Hawthorne and I are old friends."

"Good evening, Colonel." Eve extended her hand, smiling. "This is a welcome surprise. I am happy to see you."

"No happier than I, my dear Mrs. Hawthorne. When Lord Humphrey told me you were visiting Willowmere, I told him I could not leave without seeing you."

"I am very glad that you did."

Fitz's eyes narrowed as he watched the older gentleman take Eve's hand and bow over it. "How fortunate that you have *two* friends here, Colonel. How is it that you and Mrs. Hawthorne know each other?"

"My husband, Major Hawthorne, served under the colonel," Eve explained.

"An excellent man. None braver." Colonel Willingham shook his head admiringly.

"Yes. Bruce was always brave."

"Come. You must tell me all about what you have been doing since I saw you last." Colonel Willingham edged Eve a little away from the others. "I asked Lady Sabrina not to tell you who their guest was. I wanted to surprise you."

Eve noticed that Vivian's eyes followed them curiously, as did Sabrina's, though the latter's gaze carried venom as well. Eve sighed inwardly. She felt sure that Sabrina had not taken kindly to the colonel's not only knowing Eve but wanting to see her again. Sabrina was the sort who liked to keep any gentleman's attention solely on herself. She would not care that Colonel Willingham valued Eve because of his regard for her late husband. She would see only that a male who was supposed to be admiring *her* was happily chatting with Eve.

However, Eve was not about to turn the colonel over

to his hostess. The colonel had always been a good friend to her, especially after Bruce's death. He had helped her through the funeral, taking on many of the things that had to be done after someone died. His own wife had passed away four years before that, and he was, he assured her, well aware of the grief that faced her.

Eve had turned down most offers of help, preferring to pack her clothes and to sort through Bruce's things herself; she was not a woman who shared her moments of grief. But the colonel's help had been as efficient as it was kind, and she had been grateful to him.

"I fear that I have done little of interest, sir," she told him now. "I returned to my father's house."

"But now you are here. And I understand that you intend to be in London next Season."

"Yes." No doubt Sabrina had been happy to tell him that Eve was now a lowly chaperone. "Lord Stewkesbury was kind enough to hire me to be a companion for his cousins during their first Season. Lady Vivian plans to sponsor them."

"So she told me. I had not realized that you and Humphrey's niece were friends."

"We went to school together. I have not seen her as much as we would have liked in recent years."

"Yes." He smiled faintly. "One goes where the army sends one."

"You are familiar with that, of course."

"I am glad to see you looking so well. Obviously helping these young girls agrees with you."

"You are kind to say so. But yes, I am enjoying my time here. And how have you been these last two years?" Eve asked, ignoring the eyes that she could feel burning a hole in her as they continued to chat.

She would have been surprised, had she turned to look,

to find that Sabrina was not the only one watching them. Fitz was gazing at them, too, leaning against the far wall, his face knotted in a scowl so fierce that the others at the party left him to himself.

What the devil was Eve doing talking to the fellow so long? he wondered. The colonel was old enough to be her father. Surely she could see that. She could not be interested in him. The colonel, Fitz could see, was certainly interested in her. He had neatly cut her from the rest of them and maneuvered her over into a corner by herself. If she was so worried about her reputation, she ought to consider that it would not help it to be seen cozying up to this man.

If he had been himself, Fitz would have seen the absurdity of his thoughts, the comedic properties of his position. But the truth was, he was not himself. He hadn't been for days now. It had annoyed him that Eve wanted to end the budding romance between them, but he had also known, with some degree of guilt, that she was right in her assessment of the situation. It would go much harder on her if rumors got out about her and Fitz. And however hard they tried and however faithful the servants were, there was always the possibility that something would get out. He had decided to be the gentleman and cease his pursuit of her. After all, he was not the lightweight, amoral chap she assumed him to be. He would not try to seduce her into going against her own wishes.

But he had been unprepared for the odd hurt that had settled on him. She, it seemed, could quite easily give him up. She just went on about her duties, smiling and talking to the others, bustling about her business. It was painfully obvious that she did not miss his presence at all. Whereas he . . .

He had been awkward and ill at ease around her—he,

who had never been awkward around a woman in his life! He could not look at her without remembering their kisses and caresses. And he could not remember those things without wanting to take her into his arms again. Hunger rose in him whenever she was around, so that he had begun to avoid the places where he might run into her—though clearly that did little good, as he spent all his time thinking about her anyway. He had even taken to brooding, actually brooding, in Oliver's office or the smoking room, avoiding everyone and attempting to forget his problems by plunging into work. (Though he could not understand how his brother could find solace from whatever beset him, as he said he did, by plunging into such deadly dull stuff.)

And while he was standing there, watching her, and aching because he longed to touch her and knew he could not, she was flirting with some old warhorse. It was, he thought, the outside of enough. The height of unfairness. And while he knew in some remote part of his being that he was probably being ridiculous, he could not suppress the thrust of jealousy, like hot iron, through his chest. With a low noise that rather resembled a growl, he levered himself away from the wall and strode across the room toward the other couple.

"Mrs. Hawthorne. Colonel."

Eve jumped, startled at the sound of Fitz's voice behind her. She turned and was amazed to see Fitz smiling in a determined way at Willingham, though she was not sure that *smiling* was the proper term for the grim baring of teeth that Fitz displayed.

"Fi—I mean, Mr. Talbot." Eve schooled her voice to a pleasant tone. "Please join us."

"Thank you." He turned to the colonel. "I am so pleased to meet a friend of Mrs. Hawthorne's. Are you stationed nearby?"

"Oh no. I am on leave and was going to Lancaster to visit some relatives. It gave me an opportunity to see Lord Humphrey."

"It must have been a welcome surprise to learn Mrs. Hawthorne was staying here."

"Yes indeed."

"You are alone? Mrs. Willingham did not accompany you?" Fitz went on.

Eve stared at him. Fitz was acting most unlike himself. The easygoing charm was nowhere in sight. His face was set, his eyes intent on the colonel's face. In fact, he seemed to be almost interrogating the man.

"I am a widower, sir. My wife died many years ago."

"My condolences."

Colonel Willingham accepted his words with a stiff nod.

"The colonel was most helpful to me when Major Hawthorne died," Eve said, trying to turn the conversation onto a friendlier path. The two men did not seem to get along, which was scarcely surprising. Fitz and Willingham were utterly different. What was surprising was that Fitz was trying to talk to him at all.

"Was he?" Fitz's eyes flicked over to the older man, his gaze assessing.

"I did what I could," Willingham said modestly. "The major was one of my best soldiers."

"No doubt." Fitz nodded. "Have you, um, kept up with Mrs. Hawthorne through the years, then?"

"No, I fear we quite lost track of each other," Eve inserted. Fitz's manner was almost rude.

It was a relief when Vivian and her uncle joined them. "Come, come, gentlemen, I cannot allow you to take up all of Mrs. Hawthorne's time," Vivian said. "I have been most eager to see her again. Uncle Humphrey, you should tell Fitz about the hunt you were thinking of organizing."

Deftly Vivian edged Eve away from the group, leaving the three men together.

"Thank you," Eve told her friend. "I was feeling decidedly uncomfortable. Fi—Mr. Talbot was behaving in a most peculiar way."

"I could see. I believe our dear Fitz has scented a rival."

"What?" Eve glanced at her. "What are you talking about?"

"Fitz is feeling a bit jealous of Colonel Willingham."

Eve stared, then said abruptly, "Don't be ridiculous. He isn't jealous. Why would he be jealous?"

Vivian did not reply, simply gave her a speaking look.

"Fitz Talbot is not interested in me," Eve told her flatly. "If you had been around the last few days you would know how unlikely that is. We have not been in each other's company except at mealtimes, when everyone is there. He makes not the slightest effort to seek me out or—" Eve broke off abruptly.

"Then he's something of a dog in the manger because he definitely looked to me as if he was warning the colonel off."

"Really, Vivian . . ."

Vivian raised her brows. "You think I don't recognize the signs? My dear Eve, I will remind you that I am something of an expert in this regard. Men frequently try to establish their claim to the daughter of a duke."

"But we are talking about me, not you. I've told you how Fitz has dropped his pursuit—for which I am most grateful, I assure you—and the idea of Colonel Willingham thinking that I—it's absurd. He is almost old enough to be my father."

"Some women like a distinguished-looking man and an air of authority. And fifteen years is certainly not enough to give men pause. Why, look at my uncle and Sabrina. There is a far larger gap there."

"Yes, well, I am not Sabrina."

"Thank God." Vivian gave Eve's arm a friendly squeeze. "But truly, do you have no interest in the colonel? I must say I wondered myself. You looked so happy to see him."

"It was nice to see an old friend. And it was such a surprise. But no . . ." Eve shook her head. "I have no interest in the colonel. He is but a friend."

"What of Fitz?"

"He is a friend as well." At Vivian's skeptical look, Eve went on, "What else can he be? You were the one who warned me about him."

"Yes, I know." Vivian turned her head toward the group of men they had left. "But Fitz seems different. I have never seen him act this way about a woman before. Even the fact that he has stopped pursuing you is unlike him."

"I am sure he has grown uninterested in women before."

"I don't think it's a lack of interest. It might be that this time he cares more about the woman than his own desire."

Eve could not quite quell the spurt of hope that rose inside her at Vivian's words, but she firmly shoved it back down, shaking her head. "No. 'Tis foolhardy to think that way. I have told Lily that she must be practical. I must be that way as well. I cannot, I will not, fall in love with him."

The rest of the evening passed slowly. Dinner was long, and Sabrina made herself the center of attention. Whenever Vivian or Colonel Willingham or Neville made an effort to move the conversation to some other topic, such as the balloonist who had landed in their meadow, Sabrina immediately found some way to turn the talk back to herself. She flirted madly, fluttering her lashes and plying her fan not only with Fitz and Neville but also with Colonel Willingham. What Lord Humphrey thought of her performance Eve could not imagine. He looked frankly bored most of the time and was at his liveliest when he and the colonel fell to talking about old times. However, since Sabrina's mouth immediately began to turn down sulkily and the looks she sent her husband became longer and harder, he soon subsided into silence.

For once Fitz made little effort to keep the conversation going. He ignored Sabrina's flirtatious efforts and spent most of the time talking to Vivian or Lord Humphrey on either side of him. Eve kept most of her attention on her two charges. She could sense Lily's anger building beside her as Sabrina flirted with Neville, while across from her Camellia appeared to wilt as the evening passed, listlessly pushing food around on her plate but eating little. Neither girl seemed concerned with the success of their party, and indeed Eve had to admit that it hardly seemed as if it *was* their party, what with the way Sabrina was monopolizing the conversation. The best thing she could say about the evening was that Sabrina was so busy flirting that she did not send any barbs their way.

After dinner the women retired to the music room while the men spent an inordinately long time over their port and cigars. Eve was inclined to think that they were simply avoiding joining the women again. She could scarcely blame them. Sabrina began to play the piano, and when the men finally returned she pounced on Neville, insisting that he turn the pages for her. He countered by asking Lily to come stand with him and sing the songs. Eve had to smother a smile at the neat way he had outmaneuvered Lady Sabrina, but from the expression on Sabrina's face, Eve was certain that she would find some way to make Lily pay for this in the future.

Colonel Willingham seized the opportunity to seat himself in the chair beside Eve, but Fitz came up and sat on her other side and once again inserted himself into their conversation. To Eve's relief he did not resume his interrogation of the colonel, but his presence made the situation awkward and the conversation stilted.

Eve was soon wishing that the evening would draw to a close. She was tired, and Camellia looked as if she might fall asleep in her chair. Eve could not help but worry that the girl had fallen ill. However, she could not take her upstairs with their guests still there, and it did not look as if Sabrina was ever going to suggest leaving. Finally, however, Vivian rose and began the polite routine of departure, taking the decision out of Sabrina's hands. After a round of thank-yous and good-byes the guests finally left.

Eve whisked Camellia up to bed. Though Camellia assured her that she was only tired, her forehead was hot to the touch, and Eve found it telling that Camellia did not protest Eve's fussing over her. Instead she simply undressed and crawled into bed and let Eve wring out a cool cloth and lay it across her forehead.

"I'll feel better tomorrow," Camellia said as she closed her eyes.

"Of course you will." Eve watched as the girl drifted immediately into sleep.

Frowning, she left the room. Camellia was normally so healthy and strong, so it was worrisome that she was not feeling well. Eve went across the hall to check on Lily. If Camellia had caught some fever, it seemed likely that her sister would come down with it as well.

She stopped with her hand raised to knock. She could hear the soft sounds of Lily crying inside. Sympathy flooded Eve, and she knocked, then opened the door without waiting for an answer. Lily was lying facedown across the bed, and she turned, sitting up and wiping her eyes, when Eve entered the room.

"Oh, Lily . . ." Eve hurried across the room and sat on the bed beside Lily. The girl threw her arms around Eve, putting her head on her shoulder, and gave way to tears. Eve patted her on the back, murmuring soothing words, and finally Lily's tears subsided.

Lily pulled away, wiping at her face and offering Eve a watery smile. "I'm sorry. I did not mean to cry. It's just—she made me so angry."

"Sabrina?" Eve asked, surprised. She would not have thought the girl's tears were over Sabrina.

Lily nodded. "Yes, the way she was flirting with Neville tonight! I was furious—though I think it sweet of him to ask me to sing while she played. Don't you?"

"Yes, of course."

Lily smiled to herself, her eyes turning dreamy. Then she straightened, returning to her earlier thoughts. "It was terrible, the way she acted—and her a married woman. When I came up to bed I was thinking of all the things I wanted to say to her. And then . . . then I realized I haven't any right to be upset. I have no claim on Neville, and I never will."

She did not start to cry again, but her face turned so woebegone that Eve could not keep from reaching out and taking one of her hands. "I am so sorry that you are hurt. I wish Mr. Carr had never come here."

"Don't say that!" Lily's eyes widened. "Then I would never have known him at all, and that would be awful."

Eve had her doubts about that, but she wisely kept silent.

"I know there is no hope for us," Lily went on tragically. "But I fear that Cousin Oliver will find this Season wasted on me. Perhaps Camellia will find a husband, but I do not think that I could ever meet someone who could measure up to Neville."

"It is some time until the Season starts."

"Time will not change how I feel about him." Lily looked at her with great, limpid eyes.

Eve knew better than to argue with such a statement. "No one is expecting you to leave the Season with a husband in tow. You are young, and all you need to do is enjoy the parties. There is much to enjoy—dancing, plays, the opera, new clothes."

Lily nodded. "Yes, I think I shall like all of that very much. I will not let on to Cousin Oliver that I am anything but happy with everything he has done for us. But . . ." She broke off, her eyes shadowing.

Eve leaned over to give her a quick hug. "Try not to worry overmuch about it. Get some sleep. I am sure that everything will seem better tomorrow morning. Where is your maid? Shall I ring for her?"

"No. She was asleep on that chair when I came in, so I sent her to bed. I'll get Cam to unfasten the hooks."

"I'll do them. Camellia is already asleep, poor thing. I think she may be sick. You are not feeling under the weather, are you?"

Lily shook her head. "No. I thought Cam was quite lively earlier. But maybe she was merely feverish."

Eve quickly undid the series of hooks-and-eyes that ran down the back of Lily's gown and left the room. She started down the hall to her own bedroom, then stopped, swung on her heel, and ran lightly down the steps.

It was dark downstairs, but the light from the open door halfway down the corridor was enough for Eve to see her way. Her steps slowed as she neared the door, and she stopped before she reached it, listening for masculine voices. The last thing she wanted was to enter the study and find Fitz talking to Neville.

She heard nothing, so she slipped closer and paused in the doorway. Fitz was seated behind Oliver's desk, a glass of liquor in front of him, and he was staring sightlessly across the room into the fireplace. He looked . . . unhappy.

Eve's heart squeezed in her chest, and she took an involuntary step into the room, saying, "Fitz?"

"Eve!" He sprang to his feet, a smile on his lips, and started toward her. "Come in. Sit down."

He reached for her hand, and Eve let him lead her to the set of chairs in front of the fireplace. She could smell the scent of the alcohol on him, but there was nothing to indicate that he was inebriated. His hand was as steady as ever, his eyes as bright.

"I am glad to see you," he told her. "But I can see that you are troubled."

"Camellia is ill."

"Really?" His brows rose in surprise.

"Yes, she has a fever, I think. But that is not what brought me here. It is Lily who worries me. I fear she has fallen in love with Mr. Carr. I found her crying in her room tonight."

He sighed. "Lily is given to high emotions. Do you think her heart is truly captured?"

"I'm not sure," Eve admitted. "She does relish a dramatic situation. I think she enjoys, a little, the tragedy of it. But I believe she really cares as well. She was saying tonight that she feared her Season would be a waste, that she would never fall in love with any other man but Mr. Carr. I know that young girls say such things and two months later are head over heels about another gentleman, but . . ."

"He means no harm to Lily. Neville cares for her. He promised he would make no advances to her, and I believe him."

"Perhaps not. But this afternoon I came upon them alone in the herb garden." She colored and glanced away, remembering what had transpired between them in the same place.

It was a moment before Fitz spoke, and Eve wondered if he, too, was thinking of the night of the wedding. Did it warm his blood to remember her mouth opening beneath his, her skin heating to his touch?

"I see." There was a certain huskiness to his voice that made Eve think that he had not forgotten. "Were they—"

"No," Eve assured him quickly. "They were not in a compromising position. But it is a secluded area, and they were alone. The way they stood bespoke . . . longing."

The word hung in the air between them, naked and evocative. Fitz's gaze held hers; Eve could not look away. There was something in his eyes that melted her inside, and she was aware of a treacherous desire to curl up in his lap and lay her head against his chest, to have his arms shelter her.

"Sometimes," Eve said, her voice barely more than a whisper, "words can be as dangerous to a girl's heart as any kiss." She knew she was no longer talking about Lily but herself. "She knows there can be nothing between them, and yet she cannot help but hope, cannot keep her heart untouched."

"He may feel the same. It is difficult to live in such close proximity and not have feelings grow stronger." He leaned toward her. "It is hard not to want her when you see her at every turn. When you smell the scent of her perfume on the air when you walk into a room. The most foolish things can make your pulse race, like finding her glove dropped, unnoticed, on the floor."

Eve swallowed. What he had said stirred her as much as if he'd stroked his hand down her arm. She pulled her gaze away, struggling not to show the emotions racing through her.

"I've missed you," Fitz said, and the simple words sent a shiver through her. "The past few days, not being around you . . ."

"Not through any doing of mine!" Eve flared. "You are the one who has stayed out of my company. When I come into a room you leave. One would think I have the plague."

He stared at her. "You think I have done that because I wanted to?"

"I cannot imagine why else you would. Obviously you have tired of the chase." Eve knew she sounded sulky, but surely she had good reason. It was annoying that he had paid no attention to her for days on end, as if she were the veriest nothing, and now he was speaking sweet words about perfume and pulses racing. It was even more galling that she responded so easily to it.

"I did it because *you* asked me to." Something flashed in Fitz's eyes, and he stood up abruptly. He took a step toward the fireplace, then swung back. "You asked me not to seduce you. You told me you could not have an affair with me. You could not afford the risk to your reputation. Did you not mean that? Was that merely a ploy?"

"No!" Eve shot up, too, pierced by guilt as much as by anger. She *had* told him to stay away from her. But had she, deep inside, hoped that he would not do so? "No. It was no ploy. I cannot have an affair with you. But I did not mean that I never wanted to see you again. That we could not be friends."

"Friends? Well, that may be easy for you, but it's bloody difficult for me. What am I supposed to do, sit with you, dance with you, talk with you, and not want you? How am I supposed to do that? Just the sight of you makes me—" He broke off and swung away, picking up the poker and shoving it into the fireplace.

The charred logs broke and flared into life again, glowing red and shooting up sparks. He continued to poke at them, saying, "What about the colonel? Am I supposed to watch him flirt with you and not care?"

"Flirt with me!" Eve stared. "Colonel Willingham was not flirting with me."

"The hell he wasn't." Fitz turned back around, slamming

the poker down into its stand. "You may think he's nothing but your dead husband's commander, but I saw how he looked at you. I watched the two of you, sitting there laughing and talking."

Eve planted her fists on her hips. "Now I'm not allowed to talk to anyone? Or is it just the colonel? Pray, give me a list of who—"

Her words were cut off when Fitz, muttering an oath, took a quick step forward and grabbed her wrist, jerking her to him, his mouth coming down to seize hers in a searing kiss.

Chapter 13

His kiss did not startle Eve. She realized even as his lips touched hers that she had been waiting for this moment. However wrong it might be, however foolish, she wanted him to kiss her. She wanted the heat of his body pressed against hers, the hard iron of his arms around her. No amount of reasoning and logic could hold sway against the primal hunger surging up in her.

Eve's hands went to his shoulders, not to push him away but to cling to him. He lifted her up and into him, and she felt the heavy throb of his desire. And though she suspected that it was quite shameful of her, she reveled in the feeling. Mouths locked together, they kissed as though they could fuse and join, their bodies melting into a single flame of passion.

Fire danced along her veins, and she wanted only to feel more, to burn brighter. Her brain whispered that it was madness, but Eve ignored it. She kissed him, her tongue twining with his, and ran her fingers down his chest and beneath his jacket, gliding over the satiny cloth of his waistcoat. She wanted more; she wanted to feel his skin beneath her fingertips, to touch and explore without restraint.

Deep down she knew that this was why she had come

here tonight. None of the reasons that she gave herself was the truth—or at least only skimmed the surface of the truth. She had felt Fitz watching her tonight; despite her denials to Vivian, she had sensed his jealousy and the desire that lay beneath it. She had yearned for that hunger to flare into life, to sweep her up into the inferno that raged through them now.

He murmured her name as his hands moved over her, exploring the soft curves of her body. Even through the fabric of her dress and underclothes, Eve felt the searing heat of his hands, and she shivered, her nipples hardening. He made an inarticulate noise and reached up to strip off his jacket and fling it away. Her fingers fumbled at the buttons of his waistcoat, opening it, but still it was not enough for her. She tugged his shirt from the waistband of his trousers and slipped her hands beneath the soft cambric, gliding over the smooth skin of his stomach and up to his chest.

A tremor shook him at her touch, and his fingers dug into her hips, holding her to him. They kissed hungrily as Eve's hands roamed over his body beneath his shirt, skimming the curves and lines of thick muscle and harder bone, delighting in the textures of satin-smooth skin and wiry curling hairs, the fleshy nubs of his masculine nipples.

With an oath he broke away, raking his fingers back through his hair. "No. If we go on, I won't be able to stop."

"I don't want you to stop." Eve followed him.

He let out a groan, his eyes flashing. "Don't say such things. I'm on the edge of my better nature here. If you don't leave now . . ."

"I don't want to leave. Look at me." She took a step closer, stopping directly in front of him, only inches away, and looked up into his eyes. "I am telling you, I don't care about all those things I said before. I won't regret this in the morning; I have made my decision. I don't want to grow old and fade away, never knowing what I could have had, what I could have experienced. I want to know, to feel, to have . . ." She made a vague gesture. "Everything. Whatever happens, I don't want to spend the rest of my life regretting what I gave up."

He looked at her, his body taut, his eyes the burning blue of the hot center of a flame. "Eve, think . . ."

"I'm done thinking. I want you." Eve's hands went to his shirt, grabbing hold and crumpling it in her clenched fists as she pulled him toward her, going up on her toes to touch her lips to his.

His arms lashed around her like iron, and his mouth dug into hers. He kissed her as if he would never stop, as if he could not get enough of the taste of her mouth. Eve felt as if she had gone up in flame, as though the heat of his hunger raced through her, fueling her own fire.

Her hands went beneath his shirt again, running over his muscled back and down, seeking out the indentation of his spine and following it until the waistband of his trousers blocked her exploration. She came back up his sides, tracing the ridges of his ribs, and around to the front of his chest. She wanted to see him, to watch her hands on his flesh, to explore his body with her lips and tongue. As she thought of these things, an ache grew between her legs, heated and damp, pulsing with a primitive hunger she had never experienced.

With an impatient noise she broke their kiss, her hands going to the ties of his shirt. He stepped back, shrugging out of his waistcoat and fumbling at the ascot around his neck, cursing as it tangled, and finally jerking it free. Fitz whipped the shirt off over his head, then returned to her, his fingers going to the multitude of small buttons down the back of her dress.

Eve, finding herself in a perfect place to do exactly as she wanted, put her hands on him, drinking in the sight of his bare flesh as her fingers glided over the curves and planes of his chest. She twined her fingertips through the V-shaped patch of curling hair at the center of his chest and skimmed her nails over the flat masculine nipples. A chord thrummed through her as she watched the buds tighten, increasing the ache in her loins. Boldly she leaned forward, pressing her lips to his skin.

He jerked, and his fingers dug into the cloth of her dress. Eve started to pull back, but he whispered, "No, no, stay."

Fitz curved down over her as her mouth made its way across his chest, his fingers tugging at her buttons. Now and then he let out a little sigh or groan, and his fingertips dug into her back, and once he stopped and pulled her up for another deep, searching kiss. In this manner it took some time for him to undo her dress, but at last he did, and he shoved it down to pool around her feet, quickly untying her petticoats and sending them after it.

"Now," he told her, his eyes slumberous with passion, "it's my turn."

He reached down and unfastened the ribbon of her chemise, pulling the satin bow undone. The top of the garment sagged slightly, revealing more of the soft curves of her breasts above it. Fitz spread his hands out on her chest and slid them slowly down, turning to slip his fingertips beneath the chemise and draw the cloth lower and lower.

Eve felt the texture of his fingertips on the sensitive flesh of her breasts, the tug of the fabric as it caught on her nipples, then dragged over them. Even that small touch heightened her arousal, centered in the heat between her legs. Her eyes closed, and her head fell back as she lost herself in the sensation. He stroked his hands over her smooth breasts, shoving the loosened chemise down over her hips. The material stuck for an instant, and he pushed it the rest of the way, setting off a little ripping noise. But neither of them cared.

Fitz caressed her breasts, gazing down at her soft, enraptured face. Her tongue crept out to wet her lips, and a tremor shook him, his hunger swelling. But still he moved slowly, adoring her with his fingertips. Her breasts swelled, the hard centers thrusting out. Eve trembled, loving the engorged ache of her nipples yet wanting more, needing more. Her breath caught in her throat, and for an instant fear flashed through her that once again she would be left wanting, that this longing that built and throbbed inside her, a yearning far greater than any she had ever known before, would never be fulfilled.

Then he bent and took one nipple in his mouth, and heat flared through her, taking her past fear or thought. She was suddenly raw need, naked pleasure, and with every stroke of his tongue, each pull of his mouth, she was flooded with passion.

Fitz bent and picked her up. He carried her over to the fireplace. After spreading out her petticoats to shield her from the rough texture of the wool rug, he laid Eve down. Kneeling beside her, he untied her pantalets and drew them down, his hands sliding the material over her thighs and calves. He lifted her feet one by one and took off her slippers, pulling off each garter and sliding his hand beneath the stockings to remove them.

He sat back on his heels, looking down at her with eyes that glowed hotter than the embers in the fireplace. The red light bathed her pale skin. The circles of her nipples were swollen and red, damp from his kisses. As he gazed at her, they tightened even more, and she moved her hips restlessly, squeezing her legs together. He stood, quickly divesting himself of the rest of his clothing.

His member sprang free, thick and quivering, and Eve's

eyes were drawn to it. Her mouth opened a little, and she drew a quick breath. Her teeth caught her bottom lip. She could not look away, could think only of him inside her. This was new to her, completely unfamiliar, and she was filled with a roiling excitement that was part fear, part eagerness. Her body ached for him, the yearning between her legs spreading, throbbing. Yet she thought, too, of the pain, the breaching that she had never experienced, and suddenly she wished that she had told him, had explained . . .

But then he was beside her again, stretched out, his knee insinuating itself between her legs, opening her to him. He leaned over her, his arms braced on either side of her body, and bent to kiss her. Eve flung her arms around his neck, trepidation flying away from her as his mouth took hers. As they kissed, his hand glided down her body, caressing every inch of it. His fingers twined through the curling thatch of hair between her legs, and when she clamped her legs together he teased them open. She could feel the smile upon his lips.

Eve could not hold back a noise deep in her throat as his fingers slid over the most intimate part of her, exploring and caressing, opening her to him. She blushed, embarrassed at her own response but too aroused by his touch to let the embarrassment hold sway. If she was consumed by desire, no less was he. She could feel the insistent pulse of his manhood against her leg, hard and urgent. Eve wanted to curl her hand around him, to feel him swell and pulse within her grasp, to learn the texture and thickness of him, but such boldness was beyond her, even in her passion-drugged state.

His mouth left hers, traveling to nibble at her earlobe. Eve shivered in delight as he explored her with his lips and tongue. All the while his fingers never ceased to roam between her legs, stroking her thighs and moving down to her calves, then returning to the hot center of her. Her breath rasped in her throat as he moved lower and lower, his mouth traveling over her breasts and down onto her stomach. She arched up against his hand, almost sobbing with the need that pulsed inside her. She clutched at his back, her legs opening to him.

Fitz moved between her legs, his face stark with hunger. Positioning himself, he thrust deep into her. The pain came then, and Eve flinched, making a low noise. He froze, staring at her in amazement.

"Eve!" His voice was low and hoarse. His fingers curled into the cloth beneath her, and he began to pull back.

But Eve swiftly wrapped her legs around him, holding him to her. "No. Go on. Please . . ."

He hesitated for an instant, but when she moved beneath him he gave in with a groan, thrusting even deeper inside her. Eve let out a soft sigh, the pain ebbing, replaced by the deep satisfaction of him filling her, stretching her. She had not dreamed of this—the emptiness filled, the void she was scarcely aware of gone, the utter completion.

He began to stroke within her, moving in and out in a building rhythm, and the sensations within her changed again, turning into a pleasure so intense she had to dig her fingers into the petticoats beneath her, holding on against the fierce need growing inside her. She whimpered, desperately wanting something without knowing quite what, yearning eagerly toward it as the heat built within her, until it seemed that she must shatter from the intensity of her need.

And then she did shatter—pleasure bursting within her and in him at the same time, for he let out a hoarse cry and buried his face in the side of her neck as he shuddered against her. The bright joy slammed through her, sweeping out in a wave in all directions, convulsing her as it did him.

In an instant the world was gone, and there was nothing but this pleasure, this explosive bliss, blinding and complete.

*   *   *

Fitz collapsed upon her, and they lay, tangled and sweating, beyond words, drifting in a fog of contentment. For a long time they stayed that way, too replete to move, but finally he rolled from her.

Curling his arm around her, Fitz pulled her close to his side. Eve nestled her head on his shoulder, floating in a warm sea of lassitude. He stroked his hand down her arm and back up and bent to press a kiss to her hair.

"I had no idea," he murmured. "Why did you not tell me? I would have . . . done things differently."

Eve shook her head. "I—'tis hardly an easy matter to bring up in conversation. I am a widow, but I've never—" She broke off, blushing.

He levered himself up on his arm, gazing down into her face. "Why? How could your husband not have—" He broke off as she closed her eyes and turned her face away. "I do not mean to embarrass you. I should not ask."

"No. It's all right. It's only natural to wonder. The thing is, I don't know why. I'm not sure Bruce did. He was never able to . . . to consummate our marriage. He told me that he hoped that with me it would be different. But he was incapable. He had never been able to complete the act. He thought it was because of an accident when he was young. But honestly I don't know. He would scarcely talk about it, even to me."

"I pity the man. To have been so close to you and be unable to—it must have driven him mad." Fitz caressed the side of her face. "I am so sorry. If I had known I would not have acted as I did. I assumed you were a woman of experience. Not an innocent."

"I am not sure that I would qualify as an innocent." Eve grinned up at him, her eyes twinkling, and linked her hands behind his neck. "Certainly not now." She reached up to plant a feather-light kiss upon his mouth. "I am glad. I did not want you to act any differently. I am exactly where I want to be."

A slow, sensual smile spread over his lips, and Fitz bent to kiss her again, more lingeringly this time. He raised his head and lay, looking at her, tracing his forefinger down her face, skimming over her forehead and down the line of her nose, brushing across her lips.

"I will protect you," he assured her. "We will be very careful after this. I will not allow even a hint of gossip to attach to you."

"No sneaking off alone together to the maze?" Eve asked flirtatiously.

"No, you minx. No meaningful glances across the drawing room, either. Or popping into the library for a stolen kiss. No assignations of any kind unless we are absolutely certain no one will know." At those words he glanced toward the door and let out a soft oath. Rising lithely to his feet, he strode over to turn the key in the lock. He turned back, looking grim. "No more of that. Anyone could have walked in on us."

Eve could not help but giggle. "I fear they would have had quite an eyeful."

His smile was rueful. "Indeed they would have." He sank beside her again and gathered her up in his arms. "But we must be more careful."

Eve lifted her hand and laid it against his cheek. "We will be. Tomorrow."

"Yes." His eyes darkened, and he leaned down again to take her lips. "Tomorrow."

Eve awakened the next morning and lay for a moment staring at the tester above her, a smile playing about her lips. There was a soreness between her legs as well as a heaviness deep in her loins that was unaccustomed, but these feelings brought more pleasure than pain. She laid her hand on her abdomen, her mind going back to the night before.

They had made love again and lain together, talking in soft, loverlike murmurs, but finally they had risen and dressed. Fitz had checked the hallway to make sure that there were no servants about, and Eve had slipped up to her bedroom, sure she would be unable to sleep with all of the joy bubbling inside her.

But surprisingly she had fallen asleep almost immediately and slept solidly through the night, even awakening a bit late this morning. She got up, stretching, and went to open the drapes, letting in the morning sun. It was then that she realized the maid had not come into her room to open the drapes and bring a pot of tea as she usually did. It was not surprising that she had slept later than usual.

She dressed, choosing a sprigged muslin round gown with graceful long sleeves that Fitz had complimented the first time she wore it. After that she could not keep from taking a little extra time to wind her hair into a softer style than the knot she frequently coiled atop her head. Teasing out little feathery curls beside her face, she studied herself in the mirror.

Did she look different? She could not keep a smile from her face no matter how hard she tried to pull her features into serious lines. She hoped no one would question her cheerfulness. After tucking a fresh handkerchief into her pocket, she swept out of the room. She was halfway to the stairs before she remembered Camellia.

With a stab of guilt, she turned and hurried back to the girl's room. How could she have let her happiness carry her away so much that she had not even thought of poor Camellia in her sickbed?

She tapped softly on the door, opened it a crack, and

peered inside. Camellia stirred in her bed and turned toward her.

"Eve?" The girl's voice came out in a croak.

"Yes, dear, it is I." Eve came over to the bedside. "Has Jenny come in to bring you any tea?"

Camellia shook her head. Her face was flushed, and she frowned when Eve leaned over to open the drapes.

"No, please, the light hurts my eyes."

"Cam, dearest . . ." Eve laid her hand on Camellia's forehead. She was hot, her eyes feverishly bright.

"My throat hurts."

"Poor dear." Eve wet a rag at the washstand and wrung it out to lay it on Camellia's forehead.

She was just about to ring for the maid and ask for tea and toast for Camellia when the door flew open, and Betsy, one of the downstairs maids, popped in.

"I'm sorry, miss. Jenny's sick this morning, and Mr. Bostwick sent me up to do for you." The maid drew a breath and paused to look at Camellia for the first time. "Ooh, are you sick too, Miss Camellia?"

"Yes, I fear she is," Eve answered. "If you would be so good as to fetch her a pot of tea and some toast, perhaps she'll eat a little."

"Yes, ma'am."

After the maid left, Eve continued to bathe Camellia's face, dipping the cloth in water and wringing it out several times. When the door opened again a few minutes later Eve swung around, surprised that Betsy had returned so quickly. But it was Lily who slipped quietly into the room.

"I came to see how Cam is doing." She came closer. "Oh, goodness, Cammy, you don't look well at all."

"I feel worse," Camellia assured her sister with some of her usual spirit.

Lily turned frightened eyes to Eve. "What's the matter with her?"

"I'm not sure. You are not feeling ill at all? I understand that one of the maids is sick as well."

Lily shook her head. "No. I'm fine."

Eve folded the cool, damp cloth and laid it over Camellia's eyes. "I was expecting to find Camellia feeling better this morning. I'm afraid perhaps we should send for the doctor."

Camellia groaned, and Lily explained, "She doesn't like doctors."

"I don't want a doctor," Camellia muttered from her bed, setting her jaw.

"Now that your eyes are covered, I'm going to open the drapes a bit so I can see you better," Eve told Camellia.

She twitched aside a corner of the drapes, sending a shaft of sunlight across the floor. It did not reach the bed, but the light was enough to show Camellia's flushed face more clearly. Eve returned to the bed and bent over Camellia. Her eyes were drawn to a red dot near the girl's hairline. There was another at her jaw.

"Oh dear." She leaned closer.

"What?" Lily looked alarmed.

"What's the matter?" Camellia picked up the bottom edge of the cloth to look at her.

"Don't worry. I'm sure you'll be fine." Eve smiled with a great deal more calm than she was feeling. She did not want to alarm the girls. "It's just . . . I think you've caught the measles."

Chapter 14

Eve arrived downstairs twenty minutes later, Lily trailing behind her. They had stayed with Camellia and persuaded her to sip a little tea and nibble at some toast. On the promise that she would try to sleep again, they left her with Betsy sitting watch and went down to eat.

"We are going to need to keep up our strength," Eve told Lily as they walked toward the dining room. "My guess is that Jenny is suffering from the same complaint, and there may be others."

"Cam is going to be all right, isn't she?" Lily asked, frowning worriedly. "I've heard of people dying with the measles."

"Usually not strong, healthy young women like your sister," Eve replied. "It is the weaker ones who succumb—young children, old people, those who are underfed or ill. But I cannot lie to you; it is harder, I think, on those who get it when they are grown than it is on people who catch it when they are younger. I am afraid she will feel quite ill for the next couple of weeks. We will need to watch over her carefully and keep her fever down. Get her to eat some soup or gruel if she can."

She put her arm around Lily's waist and hugged her,

assuring her with a smile that something like the measles could not lay Camellia low.

Fitz was still sitting at the table when they entered the dining room, a nearly empty plate before him. It was late enough that even Neville was there. Both men were listening to the butler, whose usually imperturbable face was creased with lines of distress.

Fitz turned when Eve and Lily entered the room, his face brightening. "My—Mrs. Hawthorne." His eyes met hers, warm and intimate, before he pulled his gaze away and looked at his cousin. "Lily. We were beginning to worry that perhaps you ladies were not feeling well. Bostwick just informed me that some of the servants are down with the measles. How many, Bostwick?"

"The pot boy, a scullery maid, an upstairs maid, and the housekeeper." He released a heavy sigh.

"Oh dear," Eve commented. "I am sorry Mrs. Merriwether is ill. I do hope she will not have too hard a case of it." The housekeeper's age, she feared, might make her more likely to succumb to the illness.

"I am sure she will be fine," Bostwick stated. "But I fear the household may not run as smoothly without her. I apologize for any disruption in advance, Master Fitz, but 'twill be difficult to maintain our usual standard of service. We shall endeavor to do so, of course."

"No need to apologize," Fitz replied easily. "Do the best you can."

As they talked Neville had seated Lily, and Fitz now offered the same gesture to Eve. She felt the faint brush of his fingers against her shoulder as he pushed in her chair. She turned to look at him as he walked away, then remembered that they were supposed to be very discreet.

She had a suspicion that they had not started off well in

that regard. Eve stole a glance at Lily and Neville, but they were looking at each other, not at her. She could not help but breathe a sigh of relief.

"I hope that you ladies have both already had measles," Fitz told them. "We may be in for a bit of an epidemic. I remember the other day when I was at the estate manager's cottage, both of his daughters were ill."

"I had them a long time ago," Eve said. "But I fear Camellia is not so lucky. We just left her upstairs. She's running a fever, and she has a few red spots."

Neville turned to Lily, frowning. "Have you not had them?"

"My mother said I had them when I was a baby, although I don't remember it. It seems odd that Camellia did not catch them at the same time, though. But wouldn't I have caught them from Cam by now if I had not had them already?" She glanced around at the others, a line forming between her brows. "I should hate to come all over in spots."

"What about that other chap?" Fitz asked. "The balloonist? Bit of bad luck for him if he catches them."

Eve drew in her breath in a gasp. "Oh dear! I completely forgot about Monsieur Leveque. I wonder if the servants remembered to take him a breakfast. With Camellia ill he has probably been quite neglected. I shall look in on him after breakfast."

"I can read to him," Lily offered. "Cam listens to all that ballooning talk, but that is too boring." She wrinkled her nose.

"I'll join you," Neville suggested. "Perhaps we could play a game. Or talk of something besides balloons. He's a pleasant enough chap if you get him on another topic."

"You've visited him?" Eve asked, surprised.

"A few times. One cannot desert a man one's shared a bottle of brandy with, after all."

"But surely, Nev . . ." Fitz said casually, leaning back in his chair. "You don't mean to stay on now, do you?"

"No!" Lily exclaimed, looking alarmed. "You cannot go!"

Neville turned an appraising gaze on his friend. "What's this, Fitz? Trying to chase me off?"

"It can't have been much of a stay for you," Fitz went on. "And now that we've been struck by measles, it's positively dangerous. Have you had the disease?"

"I haven't any idea," Neville returned.

"Then you should make haste. You would not want to catch them." There was a challenging light in Fitz's eyes.

"Indeed not. But who will communicate with your Frenchman when he gets excited and forgets his English? Your French has always been execrable. No, I cannot desert you in your time of need." Neville's light blue eyes glinted with amusement.

"I appreciate your devotion." Fitz's mouth curled sardonically. "But think, man, your valet might fall ill."

"I shall have to do without his services." Neville assumed a look of noble sacrifice.

"The meals will perforce be casual affairs. No more than four courses, probably. Fires may go unlit. Linens unpressed."

Carr shrugged. "I expect I shall endure the deprivation. What sort of a chap would I be to desert you now?"

"One who thinks of the future," Fitz retorted drily. "I cannot allow you to put yourself in harm's way. If you should catch the disease . . ."

"Indeed I may already have," Neville pointed out. "What would I do then? 'Twould be most uncomfortable to fall ill on the road."

"He cannot do that, Cousin Fitz." Lily leaned forward earnestly. "That would be awful, to be alone and ill in some ramshackle inn."

"Mm. Doubtless it would be ramshackle."

"He could spread the illness to other people," Eve admitted with a sigh. "It would be thoughtless of us to endanger others."

"Well, of course, when you put it that way, Neville must stay."

"You are so kind," Neville responded in a bland tone.

"It is the least I can do."

"I know." Neville chuckled, and Fitz could not keep from grinning ruefully.

After breakfast Eve went upstairs to Monsieur Leveque's room. At her knock he called out *"Entrez!"* and Eve stepped inside. The Frenchman was sitting propped up against his pillows, a tray on the bed beside him.

"Bonjour, monsieur," Eve said, exhausting a good portion of her knowledge of French. "You are looking better."

"Merci. I feel better."

"I came up to see if I could do anything for you. I see they brought your breakfast."

"Oh yes. Very English breakfast. But it is not the usual—Jeanne, is it?"

"Jenny. No, I fear Jenny is sick."

"And Mademoiselle Camellia? She is not sick, too?"

"I am afraid so. Apparently the measles are going around."

There followed a few minutes of Eve trying to explain the word to the mystified Frenchman, but at last his face cleared. "Ah! *La rougeole!*" He shook his head. "*La pauvre* Mademoiselle *Camellia.* This is very bad."

Eve was a trifle surprised at the intense concern on the man's face. Could it be that an attachment was forming between Leveque and Camellia, as she and Fitz had joked? She hoped not; she could just imagine the earl's face if he found that both of his cousins were falling into unsuitable infatuations.

"Who now will see to my balloon?" Monsieur Leveque went on. "Mademoiselle Camellia promised me she will do it."

Eve almost laughed. Perhaps she need not worry about Camellia and Monsieur Leveque after all. "I am sure your balloon is fine. They carried it into the barn. Camellia watched over them to make sure that they did everything exactly as you said."

"Yes, but she said she would make sure no one moves it or—or lays something on it. There are tools in the barn, I believe." He shook his head, envisioning the variety of disasters that could befall his balloon while it lay sheltered in the barn.

"Perhaps later Mr. Carr will go down to check on it." Eve offered up Neville without a qualm. "He said that he would come to see you today. You could tell him what he must look for."

"Yes. Yes, perhaps I could." He seized on this idea gratefully.

"At least he speaks French."

Monsieur Leveque grinned and gave a very Gallic shrug. "His knowledge of drinking songs is good, that is true." He heaved a sigh. "I am glad of his company. The broken leg is very boring, I find."

"Yes, I imagine you do. Could I bring you any books? Writing paper and pencil?"

He shook his head. "*Merci.* Mademoiselle Camellia has kindly done that for me. I am not much with the paper and book. Better to be outside, no?"

"No doubt. Well, you have a bell there, I see. Ring if you need anything."

She picked up his tray and laid it on the floor outside, figuring to save the maids a bit of work, then made her way to Camellia's room. Opening the door a crack, she peered in.

The room was dark, and Camellia was asleep. Not wishing to disturb her, she quietly closed the door and went down the stairs to check on the housekeeper, Mrs. Merriwether.

Like Camellia, Mrs. Merriwether was feverish, with an aching head and sore throat, and several spots had popped out on her arms and face. In her fevered state, she kept trying to get up and go about her duties, moaning about the state of the house without her. Eve assured her that she would take over the housekeeper's duties as best she could, which seemed to ease the woman's fears somewhat—though Eve could tell that the middle-aged woman had her doubts about the ability of a lady to oversee a household adequately.

Eve would have thought that the household, under Mrs. Merriwether's and Bostwick's exacting rule, was so well organized as almost to run itself, but she found that the servants relied more on the housekeeper's authority (and her eagle eye) than they did on themselves. At the loss of one of the people who told them what to do at the very moment when they were facing a crisis, they had fallen into a panic. What they needed, Eve realized, was a calm demeanor and confident answers, both of which she was able to manage. She took care of most of their questions by extracting from them what Mrs. Merriwether would expect them to do, and for the rest she relied on common sense.

Doing so, however, took most of the rest of her morning. She returned to Camellia's side early in the afternoon and found Lily there, bathing Camellia's face with cool lavender water. She was glad to see Lily with her sister, not only for Camellia's sake but also because she was afraid that without Eve's supervision Lily might seize the opportunity to spend every moment with Mr. Carr.

"How is she feeling?" Eve asked, moving quietly up beside Lily.

"She's very feverish. She's been sleeping most of the time

I've been here. Betsy has looked in on her all morning, as well as taking care of the maids upstairs who are sick. So I sent her down to get something to eat and a bit of rest. When she comes back Mr. Carr and I are going to visit with Monsieur Leveque to keep his spirits up."

"Thank you, dear."

"I don't mind. I'm just worried about Cam." Lily cast a glance over at her sister, her forehead knitting. "She's never sick. I don't remember when I've ever seen her this way."

"I'm sure she will recover. Camellia is a strong young woman—healthy and strong-willed. It would take more than measles to defeat her."

Lily smiled. "I know. She'll feel better soon."

"Of course I will," said a scratchy voice from the bed, and both of them turned to look at Camellia, whose eyes were open. She smiled weakly.

"Oh, Cam, are you feeling better?" Lily asked.

"I'm not any worse. But my throat hurts something awful."

Lily poured her a glass of water from the pitcher beside her bed and helped Camellia sip from it.

"Stupid," Camellia said. "I feel so weak. Why is it so hot in here?"

"It's you, silly," Lily told her. "You're hot, not the room."

There was a shriek in the corridor outside, followed by a crash. Lily darted to the door and opened it, followed by Eve. The maid Betsy stood outside, a tray on the floor before her, along with a small earthenware jug, which somehow was miraculously not broken but was turned on its side, spilling out a pale liquid.

"Who're you!" Betsy was saying as they opened the door. She was facing a young man who appeared equally as frightened as the maid. "What're you doing here?" Betsy whirled as the door opened, and her face registered relief. "Mrs.

Hawthorne. Miss Bascombe. I found this stranger in the hall. I'm terribly sorry. It gave me a turn."

She squatted and began to clean up the mess on the floor.

"But I'm Gordon," the young man was saying, almost pleadingly. "I've been here before." He turned to Eve and Lily, and his face creased with puzzlement. "I say, do I know you?"

The young man was dressed all in black except for a white shirt and the snowy cravat at his neck. His brown hair was carefully tousled, and a curl fell artfully forward onto his forehead.

Lily gazed back at him with great interest. "I think I know you," she told him. "Aren't you that man who was with Sir Royce when we met him? Only you were dressed very differently. You probably don't remember; you were drunk as a wheelbarrow. We are cousins, aren't we?"

The young man blushed and cast a mortified glance at Eve. "Beg pardon, ma'am."

"Lily, that is the sort of thing young ladies don't announce to the world."

"But it's just us," Lily replied mildly. "I wouldn't say so to a stranger. But *I* was the one who saw him in his cups, and *he* was the one who was inebriated, so we both know about it already. You are the only one who didn't, and you won't get all high in the instep over it, will you?"

"No, but I fear your—cousin, is it?—might not be accustomed to your way of speaking." Eve looked toward the young man.

"I'm sorry. I should introduce you, shouldn't I?" Lily said. "Eve, this is Gordon—only I don't know your last name. You're Aunt Euphronia's son, aren't you? Or is it Aunt Phyllida?"

"Mr. Gordon Harrington, ma'am." The young man executed a bow. "At your service." To Lily he added, "I am Lady Euphronia Harrington's son."

"I thought so."

"It's the dandy," Camellia offered from inside her room.

Gordon looked startled and moved closer to the door, peering into the room.

"He's the fop. The one who knew that silly man who kicked Pirate." Camellia pushed herself higher in her bed.

Gordon's eyebrows went up. "Kicked a pirate? I'm sure I don't know anyone . . ."

"No, not *a* pirate. Pirate the dog."

"Ah." He looked more confused than ever, but before he could speak a door opened down the hall, and Neville Carr started toward them.

Carr stopped at the sight of the group in the hall. He stared at them for a moment, then his eyes opened wide, and he exclaimed, "Good Gad! Gordy? Is that you?"

Gordon whirled, his face flooding with relief. "Carr! I'm devilish glad to see you. What's going on here? No one answered the door, so I finally just came in, and there were no servants about until that maid screamed when she saw me. Then, of course, I met you ladies—" He offered an apologetic smile to Eve and Lily, with a wary glance toward Camellia in the darkened room. "But I'm afraid I don't know you, either, though, of course, if you are my cousins, I am very glad to meet you." He swung back toward Neville. "Did you know that there's a Frenchman in a room down the hall?"

"I did," Neville allowed, sauntering toward them.

"He came here in a balloon and broke his leg," Lily offered.

"Ah, I see," Gordon replied faintly, eyeing his cousin as if he thought she might be half mad.

Neville chuckled. "It's the truth, my dear fellow." He joined the group and leaned his head into the room. "How are you, Miss Camellia?"

"It's terribly hot in here," Camellia told him.

"Yes, dear, and you should try to sleep," Eve said. "We're going to leave you alone now. Betsy . . ." She turned toward the maid, still crouched on the floor. "As soon as that's done would you sit with Miss Camellia?"

Eve closed Camellia's door. "Why don't we repair to the drawing room? Lily, you can ring for tea."

"What's happened?" Gordon asked again as they trooped down the stairs to the drawing room. "Where is everyone? Is that girl sick?"

"Miss Camellia Bascombe? Yes, she has the measles, I'm afraid."

"The measles!" Gordon's eyes threatened to pop from his head. "Good Lord. Well. Oh dear."

"Have you ever had the measles, Gordon?" Neville asked.

"I don't know." The young man looked distinctly nervous. "I'd have to ask my mother. But I surely—I must have."

"Mm. One hopes."

When they had settled in the drawing room and Lily had rung for tea, Neville turned to Gordon, saying, "What's happened to you, lad? It's no wonder the maid didn't recognize you. I barely knew you myself."

"I haven't changed that much," Gordon replied somewhat defensively. "The girl must be new."

"She's been here for years. She told me," Lily informed him. "Didn't you recognize her?"

Gordon looked at her oddly. "Well, no. But . . . she's a servant."

Lily gazed back at him blankly.

"Sorry, Gordy," Neville drawled. "I'm afraid Miss Bascombe has not been an aristocrat long enough to understand the difference between a person and a servant." Eve smothered a chuckle, but Gordon merely looked at Neville with such blankness that Neville sighed and said, "Never mind."

"You do look quite different," Lily told him. "You were wearing a yellow jacket before and lilac-and-white striped pan—I mean, inexpressibles." She cast an apologetic glance toward Eve.

"Indeed. Has someone died?" Neville added, running an eye down the young man's somber attire. "Or perhaps you turned Quaker."

"No, of course not. I'm just—well, I haven't the time for such frippery anymore. That was just schoolboy foolishness. Merely color to mask the personal tragedy." He looked downward, his face falling into lines of sorrow.

The other three regarded him blankly for a moment, then Lily said, "What tragedy? I thought you said no one had died."

"They haven't," Gordon replied a little impatiently. "I meant, you know, the tragedy of life in general. Man is here and then gone in an instant, a brief spark. No more."

"Indeed." Neville's lips twitched at the corner. "Like Byron."

"Exactly. Genius snuffed out before its time. I wrote an ode to his struggle last week."

"You are writing poetry, then?" Neville laid his hand across his mouth in a contemplative pose.

"Oh yes, it has been veritably pouring out of me the last few weeks. Ever since I discovered my talent."

"I see. And how did that happen?"

"Why, I knew it as soon as I met my muse."

"Ah." Neville nodded sagely.

"Miss Emily Pargetter."

"Not Jasper Pargetter's sister?"

Gordon nodded eagerly. "Yes! Is she not the most divine creature? She opened my eyes to the world I had been missing."

"Read poetry to you, did she? Tried that with me one time, but I ran."

"I tried to myself," Gordon confided. "But I couldn't; Langton was blocking my way. Then she started reading, and I looked at her entrancing countenance, and I realized how wrong I had been all my life. How foolishly I had frittered away my days on trivialities."

What Neville might have replied to this statement was lost, for at that moment Fitz strode into the room. "Ah, there you are. Hope you've rung for tea. I've just been down at the estate manager's. Poor devil, he's come down with it, too—" He came to a halt, finally noticing Gordon. "The devil!"

"Hallo, Fitz." Gordon rose to his feet.

Fitz stared at him for a moment, then asked, "Good Lord, did someone die?"

"Just what I thought," Neville told him. "But it seems our Gordon has turned serious. He's eschewed the foibles and fripperies of life."

"Well . . ." Fitz carefully avoided glancing at Neville. "You're, um, going to study for the clergy?"

Neville made a strangled noise.

"No, he's fallen in love and decided to become a poet," Lily explained helpfully.

"Naturally." Fitz glanced around. "I think something stronger than tea is in order. Neville?"

"My exact thoughts."

The tea was brought, as well as alcohol. Apparently Gordon's new approach to life did not include avoiding alcohol, for he joined the other men in a glass of sherry.

"I'm surprised you're here at Willowmere if you've taken a fancy to a young lady in London," Fitz told his cousin.

Gordon blushed. "It isn't just a fancy, Cousin Fitz."

"She's his muse," Neville added. "Isn't that right, Gordon?"

"Yes, of course," Gordon agreed, pleased at the other man's ready understanding.

"Even more reason to stay in London, I'd think," Fitz commented.

Gordon shifted uneasily. "Well, that is . . ."

"Told your mother about her, did you?" Fitz guessed.

"Good Gad, man, of course not! I'm not mad, you know."

Fitz shrugged. "I thought she might have refused to let you marry the girl, so you were turning to Oliver for help."

"Stewkesbury?" The young man looked only slightly less terrified than he had at the mention of his mother. "No. No."

"Well, he isn't here, at any rate."

"I know," Gordon blurted out. "I saw him in London the other day."

Fitz's eyes narrowed suspiciously. "Did *he* send you here?"

"I didn't *speak* to him." Gordon looked at Fitz as if he'd lost his mind. "I just *saw* him. He was turned away, thank heavens, so I went the other direction."

"I see. So you decided to come to Willowmere because my brother wasn't here."

"Exactly."

Fitz nodded but did not pursue the matter. After a few more minutes of chat Neville offered to show Gordon to a bedchamber, and Lily quickly volunteered to help. Eve did not bother to try to circumvent it; ushering Cousin Gordon about was scarcely conducive to dalliance.

"We'll introduce you to Monsieur Leveque, as well," Neville offered, clapping Gordon on the back as they left the room. "He's French; no doubt he'll be quite knowledgeable about love and poetry."

As they heard the others' steps recede down the corridor, Fitz leaned forward in his chair, bracing his elbows on his knees and dropping his head to his hands. "I have been cursed."

Eve chuckled. "Is he really that bad?"

"You don't know Gordon," he told her darkly. "There's some reason he's here. He bolted as soon as he saw Oliver was in town. He's probably in the basket. His mother keeps him on a short rope—easy to see why. He's perfectly birdwitted, always has been. But the result is that he comes to me or Royce when he's run off his legs. I'd give him the money simply to be rid of him, but now he's been exposed to the measles, and you will tell me I can't let him loose on the world."

"You know you wouldn't even if I didn't tell you that." Eve smiled.

Fitz looked at her, and the irritation seemed to fall away. He smiled and went to sit beside her, taking her hands in his. "What an idiot I am, wasting time talking about Gordon. I have been thinking about you all day, wanting to see you." He raised her hands to his lips and pressed a fervent kiss upon them.

Desire stirred in Eve. She had been thinking about him, too, remembering his kisses, the way he had touched her, the passion that seemed to melt her very bones. Now the yearning that had lain barely beneath the surface all day sprang to life. She wanted, quite badly, for him to kiss her.

She let out a soft sigh. He kissed her hands again, then turned them over to press his lips against each palm.

"I don't think this is very discreet," Eve murmured.

"I know. But I cannot help myself." With a soft groan he pulled her up and over onto his lap. Cupping his hand behind Eve's neck, he kissed her thoroughly.

It was some time later that Fitz finally raised his head. "Bloody hell. We cannot do this."

He set her away from him and rose to his feet, walking several paces away. Eve laced her hands in her lap to hide their trembling and watched him. She suspected that everything she felt must show in her face. But at least they were a decent distance apart if someone should happen to walk in on them.

Fitz swung around to face her, his face tight, jaw set. "This blasted illness has thrown everything into disarray. And now Gordon's here."

"Does that matter so much?"

"It changes everything. Last night we needed to be discreet, but if we slipped up it wouldn't be disastrous. I can trust Neville's discretion, and Lily and Camellia are loyal to the extreme. They'd never reveal something that would hurt you. I trust the servants, too, and in any case they are up here, not in London, which is where silence is essential. But Gordon! He's not a bad fellow, but he has little sense; he's one of the last people I would trust with any sort of damaging knowledge. I fear if he suspected something it would be all over the city before we returned. No, with Gordon here we have to be absolutely perfect." Fitz sighed. "I fear there's nothing else for it. As long as my dratted cousin is here we must not . . . be together."

Eve was surprised at the way her heart fell inside her. It would be no different from the way she had been living before last night, after all. It should not matter so. Yet now that she had discovered such happiness, she found herself most reluctant to set it aside.

"I suppose it's for the best," she said, struggling to hide her disappointment. "It will be difficult enough to chaperone Lily and Neville the next few days, with all we have to do. It's better if we are not distracted by our own, um, indiscretion."

"It was not an 'indiscretion.'" Fitz strode across the room and leaned down, bracing his hands on either arm of Eve's chair and looking straight into her eyes. "That is far too tepid a word for what happened between us last night. And when Gordon is gone, I promise you, there are going to be many more nights like it."

Chapter 15

The following day Eve was kept even busier. Two more of the kitchen servants and a downstairs maid fell ill. Eve set Betsy solely to tending the sick servants, and she spent most of the day taking care of Camellia, leaving her bedside only to consult on household matters with the cook and the butler. Lily relieved her several times throughout the day and also took it upon herself to look in on the Frenchman now and then.

"I tried to talk to Cousin Gordon, too," she told Eve. "But he is an odd fellow. He keeps spouting the most peculiar things, which makes Neville laugh, but really, they are quite foolish. He goes on and on about poetry, so I thought he might like to read something, but when I offered to lend him a book, he looked as if I had handed him a snake."

"I think your cousin is less into reading than feeling."

"And he made Monsieur Leveque so angry yesterday that the man threw a cup at him."

"Oh dear. What did he do to enrage Monsieur Leveque?"

"I wasn't really listening too well, for it was deadly dull. Cousin Gordon was talking about soaring above the clouds—you know, in some poetical sort of way, and Monsieur Leveque thought he must be interested in *actually* sailing in the air. So he started talking about balloons and wind currents and, oh, all sorts of things I can't remember. I can quite understand why Cousin Gordon found it boring, but then, of all the silly things to do, he told Monsieur Leveque that he was talking about the 'flight of the soul, not tossing about in a balloon.' And Monsieur Leveque told him that Gordon had no soul if that was what he thought about flying in a balloon. Then Gordon said that balloons were not important in the whole scheme of things."

Eve could not help but giggle. "I am surprised Monsieur Leveque threw nothing more than a cup."

"He could not reach anything else, or I'm sure he would have. I was very sorry Cam missed it." She turned to look at her sister, sleeping on the bed, and her forehead knotted in worry. "Is she all right, do you think?"

"I believe she is better today, though she's covered in spots worse than ever. But her fever seems down, and she's sleeping more peacefully. If she wakes up and frets, there's a soothing lotion to put on her spots."

Lily nodded. "I'll be fine. You should lie down and rest. Cousin Fitz said I should make sure that you don't tire yourself." She paused, looking at Eve speculatively. "I think Cousin Fitz is a little sweet on you."

Eve felt a traitorous blush steal into her cheeks. "What? Don't be silly."

Lily smiled archly but made no reply. She walked toward the chair beside the bed, but as she started to sit down she made a face and exclaimed, "Oh! I almost forgot."

Lily reached into the pocket of her skirt and pulled out a square of white paper, which she held out to Eve. "There was a letter for you on the hall table downstairs, so I brought it up."

Eve froze, her heart seeming to flip in her chest. Lily

looked puzzled, and Eve forced herself to take the letter from her. "Thank you, dear."

Her eyes went to the writing. It was the same strong masculine hand. She managed to give Lily a smile before she walked away. She could not remember afterward if she had even said good-bye to the girl.

When she reached the privacy of her own room Eve ripped open the letter.

Your husband was a thief.

Eve gasped as she read the first bold line of the note, and her hand flew to her mouth. She made herself read on.

The watch you wear is proof of his thievery. I could reveal his transgressions to the world. How do you think the mighty Earl of Stewkesbury would like having a chaperone who is the widow of a thief? What do you think he would do if he knew the watch you flaunt is stolen? Or that Major Hawthorne was about to be cashiered from the army? That he killed himself rather than face that shame? Do you really think his fall was an "accident"?

Eve sank onto the side of her bed, pressing a hand to her stomach, as if to hold in the turmoil inside her. *Bruce, a thief?* It couldn't possibly be true. Bruce had always been one of the most honorable men she knew. She was not the only one who thought so—he was respected by the men under him, his fellow officers, and his superiors. However extravagant he might have been, however lavishly he might have spent, he had never lied about it. He had never tried to cheat anyone. He paid his gambling debts immediately. And when he made a promise he followed through on it.

She could not, she would not, believe that Bruce had been a thief. He could not have been in danger of being thrown out of the army in disgrace. It was impossible, unthinkable.

It was easier somehow to believe that he could have killed himself. His failure to consummate their marriage had haunted him, she knew; he had felt himself inadequate, his condition shameful. There had been times when Eve had wondered if his reckless riding, his wild courage, had been at their heart as much attempts to end his life as proof to the world that he was a real man. If he had done the things the letter accused him of, if he had faced being publically disgraced and cashiered from his beloved army, then she could conceive of him kicking free from his stirrups and rolling from his saddle as his horse sailed over the stone wall. As long as he was certain that his mount would not be harmed, he would have faced death willingly. But throwing oneself off a horse would be a far from certain method. Bruce would have known that and chosen a gun, surely.

Her heart clutched as she thought of it, and tears sprang into her eyes. But no, she could not believe it. Besides, Bruce would not have been in that situation. He would not have stolen. He had not been teetering on the edge of disgrace. She would have known it surely if he had been worried and tormented. She could not have been so blind to what was happening to him.

No, she thought. She was certain that the person who had written the letters was lying.

But why? It made no sense. The first letter had told her to leave. The second had hinted at Bruce's wrongdoing and told her to get rid of the watch. And this one accused Bruce of thievery and threatened to tell Lord Stewkesbury what the major had done. But it had not asked for anything or instructed her to do anything. Usually when people threatened one it was in order to get something. Yet this letter seemed intended merely to frighten her.

Well, it had certainly accomplished that. If the person who sent the letter should tell Lord Stewkesbury his claims or even start rumors about Bruce that got back to Lord Stewkesbury, it would be disastrous for Eve. She knew that whether or not the rumors were true would make little difference. It would be difficult to disprove them, and even if she could, the mere fact of the rumor would follow her the rest of her days. A chaperone's most valuable asset was her reputation; no one would want a widow who inspired whispers of gossip to usher their daughters through the *ton*.

The earl would dismiss her, and she would be doomed to spend the rest of her life at her father's house. Her stomach lurched at the thought of leaving Willowmere, of never again walking through its lovely gardens or idling away an hour or two in the magnificent library, of never seeing Lily or Camellia—or Fitz.

She had not realized until this moment how much she had come to love this place in the last few weeks or how easily the Bascombe sisters had stolen their way into her heart. As for Fitz . . . well, it was better not to think of that.

But what could she do? How could she combat the creature who was sending these letters? She had no idea who it was or what his purpose might be. She had little attachment to the watch and would be just as happy not to have it. But she could not imagine how the letter writer would know that she had gotten rid of it. Besides, she had a stubborn reluctance to cave in to the beast's demands, as if she would be failing Bruce, admitting that she believed the wicked things he had said about her husband.

Eve took the letter and placed it with the other two and the watch, deep in the drawer beneath her nightgowns. Then she sat in the chair beside the window and stared out, trying to think. Who could hate Bruce so much? Or perhaps it was Eve herself who was hated. But she could not think of anyone who hated her to such an extent. Lady Sabrina obviously disliked her, but this seemed extreme for someone who barely knew Eve, even someone as unpleasant as Sabrina. Perhaps a soldier whom Bruce had disciplined had held it against him all these years? She felt sure that her husband had made decisions that others had resented, and there might be those who would hold a grudge so long.

But she could not understand why they would have waited until now to bring it up. And what in the world did it have to do with the watch that Bruce had gotten for her just before his death?

She wished quite badly that she could talk to Fitz about the letters. He would smile and toss off a remark that would make her smile, too, and her fears would ease. Fitz had that way about him, the ability to shrink fears and problems down to a manageable size. He would kiss her and take her into his arms, and she could lean her head against his shoulder, and somehow everything would be better.

But even as she thought of going to Fitz with her problems, she knew that she could not do so. He was the earl's brother, and she would be putting him in a terrible position. Stewkesbury would have no choice but to dismiss a chaperone with such scandal in her past, so Fitz would feel compelled to keep her secret from his brother. She could not ask him to choose between her and his family, and indeed she was not sure she wanted to learn what his choice would be.

Besides, she disliked the thought of exposing her late husband in that way to another man. Fitz had not known him. He might assume that Bruce had been exactly the sort of man the letter writer had described. She had loved Bruce, and she had been loyal to him for ten years. However much she might feel for Fitz—and she was not yet certain what that was—she could not bear to hear Fitz express contempt for Bruce.

No, Fitz was out of the question, she told herself, and there was no one else. She could scarcely burden Lily or Camellia with it, and she could not justify taking time off from her many duties here at Willowmere to visit Vivian and pour out her troubles to her. She needed to resolve this on her own. Unfortunately she could think of no way to do so.

Eve stood up, mentally shaking off her unproductive thoughts. It was useless to worry over a letter sent by someone who would not even reveal himself. Until she knew more, there was nothing she could do. She looked at the clock. It was almost time for tea.

Despite the disarray of the household the past few days, she had tried to keep them to a traditional schedule. It was helpful for the Bascombes, she thought, who were trying to catch up on twenty years of life experience. And she suspected it was good for the rest of them, too. If there was anything she had learned from her years as a military wife, it was the importance of tradition and discipline.

Eve washed her face and hands, then brushed out her hair and repinned it in the simple knot she usually favored. Feeling somewhat refreshed, she made her way downstairs to the drawing room where they usually had afternoon tea. Neville was standing at one of the windows, looking out, and he turned at her entrance.

"Ah, Mrs. Hawthorne. Good afternoon."

"Mr. Carr." Eve was never sure quite how to act with Neville. He was amusing, and in other circumstances she would have probably enjoyed a conversation with him. But because of Lily she always felt as if she needed to be on her guard with him.

"I was hoping we might have a chance sometime to speak alone," he said now.

"You were?" She looked at him, surprised and a trifle wary.

He smiled faintly. "There is no need to look suspicious. I do not mean to make a nuisance of myself."

"Mr. Carr . . ."

"Please, just hear me out. I know that you disapprove of me, and Fitz has told me why." He looked into her face, his gaze direct, without pleading or artifice. "I have not been the best of men; I admit that. And I cannot change what I have done in the past. But I can tell you that I am not the same man I used to be. My feelings for Lily are deep and strong. I love her, Mrs. Hawthorne, and the last thing I want to do is hurt her. No doubt there are better men than I who would fall in love with her—indeed how can anyone not?—but I promise you that none would try harder than I to make her happy."

Eve sighed. "I have no doubt that what you say is true. But there is an impediment to any relationship with Lily, is there not?"

His face darkened. "Yes, but I have hope—if I can but talk to—" He muffled a curse as Gordon walked into the room.

The moment was gone. Neville could do nothing but bow to Eve and move away. She was frankly relieved. She could not help but feel sympathy for the man, but there was nothing she could do. Her first consideration must be Lily and what would happen to her. And in any case, she had nothing to say in the matter. Eve could only turn it all over to Fitz.

She turned to greet Gordon, and the three of them sat down, making social chitchat. Lily came rushing in to join them just as Bostwick and one of the footmen carried in the tea trays. "Sorry I'm late," she said, prettily flushed, and sat beside Eve on the sofa. "Camellia awakened, and I wanted to make sure she did not need anything before I left."

"How is she feeling?" Neville asked.

"Better, I think. This time when she awoke I really thought she seemed less warm. Her color was not as high, and she sounded more like herself."

"Excellent. Let's hope we can look forward to a speedy recovery."

Gordon glanced around. "Where is Fitz? Isn't he joining us?"

"He was riding out to visit some of the tenants this afternoon, I believe," Eve told him. "He said not to expect him before tea."

"I don't understand. Why is Fitz doing all this work?" Gordon asked rather plaintively. "I had hoped we might get in some hunting while I was here."

Eve was not sure how to reply to this statement. "It's a bit of an urgent situation right now, I'm afraid. Mr. Talbot is standing in for his brother, and the estate manager has taken ill."

Gordon shrugged. "The place would hardly fall apart while Stewkesbury's gone."

"Yes, Fitz has become distressingly level-headed," Neville agreed. "Perhaps you can exercise some influence on him, Gordon."

"I wouldn't think so," Gordon replied seriously. "Never known him to pay any attention to me."

Eve, suppressing a smile, leaned over to take the cup of tea Lily handed her. As she did so she became aware of voices in the foyer. They rose in volume, a man's voice, polite but insistent, countered by a woman's, growing louder and higher, until finally they resolved into audible words.

"I am sorry, miss, but—"

"Don't take that tone with me!" The woman's voice came back sharply.

Eve glanced at Lily in surprise. As she turned toward the doorway Eve caught sight of Gordon's face. He had paled and turned rigid, his teacup held stiffly out in front of him.

"Here! You can't—" Eve recognized the man's voice now as that of Paul, one of the footmen.

"Don't tell me what I can't do!" The woman's voice was unfamiliar, high and rather harsh, and while the accent was that of a lady, there was something about it that rang false. "I tell you, Mr. Harrington will be glad to see me. Now, get out of my way, unless you want to explain to him why you're not letting in his fiancée!"

Something like a bleat escaped Gordon's lips as the other three occupants of the room swung around to look at him. With a clatter he set the cup and saucer on the small table before him and jumped to his feet. Face white, eyes large, he looked rather like a hare with the hounds after him. He glanced toward the door, where the sound of footsteps was fast approaching, then swung back, casting a desperate glance around. He darted across the room, shoved up the lower section of one of the long windows overlooking the front garden, threw his leg over the sill, and went out the window.

Lily and Eve stared in astonishment at the window through which he had disappeared. Neville cried, "Yoicks away!" and began to laugh.

The women swung back to the door as the footman and a woman entered in a kind of peculiar dance. The footman, facing her, was shuffling backward, trying to maintain his position between the visitor and her goal, while she tried to circle around him, first to the left, then to the right, all the while gaining ground on him.

The woman looked to Eve to be around her own age,

several years older than Gordon Harrington. Her hair under the stylish blue bonnet was a froth of golden curls, and her face was rather pretty, with a rosebud mouth, round blue eyes, and a small, tip-tilted nose. She was dressed in girlish white dimity, with a great deal of fluttering blue ribbons and ruffles. But startlingly, the neckline of the dimity dress was cut quite low, exposing much of her bosom, without a fichu or even a ruffle to cover it up. Her pink lips and blushing cheeks obviously owed more to a rouge pot than to nature. A blue cloak shoved back behind her shoulders, short white gloves, and a blue-and-white-beribboned parasol completed her outfit. She looked, Eve thought somewhat uncharitably, like Bo-Peep without her shepherdess crook.

"I'm sorry, ma'am, miss." The harassed footman turned toward Eve and Lily. "I tried to explain to this lady that visitors must be announced, but—"

"He would not let me in!" The woman exclaimed, seizing the opportunity to step around the footman. She clasped her hands at her bosom and turned her beseeching gaze upon Mr. Carr. "I've never been so surprised in my life. I know that my darling Gordy will be very much distressed to learn how I have been treated."

Eve nodded to the footman, and he bowed and turned away, his footsteps ringing a quick retreat toward the back of the house.

"Indeed I believe he is already greatly distressed," Neville replied gravely. "I fear that I do not have the honor, Miss . . ."

"Oh! I am so sorry." She let out a little titter, raising one small gloved hand to cover her mouth shyly. "Of course I should have told you my name. Gordy is forever telling me I am a goose."

"Is he?" Lily asked. "That sounds very rude."

Eve detected a bite in Lily's polite tone, and she sensed

that Lily had taken an immediate dislike to the woman. Just, Eve admitted, as she had.

The woman cast a faintly disconcerted glance at Lily. "What?"

"Calling you a goose. I think I would take exception."

The woman looked at her, and Eve saw a moment of calculation in the baby-blue eyes before they resumed their previous vacuity. "Oh no, it is only Gordy's way. His little affectionate term."

"Mm." Lily's tone was noncommittal.

"I am Elizabeth Saunders." The visitor turned once again toward Neville, simpering as she said, "You must be my Gordy's cousin. I am so happy to meet you." She held out her hand to Neville.

"Must I?" His eyebrows rose a little, but he stepped forward to take her hand and sketched a very brief bow over it. "I fear I am quite unrelated to young Harrington."

"Oh, silly me." She looked toward the women inquiringly, but Carr made no move to introduce the woman to either Eve or Lily, which confirmed Eve's suspicion, growing stronger by the moment, that Miss Saunders was anything but a lady.

Even though Miss Saunders had adopted a number of young, even shy mannerisms, from downcast eyes to sweet smiles to covering her mouth in an embarrassed way, there was something quite bold about her. No young lady would have forced her way in past the footman, nor would she speak of her fiancé by a diminutive name in front of strangers. Most of all she would not have introduced herself to a strange man and stuck out her hand. Eve knew that any of these things might have been done by her own charges, at least when they first arrived in England. But there was a fresh, innocent quality to Lily and Camellia that was utterly missing in Elizabeth Saunders. And none of the Bascombes would have exposed her bosom in such a manner, even when they first arrived.

Miss Saunders was not deterred by Neville's lack of introduction. She merely turned to Lily, then Eve, repeating her name and holding out her hand.

Lily, of course, responded with her own name and a handshake, though there was a reserve in her that Eve had never seen before. Eve felt sure that though Lily might not know why, Lily suspected something was off about their visitor. Eve merely nodded and said hello. She could see the other woman assessing her. Then Miss Saunders bared her teeth in something that was as much a challenge as a smile. Without waiting to be asked, she sauntered over to a chair and sat down.

"Well, I am sure you must all have been agog when Gordy told you that we were engaged."

"No doubt we would have been," Neville replied, "had the lad told us."

"What?" Her hands flew to her cheeks in an expression of astonishment. "That bad thing! Not to have breathed a word of it! Oh, I shall have to scold him about this. Where is that wicked boy?" She glanced around as if she might find Gordon hiding behind some chair.

"He was around only a moment ago." Neville's eyes gleamed with amusement.

"I shall take him to task as soon as I see him. Just you wait."

"Oh, I shall," Neville assured her.

"Have you and Cousin Gordon been engaged long?" Lily asked.

"My, no. It has been a whirlwind courtship. I blush to think of what his mother will say."

"Aunt Euphronia doesn't know?" Lily's eyebrows sailed upward.

"I think you must be the first to know," Miss Saunders answered.

"But we didn't know," Lily responded.

"Until now."

"Yes, well." Eve stood up. "Indeed it is too bad that Mr. Harrington is not here to meet you. One scarcely knows what to do." She turned toward Lily. "My dear, perhaps we should go look for your cousin."

"Me? Us? But why? Surely Paul could look for Cousin Gordon."

"Much better, I think, if we do it." Eve sent her charge a firm look. She had little idea what to do with the bold Miss Saunders. But she had no doubt that Lily should not be chatting with the woman.

Lily's face was beginning to set mulishly, and Eve feared she might argue, but at that moment there was the sound of footsteps, and Fitz appeared in the doorway, followed by the butler. His eyes flickered around the room, taking in the situation.

"I see we have a visitor," Fitz said in a mild tone.

"I am Miss Saunders," their guest said, rising and advancing toward Fitz. "I am Gordon Harrington's fiancée."

"Are you?" Fitz returned her gaze blandly. "I am sure that will come as a surprise to his mother and father."

She giggled, covering her mouth coyly. "Indeed I fear it will. It was bad of us not to tell anyone, but it happened so fast. My Gordy is most impetuous."

"Indeed. 'Your Gordy' is also a minor, requiring his parents' permission to marry. And if you knew Gordon's mother, you would have little expectation of receiving it."

Miss Saunders's eyes flashed. "I think she'll not like having it known that her son gave an innocent maid a slip on the shoulder, then refused to honor his obligations."

"If you think anyone, including my aunt, will swallow that Banbury story, you are more naïve than you look," Fitz replied.

"He owes me!" The most sincere emotion Eve had seen yet bloomed on their visitor's face. "He promised to set me up—a house and carriage and everything. A *carte blanche*. Then he ups and starts chasing after that dreadful bluestocking. All of a sudden he's spouting poetry all the time and ignoring me. And where is my house? All I've gotten from him is this paltry bracelet." She raised her arm and shook it to show the circlet of pearls. "I told him I wouldn't let him get away with it!"

"That is quite enough." Fitz's clipped voice was deadly cold, his eyes equally frigid. Eve noticed that even Miss Saunders went a little pale and closed her mouth on whatever she had been about to say. "Now . . . whatever Mr. Harrington promised or didn't promise you, the issue does not belong here. It will not be discussed in front of Mrs. Hawthorne and my cousin. Bostwick will show you to my study. I have sent a servant for Mr. Harrington, and as soon as he arrives we will sit down and discuss the matter. In private."

He made a gesture toward the doorway, and the butler came over to stand beside Miss Saunders. She set her jaw, and for a moment Eve thought she might refuse, but then she swept out of the room, moving so quickly that Bostwick had to hurry to keep up with her.

Eve and Lily turned to Fitz.

"Cousin Fitz, who was that awful woman?" Lily asked. "She isn't really engaged to Cousin Gordon, is she?"

"I sincerely doubt that even Gordon is so foolish. And you, my dear girl, should forget that you ever saw her."

"I can't do that," Lily protested. "What did she mean, he

gave her a *carte blanche*? And why did he promise to give her a house?"

Fitz, looking somewhat harassed, turned toward Eve. "Mrs. Hawthorne . . ."

Eve swallowed her amusement. "Yes. Come, Lily, I think it's time we finished our tea." She gestured toward their cups, cooling on the table.

"But . . ." Lily protested, looking toward Fitz. "I want to talk to Cousin Fitz."

"Yes, well, I think that is precisely what your Cousin Fitz does not want." Eve glanced at him with a smile.

"You are, as always, most astute. Ladies, I bid you *adieu*. Carr?" He turned toward Neville.

"Coming." His friend rose with alacrity, and the two men left the room.

"Well, if that isn't the outside of enough!" Lily exclaimed, putting her hands on her hips and staring out the door after them. "No doubt they're going off to discuss everything."

"Most annoying."

"It is. That is exactly what *I* wanted to do." She paused, considering. "What I'd really like is to hear what Fitz tells Gordon. Wouldn't you?"

Eve had to grin. "Yes, rather. But I suppose we must respect Mr. Harrington's privacy."

"I suppose. But I bet Cousin Fitz will tell Neville what he plans to say."

"Mr. Carr probably has a good idea already."

Lily chose a tea cake and bit into it, chewing thoughtfully. "Miss Saunders is a lightskirt, isn't she?"

"Lily! Wherever do you learn such things? Did Mr. Carr tell you—"

"Goodness no. Neville can be positively stodgy about such matters. Which is really quite odd, since Cousin Gordon assured me that Neville has a reputation as a rake. Well, he says Cousin Fitz does too, but Gordon says that Neville is loose in the haft, which I gather is worse."

"At least he isn't bird-witted enough to say such things to a young girl, as Gordon did."

"Look, there is Gordon now." Lily was looking out the window through which her cousin had so precipitously left, and she hopped up now to go closer. "He doesn't seem happy."

Eve came over to stand beside her. Gordon marched across the lawn toward the front door, followed by the grim-faced Paul. "Gordon has good reason not to be happy. I suspect your cousin is going to ring a peal over his head."

"If they are not engaged, why did Miss Saunders pretend to be? Did she think Cousin Gordon would fall in with her plans?"

"I imagine she was trying to embarrass him. She claimed he had made certain promises to her."

"To set her up in a house," Lily supplied.

"Yes, but please remember never to talk about such things in front of others."

"I shan't, but what a lot I'm going to have to tell Cam when she feels better!" Lily chuckled. "She will be furious she missed all the excitement."

"I am sure she will be."

"But go on. When Gordon didn't live up to what he promised, she thought to make him do so by pretending they were engaged?"

Eve shrugged. "That would be my guess. She probably told him she would go to his parents. Perhaps he dismissed her or said she wouldn't dare. So she decided to confront him."

"Why travel all the way to Willowmere to do it?"

"If she has any inkling of what Lady Euphronia is like, she would not have wanted to take her on."

"No." Lily gave a little shudder.

"Besides, she would have lost her bargaining power. Miss Saunders had nothing but the threat of embarrassment to use against Gordon. Once she embarrassed him in front of his parents, that would be the end of the threat."

"But she said she was going to tell everyone, make a great scandal."

"Who would she tell? She scarcely runs in the Harringtons' circle. And who is going to pay any attention to a woman such as she, claiming to be Gordon's fiancée? No, I think her best threat with Gordon was to get him in trouble with his mother. So she came to others in his family, hoping to show Gordon what she would do at his mother's house. I am sure she hoped it would frighten him enough to give her some sort of settlement."

"Instead it frightened him enough to run like a rabbit." Lily giggled.

Eve had to smile at the memory of the young man bolting out the window.

They resumed their seats and returned to their tea, but a few minutes later they were drawn to the window again by the sight of Miss Saunders walking out to her carriage.

"Do you think Fitz gave her any money?" Lily asked.

"He may have. She looks . . . not pleased but not furious, either. From what Fitz said, he has rescued Gordon from other scrapes."

"He didn't sound happy to rescue him today." Lily gave an expressive shudder. "I vow he quite scared me when he told her to go with Bostwick. I never would have guessed Cousin Fitz could look so hard."

"Mm. I would not wish to be Cousin Gordon right now," Eve agreed.

Chapter 16

Eve was not the only one who did not wish to be Gordon Harrington. The young man himself was slumped in a chair in the earl's study, chewing at his thumbnail, regarding his cousin with a sullen blend of resentment and trepidation.

"I don't know why you're going on at me so," Gordon whined. "How was I to know the silly girl would take it into her head to chase after me up here?"

"Silly? Shrewd is more like it. You are the one who has displayed silliness to an excessive extent." Fitz leaned against the edge of the desk, his ankles crossed, but there was no relaxation in his manner. His blue eyes were glacial as they bored into his cousin's.

"I don't know why you've turned into such a stickler. It's not like you and Royce never traded in the muslin company."

"I never made promises I had no intention of keeping. Could not keep, in fact. You could no more have bought that bird of paradise a house than you could shoot a pip off a card at twenty paces. I don't care if you keep a mistress. I don't care if you keep a dozen. But I do care—" Fitz straightened suddenly and took a step forward, looming over the young man. "I do care when your frivolous, thoughtless actions bring a doxy into this house. Into the same room as Miss Bascombe and Mrs. Hawthorne!"

Gordon swallowed convulsively and began to stutter.

"Don't bother to come up with an excuse." Fitz swung away from him. "It is clear to me that I have done you a disservice the past few years, helping you out of scrapes, clearing up your messes. Royce and I felt sorry for you. We didn't want you to have to face Aunt Euphronia with your mishaps. But it is obvious that as a result you have learned absolutely nothing."

"You're not going to tell my mother, are you?" Gordon turned ashen, his eyes bulging.

"No. At least not yet. But I can assure you that if you do not follow what I say exactly, I shall lay it all in her lap."

Gordon stared at him, his mouth opening and closing convulsively. "But . . . but . . ."

"Here is what you have to do. You will repay me every cent that I gave Miss Saunders."

"What?" Gordon found his voice, though it rose at least an octave. "But how?"

"Out of your allowance from your father, I imagine. He gives you money to live on."

"Yes, but I spend it all."

"Well, now you will spend some of it paying back the money I just gave Miss Saunders."

"I don't see why you had to give her so much."

"Because you made promises to her. A gentleman keeps his promises, whether he's made them to a king or a dustman . . . or a lightskirt. If you don't mean to carry them out do not make them. If you continue to go on in this manner you will become known as a man whose word cannot be trusted."

"But you'll never miss it; you've got piles of blunt."

"Which I have no intention of giving to you the rest of

your days. I realize that your parents do not shower you with money, but they give you enough, and I don't expect repayment all at once. However, you will have to give up your gambling and drinking for a while so that you can repay me a little every month. Is that clear?"

"Yes." Gordon crossed his arms, his chin sinking onto his chest.

"This evening you will apologize to both our cousin Lily and Mrs. Hawthorne for bringing that woman into their presence."

Gordon's eyes bugged out again, but after one look from Fitz he muttered, "All right. I will apologize." He lifted his chin, saying in the tones of a martyr, "After that I will remove myself from this house, since it is clear that I'm not wanted here."

"No, you will not. You have been exposed to the measles, and I won't have you responsible for spreading them everywhere you go. But while you are here you will help out."

"Help? What do you mean?"

"I mean that we have several sick servants and two patients upstairs. Monsieur Leveque needs to be lifted in and out of bed." When Gordon started to protest, Fitz lifted one eyebrow and said, "Neville doesn't seem to find it beneath his dignity to help the fellow."

"All right, all right, I will help."

"You might even go in to chat with him now and then or play a game of cards. And when the illness is over I expect you to return to college and apply yourself to your studies. Or at least do not get yourself expelled again. Stay away from gambling halls and Haymarket ware until you have repaid every cent."

"Well! I never thought I'd see the day." Gordon rose huffily. "You've turned into Stewkesbury."

"There are far worse people to be, I assure you."

"You used to be a bang-up cove," Gordon told him bitterly. "I don't know what happened to you."

Fitz looked at him for a long moment. "Maybe I grew up."

Eve was in the small sitting room the next day, studying the reduced menu plans from the cook, when Bostwick announced that Colonel Willingham had come to call. She looked up, startled, and felt a moment of guilt that in all the turmoil of the last few days she had completely forgotten that the colonel was in the area.

"Please show him in," she told the butler. "That is, he does know about the illness in the house?"

The butler nodded. "Yes, ma'am. He was inquiring after the health of our household."

A moment later the colonel strode in. Eve went forward, holding out her hand. "Colonel. What a delightful surprise."

He bowed over her hand with military precision, his face grave. "I hope I find you well."

"Yes, thank you, though poor Camellia has been struck down with the measles and several of the servants as well. I take it they are spread all over the village."

"Yes, to the best of my understanding."

"How do you fare at the hall?"

"As you do here. A few have been stricken. Lady Vivian and Lord Humphrey and I are fine, but poor Lady Sabrina, I fear, has been severely stricken with them."

"I am so sorry."

"Yes. There has been much ado. Her ladyship fainted the other night, just after we returned from our dinner here, and I had to carry her up to her room. I confess I assumed that she had simply become . . . overexcited."

Eve suspected that his words were a graceful euphemism for his assumption that Sabrina had been making another effort to capture his attention. A graceful faint into his arms sounded like just the sort of ploy she would use.

"But by the next afternoon she had a fever, and now, as I understand, she has come all over with spots."

"Oh dear." Eve firmly quelled the little devil of amusement that came to life at this pronouncement. She could not laugh; it would be too wicked. Measles could be extremely painful, even dangerous, to adults. But she could not help but imagine Sabrina's outrage at the appearance of red dots all over her lovely countenance.

"Yes. I understand Lady Vivian had been ready to take her leave of us, but when Lady Sabrina was stricken she had to lay aside her plans and stay to care for her."

"Oh my." Eve firmly pressed her lips together. This was almost too much, to think of Vivian playing nursemaid to Sabrina.

"Yes." The colonel's grave expression was belied by a twinkle in his gray eyes. "It, um, fairly boggles the mind. This morning there were a number of crashes coming from the lady's bedchamber."

A gurgle of laughter escaped Eve, and she clapped her hand to her mouth, but Colonel Willingham joined in. He quickly sobered, however, and leaned toward her.

"Mrs. Hawthorne, I cannot help but notice that you look rather pale and tired. I hope you are not overtaxing yourself. You must not work too hard. I hate to see you in this position, run ragged by the demands of others."

"You are most kind, sir, but indeed I assure you that I am not 'run ragged.' Nor do I mind helping out a bit beyond my duties. Lord Stewkesbury is a fair, generous employer, and during this emergency I am more than happy to do my part."

"Of course you would be." He smiled. "But come, could I not persuade you to take a turn about the garden with me?

It is a bit crisp but still a fair day. It would help to put some color in your cheeks."

"That sounds delightful."

Eve got her bonnet and a light pelisse, and they went out into the garden. It was, as he had said, a fair day, with the sun shining to counteract the nip of autumn in the air.

"Thank you for suggesting this," Eve said, smiling. "It is exactly what I needed."

"I hate to see you troubled." Willingham gazed down at her gravely. "There is something else that bothers you, is there not? It is not simply the work you have been doing."

Eve glanced at him, a little surprised by his perspicacity. She would not have considered Colonel Willingham a particularly intuitive or sensitive man. He had been kind to her but in a rather uncomfortable, masculine way. She realized now, somewhat abashed, that he must have more depth to him than his strict military manner showed.

She thought of the letter she had received the day before and the worries that had plagued her since, thoughts that she was afraid to share with anyone else. But Colonel Willingham had known Bruce; he was aware of the kind of man her husband had been. He would know better than anyone that Bruce could not be guilty of the things he had been accused of in the letter. He would be able to consider the matter judiciously and help her decide what to do.

Impulsively she said, "Yes, I have received letters . . . about Bruce."

"About the major?" His eyebrows went up. "What do you mean? From friends of his?"

"No. Quite the opposite. If you will wait here just a moment, I will get them for you to read."

"Of course." He looked puzzled but nodded in agreement.

Eve flew up to her room and retrieved the letters from

their hiding spot, then hurried back to the garden. The colonel was pacing back and forth among the bare rosebushes, and he turned at the sound of her approach.

"Let us go farther along the walk, where we can sit and you can read the letters." She gestured ahead of them, and they strolled along until they came to the long arbor, where they sat down on a secluded bench and Eve handed him the three letters she had received.

He read through them carefully, in order, and when he had finished he folded them and sat for a moment, staring off to the side. "Poor Bruce," he murmured at last, and heaved a sigh. Turning, he offered her a sad smile. "Poor Eve. I had hoped you would never find out."

Eve felt as if she had been punched in the stomach. "Wh-what? What are you saying? You think it is true?"

"Your husband was a good man," he told her earnestly. "I am sure he would never have set out to do anything dishonest. But he was not wise with his money."

"Yes, I know, but—"

"He had gambling debts. I had heard rumors that they were very high. And some said, well, that he had taken to some shady activities to get the money to pay them. Even robbery."

Eve stared at him, unable to speak. She could not believe what she was hearing. "Do you know this for a fact? Or was it only rumors? Did he admit to you that he had stolen that watch?"

"Bruce did not tell me that. He would have been too ashamed, I'm sure. But I have heard the stories from people I trust. I am sure you must have noticed the change in him before his death."

Eve thought back, trying to remember. It did seem that Bruce had been quieter, even sad, the last day or two before he died. But she was not sure if she actually remembered that or if she was simply responding to the colonel's suggestion.

"You think he killed himself?" she asked in a choked voice.

"I do not know. I think those of us who loved him must remember him as he was. You must not think of those last days or what Bruce might have done. If he stole, he was not himself."

Eve stared down at her hands, knotted in her lap. She could not bring herself to look at the colonel. She was, she realized, furious at the colonel for not trusting Bruce, for believing that he could have violated his honor by stealing. It was illogical, she knew. Obviously there must have been many rumors, and they must have been very convincing for the colonel to accept them.

"Perhaps this watch was something he stole," Willingham suggested.

"But it says 'For my beloved wife.'" Eve's voice was barely above a whisper. "I . . . thought he was going to give it to me on my birthday."

"Dear Eve." The colonel leaned forward, taking her hand comfortingly between his. "Do not grieve. I hate to see you unhappy. Let me help you. I will take this watch and get rid of it for you—toss it in the river."

"No!" Eve cringed at the thought. "I cannot. I cannot believe that he stole it."

"But it could have been engraved for some other wife," Willingham pointed out gently. "Did it say your name?"

Eve shook her head. "No, but—"

"I don't know how Bruce would have had the money to buy you so expensive a present, especially given his straitened circumstances," the colonel went on. "Please, my dear, do not fret yourself. Would you not feel better if I took the object away? That seems to be what this person wants."

"But I don't want to give him what he wants!" Eve's temper flared. "What kind of person would threaten me this way? He wants to blacken Bruce's name and ruin my life. I cannot buckle under surely. It would be an insult to my husband's memory."

"But you cannot want this to come out," the colonel said, and Eve thought she heard the slightest crackle of irritation in his voice. "What if he tells the earl? Or spreads this rumor through the *ton*? It could ruin you. I do not want to see that happen."

"Neither do I," Eve agreed. "Perhaps you are right. It would be more practical to do as he says. But he would still have that threat to hold over me. There is no way I can stop anyone from spreading gossip. And how is he to know that I've gotten rid of the watch? Why would he want me to anyway? It makes no sense. He does not even ask me to give up the watch in the last letter."

"That is true." He was silent for a moment. "It is your decision, of course. Perhaps you ought to think about it a bit more. I am, of course, ready to help you in whatever way I can. Just send me word, and I shall do everything I can to help you."

"Thank you, Colonel." Eve gave him a weak smile. "I think that I shall stay here for a while, if you don't mind."

"Of course. You need to get your thoughts in order. I shall see myself out." Willingham bowed over her hand again and walked away.

Eve closed her eyes and leaned her head against the wooden latticework frame of the arbor. She suspected that the colonel was a bit miffed with her for not taking his advice. No doubt it was the sensible thing to do.

But she could not bring herself to believe what the letter said about Bruce. He could not have been a thief. He could not have been so dead to honor. And he would not have killed himself, leaving her alone to face possible scandal. Bruce had been a far better man than that, and it hurt, she realized, that his commanding officer believed him to be a thief and perhaps a suicide.

Tears leaked from the corners of her eyes and trickled down her cheeks. She ached for the pain that Bruce would feel if he knew that his good name was being trampled. She could not turn against him, too.

"What, crying, my dearest?" Fitz's voice sounded softly above her head, and his hand brushed her cheek, wiping away the trail of her tears.

"Oh!" Eve's eyes flew open, and she sat up, hastily dabbing at her cheeks. "I'm sorry. I did not know anyone was about."

"Only me. Don't worry." He sat down on the wooden bench beside Eve and looked into her face, frowning a little. "Why are you out here crying? Camellia has not taken a turn for the worse, has she?"

"No, oh no, nothing like that. Indeed I think Lily is right and she is improving."

"Lily and Neville? I may have come up with a way to help in that regard."

"Really?" Eve looked at him with interest. "How? What are you going to do?"

He shrugged. "I will tell you if it works. But right now the important thing is what is troubling you. Has someone hurt you?" His brows snapped together darkly. "If that idiot Gordon has said something to offend you, I'll have his hide."

"No." Eve chuckled and reached out to lay a pacifying hand on Fitz's arm. "Do not take poor Mr. Harrington to task. He is much chastened today and has not given me the least insult, I assure you. Indeed, he even offered to read to Monsieur Leveque this afternoon. Though," she added judiciously, "I am not sure that went as well as one would hope, as I heard Monsieur Leveque shouting, *'Imbecile!'*"

Fitz grinned at her words. "Gordy must have been in Leveque's room, then." He sobered and reached out to take her hand in his. "Tell me, if it is not my foolish cousin, what is it that has brought this unhappiness to you?"

Eve hesitated. She had told herself that she would not reveal the letters to Fitz. There had been, as she remembered, many reasons she had thought it would be a bad idea. But looking at Fitz now, she could not remember any of them. Of all the people in the world, she realized, she trusted Fitz the most.

"I got a letter the other day," she said finally, and the hard knot in her chest eased even as she said the words. She went on to explain the letters she had received, reaching into her pocket to pull out the three sheets and hand them to Fitz.

He read them through one by one, and as he read his expression grew darker. Eve braced herself for his denunciation of Bruce. Instead, when he finished, he crumpled the last letter in his hand, saying, "I'd like to get my hands on the neck of whatever scoundrel sent these!"

Eve relaxed, a faint smile touching her face. "I'm not sure that would be the best idea."

"Who the devil would try to upset you this way?" he went on. "Sabrina is spiteful, and it's clear she's jealous of your beauty, but I cannot imagine even her playing such a vicious trick. What purpose would it serve?"

"I don't know. I have no idea who it could be. I don't understand what he wants. He has not asked for money—not that I have any to give him. He didn't even ask for the watch, which is the most expensive thing I own. He suggested I destroy it."

"It makes little sense," he agreed, shaking his head as he ran his eyes over the last letter again.

"I keep wondering if it could be true. If Bruce really

could have done such a thing. He was foolish with his money; there were times when it drove me mad. But his honor meant more to him than life itself, I think. Could he have stolen? Could he have taken his own life?" Eve turned to look at him, aware suddenly of how much his answer meant to her.

"I never met your husband, so I don't know anything about him except that he had the great good sense to marry you." Fitz smiled and raised her hand to his lips. "But you loved him."

Eve nodded. "Yes, I did."

"I do not believe that you would love a weak or immoral man. So no, I don't think Bruce did these things."

"Oh, Fitz!" Eve felt as if the sun had suddenly risen inside her. She threw herself into his arms and kissed him.

His arms tightened automatically around her, and for a few minutes they were lost to the world. When at last their lips parted Eve settled herself against his chest, warm and contented.

"I am so glad you said that," she told him. "So very, very glad."

She could hear the low rumble of his laughter against her ear as it rose from his chest. "So am I, now. Did I pass a test?"

"No." Eve smiled. "It wasn't a test. But the instant you said it I realized how much I wanted you to believe as I did. To see that Bruce was not a thief or a scoundrel. Even his colonel believed the rumors."

"His colonel? Willingham? What does he have to do with it?"

"He paid us a visit. He guessed something was wrong, so I showed him the letters. That's why I had them in my pocket. He told me there had been rumors that Bruce had been stealing things to pay his gambling debts. Even rumors that he had killed himself, as that letter said."

Fitz snorted. "I knew there was a reason I didn't like that man." He tightened his embrace and pressed his lips against her hair. "Darling girl, I fear we are not being prudent."

"I know." Eve sighed. It had been so pleasant, so warm and comforting—and yes, just a little bit arousing—to cuddle with Fitz this way. She wished that she could kiss him again, that she could lie in his arms and listen to the steady thud of his heart beneath her head.

She could feel the heat stirring in her loins, the prickling and anticipation. That one night had not been enough, not nearly enough. It had not been even a week since they had made love, but it seemed like forever. Eve squeezed her legs together against the small throbbing ache that had started there and thought about the possibility of tiptoeing down the hall tonight. If she went to Fitz's room, she suspected he would not send her away. Did she have the nerve?

She forced herself to pull away and sit once again on the bench beside him. She brushed at her skirts and hair, doing her best to control her unruly thoughts as well.

Fitz turned to her, and there was a warmth in his eyes that told Eve that he had no more wanted to end their embrace than she had. "I have the devil of a time keeping my hands off you. I can hardly follow the conversation at the dinner table for thinking about you."

"Everyone is retiring earlier these days. Perhaps . . ."

He reached out and took her hand, twining his fingers through hers. "You tempt me." He was silent for a moment, his thumb rubbing the back of her hand. "But no, I swore not to put you in danger. That blasted Gordon would be sure to take it into his head to go downstairs for a brandy at exactly the worst moment. And he is annoyed enough with me to do me harm if the opportunity presents itself."

With a sigh he set her hand away from his and stood up. "The thing to do, I think, is to concern ourselves with your other problem."

"The letters." Eve nodded, suppressing her disappointment. "You are right. I have thought and thought about it, but I remain confused."

"Did Major Hawthorne have enemies?"

"I presume he did. When one commands soldiers, there are always those who disagree with you or resent you. Men he might have disciplined. Maybe other officers who were jealous of him or who felt they were unfairly passed over. But in general he was well liked, and though I have tried to think of someone who might have a grudge against him, I have been unable to come up with a name. Of course, if someone had threatened him, he probably would not have told me. He wouldn't have wanted to worry me."

Fitz nodded. "What about his death? I know this is painful for you, but was it possible that it wasn't an accident?"

"That he killed himself?" Eve asked.

"I was thinking more of whether someone might have done him harm."

"Oh." Eve's eyes widened. She thought for a moment, then shook her head. "No, I do not think so. He was with some friends. They said he lost his stirrup over a high fence and came out of the saddle. He fell, and his neck was broken. They checked the equipment, and there was nothing wrong. I don't see how someone could have staged that."

"So all we know is that he died accidentally, that he gave you this watch, and that someone is accusing him of having stolen it—for what purpose we don't know."

Eve nodded, then paused. "Actually he did not give me the watch. I found it afterward. I had never seen it before, but it was obviously a woman's watch. So I opened it, and I saw the inscription, 'For my beloved wife.' My birthday was only a few days after he died, and I assumed it was a birthday present for me." She frowned. "I don't really know that it was meant for me. But what else could it have been?"

"I don't know. No doubt it was a present for you. But what if the major didn't buy it? What if someone lost it to him in a card game and now he wants it back? Or he sold it to the major and regretted it later."

"I suppose that could be." Eve frowned. "But he could have come to me and explained, offered to buy it back from me."

"Unless he hadn't the money to do so." He grimaced and dropped back onto the bench beside her. "But if he was so desperate to have it, why wouldn't he have tried to steal it right there and then? There are bound to have been a number of people in and out of your house at that time."

"Oh yes, so many people called on me and offered help. Someone could have slipped away and searched for it, I suppose. And some of the men were even in the bedroom at times, getting his uniform and such. But it wasn't where it was easily seen, you know."

"So perhaps they did try to find it but couldn't."

"Then I moved back to my father's house. But whoever it is could have written letters like these to me earlier. Why did he wait until now?"

"I'm not sure."

"And if he wants to recover the watch, why didn't he say so in the last letter? Why did he tell me to get rid of it, even to destroy it? It's almost as if he doesn't care whether he gets the watch, so long as I don't have it. That is why I first thought of Sabrina—because it seemed so spiteful."

"I think there's something more here than just spite. What if it's not that this person wants the watch back, but he just doesn't want it seen? You'll be going to London for the Season with Lily and Camellia. Maybe he figured no one would ever see the watch if you were at your father's house in the country, but in London someone might recognize it."

"So if this person wasn't supposed to have sold it or gambled it away, he would be found out if someone saw me wearing it."

Fitz nodded. "Or maybe it really was stolen, and the real owner might see it."

Eve looked at Fitz in dismay. "But I thought you didn't believe that Bruce—"

"No, I didn't mean that Major Hawthorne stole it. What if someone sold him a stolen watch? Or used stolen jewelry as collateral for a gambling debt?"

"But I would be the one wearing it. Why would this other person be in any danger?"

"He may not know that the major did not tell you how he obtained the watch. For all he knows you may know exactly who sold it to him or gave it to him. But he hopes to frighten you and intimidate you. And perhaps to deflect suspicion from himself. If there are already rumors floating around that Major Hawthorne was a thief, then who will believe you if you tell them that he bought the thing from someone else?"

Eve nodded. "It makes an awful kind of sense. No doubt he started the rumors after Bruce's death. That's why Colonel Willingham thought the letter was true—though I cannot quite forgive him for believing that of Bruce. But how does this man know that I am about to return to London?"

"Word travels fast through the *ton*. I am sure that Vivian has written her friends and mentioned it. As has your stepmother, no doubt. Or Sabrina. There were a number of people here for the wedding, and I am sure that they heard you would be chaperoning the girls. They mention it to their friends when they get back . . ."

"Yes, you are right. Any number of people could have learned of it." She hesitated for a moment, then said, "Do you think it is possible that the man who sneaked into the house, the one who frightened the maid, could have—"

"Been looking for your watch?" Fitz finished. His eyes narrowed in speculation. "I don't know. Perhaps. At the time I just thought—"

Eve looked at him curiously. "Thought what? Did you suspect someone?"

"No one I know, really." He sighed. "But I thought it might be Camellia's and Lily's stepfather."

Eve's eyebrows rose. "I didn't know they had a stepfather."

"Mm. A rum touch, from all accounts. Jenny's description sounded much like the way the girls described their stepfather, and he had tried to do them mischief before. And Lily and Cam looked at each other in a significant way."

"Yes, I saw that too, but when I asked them they said they had no idea who it was."

"He is an embarrassment to them. Not the sort you want turning up when you're making your debut. I assumed he had tried to get into the wedding to try to wheedle money out of Stewkesbury and that later he came back to get some from Lily and Camellia. I sent men to look through the village for him; I intended to pack him off with a bit of money and a warning. But he was nowhere to be found. So I thought perhaps Oliver had already taken care of him. But now I wonder . . . maybe it wasn't him at all."

"But if it *was* the man who's been sending me these letters, we are still no closer to him. I mean, your men did not find any stranger in the village, did they?"

"No, but he may have left by then and decided to do the rest of it by the Royal Mail. But there is one thing we have on our side. I don't think he will be content with hoping you throw away the watch. He will have to know for certain.

And that means that he is going to contact you again and eventually, one way or another, try to get his hands on that watch."

"You think he will try again to steal it?"

"Perhaps. Just in case, from now on I'll make sure the servants are on the alert. But I wouldn't be surprised if he writes a letter telling you to take it somewhere or mail it somewhere. And if he does that . . ." Fitz grinned wickedly. "We'll catch him."

Chapter 17

During the days that followed Eve was too busy most of the time to think about the threatening letters or who might be responsible for them. Though her eyes were still sensitive to light, Camellia's health steadily improved. Unfortunately she was a poor patient, too accustomed to activity to take easily to staying in bed yet too weak and feverish to get up. Therefore a good deal of Eve's time was spent sitting by the girl's bedside, trying to keep her quiet and entertained. Lily relieved her now and then, but Lily was too used to Camellia's doing as she pleased to exercise much authority over her sister, so Eve tried not to leave Camellia under Lily's care for too long.

When Eve was not with Camellia she looked in on Mrs. Merriwether, who was not progressing as rapidly. What with taking over much of the ailing housekeeper's duties and trying also to keep apprised of the health and care of the sick servants, Eve had little time to spare.

It was a constant source of worry to her that she did not have enough time to chaperone Lily adequately. Lily spent two or three hours each day reading or chatting with her sick sister, and she had taken up the chore of dusting to ease the burden on the staff—a kindness on the girl's part that Eve

refrained from mentioning to the ailing housekeeper for fear
the news would send Mrs. Merriwether into a severe decline.
Lily also dropped in on Monsieur Leveque occasionally.

The rest of the time, however, Eve had no idea where Lily
was—or with whom. As Fitz was out most of each day, trying to help his tenants and stand in for the estate manager,
the only chaperone for Lily and Neville was Gordon, and
Eve had little hope that Gordon was adequate to that task.
Though Gordon had, somewhat to Eve's surprise, followed
through on his promise to Fitz to help out, especially with
Monsieur Leveque, he was not the sort to interest himself
in anyone else's life. He spent most of his free time in the
library writing poetry or in his room, presumably brooding
in a poetical way.

That left Lily and Neville on their own most of the time.
Indeed even when Lily was visiting Monsieur Leveque, Eve
suspected that she did so with Mr. Carr by her side. Eve did
not fear, really, that Carr would try to seduce Lily, but she
did fear quite strongly that Lily would wind up deeply in
love with a man bound to marry another.

These fears were reinforced one morning when Eve came
into Camellia's room and found her and Lily engaged in a
low-voiced but fierce argument. Eve heard only a few words
of their conversation, but one phrase leaped out and struck
her with cold clarity: ". . . marry Neville."

Camellia was flushed, her eyes too bright, and she was
sitting up, looking poised to jump out of bed. Eve moved
first to defuse the situation, suggesting to Lily that she run
and fetch her bonnet and pelisse.

"I thought we might take a stroll in the gardens," she told
the girl with a smile. "Camellia should probably rest anyway.
How are you feeling, dear?" She turned back to Camellia.

"I'm fine." Camellia's jaw jutted out stubbornly. "I don't
need to sleep."

"I am sure you are getting quite tired of it really," Eve replied sympathetically. "But you know, rest helps heal one, and I know you want to get back to your full strength as soon as you can."

"That's certainly true." Camellia glanced involuntarily toward the door through which her sister had left.

Eve laid a gentle hand on her arm. "Don't worry, Cam. I will keep an eye on Lily."

Camellia glanced at her, her face a study in frustration. Eve knew that Cam could not bring herself to tattle on her sister, and Eve had no intention of trying to worm any information out of her. On the other hand, Cam was clearly worried.

"She's always so full of romantic notions," Cam muttered.

"I know. But you needn't worry. Fitz and I are here to watch over her. You concern yourself with restoring your strength."

Camellia sighed. "And getting rid of these blasted spots. I look like a leopard."

"They're very beautiful animals," Eve pointed out.

Camellia had to grin a little. "I think I'd prefer to remain the way I've always looked." She frowned, looking unaccustomedly vulnerable for an instant. "You don't think—I mean, the spots won't stay, will they? I mean, I won't be—"

"Scarred? No, I shouldn't think so. You've been quite good about not scratching. The lotion has helped, hasn't it?"

Eve stayed for a few minutes, chatting cheerfully with Camellia, and the girl soon relaxed and agreed that perhaps she could sleep for a little while. Eve slipped out of the room and, grabbing her own bonnet and pelisse, went in search of Lily. She found the girl in the conservatory, staring moodily out one of the many windows. Lily turned and cast a searching glance at Eve's face before pivoting back to pick up her bonnet and gloves from the small stand beside her.

There was a distinct nip in the air outside, and Eve was glad for the warmth of her pelisse. Before too much longer, she thought, they might need woolen cloaks for a walk through the gardens. They were silent for a time as they strolled along the winding paths. Eve searched for a way to bring up the topic that concerned her. Finally she could think of no diplomatic way to say what needed to be said, so she decided simply to plunge right in.

"Lily, are you and Mr. Carr making plans?"

"She told you, didn't she?" Lily turned to look at Eve, her eyes flashing.

"Cam? No, you know she would never betray you. But it was clear that she was upset, and I heard a few words that you said. I have to know, Lily, has Mr. Carr asked you to marry him?"

"Yes!" Lily raised her chin defiantly. "And I accepted. He loves me, and I love him."

"But Lily, you know that he is promised to another."

"He didn't propose to her. It is only a plan cooked up by his father and her mother. Neville never wanted to marry her. But he agreed to, believing that he would not fall in love. It's not fair that he should be stuck with marrying someone he's never even proposed to."

"But there was an understanding between them."

"Neville says that she doesn't want to marry any more than he does."

"That may be; I don't know. But I do know that it will be the talk of London if he does not follow through on what everyone knows has been intended for years."

"Oh, I know there will be something of a scandal," Lily admitted airily. "But it will eventually blow over. Neville says as soon as the next scandal comes along everyone will stop talking about it. Besides, I don't care a fig for what the *ton* thinks. I don't know any of these people, and they don't know me. Why should I care if they gossip about me? I won't hear it. I'll be with Neville. And if it's too bad, he says we will go to the Continent to live for a while."

Lily's carefree answers nearly took Eve's breath away. How was she to combat this breezy surety? "But what about Mr. Carr's father? He will not be pleased with Mr. Carr defying his wishes. Until his death he has the title, the estate; I fear he controls the purse strings."

"I am not used to being rich," Lily reminded Eve solemnly. "Neville's father will come around, and in any case he says he has a small bequest from his grandmother. We shall not starve."

"Lily, think!" Eve's voice came out more sharply than she had intended, and she could see Lily's jaw set more stubbornly, reminding Eve of Camellia a few minutes earlier. She softened her tone. "Dearest, you are not of age. Stewkesbury is your guardian. Do you really think he will allow you to marry into scandal?"

"If we have to we will run away." Lily's pretty face was stormy now.

"Elope? Oh, no . . ."

Lily stopped, turning to face Eve. "Everyone acts as if that is the worst thing in the world. But it isn't! The worst thing is to live without love. My mother eloped, and she *never* regretted it. She and my father were happy; it didn't matter that they didn't have titles or wealth or any of that. They had each other. As Neville and I will."

"Perhaps you don't care about the scandal. But surely you must care about Camellia."

"She's being silly. I cannot imagine why she's so against it. Usually Cam's the bravest of us all."

"I am sure she is concerned that you may make a mistake that will haunt you the rest of your life. However, I am thinking not just of you but of Cam as well. You may take off to the Continent as you said and weather the storm with your husband, far from the wagging tongues. But Camellia will be left here to endure a Season marked by scandal. The scandal will damage all of your family—Mary and Sir Royce, Fitz, the earl. Most of all it will hurt Camellia. It would be bad enough for Carr to jilt Lady Priscilla. But if you were to elope . . . well, the tongues would not cease wagging."

"Camellia won't care about that. I told you she is the bravest of us all."

"And the one likeliest to fly to her sister's defense. Do you honestly think she will hear anyone speak ill of you or your actions and not take that person to task? She could ruin herself socially if she starts pulling caps with one of the patronesses of Almack's. And you know that Cam would never pause to consider the damage to herself; she is too loyal."

Lily's surety faltered. "But . . . there would be no need. I will tell her not to do so."

In answer Eve merely quirked an eyebrow. Lily looked away. Eve pressed her advantage, moving closer to the young girl and putting her hand on Lily's arm.

"I know you have no wish to harm your sister or any of the others. Please promise me you will not elope. Wait and talk to the earl when he comes home."

Lily's eyes grew wider. "Stewkesbury! Oh no, I cannot talk to him. He—well, I do not think he is unkind, but he scares me a little."

"Mr. Carr will go with you when you speak to him. I am sure he would not leave you to face the earl alone."

Lily looked a little comforted at that prospect, but still she hesitated. "I don't know . . ."

Eve made her last stand. She hated to use her own problems to sway Lily, but she felt desperate. She could not allow

Lily to run full tilt toward such disaster. Even if Lily was right and her parents' life had been far happier for eloping, Eve was well aware of the fact that Miles and Flora Bascombe had fled to the United States and raised their family far from any of the gossip that ensued. It had been the family members they left behind who had weathered the gossip. But there was little likelihood that Neville would flee his title and the world he had always known. Lily would spend the rest of her life as the woman who had stolen Priscilla Symington's fiancé. Even as Lady Carr people would cut her, and there would always be whispers about her. It would hurt her, and because Eve knew Lily's kind heart as well as her impulsiveness, she knew it would hurt Lily, too, that she had caused damage to her family.

"Lily, please wait," Eve entreated. "What am I to do if you leave? Camellia is still sick. Mrs. Merriwether is not improving quickly. I have so much work, yet how am I to get anything accomplished if I must worry about your running off?" She stopped there, unable to bring herself to point out that Lily's elopement would be the sure end of Eve's job as chaperone to Camellia. She would have failed in the most important task she had been given.

To her relief Lily nodded. "I will not leave while everyone is still sick. I wouldn't desert Camellia or you that way. I promise."

"Thank you." Eve breathed a little easier. At least now she had some time to try to figure out how to thwart Lily's and Neville's plans.

Eve spent the rest of her day going through her usual tasks, waiting for the evening. Since the measles had struck the household they had stopped gathering in the drawing room after their shortened evening meal. Lily went upstairs to sit with Camellia until she fell asleep. Fitz would drink a glass of port with Neville and Gordon, then go to his brother's study while the other two men stopped by Leveque's room before retiring. Eve usually dropped in to see all those who were ailing, then spent a few minutes in consultation with the butler. She had become accustomed to ending the evening visiting with Fitz in the study.

It was not, she supposed, an entirely wise thing to do, for being alone with Fitz only seemed to fuel her desire to be with him even more, yet she could not bring herself to stop. She looked forward to this visit all day long. A few minutes with Fitz picked up her spirits, and only his presence could fill the lonely spot within her. It frightened her a little that Fitz had become so necessary to her life. She hated to think about the future that would stretch out in front of her when he was no longer there.

Tonight, however, she looked forward to their time together for more practical reasons than the simple pleasure of being with him. She needed his help with Lily. It went against the grain to reveal the girl's secrets to her cousin, and if Lily found out Eve was afraid that Lily would never forgive her. But Eve had no real authority over Lily and no influence with Neville, as Fitz did. Besides, she was coming to learn that Fitz was a good man to have around in a crisis.

When she went into the study she found Fitz reading at the desk, his jacket tossed over a nearby chair along with his cravat, and the buttons of his waistcoat undone. A short, rounded glass containing an inch of brandy sat before him. Fitz's elbows were braced on the desk, and his fingers were plunged into his hair as he read the account book before him.

At the sound of the door snicking shut, he raised his head, his hands falling away, and a delighted smile crossed his face. "Eve."

She smiled back, her heart warming in her chest at the

sight of him. His hair was adorably mussed, giving his modeled face a boyish look, but there was nothing boyish about his long, lean body as he rose from his chair and started toward her. He exuded masculine power and grace. The top tie of his shirt was undone, so that the sides fell open a few inches down, revealing a V of his chest, and Eve's eyes were drawn to that patch of skin. She remembered how it had felt beneath her fingers and her mouth. How warm and slightly salty his flesh had been, how firm the muscle that lay beneath it.

Resolutely she pulled her mind away. "Hello, Fitz."

He wrapped his arms around her, pressing her against his chest, and for a few brief moments she luxuriated in the warmth and comfort of his embrace.

"I've been wanting to do this all day," he murmured. "I saw you walking back from the garden this afternoon, and you looked tired and worried. It was all I could do not to go out there and put my arms around you."

"I would have liked that." Eve nestled closer, linking her arms around his waist.

"What troubled you? Can I help?" He kissed the top of her head, and they turned, walking toward the chairs that sat before the fireplace.

"I hope you can. I talked to Lily today. The situation is worse than I thought."

"What do you mean? What has happened?" They had reached the chairs, and he released her, turning to look at her with a sharpened gaze.

"Mr. Carr has asked her to marry him."

"What?" Fitz's voice boomed out, and he went taut, his arms stiff at his sides. "Neville proposed to her?"

"That is what Lily told me. She said they are prepared to weather the scandal."

"Oliver will never allow it."

"I do not think that will stop them."

His eyebrows vaulted upward. "They plan to run to Gretna Green?"

"Lily is willing to. I cannot speak for Carr. But she says that her mother and father did so and were very happy."

Fitz let out a snort. "Oh yes, starving to death in America. Raising four girls on a shoestring and then having to marry a scoundrel to support them. I am sure that my aunt would wish that life for her daughter."

"Lily is a complete romantic, as I assume her mother must have been. And there is a certain headstrong quality in the Bascombe sisters."

"You mean they are all willful and hardheaded." He set his jaw, his eyes dark with anger. "But it is not her I blame. She is only eighteen. She's never even experienced a Season. Bloody hell, I never thought Neville would be such a blackguard."

He pivoted and began to pace up and down the room. "I'll call him out. No, I'll toss him out of the house on his ear. But first I'll give him the thrashing he deserves."

"I doubt those solutions will benefit Lily's reputation," Eve pointed out drily. "Besides, it won't stop her from running away with him."

"I'll lock the girl in her room if I have to," he threatened, scowling.

Eve raised her hand to her mouth to cover a giggle.

"Are you laughing?"

"I'm sorry. You sound like the overbearing father in a bad play."

Fitz glared at her, but then the corner of his mouth twitched, and he relaxed, letting out a noise that was part groan, part laugh. "So I do." He collapsed into a chair and leaned his head back with a sigh. "I didn't realize Neville was this far gone. I understand—he never thought he would fall in love, and now he finds he can't live without her. Damn. I hate to be the one to condemn him to his lonely fate." He looked at Eve. "He does love her, I think."

Eve nodded. "And I fear she loves him. I don't think it would be a bad match if it weren't for the problem of his engagement. Lily would not be happy married to a staid, respectable sort. Mr. Carr will always provide her with excitement."

"He will that. But, completely aside from the scandal, how would they live? His father will not stand for him throwing over Priscilla, not after all this time. And Lady Symington—" He gave an expressive shudder. "No, if Neville marries Lily, it will be a dreadful scandal. Lord Carr will cut him off. Oliver will be furious—though, of course, he would never allow them to starve. But Camellia's debut will be completely shadowed by it. Everyone will bring up the old scandal with Aunt Flora's running off."

"I am so sorry." Tears started in Eve's eyes. "I fear I have failed Lily and . . . and all of you. I should have watched her more closely."

"No. No, dearest Eve . . ." He leaned forward and took her hand. "Do not think that. All of us, including Oliver, knew what a difficult task it would be to chaperone the girls. Especially now that they are without Mary's and Rose's steadying influence. And with this crisis upon us no one could expect you to oversee her every minute of the day. Indeed if anyone is at fault—besides the two of them, of course—it is I. You warned me what might happen. I should have made Neville leave the instant you told me. Clearly I put my trust in the wrong person."

Eve squeezed his hand. "I fear your brother may not be so kind."

"He will ring a peal over my head, I'll tell you that." Fitz released her hand and settled back in his seat. "But I am not ready to concede defeat just yet. Surely they are not planning to escape tonight."

"No. Lily promised that she would do nothing while the household is still so disrupted. She said she would stay and help. Measles don't run their course for two weeks, so with the ones who came down with it later, I should think we have at least another week."

He smiled, his eyes lighting mischievously. "Then there is still time for my plan to work."

"You have a plan?" Eve brightened.

He shrugged. "I set one in motion a few days ago. Now, whether it will work out, I don't know."

"What is it? What did you do?"

He grinned. "I cannot say. You will see it as it plays out."

"Don't be so mysterious! Tell me."

Fitz chuckled at her expression. "No, it will be better if you don't know. Your reaction will be much more natural."

"Oh! You are so aggravating." But Eve felt the cold knot of worry within her chest ease. Perhaps everything would turn out all right after all. It was much easier to feel that way when she was around Fitz.

"So I have been told." He stood up. "Would you like a drink? Sherry perhaps?"

Without waiting for an answer he went to the liquor cabinet and poured a glass of the golden liquid. Desultorily they talked about their day as they sipped their drinks. She told him about Camellia and her progress, as well as the housekeeper's slower healing. He described a dispute he had to settle between two of his brother's tenants over a cow that had gotten into his neighbor's field.

"You look tired," Fitz told her. "You work too hard."

"Not so hard." Eve smiled faintly. "I spent most of my day sitting beside Camellia's bed, reading or talking."

"Mm. And the rest of it scurrying about trying to take care of all the rest of the problems in the house. I wish I could take your problems from you."

"I would be very happy to relinquish them, I assure you," Eve retorted. "Unfortunately I think they are squarely in my hands."

He set aside his glass and stood up. Coming around behind her, he put his hands on her shoulders and began to rub them, his thumbs and fingers working at the knots in her muscles. Eve let out a sigh of pure pleasure as the tightness eased. He moved to her neck, then returned to her shoulders and upper back.

"Here, stand up," he said, and she obeyed.

He continued his work down her spine. Eve felt herself loosening, the muscles easing. The worries that had plagued her drifted away, along with her weariness. Her very bones seemed to melt, and she sagged, leaning back into the strength of his hands. Heat flickered within her and grew, warming her loins and traveling along her veins. A pulse began to throb deep within her, and her breasts felt full, the nipples hardening. Her breasts ached for the touch of his hands on them; she longed to have him cup the heavy orbs as he had before, to feel his thumbs stroke her nipples.

"Oh, Fitz . . ." She let her head fall back against his chest as he slid his arms around her from behind, circling her waist.

He nuzzled the crook of her neck, his lips bringing her skin to tingling life. He murmured her name as his mouth traveled over the side of her neck, nibbling at the taut cords. His hands slid up to cup her breasts, and Eve let out a little shivering sigh at the touch she had hungered for. The ache grew between her legs, pulsing and eager. She wanted him to take her, to pull her to the floor and cover her with his hard male body. She longed to feel him inside her, filling her, and she imagined wrapping her legs around his back, holding him closer.

Footsteps sounded on the back stairs, loud in the still house. Fitz released her and spun away, moving like a shot to the door. He fumbled at the lock but did not find the key, and, letting out a low curse, he put his hand on the knob and stood still, listening. After a moment he opened the door and stuck his head out, looking up and down the hall.

He turned back, closing the door after him. "Someone's gone to the kitchen, I think." He faced her, back against the door. "I was a fool. I don't even know where the bloody key is."

Fitz strode across the room and took his jacket off the back of the chair, pulling it on. Eve watched him, unsatisfied passion still thrumming through her.

"I have the key to my door," she said boldly.

Light flared in his eyes, but he shook his head. "No. Please don't tempt me. I swore I would not do anything to bring you harm. There are too many people in the house, too much going back and forth. I am certain that Cousin Gordon pops downstairs in the middle of the night to raid my brother's supply of port."

Eve smiled faintly at his words. "I know. You are right. It is just . . ."

"Soon," he told her, crossing the room and taking her by the shoulders. She looked up into his face as he repeated, "Soon this will all be over, and our blasted guests will be gone. And you and I . . ." He did not finish his sentence but bent and kissed her, hard and fast, then stepped back. "You'd better go now."

Fitz went to the door and opened it, once again checking the hall, then stood aside with a nod. Eve went lightly through the door and down the hallway, not looking back.

* * *

Camellia seemed much improved the next day. Her fever was gone now, her forehead cool to the touch, yet conversely she seemed much more aware of her own tiredness and less inclined to fuss about sleeping. Eve was able to leave her and slip away to write a few letters that she had been putting off for days, including a note to Vivian to inquire after her health and that of the others at Halstead House. She looked around for Lily, hoping to persuade the girl to sit with her and chat while she penned the letters, but she could not find her. Eve suspected that Lily was with Neville, probably in the garden. She could waste the entire afternoon searching the gardens without finding them, and she wasn't sure it would do any good anyway. So she settled down at the desk in the drawing room to tackle her correspondence.

She looked up at a noise outside and was startled to see a large, old-fashioned carriage rolling up the long driveway toward the house. It was not a carriage she had ever seen before, certainly not Lord Humphrey's nor the smart equipage Lord Stewkesbury had taken to London. But whoever it might be, she realized, she must stop them before they dismounted and entered the house, lest they be exposed to the measles.

She jumped to her feet and started out of the room. Before she reached the front door Fitz came hurrying down the hallway to intercept her.

"No, no," he said in a low but carrying voice.

"But there's someone co—"

He held up his forefinger to his lips in a hushing gesture and seized her wrist with his other hand. Carefully he peered out the long, narrow window beside the door and stepped back, a grin spreading over his face.

"I knew it!" he exclaimed softly, and he pivoted, pulling Eve down the corridor after him.

"Fitz! What are you doing? Do you know who that is?"

"Our salvation, I hope." He turned the corner, walking swiftly toward the conservatory. "I believe that you and I are far too busy elsewhere to hear the knock at the door."

"You want someone to come in even though they'll be exposed to the measles?"

"I am without conscience, I know," he told her blithely. "Shall we sit?" He directed her to an uncomfortable wrought-iron bench beside a large fern and himself took up position at one of the long paned windows. "Ah, there are Neville and Lily coming along now. He appears a bit agitated." His grin grew.

He looked, Eve thought, like the cat that had gotten into the cream. She opened her mouth to question him, but at that moment she heard the sound of voices in the distance. Then a woman's stentorian tones echoed through the hallways. "Fitzhugh! Fitzhugh Talbot!"

A spasm of unease crossed Fitz's face. "Perhaps I went too far."

He turned around to face the doorway as footsteps sounded outside. Two women strode into the room, followed by Bostwick, literally wringing his hands. Eve stared at the visitors in surprise. From the sound of the voice she had been expecting a woman of large stature. Instead she saw a petite middle-aged woman. She had thick brown hair done up in an intricate style, with two dramatic streaks of pure white swooping back from her temples, and she was stylishly dressed, from the top of her bottle-green silk bonnet to the bottom of her kid half-boots. The expression on her face, however, matched the demanding voice, for it was set in deep lines of hauteur.

Trailing after her was a much younger woman of similar size. She was not unattractive, having rather large brown eyes and a trim figure, but she did little to aid her looks. Her eyes were obscured by glass spectacles, and her hair was in a simple bun at the nape of her neck. She kept her eyes on the floor as she walked, glancing up anxiously from time to time at the woman in front of her.

"What's the meaning of this?" the older woman snapped at Fitz. "Your fool butler tried to keep me out of the house. Since when have I not been welcome at Willowmere?"

Bostwick moaned, his hand wringing increasing. "No, no, my lady . . ."

"Mama . . ." The younger woman blushed, casting an agonized look at Fitz. "I am sure he did not mean that."

"The late earl must be turning over in his grave if hospitality at Willowmere has come to this." The girl's mother ignored her, continuing at full steam. "Reginald was ever a gentleman. I had always thought Oliver was too, but the young have no manners apparently."

Fitz strode forward, saying easily, "Please accept my apologies. Of course you are welcome here anytime. I am sure that what Bostwick was trying to tell you is that measles are rampant in the house and indeed throughout the area. I am sure that Bostwick was only concerned about your health."

The woman compressed her mouth, letting out a little "humph," as though she was not at all convinced of Fitz's explanation. At that moment the door from the terrace flew open, drawing her attention. Neville Carr rushed in, with Lily right on his heels.

"Fitz, I thought I saw—" Carr's gaze went past Fitz to the group at the door, and he stopped so abruptly that Lily bumped into his back. "Good Gad!"

"Neville. So nice to see you finally," the woman said with asperity.

Neville recovered enough to close his mouth and make a courteous bow. "Lady Symington. Priscilla. What a surprise."

Chapter 18

Neville's words confirmed the suspicion that had been grow-ing in Eve from the moment the two women entered the room. Lily, however, let out a little squeak of dismay.

"Yes, isn't it?" Fitz agreed blandly, and Neville shot him a suspicious look. Fitz turned to Lady Symington and her daughter, saying smoothly, "Mr. Carr you know, of course, but pray allow me to introduce you to my cousin Miss Lily Bascombe and Mrs. Hawthorne. Cousin Lily, Mrs. Haw-thorne, this is Lady Symington and her daughter Lady Pris-cilla."

Eve came forward to curtsey to the two women and was pleased to see that Lily, despite her shock, also made a credit-able curtsey and murmured a polite greeting. Lady Syming-ton favored them with a frosty nod, but her daughter smiled shyly and offered her hand in greeting.

"Pleased to meet you," Priscilla murmured. "I am so sorry to intrude upon you like this. Particularly with illness in the house."

"Nonsense, Priscilla. We have both had the measles," her mother told her. "We shall be fine." Clearly the problem their visit might cause for the residents of Willowmere did not concern her.

Priscilla quickly looked away, coloring—whether in embarrassment for herself or her mother Eve wasn't sure.

"Still," Neville said, joining them, "'tis quite a virulent episode of the disease, I believe."

Lady Symington favored him with a long look that could have frozen running water. "One can only catch it once, Neville, no matter how strong it is."

"Indeed, but many of the servants have fallen ill to it. The earl's household is much reduced. I think you'll find that the accommodations will be rather less than you are used to."

"Are you insulting the quality of my hospitality?" Fitz asked, eyes dancing with amusement.

"Of course not." Neville sent him a fulminating glance. "I am merely pointing out that Lady Priscilla and Lady Symington would find it much more to their taste and comfort to stay at the inn in the village."

"Yes, Mama, perhaps we should—" Priscilla began.

"An inn?" Lady Symington's chin lifted, and her tone suggested that Neville had suggested she stay in a pig sty. "I dare say Willowmere would outdo a village inn, even in the midst of an epidemic. Really, Neville, you must learn to curb your penchant for theatrics. Nor, Priscilla, is it necessary for you to agree to every madcap thing he says." She fixed her daughter with a basilisk glare. "You will be in for a very long marriage indeed if you begin that way."

Priscilla was now an unbecoming shade of red. "But I did not—" she started, then subsided, turning away and folding her hands tightly in front of her.

"I will see to it that rooms are made ready for you right away, my lady," Eve assured Lady Symington. She would have preferred to make the obnoxious woman cool her heels, but Eve felt too sorry for Lady Priscilla not to do whatever she could to ease the situation. "Bostwick?"

She cast a glance at the butler and another at Lily, both of whom followed her out of the room with every appearance of relief. She and Bostwick conferred quickly in the corridor. Then he headed for the kitchen and the servants' area while Eve and Lily hurried up the stairs to the bedrooms.

"That is Lady Priscilla?" Lily asked breathlessly as she trotted alongside Eve. "The one Neville is—is supposed to propose to?"

"Yes." Eve cast a look at the young girl. "I am terribly sorry, Lily. I know it must be upsetting, but—"

"I know. I—I'll have to face much worse than that, won't I?" Her young face was more doubtful than it had been the day before. "She, um, seemed quite nice."

"Yes, she did, though her mother is a tyrant." Eve led Lily into her bedroom and went to the wardrobe to pull out her bags.

"Yes indeed." Lily went through the drawers quickly, pulling out Eve's things and piling them on the bed while Eve packed. "But—what you said to Bostwick—do you really mean to give up your room to them?"

Eve nodded. "It's the only way that makes sense. It is already clean, and it's one of the nicest bedchambers. You said so yourself. Besides, it's next door to Mary's old room, which won't need more than a dusting and new sheets, either. So Priscilla and her mother can be side by side. They're the best rooms in the house aside from the earl's room, and of course we can't put either of them in there."

"But where will you go?" Lily asked. "It doesn't seem fair."

"I think it's probably best to move my things to the nursery."

"The nursery?"

"Yes. I don't believe Lady Symington would approve of the help sleeping in the family wing, do you? And I don't wish to be at the other end of the hall, for I think Mr. Carr and Mr. Harrington frequently gather at Monsieur Leveque's room rather late at night, don't they? No, I think the best and quietest place for me will be the nursery. Don't look so mutinous, dear. I don't mind, and it's only for a short time."

"Well, I don't like it. Why are they here anyway? I don't believe that they just happened to decide to come visit."

"I am sure not." Eve decided not to mention the blend of triumph and mischief on Fitz's face when the Symingtons arrived. "I suspect that Lady Symington pursued Mr. Carr here. I understand that she and Priscilla went to his estate, and that is why he fled here. No doubt she found out he had come to Willowmere, so they followed."

"It seems very brazen to me."

"I don't think that Lady Symington is exactly retiring."

"Poor Neville—imagine having her for a mother-in-law!"

"Yes. I should think that she will make it more difficult for him to go back on his proposal."

"He isn't!" Lily responded hotly. "I mean, he never actually proposed."

"You know what I mean. Lady Priscilla doesn't look the sort to make a fuss—she seemed rather beaten-down, poor thing, didn't you think?" Eve sneaked a glance at Lily as she went on, "But her mother will hold him fast to their agreement."

"She's a horrid woman. It's no wonder her poor daughter seems so . . . so . . ."

"Tyrannized?" Eve suggested, suppressing a stab of guilt as Lily's expression grew more troubled. "I imagine Lady Priscilla quite looks forward to marrying Mr. Carr, just to get out from under her mother's thumb. But of course that's no reason for him to marry her."

"No, of course not," Lily agreed faintly.

It did not take them long to pack Eve's belongings. They could hear the maids in the room next door, getting the room in order. While they waited for the footmen to move

Eve's things, Lily and Eve set to straightening up the room, dusting and changing the sheets, so that in a very short time both rooms were ready for their new visitors.

Lily went to Camellia's room to relate the arrival of the Symingtons, and Eve made her way to the nursery wing. It was not on a separate floor, as in many large houses, but was located in one of the additions that had been built onto the main house over the years, giving Willowmere its pleasant, almost haphazard appearance.

Halfway down the bedroom corridor, opposite the bank of windows, was a short hallway to the left. At the end of it was a closed door that opened onto the landing of a staircase. If Eve were to turn right and go down the flight of stairs, she would find herself at the huge kitchen. Instead she crossed the landing and went up six steps to the nursery wing. Built over the kitchen and serving area, it was rarely used.

Eve stopped at the first door. It was the governess's bed-chamber, and like the children's rooms that stretched down the hall, it was both smaller and more sparsely furnished than Eve's former chamber. It did, however, have a comfortable-looking bed, a wardrobe, a washstand, a chest of drawers, and even a chair by the window overlooking a narrow swath of the gardens.

Eve's trunk and bags sat at the foot of the bed, and two maids were busy cleaning. The dust covers had been removed and folded away, and the maids were in the process of turning the mattress. It was clear that it would be some time before they were done, so Eve left them with a smile and a quick thanks and went down the stairs to the kitchen. Predictably Cook had been thrown into a fit of nerves by the sudden arrival of more guests.

"This'll never do for her ladyship!" she moaned to Eve. "That one's been here before, and she always complains—this is too cold, that's too dry. There's never been a meal she didn't send a dish back. And the menu we had planned will never do for her!"

"Lady Symington will simply have to adjust to the fact that our meals have been curtailed by this illness," Eve told her with more surety than she felt.

The cook shook her head dolefully. "She'll be telling everyone what a poor table his lordship keeps. I can't let Lord Stewkesbury be shamed."

"I am sure that Lord Stewkesbury is far too practical to be shamed by curtailing his menus during a time of crisis. Just add a few dishes if you feel it's necessary—a dessert or a soup. What does Lady Symington like?"

"Nothing."

Eve could not help but chuckle. Having met the lady in question, she suspected the cook was speaking nothing less than the truth. "Just try to do your best with the time and staff you have. Leave it to Mr. Talbot to charm her into better spirits." Eve had learned long ago that Fitz was a favorite with the staff.

The other woman smiled faintly. "If anyone can, it'd be Master Fitz. That one can talk the birds out of the trees, and that's the truth."

Eve left the cook in somewhat renewed spirits and sought out the butler. Bostwick had apparently accepted the visit as a test of his mettle and was polishing the best silver while snapping out orders left and right. Satisfied that he needed no shoring up, Eve went in search of Fitz. She found him in the study, leaning back in his brother's chair, contemplating the ceiling. At the sound of her entrance, he looked up and sprang to his feet.

"Eve. That is, Mrs. Hawthorne. Blast it, I shall have to be more careful. It's rumored that Lady S has eyes in the back of her head—and probably an extra set of ears as well."

"And yet I think you are responsible for her presence here."

Fitz held a finger up to his lips. "Don't let Neville hear you. He's already been in here, blasting my ears. He is certain that I arranged for Lady Symington to come here."

"Didn't you?" Eve asked with a smile. "Somehow I cannot help but connect this to that plan you spoke of yesterday."

Fitz's quick grin acknowledged her words. "It was Gordon who gave me the idea."

"Gordon?" Eve repeated in disbelief.

"Yes. When he arrived, I was so annoyed, for I knew that it would entirely ruin my hopes of being with you. But it set me thinking about all the damage an unexpected visitor could do to a romance."

"So you wrote Lady Symington telling her to come here?"

"I let it slip that Neville was visiting," he admitted, his eyes twinkling. "And I may have reminded her that she and her daughter are always welcome at Willowmere—though what Oliver will say if he returns and finds her still here I hate to think. However, I wasn't certain that she would take the bait and come. I did, after all, point out that we were under a siege of measles."

"Clearly that counted little with Lady Symington." Eve paused. "Do you think it will be enough?"

Fitz shrugged. "It was the best I could come up with on the spur of the moment. I suppose it could do the opposite and send our star-crossed lovers fleeing into the night."

"I don't think Lily will leave after she has promised me not to. She is appalled, of course, by Lady Symington."

"A not uncommon experience."

"But I could see that she felt sorry for Lady Priscilla. You were very clever to think of it. Before now Neville's fiancée was just a figure of the imagination to her. But Lily will find it much more difficult to do something that will hurt someone she actually knows. She is a tender-hearted girl."

"Neville detests it; I can tell you that. As soon as Lady

S and Priscilla went up to their rooms, he subjected me to a blistering commentary on my lack of honor, loyalty, and good sense. After spending a few minutes with Lady Symington, I am inclined to wonder about the lack of good sense myself."

"He knows that you sent for them?"

Fitz shook his head. "Fortunately he accused me of inviting them, which I was able to deny with good conscience, as I never specifically issued an invitation in my letter. He is still distrustful, but he cannot deny that Lady Symington or his father could have heard from one of the wedding guests that he was here."

"Will he change his mind, do you think, now that they are here?"

"As you said, it is harder to hurt someone you know— even harder when that person is right before you. He is fond enough of Priscilla, I think, and he knows Priscilla's mother will turn on her if he elopes, however blameless Priscilla will be." Fitz smiled wryly. "Of course the question now is whether Neville will give up his scheme before I am driven to throw Lady Symington out."

The evening meal had become much reduced since the measles had struck Willowmere, with few courses and less elaborate dishes, and the residents had taken to treating dinner less formally. They ate at an earlier time, and they wore less elegant clothes. Lady Symington, of course, came down to eat in diamonds and a silk evening gown.

She took one look around at the others assembled there, her quizzing glass raised for maximum effect. "Good heavens, Fitzhugh, what is this? You no longer dress for dinner?"

From her expression she might have asked him if he had stopped wearing clothes altogether.

"Yes, forgive me, Lady Symington, I should have told

you. It completely slipped my mind. But what with the illness and the shortage of servants we have adopted a more casual attire."

"That's all very well, but one must keep up one's standards. Otherwise what is to distinguish us from the barbarians? We might as well be Scots or Americans."

"I am American," Lily pointed out.

"Yes, well." The older woman cast an eloquent glance at Lily and turned back to Fitz. "I am sure if Stewkesbury were here he would be most horrified."

"Perhaps so," Fitz replied equably. "But as he is not, I am afraid we shall have to muddle along the way we are."

Priscilla cast a quick apologetic smile at the others. It was, Eve found, something the young woman would be forced to do many more times throughout the evening. Lady Symington, it seemed, had fault to find almost everywhere she looked. She corrected Gordon's posture and Lily's wielding of her dessert spoon. She found the table's centerpiece—the epergne Bostwick had been so ardently polishing—mundane and the dishes lacking in variety. There were too few of them as well, and she admitted she would have hoped for a better sauce for the meat. As Cook had predicted, she sent back two of the dishes she had taken onto her plate, one for being too cold and the other for not having enough salt.

Eve felt sorry for Priscilla, who grew more silent and miserable-looking by the moment. Eve could only imagine how humiliating this whole experience must be for the girl. Not only had Neville run away rather than propose to her, but her mother dragged her along as she chased Neville down with the intention of forcing him to propose. When they had arrived she had had to stand by and watch her mother wedge her way into a house where anyone with the least degree of sensitivity would have seen that visitors were merely another burden.

Clearly unable to stand up to her mother, Priscilla could only apologize for her and, Eve suspected, wish that she were anywhere but there. She wondered if Priscilla could see the feeling that had blossomed between Lily and Neville. It was quite plain to Eve, but perhaps that was only because she had witnessed it as it grew.

She watched Priscilla, trying to gauge her response when she looked at Neville or Lily. The surprising thing, Eve realized, was that Priscilla spent little time looking at Neville. At first Eve assumed that this was because of embarrassment, but as the meal ground on she began to wonder if this assessment was true. Priscilla looked at Neville when he spoke, often offered a faint smile at one of his witticisms, but she looked at Gordon when he spoke and at Fitz, too. Indeed she turned her gaze, with varying degrees of interest, on everyone at the table. And though Priscilla shot Neville an apologetic glance now and then, it was no more than she did to any of them when Lady Symington made an insulting remark.

It was a relief when the meal ended. Eve was happy that since the measles had struck they had given up the habit of socializing in the drawing room after dinner, so she and Lily were able to escape an evening of sitting with Lady Symington and her daughter.

With a polite nod and smile to the other women, Eve and Lily went up the stairs. Eve stopped first at Camellia's room. She was continuing to improve, and Eve soon left Lily to regale the patient with tales of their dinner while she made a last round of the ailing servants. Even Mrs. Merriwether was beginning to look better, having finally overcome her fever.

Humming a little, Eve proceeded to her own room. She undressed and washed, then spent some time choosing the prettiest of her nightgowns. She sat down to the nightly ritual of taking down her hair and brushing it out. Afterward, the pale gold hair lying like silk over her shoulders, she wrapped her dressing gown around her and picked up a book. Usually she went back downstairs to talk to Fitz in his study, but not tonight.

It did not surprise her when she heard footsteps on the short flight of steps up to the nursery area. A moment later Fitz appeared in her doorway, frowning.

"What the devil are you doing in here?"

"Good evening to you, too." Eve set aside her book and stood up.

"Why didn't you tell me you were planning to move into the nursery? No, never mind, I know the answer—you knew I would forbid it. Blast it, Eve, there was no need for you to give up your bedroom to Lady Symington and Priscilla."

"It made perfect sense," Eve pointed out, coming a few steps closer. "Lady Symington would expect one of the better rooms. She wouldn't have wanted to be put off down the hall with Monsieur Leveque. We could hardly place her in Lord Stewkesbury's bedchamber. She and Lady Priscilla would no doubt prefer rooms next to each other."

"I doubt Priscilla would prefer it."

Eve smiled faintly. "That may be. But I suspected that Lady Symington would insist."

"No doubt she would. But that didn't mean you had to move."

Eve shrugged. "My room is next to the empty bedchamber, and they are both very nice rooms."

"Then move Neville and Gordon out. Put the ladies in there. There's no reason for you to inconvenience yourself."

"It would look odd to house one's guests in lesser rooms while the hired help stays in one of the best bedchambers," Eve pointed out.

"You aren't hired help! I mean—" He stumbled to a stop and scowled blackly. "I don't like you putting yourself in a place like this." He cast a disparaging look around the small, spare room.

"It's not so bad." Eve sauntered past Fitz to the door. "And it's very out of the way. Or perhaps you didn't notice."

She closed the door softly and twisted the key in the lock, then turned back to face him, a slow, seductive smile curving her lips.

"Eve . . . what the devil are you about?"

"It occurred to me that the nursery was separated from the rest of the bedrooms. One has to go down a hall and through a door and up six steps. Indeed it's in an entirely different wing. One could almost say that it's secluded." As she spoke Eve's hands went to the tie of her dressing gown, slowly sliding the sash undone.

Fitz's eyes followed the movement of her fingers, the color rising in his cheeks as she released the sash and grasped the sides of the robe, slipping it back and off her shoulders. He watched as the material glided down her arms and she caught it in her hands, tossing it aside. His eyes moved slowly down her body, taking in the hint of curves beneath the thin material, the darker circle of her nipples.

"No." The word came out slowly, his voice a trifle hoarse. "We cannot. I told you—I swore—I refuse to expose you to the gossip of others. The house is too full."

"But that is the beauty of the nursery." Eve looked at him as she raised her hands to the top tie of her nightgown. "Who is to see us over here? Who is to know?" She could see the rise and fall of his chest, more rapid now. His eyes glittered, his hands clenched at his sides. She pulled the next tie undone. "We are all alone here, Fitz. And I am tired of waiting."

She opened the last tie, and the gown gaped, revealing a swath of skin down her front almost to her waist. The simple white cotton cut across the inner swell of her breasts, revealing and concealing, hinting at the delights that lay still hidden.

Fitz's face was stark with hunger, his skin stretched tight across his cheekbones, and he could not keep his eyes from feasting on the flesh her brazen gesture had revealed. "Good Gad, do you think I am not? I feel as though I have been waiting half my life!"

"Then make love to me," Eve said simply. "I don't care about the others. Where they are or who they are or what they think. I want you to make love to me. Here. Now."

With those words she stripped off her nightgown and dropped it to the floor. Fitz made an inarticulate noise deep in his throat and crossed the room to her in two quick strides, yanking off his jacket as he came. He pulled her into his arms and took her mouth in a long, deep kiss, days of unsatisfied passion surging into an almost desperate embrace. The slick satin of his waistcoat gently abraded Eve's nipples. It felt exotic and decadent to have her bare flesh against his clothed body, and it aroused her already smoldering desire.

Eve moved slightly, titillated by the smooth satin gliding over her breasts. He pulled her even more tightly to him, his hands sliding down her back and over the swell of her buttocks, fingertips pausing to dip into the dimples at the base of her spine. His mouth left hers to kiss her cheek, her ear, her throat, trailing like velvet fire down her neck. He kissed his way along her collarbone to the point of her shoulder and back, using lips and teeth and tongue. Eve's skin flamed to life wherever his mouth touched her. She was shaken by the need that poured through her.

She wanted to touch him, to feel his skin beneath her hands, to taste and explore him. Her hunger for him was an ache deep within her, a pulsing, insistent eagerness. Eve pulled away, her breath rasping in her throat, and she reached out to the buttons of his waistcoat. Her fingers trembled as she moved down the line of buttons; there was a driving force within her that wanted simply to rip at them, but she maintained enough control not to do that.

Fitz, too, was clearly eager to rid himself of the impediment of his clothing. He yanked at his neckcloth and flung it aside, then shrugged out of the waistcoat. It took him only a moment to unbutton the top few buttons of his shirt and finish the job by pulling it off over his head. Kicking off his shoes, he started on the buttons of his breeches, but Eve had begun to run her hands over the bared expanse of his chest, and his fingers faltered and fell still as she caressed his skin.

She leaned forward, pressing her mouth to the hard bone down the center of his chest, and Fitz shuddered and dug his hands into her hair. Eve kissed her way across his chest, teasing and tasting as he had done with her only moments earlier. Her hands caressed the firm muscles of his back and ran down the hard line of his spine, slipping around to his sides. She wanted to feel more; she wanted all of him.

Her hands slid down to the fastening of his breeches, unbuttoning them as her mouth continued to roam his chest. She shoved the breeches down, her hands curving over his buttocks, and the garment fell to his feet. His member prodded and pushed. She smiled a little at the feel of it, remembering how she had wanted that first night to wrap her hands around him and learn this most intimate part of him.

She did so now, one hand coming up to curve around him, amazed at the soft, satiny texture of the skin and the underlying hardness beneath it. Her fingertips stroked the delicate skin underneath, following the slight curve, and he jerked, sucking in his breath. But when she raised her head and looked at him he shook his head.

"No, don't stop," he murmured, his eyes dark with desire. "Don't stop."

She continued her gentle exploration, her fingers sliding

back between his legs. His breath came harder and faster, and his hands clenched in her hair. She stroked him, teasing his legs apart and running her fingertips down the insides of his thighs.

Fitz groaned her name and took her face between his hands, turning it up to kiss her. His mouth ravaged hers, claiming her with all the passion flooding his body. His arms went beneath her, lifting her up, and Eve moved with him gladly, wrapping her legs around his waist. She clung to him, her arms around his neck, as lost in him as he was in her.

Kicking his breeches aside, he carried her to the bed, and they tumbled down upon it, still kissing as if they could never have enough of each other. They rolled across the bed, kissing and caressing each other, heightening their pleasure almost to the breaking point, then building it again. He explored her with his mouth as she had done with him, sliding ever lower down her body, until at last she jolted in surprise when he parted her legs and slipped between them.

He looked up at her when she gasped, and he grinned. "No? Wouldn't you like to try?"

She looked at him, eyes rounded in amazement, but already the idea was humming through her, teasing and arousing her. "I am a vicar's daughter, you know."

He chuckled. "Haven't you ever heard that vicars' daughters are the best?" He stroked his finger down the soft, satiny fold, sending pleasure shooting through her. "They're so ready to learn."

He continued to move his finger teasingly over the slick, sensitive flesh, and she could not help but moan and move her legs restlessly against the bed. The ache inside her was gathering, knotting. "Please . . ." she murmured.

She felt his smile as he kissed the inside of her thigh. His mouth moved over her thighs, coming ever closer. She tensed, wanting, aching, afire with passion, yet uncertain as well. Then his lips were on her, his tongue working magic on the hard little bud between her legs, and she gasped, digging in her hands and heels, lifting herself into that pleasure.

Desire coiled and twisted inside her, building and building until she thought she could not bear it any more, and yet still she wanted more. It exploded in a storm of pleasure, sending waves of satisfaction coursing through her, and Eve went limp, suddenly boneless and replete.

But then Fitz was between her legs again, this time sliding into her, filling her, and she knew that her pleasure had not been complete until now, when she took him deep within her. To her astonishment, as he began to stroke in and out, his movements steady and powerful, she felt that knot of pleasure begin to grow in her again, pulsing and building. Surely, she thought, it could not happen again, but the pleasure took over, and she was no longer thinking, only feeling. Passion wound tighter and tighter inside her, and she wrapped her legs around Fitz, clinging to him, until at last the dizzying storm crashed through her again. He shuddered and cried out, and they held on tightly to each other through the tempest, coming to rest at last in blissful oblivion.

Chapter 19

Nothing, not even the sight of Lady Symington at the breakfast table the next morning, could dampen Eve's mood. Fortunately for her the imperious older woman had little interest in speaking to anyone other than Fitz. Since Eve was carefully avoiding even looking at Fitz, much less sitting close to him or talking to him, she was quite happy to be excluded from the conversation.

Instead she turned to Lady Priscilla and inquired whether her room was satisfactory. Priscilla smiled shyly and said, "Oh yes, it is a lovely room. But I learned that it is your bedchamber. You need not have moved for me. I'm sure another room would have done as well."

"Please, do not worry. It was no problem at all. I felt sure that Lady Symington and you would wish to be next to each other."

"Yes, of course," Priscilla agreed unenthusiastically. She waited as a footman poured a cup of tea for Eve, then said, "I am afraid that we have caused you extra trouble, arriving at such a time."

Eve smiled at the girl. "I fear we are doing little enough for you. It will likely be deadly dull around here the next few days."

"I would like to help you if I can," Priscilla went on earnestly.

"I am sure Mr. Talbot would not want one of his guests put to work."

"No, really, I should like to. I—I am not one who likes to sit about doing nothing, and I am not very good at polite conversation. When I am home I am always engaged in some activity or other. Please, you must allow me to help with the patients in some way. I could read to them if they are recuperating or watch them if they are still ill."

"I don't suppose you speak French?"

"Why, yes, I do." Priscilla brightened. "Is your cook French?"

"No. One of our patients is. But he hasn't the measles." Eve went on to explain about Monsieur Leveque's arrival at Willowmere and the broken leg that kept him languishing in a bed upstairs.

"But poor man," Priscilla said feelingly. "He must be dreadfully bored."

"I think that Mr. Carr checks in on him now and again. Miss Bascombe's sister Camellia used to drop by to talk to him, but since she has been confined to her bed I am afraid his days have been a trifle empty."

After breakfast Eve took Priscilla up to the Frenchman's room. Leveque, having just finished eating, was sitting in his bed, unenthusiastically leafing through a book, and he brightened a little at the sight of visitors. But when Priscilla shyly greeted him with *"Bonjour, Monsieur Leveque,"* he became positively transformed and began a lengthy spate of French. Unlike Neville and Fitz, however, Priscilla did not appear overwhelmed at the rush of foreign words, and when he finally paused, she replied in French, an action that had the Frenchman grinning broadly.

Eve left the room and set about her usual routine. Everything, she discovered, had grown easier. She was aware that no task today would have seemed hard given the happiness that was brimming inside her. But it was also true that her burdens were eased.

Camellia was feeling much better, as was Mrs. Merriwether. No one had come down sick for a week now, and she was beginning to feel that the end of their epidemic was in sight. And somewhat to her surprise, as the days passed Lady Priscilla proved to be a great help. It was not that Eve had thought the young woman was insincere in her offer, but she had assumed that Priscilla would soon grow tired of the tasks or would be forbidden them by her autocratic mother.

But Priscilla continued her visits with the balloonist. Eve heard them more than once in animated conversation as she walked down the hallway. Once when she looked into Monsieur Leveque's room to check on his welfare, she found not only Priscilla and Neville there but one of the footmen as well. The footman had upended a chair and was busy attaching a small platform with wheels to the legs of the chair, with Monsieur Leveque watching and issuing orders. When his English failed him Priscilla jumped in to translate.

"Ah, Madame Hawthorne," Leveque said, flashing a grin at Eve when he saw her in the doorway. "We are inventing, you see?"

"Yes I do. You are making a—a sort of Bath chair, I take it." Eve had seen them in Bath on occasion, though the three-wheeled conveyances there were much larger than this contraption and also possessed an umbrella-like roof to shelter the occupant from the weather.

"It's quite clever, isn't it?" Priscilla's eyes sparkled, and she looked almost pretty. "Monsieur Leveque drew the plans for it, and Neville was so kind as to help me search through the attic for one of the boys' old wagons to use for the wheels."

Eve wondered if it was Neville's company that had

brought this glow to Priscilla's face. The thought aroused Eve's pity a little, for she suspected that Neville's presence there had less to do with his liking to be around Priscilla than it did with the fact that anytime he was not with Priscilla, Lady Symington made it a point to be with him.

Since the Symingtons had arrived, in fact, Neville had taken on the look of a hunted animal. Wherever he went Lady Symington somehow managed to pop up. Eve was not sure exactly how she kept so well informed of his whereabouts. On more than one occasion Eve had run into Neville sneaking down the servants' staircase in the rear of the house or the one in her own nursery wing in an attempt to avoid the woman. He had taken to riding out with Fitz most afternoons, as it was one of the few activities in which Lady Symington would not pursue him.

Eve sternly suppressed her sympathy for the man, however, for Lady Symington's methods were effectively keeping Neville separated from Lily. These days Lily spent most of her time with Camellia, and on the few occasions when she was with Neville it was in the presence of the other young people.

Now that the Frenchman had the rolling chair, Leveque spent much of the day in the small sitting room upstairs rather than in his bedroom. Though it took Neville or Gordon to help him and his firmly splinted leg out of the bed and into the chair, after that it was easy enough for Priscilla or Lily to roll him down the hall to the sitting room. As Eve had noticed, Neville had taken to spending more time with Priscilla and Leveque, and Lily often joined them, even bringing Camellia with her as she grew stronger. Gordon, who was obviously terrified of Lady Symington, apparently realized that the one place that woman rarely appeared was wherever her daughter and Neville were together, so he too became a member of the group. As a result, within a few days after the Symingtons' arrival, the sitting room was a place of lively social discourse.

Eve often heard laughter erupting from the room as they talked or played games. When she looked in on them, she could not help but notice how much happier and more carefree Priscilla looked when her mother was not around. Lily too sparkled when she was talking or taking part in one of the games. But Eve saw that more and more frequently Lily tended to fall silent, her gaze going to Priscilla or to Neville, and then a shadow would fall over her face, the liveliness leaving it. Eve's heart ached for the girl. Lily was, Eve thought, truly in love with Neville, and it was breaking her heart to discover that love did not necessarily make everything right.

Eve felt a trifle guilty about her own happiness, given Lily's obvious misery. While Lily was crying over the course of her love, Eve was reveling in her own, spending each night wrapped in Fitz's arms. They might keep their distance during the day, pretending indifference, but each night was taken up with exploring all of the delights that love had to offer. They made love and fell asleep, tangled together and peaceful, only to wake and make love again, too eager and joyous in their passion to care about lack of sleep.

She did her best to hide her happiness, especially when she was around Lily. However, as the days went by Eve began to wonder if Lily would even notice Eve's demeanor. Lily spent more time alone. She had taken to walking in the gardens alone, usually when Neville had gone out riding over the estate with Fitz. One day Eve glanced out the windows that overlooked the herb garden to see Lily sitting by herself on the bench where Eve had once seen her with Neville. There was a look of dejection about the girl that made tears clog Eve's throat.

Throwing on a pelisse and a bonnet, Eve went down to the herb garden. Lily looked up as Eve approached, and she quickly swiped at her eyes, doing her best to muster up a smile.

"Hello, dear," Eve told her. "I saw you out here, and I thought, what a lovely time to sit in the sun. It's quite pleasant, isn't it?"

Lily nodded and swallowed hard. "He-hello." She looked at Eve, tears glittering in her eyes, then quickly away.

"Sweetheart . . ." Eve sat down beside her, taking the girl's hand. "I know you are troubled."

Lily shook her head, but she could not suppress her tears, and finally she had to reach into her pocket and pull out her handkerchief to wipe them away. "Oh, Eve—" she wailed in a small voice. "I don't know what to do. It's all such a wretched mess!"

"I know." Eve squeezed her hand. "It is. It's terribly unfair."

"I love Neville. I truly do!" Lily gazed at Eve earnestly. "I know you'll think I'm too young to know my mind, but I am certain that I love him. I'll never love anyone but him!"

"I know it feels that way."

"It *is* that way!" Lily's chin jutted out mutinously. "Just because I've never been in love before doesn't mean that I cannot recognize it."

"I don't question that you love Mr. Carr," Eve assured her. "I can see that you do. I can see that he loves you too."

"He does, doesn't he?" Lily's face shone for an instant but just as quickly collapsed into its former gloom. "But it doesn't matter. It doesn't change anything. Lady Symington is determined that he marry Priscilla, and it's clear that Lady Symington gets what she wants."

"I dare say she does most of the time."

"She *stalks* him." Lily scowled. "He cannot go anywhere without her appearing. It drives him mad, and I have not seen him in days! I mean, not without everyone else around. It's just awful."

"I know."

"But worst of all—I like her!"

"Who? Lady Symington?" Eve asked, startled.

"No, of course not. I wish Lady Symington were at the devil—well, I do. I know it's not at all ladylike to say it, but it's the truth." She sighed, slumping back against the bench. "It's Lady Priscilla I like. I didn't want to. I tried very hard not to. But she's terribly kind. She even listens to Monsieur Leveque tell all those stories about his balloon trips, and she doesn't act as if she's bored, and I know she must be."

"Perhaps she finds the tales more interesting than you do."

Lily looked at Eve somewhat skeptically but went on, "And Priscilla can be quite funny and fun, at least when her mother isn't around. I feel sorry for her, having to live with that woman. Have you heard the way Lady Symington speaks to her? It's dreadful, and poor Priscilla daren't talk back to her. But I can see she hates it."

"I am sure she does. It is too bad that she has to live with Lady Symington."

"But she doesn't, does she?" Lily said sadly. "She could marry Neville and leave. I know it's not my fault that she has a horrid mother, but it *will* be my fault if Neville doesn't marry her."

"No, that would be Neville's fault," Eve felt compelled to point out.

"Yes, but he would marry her if it weren't for me. I know he slipped away when they tried to force him to propose, but eventually he would have. I want to marry him so much it just makes me want to—to explode. But then I think about what will happen to Priscilla. She will be left all alone in the midst of a terrible scandal. None of it will be her fault. It was different when she was just a name, but now I know her. It would be cruel to take Neville from her. I think how I would feel if someone stole him from me." Lily's gray-green eyes flashed at the thought. "I would be furious. And devastated. To lose someone like Neville—and on top of that to be the object of scorn because he jilted her, even though that wouldn't be her fault at all—well, it's just too awful to contemplate."

"Yes, and imagine what her mother would say to her about the matter."

"She would blame poor Priscilla for the whole thing. Priscilla would be stuck with that woman for the rest of her life! A man would have to be mad to marry her with Lady Symington for a mother-in-law."

"That would certainly be something to consider," Eve agreed.

"But whenever I think about giving him up I just can't bear it," Lily went on in a wail. "How can I live the rest of my life without him? Oh, I know you'll say there'll be someone else for me. That's what Camellia says, but she doesn't understand. She has never been in love. You have—you know what it's like to love someone and—" Lily stopped, looking abashed. "I'm sorry. I didn't mean to bring up sad memories."

Eve shook her head. "No, don't worry. It's fine. You're right. I did love my husband, and I lost him. I know about that pain. I certainly would not try to pretend that it did not hurt or that I was not lonely or bereft after Bruce died. I cried. I missed him. I was sadder than I care to remember. But your sister is right. After a time I did recover. You will too. It isn't easy, but sorrow does not last forever. And you can love again." She smiled, warmth spreading through her chest. "Believe me, you will feel love, maybe even more love than you ever thought you could feel."

She realized with a start that she had perhaps given away more than she should. Eve sneaked a glance at Lily, but the girl was not even looking at her, just staring at the ground, wrapped up in her own unhappiness.

"I know that you get to where you miss a person less," Lily admitted. "It was that way when our mother died. But it's different, isn't it? Neville won't be dead. He won't be gone forever. I'll see him sometimes surely, and even if I don't, I will know that he is still here, just not with me. I'll know that Neville's off in some house somewhere with Priscilla, living a life with her. Perhaps even coming to love her. I will hear about him, know about him. I just won't share anything with him anymore. And it seems too awful. I can't bear it!"

Great tears pooled in the girl's eyes and rolled down her cheeks.

"Lily, my dear." Eve wrapped her arms around the girl and laid her head against hers.

Eve wished that she could tell Lily to go ahead and seize her happiness with Neville. But she could not. It would be a tremendous scandal for all concerned. Even Lily, no matter how blasé she might feel about facing the *ton,* would learn how hard it would be in reality. And it would be irresponsible indeed to drag her whole family into the quagmire of scandal, especially with Camellia facing her first Season.

Eve sighed and patted Lily's back, murmuring, "It will get better, sweetheart. It will, I promise."

Eve stayed in the garden for a time after Lily hugged her and left. She had not had much time to herself just to sit and think. Perhaps it was better that way. It might not do to think too much about what she was doing with Fitz, or she might conclude that the wild, exciting, wonderful path she was roaring along with him was simply too dangerous, not only to her reputation but to her heart as well. What she had told Lily about falling in love again had simply flowed out of her unscripted, without thought, but she knew as soon as she said it that it was the truth. She was falling in love again, and it was more intense, more pleasurable than the first time.

The only problem was that she was falling in love with a man who had no intention of marrying her or spending his life with her. She had known it from the beginning, but that would not make it any easier if—no, *when*—it ended. The fact that she had gone into this affair with her eyes wide open meant only that she could not wail and moan and blame Fitz when it fell to pieces. She had known the consequences, and she had gone ahead, unheeding.

The sun fell lower in the sky, throwing the area where Eve sat into shadows, and she realized that it would soon be time for tea. It was just as well, she thought; she had little liking for the gloomy turn her thoughts had taken. Whatever the future might bring, surely it would be better to enjoy what she had now instead of thinking about what would be.

She had barely reached the terrace when she saw Fitz. He started toward her, his face grim. Her gaze dropped to the white square of paper in his hand, and she knew why he was seeking her out. He stopped before her, holding out the letter with its now familiar handwriting.

"This was on the hall table." Fitz took her arm as her fingers closed around the square of white, and he led her to a chair at the end of the terrace.

Eve opened the letter, amazed that her hands did not shake. She was not, she realized with some amazement, frightened—not with Fitz beside her. Quickly her eyes scanned the missive.

"Same sort of things—Bruce was a 'thief,' a 'disgrace'; the sender will create a dreadful scandal; 'what would Stewkesbury think of the wife of a thief and a suicide?'"

"He would think this bloody villain ought to be caught and punished," Fitz put in. "I can tell you that."

"But here, this is new. He offers to 'relieve' me of the problem of the watch. I am to take it 'to the summerhouse and leave it inside the door, tomorrow at one o'clock in the afternoon.' I am to tell no one."

"Ha!" A broad grin split Fitz's face, and he brought his hand down sharply on the table. "The slimy little scoundrel's outsmarted himself this time."

Eve smiled. "I take it you have a plan."

He leaned over, heedless of who was watching, and kissed her full on the mouth. "You'd best believe I do. Stupid of him, really, to put his scheme into play in my territory. But of course, if you had obeyed his orders and not told anyone it probably would have worked out. He can sit at a distance with a spyglass and keep watch to make sure you leave the watch and walk away. He can see that there is no one lurking around the summerhouse."

"But . . ."

"But what he cannot see is inside the summerhouse, at least not any farther than directly in front of the door. And I shall be waiting inside the summerhouse, at the back. I'll go there before dawn, long before he could be waiting and watching—and in the dark he wouldn't be able to see me anyway."

"By yourself?" Eve asked in alarm. "Fitz, no, I cannot like that!"

He smiled at her indulgently. "Do you think I cannot take care of one rogue?"

"What if that rogue has a partner? There could be two of them. Or more."

"Ah, but I will have a brace of pistols. But perhaps you are right. I could take Neville with me. After all, I don't want to put a bullet in him—I could be off a bit and shoot him straight through his heart. Then I wouldn't be able to question him. Better to take Neville. We can grab him and truss him up, even if there are two of them. I cannot think that there is a whole gang of men involved in this haphazard bit of extortion."

Eve had to admit that any more than two men was far-fetched; nor could she believe that Neville and Fitz would not be able to overcome the man or men, especially given Fitz's skill with a pistol. Still . . .

She frowned. "It seems awfully simple."

Fitz chuckled. "The best plans often are."

Eve still could not shake her worry when she left the house the next afternoon after lunch. Fitz had left her room early the night before, saying with a smile, "I should get a little sleep this night, don't you think?" Naturally, since he had left before dawn, she had not seen him all day. Neville too was absent, a fact that Lady Symington brought up at luncheon, with an accusatory glance around the table.

When the meal was over and Eve was able to escape, she was held up at the door to the terrace by Lily, who was worried about Neville's absence. Eve did her best to reassure her, pointing out that he and Fitz had doubtless gone hunting—which, actually, was not that far from the truth. But it was difficult to detach herself from Lily, for when Eve told the girl that she was going for a walk, Lily suggested that she join her.

"No!" Alarmed, Eve shook her head. She did not think that Lily would expose their plan, but she could not take the time to tell her the entire story now. She was already a little late; she would have to hurry along the garden path to make it.

Lily looked at her oddly. "Eve . . . is something the matter?" Her brows drew together. "Something is going on, isn't there? Fitz and Neville are in on it too."

Eve stared at her in dismay. "No, Lily, please. I have to leave." When the girl opened her mouth to protest, Eve quickly shook her head. "Really. I am late. I cannot tell you, and it will ruin everything if someone comes with me. Just trust me. Trust us. I shall tell you all about it later, I promise."

Lily set her chin stubbornly, but she said only, "You'd better. Oh, this is so maddening."

She turned and stalked away as Eve opened the door and slipped out onto the terrace. Eve ran lightly down the steps and took the quickest path through the garden to the summerhouse, walking as fast as she could. Her hand went to her waistband to touch the watch pinned there. It had seemed the easiest way to make it clear to her enemy that she was bringing the watch.

When she reached the summerhouse, she stopped and unpinned the watch, then stepped inside the door and laid it down on the floor a few feet inside. She carefully did not glance toward the corner of the room, where Neville and Fitz lounged on benches. She could see them out of the corner of her eye, but she was not sure she would have if she had not known to expect them. Fitz had been right; it was dark inside the summerhouse, shuttered as it was for the winter.

Eve stepped out and cast a glance around. Surely that was natural; the watcher would think it odd if she did not. Putting her head down she walked rapidly back toward the house.

As she had expected, Lily was waiting for her when she

returned to the house. Lily met her in the corridor and took Eve's hand to lead her into the study. When Eve stepped into the study she was surprised to see that Camellia sat in one of the chairs before the fireplace. Though all of Camellia's spots had gone and she had been up and about the last couple of days, she had not yet gotten fully dressed and gone downstairs.

"My dear." Eve smiled and went over to take Camellia's hand. "I am happy to see you up. I thought you were not ready yet to come downstairs."

"I'm feeling well, really," Camellia assured her. "I could have come downstairs before this."

"But I told her she would prefer taking her meals upstairs," Lily added.

"Ah, I see." Eve nodded her head wisely. "Today you did not want to cool your heels upstairs."

"Precisely."

Eve glanced around. "But why are we in the study?"

"We didn't want to stay upstairs with the others because we knew you wouldn't tell us anything with everyone around. And if we went into the drawing room or the music room we might run into Lady Symington. So . . ." Lily spread her hands out as if showing her the study.

"Of course."

"Now." Lily plopped down onto the low stool beside Camellia's chair. "Tell us all about it."

It was pointless to prevaricate, Eve knew. It was a wonder, really, that the sisters had not already guessed that there was intrigue afoot.

Eve told them about the letters; she could remember them almost word for word, she had looked at them so many times. The girls asked questions, most of which she could not answer, and leaped to the same conclusion she had, that the man who had broken into the house weeks earlier might very well be the same person who had written the letters.

"It's so odd," Camellia said, frowning. "Who could it have been? We thought—that is, well, Lily and I were worried that it might be—"

Lily, who sat in the chair across from Camellia, sat up straight, exclaiming, "Cosmo!"

"Yes, I mean, that's what I thought, but how could it be? Why would he—"

"No!" Lily shook her head, pointing toward the door, at which she was staring, transfixed. Eve and Camellia turned, following her gaze.

There in the doorway stood Fitz, his hand grasping the arm of a middle-aged man several inches shorter than he. The man was dressed in rough workman's clothes, and his hands were bound behind him. He wore a brown cap on his head, but his hair, sandy in color and mixed with gray, straggled out from beneath the cap.

"I mean, Cosmo," Lily went on. "There he is."

Chapter 20

Camellia's jaw dropped, but an instant later she sprang to her feet and charged toward the door, her fists clenched. "You! What are you doing here?"

"Now, don't go fussing at me, Cammy honey," the stranger whined.

"Don't you dare call me 'Cammy honey'!" Camellia drew back her arm, fist doubled up, her face set in furious lines. "I ought to knock you back where you came from!"

"An admirable sentiment, my dear cousin," Fitz said smoothly, releasing the man's arm and coming up to take Camellia's. "But it wouldn't be sporting to draw his cork right now. His hands are tied, you see."

Neville took Fitz's place at the man's side, closing the study door behind him. He steered their prisoner to a straight-backed chair and shoved him down into it. Then he turned and held out his other hand. In it lay Eve's blue enameled watch. He walked over to Eve and handed her the watch.

"Thank you." Eve smiled and tucked the watch into her pocket.

"My pleasure." Neville swept her a bow. "Though I must

say the chap didn't provide much sport. He threw up his hands as soon as Fitz pointed a pistol at him."

"He would," Camellia said sourly. "All he dares to hit are women."

"I never hit you, Ca—" The man wisely stopped at the look on Camellia's face.

"Only because you knew I'd take a knife to you if you did."

"Cam, sit down, do. You'll tire yourself." Lily slipped her arm around her sister's waist and led her back to her chair.

"I take it, then, that I am right," Fitz said to Lily and Camellia. "This chap is your stepfather. Cosmo Glass."

"Yes." Lily also cast a look of loathing at the man. "I hate to admit it, but it's true. Why is he here?" She turned toward her stepfather. "Why did you come here? Why would you steal Mrs. Hawthorne's watch?"

"I didn't do nothing wrong," Cosmo protested.

"We caught you picking up the watch," Fitz pointed out.

"I was just doing a job. They paid me to come over and pick up the watch. They said it'd be lying there in that little house, and it was. All I had to do was pick it up and take it back. Why would I want to steal that little thing?"

"Because you're a thief and a liar and you've never done an honest day's work?" Camellia shot back.

Cosmo's eyes narrowed, and for a moment his face was filled with hatred, but in the next instant the expression dropped away, and he said pathetically, "Now, Camellia, you oughtn't be saying such harsh things about me. I fed you and clothed you all those years—"

"I think it's best not to get into how you treated my cousins," Fitz said, breaking into the man's speech. "This is a lovely story about someone paying you to retrieve the watch, but I have to ask, did they pay you to break into this house as well? Were you paid to steal the watch then as well?"

"I didn't break in anywhere!"

"Is it really necessary for me to bring in the maid who saw you?" Fitz asked. "I think we all know it was you. Just as it was you who tried to break in here the evening of the wedding."

"Now hold on a minute, I wasn't breaking in anywhere!" Glass straightened indignantly. "I was just trying to see my daughter get married. My little Mary. I raised her from the time she was just a little thing, and they wouldn't let me see her on her happiest day. I was doing what any father would."

"Mary was fourteen when our mother made the mistake of marrying you," Lily retorted. "You never raised her or any of us. You just used her to run that tavern, and then you took the money."

"You came to the wedding party because you hoped you could get money out of Mary or the earl, that's why," Camellia added. "We all know that, so you might as well stop lying. Why are you after that watch?"

"I don't want it!"

"Why did you write those letters? Why did you threaten Mrs. Hawthorne?" Fitz strode closer to the man, looming over him, his blue eyes cold as ice.

"I didn't!" Cosmo shrank back in his chair as far as he could, hunching his shoulders against a blow.

"You know," Lily said thoughtfully, "I think he's telling the truth about that."

"What?" Fitz turned toward her.

"About writing those letters. Eve told us what they said. And I don't know, they sounded too smart for Cosmo." She glanced at her sister. "Don't you think?"

Somewhat reluctantly Camellia nodded. "She's right. I've seen notes Cosmo's written. He could never string together that many coherent sentences. Certainly not legible ones."

"There! You see?" Cosmo smiled triumphantly.

"Besides," Eve stuck in, "it makes no sense that he would linger around here just to steal that watch. Why would he even know about it? There are far more valuable things in this house to steal than that."

"Very well." Fitz smiled down at the man in a way that boded no good for him. "I am willing to believe that you are not the instigator of this plot, only the rather dim accomplice."

"Accomplice? I didn't do nothing wrong. I was just doing what I was paid to."

"The same could be said for a hired assassin," Fitz replied. "It scarcely means you're blameless. Tell me who these people are that you were supposedly working for. Why did they hire you to steal the watch?"

A crafty look came over the man's narrow face. "How much is it worth to you to know?"

"I beg your pardon. You're trying to bargain with me?"

"You can't expect me to turn over my employer, now, can you? I mean, I won't be getting what I was promised for this, and a man's got to make a living, right?"

Fitz looked at him for a long moment. "Your gall is astounding. The only thing we know for sure is that you tried to steal this watch, not once but twice, even breaking into this house to do so. These are serious offenses, Mr. Glass. Theft. Attempted burglary. Extortion. You could spend the rest of your life in a British gaol. Or perhaps you'd be transported to Australia. Does that appeal more? Of course it's likely that you would die in the hulks waiting to be transported."

"You're not going to turn me in," Cosmo replied confidently. "That'd be something of a scandal, wouldn't it, your cousins' stepfather getting tossed into jail? I know you highfalutin' types. You wouldn't want that."

"No, I wouldn't." Fitz leaned down, bracing his hands on the arms of the man's chair. "You're right. I doubt I would report you to the authorities. More likely I will lock you up in the cellars. There are secret ones below the ordinary ones, you know. Been here for hundreds of years. I could leave you there to starve. No one would ever hear you. Of course there are also all the tarns around here. Terribly deep. A man could easily be trussed up and tied to a stone and tossed into one of them. I don't think anyone would miss you, do you?"

Cosmo Glass's eyes were wide and round, and his skin had turned a chalky color. "I—I don't know her name."

"Whose name?" Fitz asked.

"Her?" Eve and the girls chorused in surprise.

"Aye. The lady that hired me. She—her—it was her maid most of the time. She'd come and tell me what to do and give me my payment. A sharp-tongued witch, that one, I'll tell you. But once, the first time, she took me to meet the lady. The lady said she'd seen me trying to get into the house to see Mary on her wedding day. She understood, she said, when I told her about how they'd turned me away, and me just wanting to see my little girl one last time. She told me where there was a shepherd's hut on their land, see, and I could stay there. She give me food and drink, and all I had to do was wait for her to tell me what to do. Then she'd send the maid, and she told me where to go and what to do. But she didn't pay me last time 'cause she said I hadn't got the watch. Well, how was I to know the place'd be so full of people when you lot had gone out riding?" Cosmo looked highly aggrieved.

"Never mind that," Fitz told him impatiently. "What about this lady? What did she look like? Where did she live?"

Eve suspected she already knew the answer, but she held

her breath anyway as Cosmo Glass continued, "A blond lady, like this one here." He pointed toward Eve. "Real pretty and full of fine airs, but her eyes are cold, and that's the truth. She lives in that other big house over there."

"Sabrina." The word came out of Eve on a sigh. "My God, it actually was Sabrina."

Half an hour later Eve and Fitz left for Halstead House. It had taken all of Fitz's powers of persuasion to persuade Lily and Camellia to stay behind, but eventually, with Neville's help, the sisters had agreed to go upstairs and carry on as if nothing had happened. Then Fitz had rung for Bostwick and instructed him to take a couple of footmen and lock Cosmo Glass in the cellars.

"Not with the wine," he had cautioned.

Bostwick, giving no indication that bound men needing to be put into Willowmere's cellars didn't turn up every day, had simply nodded and led Glass from the room.

"What are you going to do with him?" Eve asked Fitz later as they waited for the carriage to be brought around.

"I doubt I'll toss him into the tarn. Though it is a tempting thought. I shall leave it to Oliver, who will likely wind up putting the villain on a ship back to the United States. The man's right; no one wants him hanging about, telling people he's the Bascombes' stepfather—whether in gaol or out. But a few days in the cellar should keep him from deciding to return here. I may give him a demonstration of my marksmanship while he's down there."

"You aren't going to shoot an apple off his head, are you?"

"Good Lord, what a bloodthirsty wench you are! You have been around Camellia too long. No, I was thinking more along the lines of snuffing out a candle with a single shot. That's usually impressive."

They spent most of the drive over to Lord Humphrey's

estate in a fruitless discussion of the reasons behind Sabrina's hiring Cosmo Glass to steal the watch.

"I understand that she saw him the night of the wedding and seized on him as a handy tool, someone no one would know or connect to her," Eve mused. "But why would she want that watch? And why would she write the letters? How could she even know Bruce had it?"

Fitz shook his head. "I've no idea. I'm beginning to think she must be mad as a March hare. I disliked her because of what she did to Royce, of course, but I've always thought her cold and calculating in everything she did. Not insane. But this . . . well, we'll see what she says."

As it turned out, they would not. The butler was quick to show them into the drawing room, but he told them in a hushed tone that her ladyship was still suffering from her recent illness and could not leave her bed. He left them in the drawing room, and a few moments later Vivian swept into the room. She looked a trifle tired, but she smiled broadly and held out her hands to greet them.

"Eve! Fitz! I am so happy to see you. It's been an age." She sat down in the chair at right angles to the sofa where Eve and Fitz were seated. "It is so odd that we have had to communicate by notes when we are only minutes apart. I have so wanted to visit, but I have been a trifle busy." She made a droll expression. "I know you have been too. How is Camellia?"

"She is quite well, thank you. In fact, today she got dressed and came downstairs," Eve told her. "But the truth is, Vivian, it is Lady Sabrina we came to see."

Vivian's brows rose in surprise. "I *thought* old Chumwick said that, but I assumed he was confused."

"No, we really must speak to her."

"But she's still sick. She really has had quite a bout of it. She's still in bed and not up to seeing anyone."

"Really?" Fitz asked. "If she is so ill, how is she sending Eve threatening letters?"

Vivian stared at him. "I beg your pardon? Letters?"

"Yes. These." Fitz reached inside his jacket and pulled out the letters, handing them to Vivian.

Vivian glanced at Eve, puzzled, but took the letters and began to read. Her eyebrows soared expressively, and she glanced up from time to time as she read, but she finished reading all of them before she spoke.

"I don't understand." She looked from Fitz to Eve. "Why didn't you tell me?"

"I would have, but at first I dismissed it, and then everyone got sick, and I couldn't come see you. It was far too bizarre to put in a note."

"But why would anyone make such accusations? Why do you think it's Sabrina? I know she can be wicked, but what could be her reason for spreading these lies about Bruce? And why would she want your watch? Is it so special?"

"I cannot tell it if it is." Eve pulled the timepiece out of her pocket and held it out to Vivian.

"It's pretty, but . . ." Vivian glanced at Eve. "It doesn't seem Sabrina's style."

"It's old-fashioned," Eve agreed. "I cannot imagine why Sabrina would want it." She explained to her friend the circumstances under which she had found the watch after her husband's death.

Vivian turned the watch over thoughtfully, even opening it and reading the inscription inside. "It looks faintly familiar." She frowned, then shrugged. "I suppose I must have seen you wear it. But I still don't understand why you think Sabrina had something to do with these letters. She can be vicious enough to write them, I agree, but really, I don't think this is her handwriting. It looks more like a man's, does it not?"

"We think it's Sabrina because we sprang a trap on the fellow who came to pick up the watch today. But he was clearly a tool. He told us that Sabrina hired him to do it. He did not know her name, but he said it was a fair-haired pretty woman who lives in a large house, and I cannot imagine who else that might be."

"This is so incredible. I would have sworn that Sabrina was too ill to have been up to anything. She's still abed, and as far as I know she has not stirred from it. Nor has she allowed anyone in except me and her maid. She doesn't want anyone to see her with spots all over her face."

"The man we captured said that he dealt with her maid," Fitz pointed out. "She could have given the woman instructions, and the maid took them to him."

"The first letter actually came before anyone got sick. You can see that the lettering is different. Perhaps Sabrina wrote that and the others have been what she told someone to write."

There was the sound of footsteps in the hall, and a moment later Colonel Willingham appeared in the doorway. He smiled and advanced into the room.

"My dear Mrs. Hawthorne. Such a pleasant surprise. And Mr. Talbot." He sketched a bow to Eve and shook Fitz's hand before he took a seat.

Fitz's face turned decidedly less friendly, but he greeted the other man politely. It was Eve who did not return his greeting. She could not help but remember the fact that Colonel Willingham had been willing to believe the worst about Bruce, when both Vivian and Fitz had assumed that Bruce was innocent. No, she decided, not willing—he had actually confirmed what the letter said. A worm of suspicion twisted through her.

"I trust everything is well at Willowmere," the colonel went on politely.

"No," Eve responded, her voice so flat and cold that both Vivian and Fitz glanced at her in surprise. "I received another letter."

"What?" Willingham looked startled. "No, how awful for you. Would you like for me to look at it?"

"Do you need to?" Eve shot back.

Vivian's eyes widened, and Eve felt Fitz tense beside her.

"I'm sorry?" The colonel gazed at Eve with a faintly puzzled expression.

"The letter demanded the watch," Eve went on. "I gave it up, but Fitz captured the fellow who came to pick it up."

Colonel Willingham glanced at Fitz, then back at Eve. "Really? But that's excellent news, isn't it? So you've tossed the miscreant in gaol, I take it."

"No. Actually he's at Willowmere right now." Fitz stared straight at the colonel, his eyes like chips of ice. "He's already told us that Sabrina was behind the scheme. I imagine he'll tell us more before we release him."

"Sabrina?" Colonel Willingham look astounded. "Come, come, man, this chap must be selling you a bag of moonshine. Lady Sabrina has been sick in bed these last two weeks, hasn't she, Lady Vivian?"

"Why would the fellow lie?" Fitz countered. "How would he even know who she was?"

The colonel shrugged. "Who knows how criminals think? Perhaps he wanted to spread lies about Lady Sabrina just as he did about Major Hawthorne."

"If they were lies, why did you tell me that they were the truth?" Eve sprang to her feet. Her anger seemed to add inches to her height, and her eyes blazed down at her husband's superior officer. "You told me those things were true. You said that Bruce had been stealing."

"I said I had heard rumors." The colonel stood up too, holding out a placating hand to Eve.

"When I told Fitz, when I told Vivian just now, they did not believe it of Bruce, yet you, who were closer to him than either of them, who knew him better than almost anyone— you believed the lies! You repeated the lies to me! How could you have heard those rumors if Sabrina made them up?"

"What are you saying?" Willingham stared at her, aghast.

"The writing looks like a man's hand," Fitz put in quietly. He had risen too and moved a step closer to the colonel.

"You lied to me, didn't you?" Eve pressed. "You tried to make me believe that Bruce had stolen that watch. That he was a thief and a coward. That he took his own life! Why?"

"It was for your own good, Eve. I swear to you," the colonel burst out. "Please believe me. I hated lying to you; it was the hardest thing I've ever done. But I could not bear for you to learn the truth about Bruce."

"You lied to protect me?" Eve's tone was drenched with scorn. "Why? What was the truth? What was so terrible that it was better to pretend that my husband was a thief?"

Willingham sighed. He looked around, then turned back to Eve, his face grave. "My dear, it grieves me greatly to tell you that the watch that you believe your husband gave you actually belongs to Lady Sabrina. It was a present to her from her husband, Lord Humphrey. She bestowed it on her lover as a token of her affection for him. That lover was Major Hawthorne."

For an instant the room was utterly silent. Then Eve stepped forward, and her hand lashed out, slapping the colonel full across the cheek. "You liar!"

Willingham's face surged with color, and he drew back his hand. Fitz stepped quickly between him and Eve and planted his fist in the colonel's jaw. Willingham stumbled backward and went down with a crash. Fitz stood over him, fists clenched and raised.

Colonel Willingham shook his head. "No. I don't intend

to fight you. You were right to hit me." He stood up slowly and turned toward Eve. "I apologize, my dear. I would never have struck you, of course; it was simply an instinctive reaction to being called a liar. But I should not have even raised my hand. I know how hard it must be to find out about your husband. I am sure he loved you very much, but Lady Sabrina is a . . . very persuasive woman."

"I am sure she is. Obviously she persuaded *you* into a great deal. I know for a fact that you are lying. My husband had no affair with her or anyone. It was you, wasn't it? This whole story of the affair and the watch—it was you who had the affair with your good friend's wife! It was you to whom she gave the watch. That first note with the printing, that was probably Sabrina's doing, trying to disguise her hand. But she sent a message to you too, didn't she? Telling you that she had seen me wearing the watch she had given you. She probably even demanded to know how in the world I had wound up with it. Then you came pounding up here, ostensibly to drop by to see your old friend, but in reality to help her get the watch back. You must have written the other letters, and then you dropped by in the hopes that I would pour out my story to you and you could encourage me to believe that Bruce had stolen the watch. No doubt you were sure I would crumble and hand the watch over to you. So sure you did not even bother to disguise your handwriting."

The colonel stood, nostrils flaring, color rising, as Eve's accusations hit him, one right after the other. Finally he roared, "Yes! The devil take it, yes! I lost the watch to Bruce in a card game. I had run out of cash, and I used it as surety. I was going to redeem it the next day, but then Bruce died in that riding accident. I let the matter drop; I thought nothing would ever come of it. Then you turn up here, of all places, wearing it." He drew in a long breath and released it. His voice was calmer as he went on, "I am not proud of what I did, and I am most sorry for causing you any upset or hurt. But you must see that I could not let you continue to go about wearing that watch. If Humphrey had caught sight of it—"

"Why didn't you tell me?" Eve asked. "Why go to such extremes? Surely telling me the truth would cause less scandal than this."

"I wanted to. I told her there was no need for the letters. I believed you wouldn't betray us, but Sabrina was convinced that if you knew you would tell Lady Vivian, and Lady Vivian would be all too happy to have a weapon to use against her."

"If that isn't just like her!" Vivian snapped. "As if I would ever do anything that would hurt Uncle Humphrey!"

"What's this?" came a jovial voice from the doorway. "Do I hear my name being bandied about?"

They all turned, struck silent. Lord Humphrey stood in the doorway, smiling benignly at them. He came forward, gesturing at them to sit.

"Why are we all standing about? Sit, sit. It's so nice to have company. It has been far too long. Dreadful business, this illness. Poor Sabrina is still laid up with it." He shook Fitz's hand and came forward to take Eve's. He stopped, staring at the watch in her hand. "My goodness! What is this? You've found it?"

"Umm." Eve glanced frantically at Vivian, then at Fitz.

"What a stroke of luck," Lord Humphrey went on, beaming. He reached out his hand to the watch. "May I?" At Eve's silent nod, he took it from her palm and held it up to examine. "Oh yes, this is definitely Amabel's watch."

"That's why it looked familiar!" Vivian exclaimed. "Aunt Amabel used to wear it all the time!"

"Yes she did. She loved it." The old man smiled in reminiscence. "Unfortunately it was in among all the family jewels, and Sabrina lost it a few years ago. She was so upset; she will be quite glad to see that you have recovered it. Where did you find it?" Without waiting for a reply he went on happily, opening up the watch. "Yes, you see? There is the inscription I had put in it: 'For my beloved wife.' And inside there is a lock of hair too. In the secret compartment."

Much to Eve's astonishment, Humphrey slipped his thumbnail into a crack in the back of the watch, a crack so small that she had never even noticed it, and he prised up the smooth golden plate on which the inscription was written. A wisp of brown hair lay inside the secret compartment, but on top of it was a tiny square of paper, folded many times. When the false back sprang open, the square popped out, falling to the floor.

The colonel, who had been watching the old man intently, sprang forward, but Fitz blocked his way, and Eve reached down to scoop up the paper.

"Why, what is that?" Humphrey asked, looking puzzled. "There wasn't any paper in there."

"It's a letter," Eve said, smoothing out the paper and quickly running her eyes over the faded ink. "A letter written, I might add, in a very similar hand to the one on those letters you're holding, Vivian."

Lord Humphrey remained confused, but Fitz and Vivian both looked at Colonel Willingham.

"What does it say?" Humphrey asked. "Who put it in there?"

"I think perhaps my late husband put it there," Eve said quietly. "It appears to be a confession, written and signed by Colonel Willingham and dated two days before my husband's death."

"A confession! To what? Why is it in the watch?"

"Colonel Willingham states that he stole a large number of things over the years in order to finance his lifestyle, which was a good bit above his means," Eve said. "He also confesses to cheating at cards and embezzling funds from the army. Rather a lot of offenses, really."

"My God!" Lord Humphrey stared at his friend in shock. "Robert! Is this true?"

"Yes!" The colonel roared. "Yes! That damnable honor of Hawthorne's! I knew the man would be the end of me." He sank into the nearest chair, a perfect image of dejection. "He knew the watch wasn't mine; it's obviously a woman's. And he'd caught me cheating as well. He had already been suspicious about the other things—the disappearance of the regiment's funds, the way things seemed to go missing among my friends. He even guessed about my aff—" He stopped abruptly as Fitz's hand descended on his shoulder. He glanced up at him, then over at Lord Humphrey. His eyes dropped again.

"He kept the watch," the colonel went on. "He made me tell him to whom it belonged, and he intended to give it back. He promised he would not tell anyone as long as I resigned immediately from the army. He wanted to avoid disgracing the regiment. Of course that would be his primary concern. Not what would happen to his friend—how I would live or how I would explain things. He insisted I write out this confession and said he would use it against me if I did not voluntarily resign. He put it into the watch to keep until I'd turned in my papers."

"It must have been a great relief to you when Bruce died," Eve said coolly. "Or did you speed the process along?"

"Good Lord, no!" Willingham looked at her with shock. "I would never have killed the fool. Bruce killed himself with his typically mad riding. The man never met a wall he didn't think he could clear." He set his jaw, and his gaze turned a trifle defiant. "But yes, I was relieved when I heard it. I thought I had been saved. You never gave any indication that you knew anything. I could breathe easier. All I had to do was get the watch back. I searched everywhere I could whenever I came over to your house in those days after his death, but I couldn't find it. Finally I gave up. I hoped he had hidden it so carefully no one would ever find it. You went back to your parents, so I hoped the bloody watch would stay there, immured in the vicarage . . ."

"Then I came here, only minutes from Lord Humphrey's house," Eve put in.

"Yes, and I knew if Humphrey saw it I was a dead man."

Lord Humphrey was still standing, staring at his friend, his fingers curled around the beloved watch. "Is this true, Robert?" His voice sounded frail, suddenly years older than he was. His face was lined with the pain of betrayal. "Did you steal Amabel's watch?"

"No, damn it!" Willingham rose to his feet, his eyes flashing, and Eve drew in her breath, afraid that he was going to tell the old man the truth, that he had been conducting an affair with Lord Humphrey's new young wife. "I—"

He had barely gotten out the words, though, when Fitz moved forward, grasping Willingham's arm at the wrist and twisting it painfully up behind him. Fitz's voice was low, but Eve was close enough to hear him say, "Careful. If you want to keep out of prison . . ."

Willingham grimaced. "Yes. All right. Yes, I took the damned watch. I found it on the floor one time when I was visiting here. I knew Sabrina must have dropped it, and everyone would assume that it was lost."

"My God. I never knew you at all." Humphrey glanced around the room vaguely. "Amabel . . ."

"Uncle Humphrey." Vivian moved quickly over to her uncle, sliding her arm around the old man's waist. Eve caught the shimmer of tears in her eyes. "Why don't we go up to your room? I'm sure Chumwick would love to bring you a cup of nice hot tea. Perhaps with a little something in it?"

The old man turned with her, and, still talking soothingly, Vivian led him out the door and into the hall. The three people remaining in the room were silent until they heard the sound of footsteps on the stairs. Then Fitz let go of Willingham's arm and came around to face him.

"Here is what is going to happen," he told the colonel, his words hard and sharp as a blade. "I am going to keep this bit of paper. It is going into the safe at Willowmere, so don't think for an instant that you can recover it. If you don't do exactly what I tell you I will reveal this confession to the world. Am I understood?"

Grudgingly the colonel nodded. "Yes."

"Good. You will resign from the army and retire to the country, where you will not breathe a word of any of this to anyone. You will not write to or see Lady Sabrina again. Nor will you try to excuse or justify yourself to Lord Humphrey or in any way attempt to worm yourself back into his good graces. Nor will you utter a word against Major Hawthorne or Mrs. Hawthorne. Believe me, if I hear a breath of scandal regarding either of them, I will know from whence it comes, and I will act. Now, go upstairs and pack your bags. I want you out of this house before I leave this afternoon."

With a sour turn of his lips the colonel nodded and stood up, then strode out of the room. Eve stood for a moment looking after him. Then she turned to Fitz, her eyes gleaming with unshed tears.

"Thank you. Oh, Fitz, it's over."

He opened his arms, and with a little sob Eve rushed into them.

Chapter 21

Eve and Fitz waited until Vivian came back downstairs after turning her uncle over to the tender care of his valet.

"I think he will be all right, but this has been a terrible shock to him," Vivian said worriedly. "It doesn't surprise me that Sabrina has been carrying on affairs behind his back." She sighed. "But I rather liked Colonel Willingham." Her green eyes flashed. "The gall of that man, coolly sitting here, pretending to be Uncle Humphrey's friend, pretending to be your friend, when all the while—I'll tell you this, if he ever shows his face in the *ton* again, he'll regret it."

"He fooled all of us," Eve told her.

"*I* never liked him," Fitz pointed out.

Vivian chuckled and cast him an arch look. "Mm. I wonder why that was."

Hurriedly Eve went on, "I thought him most kind and considerate. All those times he came by to offer his support and help after Bruce died—all he wanted was an opportunity to search through Bruce's things."

"What's most absurd is that if they had not made such a to-do about the thing I doubt anyone would have noticed the watch," Vivian said. "I don't remember seeing you wear it."

"I rarely did. It was too heavy for most of my dresses, and it wasn't in style any longer. It was just my misfortune that I wore it when Sabrina first met me."

Vivian grimaced. "I'd like to go up there and pull that witch out of bed by her hair. It makes me furious that she won't get what she deserves out of all this. But I cannot let Uncle Humphrey find out. I think he knows he made a mistake in marrying her. You could see from the way he talked about that watch that he still grieves for Aunt Amabel. But Sabrina's betrayal would crush him nevertheless."

"It won't get out," Fitz assured her. "Willingham and Sabrina won't be foolish enough to trumpet it about, and the only other people who know are you and Eve and I. None of us will say anything."

"What about Camellia and Lily?" Eve asked. "They know that Sabrina was behind the letters. I'm sure they wouldn't gossip, but . . ."

"Still, probably not a story for young ears." Fitz looked thoughtful. "We can just tell them that Sabrina admitted to playing a spiteful trick on you. I don't think they'll have any trouble believing that."

"Particularly when Sabrina comes over to make you a pretty little apology, Eve." Vivian's eyes sparkled. "Believe me, I'll make sure she does."

A few minutes later Colonel Willingham came back downstairs, escorted by the aging butler Chumwick and one of the footmen. Willingham turned toward Eve as though to say something, but Fitz quickly stepped between them. Willingham shrugged and left the house. Fitz followed to watch the man get into the carriage Vivian had ordered brought around.

Later, when Fitz and Eve were riding back to Willowmere in their own carriage, Fitz told her, "I gave the coachman instructions to take him to Lancaster. I would have liked to have dropped him off on the road and let him make his own way, but I didn't want him anywhere close to you. I hated to let the fellow go after the way he frightened you. I would have liked to throw him in gaol." He sighed. "But I'm not sure how we would have proved it."

"We could not. Certainly not without involving Cam and Lily's stepfather. And Sabrina. The scandal would have been enormous. And poor Lord Humphrey . . ." Eve leaned her head against Fitz's shoulder. "It would not do to pursue him. I'm simply glad it's over. Thank you."

"For what?"

"For everything—believing me, believing in Bruce, doing all you did."

He chuckled and bent to kiss her forehead. "What else would I do? I hope you don't think I'm the sort to let you fight your battles on your own." He kissed her again, this time on the lips, lingering until Eve felt the familiar heat steal through her. Raising his head, he murmured, "I'll always be there for you."

He curled his arm around Eve's shoulders, and she snuggled closer. It felt so warm and secure in his arms. If only she could believe that his words were true, that he would always be there for her. This idyll would end; it had to. Fitz was not a marrying man. But she told herself firmly she would not think about that now. The end would come soon enough.

"Eve . . ." he began, then stopped. "No, this is not the time or place."

A shiver of apprehension ran through her. "No," she agreed. "Later . . . later will be time enough."

They had been gone so long they had missed tea and indeed barely had time to dress and make it to dinner. Lady Symington was in a bitter mood, having been forced by their absence to take tea with the youthful group on the second floor.

"I cannot think what you were about, Fitzhugh, allowing that Frenchman to take up residence here," she said at dinner.

"He had a broken leg," Fitz pointed out mildly. "I could hardly turn him out on the road."

"But one doesn't know anything about him," Lady Symington went on. "And the French are far too easy in their speech and manners."

"He's a very intelligent man," Priscilla surprised everyone by saying. She blushed at finding all eyes turned on her, but with a little gulp, she went on, "He has been all sorts of places and knows a great deal about . . ." Her mother's gimlet gaze was turned upon her, and she wavered. "About a number of things."

"What good is that, I ask you, when you have no idea who his parents are?" Lady Symington stated. Having taken care of that minor rebellion, she turned back to her original quarry. "I can't imagine where you go haring off to all the time, either, Fitzhugh. This is scarcely the way to entertain guests."

"It's rather easier to entertain guests when one knows they're coming," Neville pointed out, then shot a glance at his friend. "Of course perhaps some of us knew about it earlier than others."

"In the old earl's day Willowmere was always prepared to receive guests," Lady Symington replied in chilling tones.

And so the dinner conversation continued. Eve did her best simply to stay out of the line of fire, and even Camellia, eating downstairs for the first time since her illness, made no attempt to counter the older woman's attacks.

"I know I should have said something," Camellia told

Eve as they climbed the stairs to her room after the meal was over. "Lily is terrified of the woman. Lady Symington made everyone miserable during tea." She sighed. "But I was too tired to argue with her."

"Of course you were." Eve slipped her arm around Camellia's waist. "You are barely out of your sickbed. Don't worry. I'm sure there will be ample opportunities to argue with Lady Symington in the future."

Camellia smiled. "I'm sure there will be. I get the impression that she's settling down for a long stay."

"However long it takes to bring Mr. Carr in line, I imagine."

Camellia nodded. "Poor Lily. She's so unhappy. I saw her and Neville whispering in the hallway earlier. They looked so . . . desperate. I don't think I'll ever fall in love."

Eve glanced at her. "But Cam—"

She shook her head. "It seems an awful lot of trouble."

Eve smiled. "I suppose it is sometimes. But it can be quite wonderful too. Think of how happy your sister Mary was, marrying Sir Royce."

"Yes, but there was a lot of unhappiness before that. I wonder sometimes if it's really worth it."

Eve asked herself the same question sometime later as she sat in her room, brushing out her hair and waiting for Fitz to knock at her door. Was it really worth it? Was it enough to have these few stolen hours of happiness? She knew it could not last. The earl would return home soon. Their guests would leave. Life would return to normal at Willowmere. It would be impossible for Fitz to keep up his nightly visits to her room. They would see less and less of each other. Then at some point Fitz would decide to go back to the excitement of London. And that would be the end of it.

She laid down her brush and looked at her image in the

mirror. She could not lie to herself. She had fallen deeply, madly in love with Fitz. It hadn't been planned. When she had started all this she had intended to remain heart-whole, to experience the pleasure and delight without taking on the heartache that would follow. Eve had told herself that she knew what she was getting into. No longer a girl, she was mature enough to indulge in an affair. She could learn about passion, experience the joy that a man could bring a woman, without giving into any girlish tendency to cloak her desire in a pretense of love.

Yet here she was, in love with a determined bachelor, a man who chose widows for his affairs because they were less difficult to deal with. Fitz was a wonderful lover. He could be gentle; he could be wild with passion. He could make love slowly, taking his time and arousing her to the point of screaming, or he could drive into her with hunger and need. But never, even in the midst of their lovemaking, had he ever said that he loved her. Fitz was a man who enjoyed life. He had fun. He was not a man to be serious. She had known that from the beginning. It was sheer foolishness to expect anything else. Sheer foolishness to give her heart to him.

The doorknob turned silently, and the door opened. Fitz slipped inside. He had already taken off his jacket and waistcoat. He wore no neckcloth or collar, and the top three buttons of his shirt were unfastened. Eve smiled and rose to her feet. The worries of the moment before fell away. There was no room inside her for anything but the sweet anticipation of the night ahead. For the moment Fitz was hers, and she was his, and nothing else mattered.

He closed the door behind him and pulled her into his arms. "It feels so good to do this," he murmured, nuzzling into her hair. "Sometimes I think if I could just hold you I would not desire anything more." He raised his head and looked down at her with laughing eyes. "That illusion always passes."

They came together in a kiss, clinging to each other, not frantic with need, secure in the knowledge that they had all the time they wanted. Their lips were soft and gentle, the exploration sweet. He kissed her face, her ears, her throat, unbuttoning her dress as he did so. His hands slipped between the sides of the dress and pushed it back slowly, his fingers sliding over the tender skin of her chest. The dress drifted down her arms and fell to her feet. Eve stepped out of it, moving forward to unbutton his shirt. She gazed up into his face as she did so, and he gazed back at her, his eyes warm with hunger. When his shirt was undone, she placed her hands flat on his stomach and slid them upward. The heat in his eyes grew.

"Eve . . . you take my breath away," he murmured, bending closer. "I want—I mean . . . will—"

There was a thud outside, followed by a muffled oath and a frantic whisper. Fitz whirled and crossed the room, opening the door a crack to look out.

"Bloody hell!" He flung the door open and charged into the hallway.

Eve heard a girlish shriek and another male oath. She started out of the room after Fitz, then remembered that she was wearing only her chemise and petticoats. She grabbed her dressing gown, throwing it on and belting the sash before she dashed out into the hallway after Fitz.

By the time she reached him he had already charged down the half flight of stairs to the landing and stood facing Neville Carr and Lily. Lily wore a bonnet and cloak, and she was holding a lantern in one hand, turned down to its lowest glow. In the other hand she held a small bag. Another bag lay at Carr's feet as he stood facing Fitz, his arms loose and ready, his gaze watchful on Fitz's face. He too was dressed for the outdoors, a many-caped coat over his clothes. A hat lay atop the bag beside him.

"You lied to me!" Fitz's voice was cold with fury. "You swore that you would do nothing to harm Lily. Now you are eloping with her! Exposing her to the contempt and scorn of the world. The scandal will follow her the rest of her life."

"I will be with her. I'll shield her from it."

"You can make them admit her at Almack's? Keep some righteous old biddy from giving her the cut direct? Can you put back together a tattered reputation? You've seduced an innocent, damn it, and you cannot shrug that off."

"Who the hell are you to take me to task?" Neville shot back. "You think you are such a paragon? Look at you." His gaze swept from Fitz to Eve, pointedly taking in their state of dishabille—Fitz's shirt hanging open, Eve in her dressing gown, her hair loose around her shoulders. "Do you think you're fooling anyone? Do you think I haven't noticed you sneaking over here when everyone's in bed? How the devil can you preach at me when you're spending every night in your doxy's arms?"

Fitz lashed out, catching Neville on the chin with his fist. The other man stumbled backward and fell with a thud, knocking the bag aside and sending it tumbling end over end down the rest of the stairs. Lily let out a shriek and started toward Neville, but he was up and charging at Fitz in an instant. Punching and cursing, the two men went after each other, crashing onto the floor and rolling across the landing.

"No! Neville! Fitz! Stop!" Lily hovered helplessly at the edge of the fight, still holding the lantern.

Eve, more accustomed from her years as a military wife to the sight of men brawling, turned and ran back to her room. A moment later she returned, carrying with her the pitcher of water that stood by her washbasin. When she reached the men, she upended the pitcher, pouring its contents over the struggling men.

Spluttering, the two men separated, and both turned to glare at Eve. At that moment a loud voice exclaimed, "Wrestling on the ground like schoolboys! Well, I must say, it's no more than I would have expected of either of you."

All four occupants of the landing turned slowly toward the hallway leading back to the main wing of the house. In the midst of the excitement they had not noticed that a crowd had gathered just beyond the open doorway. Lady Symington stood in front, Priscilla on one side of her and Camellia on the other, Gordon lurking just behind them. All were clad in dressing gowns, obviously rousted from their beds by the commotion. Behind them was a smattering of maids and footmen. Another knot of servants stood at the foot of the steps below them, gazing up curiously.

Eve's heart sank. Everyone in the household was staring at them, and she knew what a scandalous sight they must present. Eve herself was dressed for bed, and Fitz was only half clothed. Lily and Carr were both obviously headed outdoors, coats on, lantern in hand, one bag lying on the landing and the other at the foot of the stairs. Even the slowest-witted would guess what had been happening with both couples before the fight.

"You're a disgrace to your families, both of you." Lady Symington was in full sail now. Her arms were crossed in front of her, one brow arched, her face set in lines of scorn. She turned her predatory gaze to Neville. "Well, Neville, what have you to say for yourself?"

"Um," Neville began eloquently, struggling to his feet.

Fitz stood up beside him. Neither of them looked impressive, their hair soaked and dripping, blood trickling from a cut on Neville's chin, and Fitz's thin lawn shirt plastered to his body.

"I beg your pardon, Lady Symington," Fitz told her, executing an elegant bow.

He looked ridiculous, Eve knew, yet one could not help but admire his form. Even the fierce Lady Symington could not quite suppress a softening at the corner of her mouth.

"I should hope so," she told him. "But it is not your apology that interests me at the moment. It is Mr. Carr's." She turned to him.

"Please accept my apologies, my lady." Carr obliged with a bow almost as perfect as Fitz's. "I am afraid Talbot and I got into a slight argument . . . over a game of cards."

"Cards. Of course. I can see that you are both dressed for it." Lady Symington flashed a look of disdain at the men. "But I was not speaking of your fisticuffs. Nor should your apology be aimed at me. It is Lady Priscilla whom you have grievously offended this night." She gave her daughter a sharp poke in the back, sending her stumbling forward a step.

"Mother! No!" Priscilla shot her mother an agonized glance. "Neville, I'm sorry. You needn't—"

"Of course he needs to. It's clear as day what is going on here. The man is fleeing with this little hussy."

Lily gasped, and Camellia cried, "Wait a minute! Who do you think—"

But Lady Symington plowed ahead, ignoring them. "It's an affront. An insult to Priscilla and to our entire family."

"Lady Symington, there's no need for accusations or recriminations," Fitz began smoothly, smiling in his winning way.

"This matter is between Mr. Carr and my daughter," Lady Symington told Fitz firmly. "He knows what he has to do." She swung back to Neville, pinning him with a basilisk stare. "Neville, you have kept Priscilla dangling for years now. You know what she expects. What everyone expects, including your father."

"I have no intention of dancing to his tune!" Neville burst out. "Or yours. Or anyone else's."

"Very dramatic. But I would hope that you retain some sense of honor. Of what is due your name. I would hope you would have some consideration for Priscilla."

"Mama! Please!"

"If you consider yourself a gentleman, you know that you have to honor your word. You must propose to Priscilla. Now."

"No!" To everyone's surprise, the word came from Priscilla. "Don't you dare propose to me, Neville. I don't want a proposal." She turned to face her mother. She was trembling from head to toe, but her eyes were clear, her chin set as she went on. "I won't marry Neville."

Everyone, even Lady Symington, was struck dumb. Priscilla pinkened a little under everyone's gaze, but she continued, "I'm sorry, Neville." She turned back to him with a tiny smile. "I have no ill will toward you. I like you; I always have. You were kind to me."

"But Priscilla . . ." He shook his head. "Why didn't you say so? Why didn't you tell me you didn't want to marry?"

"I was willing to marry you. I didn't love you, but I never dreamed I would find anyone to love. And you, well, you seemed liked the best solution." She sneaked a sideways glance at her mother that spoke more loudly than words to what she needed a solution to. "I liked you better than other men I knew. As I said, you were kind to me, and at least you weren't prosy like most of the ones my mother favored. And you seemed to care about it no more than I did. It was nothing to do with you really, but I just . . . well, the idea of marrying and settling down with you on your estate, raising children and growing old, seemed so . . . boring. I'm sorry."

Neville looked so thunderstruck it was all Eve could do to suppress a giggle. Priscilla's statements had apparently rendered him incapable of speech, but Priscilla's mother was no longer so impaired.

"Have you run mad?" Lady Symington's voice reverberated through the hallway. "What do you think will happen to you if you don't marry Neville? You won't get any other offers. You're a spinster, and now you'll have the stigma of this . . . this . . ."

"There'll be no stigma," Neville said quickly. "She refused me. A lady has a right to turn a man down, after all."

Lady Symington ignored him. Her eyes bored into her daughter's. "Priscilla, think, for once in your life. If you throw away this chance you won't get another one. What will you do?"

"She will marry me."

Lady Symington whirled around. There, perched in his movable chair, sat Barthelemy Leveque.

Eve sat down on the steps. She had thought she was at the limit of her surprise several moments ago when Priscilla stepped forward to defy her mother. But this announcement had proved her wrong. Fitz dropped onto the step beside her.

"Did you have any idea about this?" he whispered.

Eve shook her head. "None. I thought—well, that Camellia might—" She glanced toward that young girl, who was staring at Leveque with the same astonishment that was on every other face.

"Barthelemy!" Priscilla cried, running over to his chair and dropping to her knees beside it. "What are you doing here? How did you get into your chair by yourself?"

"It was difficult, but . . . how do you say it? Needs must. I could not leave you to fight the battle alone."

"Priscilla!" Lady Symington took a step toward her. "Get up from there. What do you think you're doing? Have you completely lost your senses?"

"No!" Priscilla rose and turned to face her mother, her hand slipping into Leveque's. "I've finally gained them. Or perhaps it's just that I've found my courage. I am going to marry Monsieur Leveque. We are going to travel about the world. I'm going to go up in balloons and help him with his research. And—oh, it's going to be the most exciting life imaginable!"

"Stop this nonsense this instant. You cannot marry this man. I will not allow it." Lady Symington's cheeks were stained red, her eyes stony.

"I don't need your permission, Mother. As you pointed out a moment ago I am long past the age of consent. I shall marry whom I choose."

"But—but he's a balloonist. And a *Frenchman.*" Lady Symington delivered the final blow. "We don't know his family."

"I know *him.*"

Lady Symington stared at her daughter in astonishment as Priscilla turned away, saying, "I'm sorry, Neville, but I thought you would not mind."

"Mind?" A broad grin broke across Carr's face. "My dear Priscilla, I'm delighted!" He laughed and turned around to pick Lily up and swing her around. She laughed too, flinging her arms around his neck and holding on as he twirled giddily. When he set her back down, he went immediately down on one knee, taking her hand in his. "Miss Bascombe, will you do me the honor of accepting my hand in marriage?"

Lily gazed down at him, starry-eyed. "Oh yes. You know I will."

Neville bounded to his feet and kissed her resoundingly before he turned to Fitz. "You'll give me your approval now, won't you?"

Fitz smiled and clapped him on the shoulder. "It sounds

excellent to me, but, you know, it's Oliver you'll have to convince, not I."

In the odd way of men, Eve thought, the two of them seemed to be the best of friends once again, despite having been rolling about on the floor, thrashing each other, a few minutes earlier.

After that everyone began to talk at once. Cam went to her sister to hug her, and Eve was not far behind. The servants chattered excitedly, and Lady Symington took up her case with her daughter once more. The noise rose until suddenly several sharp barks split the air behind them. Everyone turned, startled, to see an impeccably dressed gentleman standing behind them, a scruffy black-and-white dog at his feet.

"Since I was arriving at midnight I did not expect a warm welcome," the Earl of Stewkesbury said mildly. "But I did think there might be someone to answer the door."

"Oliver!" Fitz jumped to his feet. "I have never been so glad to see you."

"Stewkesbury." Lady Symington looked almost as pleased. "Perhaps you will be able to set everything straight. This lout"—she gestured toward Monsieur Leveque—"has somehow manipulated my daughter into—"

At her words a chorus of voices rose, making it impossible to understand anyone. A pained expression crossed the earl's face. His dog, on the other hand, seemed quite taken with the commotion and began to whirl and bark enthusiastically. Finally the earl raised the gold-knobbed cane he carried and brought it down on the floor with a sharp crack.

The noise stopped instantly. "Thank you." Stewkesbury looked at his brother. "Fitz, if you will join me in my study, perhaps you can explain how we acquired all of our, um, guests. Bostwick, I'd like a small collation, if you don't mind. I suggest that the rest of you get some sleep. Good night."

With that, the earl turned and walked away. The servants scurried off, Bostwick harrying the others before him. Fitz, with an apologetic glance at Eve, went after his brother, and everyone else began to break up as well. Eve sat for a moment, watching the activity around her. Then, with a sigh, she stood up and turned back to her room.

Now that the earl was back, she had a feeling her idyll was over.

Eve's trepidation had not diminished by the next morning. She could not help but worry that her time at Willowmere was almost up. The earl would be appalled to discover that under her chaperonage Lily had been on the verge of eloping with a man all but engaged to another woman. Whatever he decided about Lily and Neville's marrying, he would be bound to view Eve as an utter failure. And if he heard the gossip that was bound to circulate about her and Fitz after last night, he would whisk her away from Camellia as quickly as possible.

It came as no surprise to her, therefore, when a footman approached her as she was going down to breakfast and requested her presence in the earl's study as soon as she finished her meal. After that summons it was impossible for her to eat. She nibbled at a piece of toast and sipped some tea, relieved to find that there was no one at the table besides Gordon, who generally required only himself to carry on a conversation.

Eve soon excused herself and walked down the hallway to the earl's study, her stomach roiling with nerves. She knocked softly and entered the room on the earl's response. He stood up, smiling, and gestured for her to take a chair.

"Ah, Mrs. Hawthorne."

"Lord Stewkesbury." She sat down in the chair across from his desk. It was better, she thought, to broach the matter and get it over with. "I am sorry that you arrived home to find such turmoil."

"A trifle more people than I had expected, but then, with this family, I have come to expect the . . . unusual."

"You must feel that I have let you down tremendously." Eve squared her shoulders and faced him. "I am aware that I have failed you in my chaperonage of Lily."

To her surprise he chuckled. "My dear Mrs. Hawthorne, I have been assured that it was your efforts alone that kept the situation from being worse than it is. Lily and Camellia would be a test of any chaperone, and with the other distractions—the balloonist, the measles, your unexpected guests—frankly I am astounded at how well you have managed the whole thing."

"Honestly?" Eve stared at him. If it had been anyone other than the earl, she would have been certain that he was bamboozling her.

He nodded. "Of course. Fitz explained it to me. He should have sent Neville away earlier, of course. Indeed I am to blame for not foreseeing the possibility of the attraction. I should have sent Neville packing before I left for London. However, I am not sure that any of us could have withstood the force that is Lily Bascombe bent on true love. In any case I have given the match my blessing. I doubt that anyone more responsible than Neville would appeal to my cousin. His name and fortune are most respectable, and now that there is no impediment, I feel sure his father will approve of the marriage. His primary concern is to see Neville married without scandal, and I am sure that an alliance with the Talbot family will suit him."

"Oh. Well . . . I am very glad, then." Eve paused. "And Lady Symington will not, um, object?"

He smiled faintly. "I think I can persuade Lady Symington to see reason. None of this was my reason for seeing you. I must not keep you, as I am sure you will be wanting to speak to Fitz before he leaves for London. But I wanted to thank you for all you have done the last few weeks. Fitz told me of the responsibilities you took on after the household was struck by measles, how hard you have worked. It was far more than anyone could have expected of you. Please accept my gratitude."

"Of course." Eve was surprised that she could speak through lips that were suddenly bloodless and frozen. *Fitz is leaving for London?* The earl's words of thanks barely registered with that news reverberating in her brain. "I was happy to do so."

She stood up, as did the earl, and took her leave, barely aware of what she was saying, knowing only that she had to get away from there and by herself before she broke down. Leaving his office, she turned and walked swiftly toward the back of the house.

Obviously the earl believed Fitz would talk to her before he left. She knew that it was the sort of thing he would do. Fitz was too much of a gentleman to leave without a word of good-bye. He would tell her he was going, would express his regrets that their affair had come to an end. No doubt he would say that he held a great affection for her; perhaps he would even leave her with a discreet and elegant gift—a bracelet of precious stones, say.

Eve could not face that right now. She was too stunned, her emotions too raw. She knew that her only recourse was to get out of the house, to go where she could sit alone and think, where she could pull her tattered pride together and prepare herself to face Fitz.

She slipped out the back door and down the steps of the terrace into the garden. It was a little chilly for the dress she wore, but she could not return to the house for a shawl or her bonnet and gloves. She had to walk as far and as fast as she could.

It was foolish, really, to be so stunned. She had known this moment was coming. It was just that she had not expected it to arrive so suddenly, so swiftly. Yesterday she had been wrapped in Fitz's arms, warm and secure. Today he was returning to London. Leaving her.

She turned toward the herb garden, knowing that she could be sure of finding both a little sun and peace there. But barely had she sat down on the bench inside the garden than she heard the crunch of feet on the gravel walk leading up to the garden. She turned, annoyed with herself for having chosen a place with no other exit. Now she would have to meet someone, exchange at least a friendly greeting before she could leave. She started forward, thinking that she could pretend to be on the verge of leaving the garden when the visitor walked in, enabling her to slip away more quickly.

The newcomer stepped through the gate, and Eve's heart sank. It was Fitz.

"Hello, Fitz." She braced herself. "I'm sorry. I was about to leave."

His brows went up. "You just walked in here. I followed you."

She tried a smile and was acutely aware that it trembled slightly. "Yes. I should not have come out without a shawl. I must go back and—"

He answered her by stripping off his jacket and wrapping it around her shoulders. "There. That's better, isn't it?"

Eve wanted to cry out that it was not better at all. Now she was enveloped in the scent and warmth of him almost as surely as if he had put his arms around her. But she could not speak; she was too close to tears. She nodded and turned away, walking back toward the bench, struggling to bring her emotions under control.

She turned when she reached the bench, straightening her shoulders and facing him squarely. She had never been a coward, and she was not about to start now. Gathering all of her courage, she said, "I know what you are about to say."

"Do you?" He smiled. "I wondered if you did. I tried to tell you yesterday in the carriage and then again last night, but I was distracted by other things."

She remembered the moments, and she wondered if it would have been easier if he had told her then. Eve didn't think it would ever have been easy for her. It pierced her that Fitz seemed so lighthearted about it.

"The earl mentioned you were leaving for London, so it didn't take great prescience on my part. It's not a surprise, of course." She struggled for a careless tone to match his. "The country must have grown boring for you. If your responsibilities had not held you here, no doubt you would have left some time ago."

Fitz looked at her, his brow knitting. "Some time ago? What are you talking about? Why would I—"

"I appreciate that you wanted to tell me before you went. You are, as always, considerate. But I am a grown woman. I knew what lay before us when this started."

"Did you? Then you're a damned sight more knowledgeable than I." Fitz scowled. "What the hell are you talking about, Eve?"

"Your return to London. The—the end of our affair. You are ready to go back, move on."

"What? How did you hit on that idea? I know Oliver never told you that. Or is this your way of thwarting my proposal?"

Eve felt the blood leave her head, dropping to her extremities. She swayed. "Pro-proposal?"

He reached out quickly and put his arm around her, easing her onto the bench. "Yes, my proposal. That's why I'm going to London—to obtain a special license from the archbishop's office. I don't intend to wait three weeks for the banns to be read. I want to marry you as soon as I possibly can." He paused, then added a trifle hesitantly, "I mean, if you will agree to marry me."

Eve put a trembling hand to her mouth. "Oh. Oh my. That is why you're going to London?"

"Yes. But I learned from Royce's mistake not to go haring off on my own without asking the lady in question first. That is what I wanted to talk to you about." He sighed. "And now here I've mucked it all up and haven't even asked you."

"No. No, it was I who sent us off down this path," Eve assured him. She tried a smile. "It is not too late, you know, to ask."

Fitz grinned and went down on one knee before her. "Eve Hawthorne, will you do me the very great honor of marrying me?"

Eve hardly knew whether to laugh or cry or throw her arms around his neck and shriek "Yes!" Instinctively she firmly tamped down all such possibilities and asked, "Are you doing this because of what happened last night? Are you sacrificing yourself to protect my reputation? I don't want or need that. And I refuse to be a millstone about your neck. I—"

He held up a hand, covering her mouth. "My darling Eve, may I remind you that I am one of those fellows who is concerned only with my own pleasure and who goes through life doing exactly as I please? I am not asking you to marry me because I am worried about your reputation or Neville's insinuations or anything other than the fact that I am desperately in love with you and I do not wish to live another minute without you as my wife!" He removed his hand from her mouth. "Now, what is your answer?"

"Oh, Fitz!" Eve could barely speak for the tears suddenly clogging her throat. "You love me? Truly?"

"Yes! Yes, I love you. Truly, forever, and every other way there is."

"Then yes! Yes, I'll marry you!" She flung herself up and into his arms, wrapping her arms around his neck.

He kissed her soundly, then set her down, and an instant later pulled her back for another kiss. After a very long time he finally stepped back from Eve and looked down into her face.

"You have not said it to me, though, Eve. Do you love me—or are you just marrying me for my dashing good looks and enormous fortune?"

Eve let out a little gurgling laugh. "Those things have some consideration, of course. But oh, Fitz, I *do* love you so." She put her hands in his, lifting their joined hands to her heart and gazing up into his eyes. Her eyes were soft and lambent, filled with a glow and promise that were unmistakable.

"I love you," she told him. "Truly, forever, and every other way there is."

"Then kiss me again," he told her, and pulled her back into his arms.

Epilogue

It was a quiet wedding, held in the small church in the village, with only Lady Vivian, Neville, and the members of Fitz's family in attendance. After all, as Eve had pointed out when Vivian and Lily had tried to lure her into a grander ceremony, she was a widow, and they were being married by special license.

"You can expend all your efforts on Lily's wedding," she had told them. The earl, though he had granted his permission, had insisted that Lily wait until after her birthday to wed.

"That's true," Lily had agreed, her eyes shining. "But that doesn't mean we couldn't also have a lovely wedding for you."

But as they waited in the small anteroom in the church, neither Vivian nor Lily could find any fault with the arrangements.

"It's perfect," Lily told Eve, eyes shining. "The candles, the ivy, even the ribbons on the pews—it's all absolutely perfect. And just right for you. You look beautiful."

She did. Eve's slender figure was encased in a gown of cerulean blue with long sleeves, puffed and slashed at the shoulders, then fitted the rest of the way to her wrists. An overpetticoat of blond lace was pulled back on the sides to expose the blue satin beneath. In the back a short train fell from the shoulders to trail about a foot behind her. A cunning little hat of the same blue was pinned to her carefully arranged blond curls, with a short veil of net that covered without concealing the upper half of her face.

Eve had expected to wear one of her better gowns for her wedding. She had no idea how Fitz and Vivian had managed it, but when Fitz returned from London in just five days, special license in hand, he had also brought with him a package from Madame Arceneaux containing the gown and matching hat.

"You are beautiful," Vivian agreed, stepping forward to kiss her friend on the cheek. "You are even lovelier than the first time you married." She clapped her hand to her mouth. "Oh! Is it bad luck to mention that?"

"I don't know." Eve chuckled. "But I am sure that nothing is going to bring bad luck to me this day."

The door to the anteroom opened, and Camellia rushed in. Her gray eyes sparkled, and her cheeks were flushed with pink, and except for the fact that she was even thinner than usual, no one would have known that she had ever been sick.

"Everyone's ready," Cam told them. "You should see the chapel, Eve. It's lovely."

They were to be married in the small room that lay to the right of the main sanctuary, separated from the rest of the church by arched pillars. Used primarily for baptisms, it seated only a few rows of people and seemed the perfect cozy spot for an intimate ceremony. They had decorated it with a wealth of white candles, garlands of ivy, and ribbons of blue to match Eve's dress.

"Are they ready?" Eve asked, and Camellia nodded.

"Everyone's here. Fitz is waiting at the altar, and oh, he looks so handsome!" Camellia rushed over to hug her too. "I can't believe you're leaving us already."

"I'll be there in London when you start your Season, never fear. I won't leave you on your own."

"I wish we were all going to London right now," Lily added disconsolately.

"I like it here," Camellia said. "I could stay at Willowmere always, I think."

"With Lady Symington here?" Lily asked, cocking an eyebrow.

"No," Camellia retorted. "Not with Lady Symington. But they're leaving in a week. The doctor says Monsieur Leveque will be ready to travel by then."

"Thank goodness. Cousin Oliver is a miracle worker. I can't believe he got Lady S to agree to the wedding."

"Stewkesbury has a way about him," Vivian said, chuckling. "I think he used the carrot-and-stick approach, pointing out how Priscilla would be a spinster if she didn't marry Leveque, then telling her that he'd looked into Monsieur Leveque's background and found his family was aristocratic before the Revolution, so she's really marrying the grandson of a count."

"Except he refuses to use any title. *That* doesn't sit well with Priscilla's mother, I can tell you."

"I don't understand why Cousin Oliver looked into his background to begin with," Camellia said. "What did it matter who he was? He just crashed in our meadow."

"That was when everybody thought you were sweet on him," her sister Lily told her, grinning.

"What? Me?" Camellia looked stunned. "Why?"

"You seemed awfully interested in him," Lily retorted.

"We thought perhaps you liked him," Eve put in.

"Well, I did like him. I do. I like Priscilla too. They've told me they'll take me up in the balloon once they get it repaired." She paused, then said to Eve, "But I wasn't interested in him that way. I told you, I don't think I'm the sort to fall in love."

"Hear, hear." Vivian clapped her hands. "We shall remain determined spinsters, you and I. We shall form a club. None of these romantic women allowed."

"Ha. As if you weren't romantic," Eve told her. "That's exactly why you haven't married—because you're so romantic. I shall see both of you married, I'm sure. You just haven't found the right men yet."

Vivian sighed and shook her head. "There is no one more interested in everyone marrying than a woman in love. But I fear with me, my dear, your efforts will be fruitless. Camellia is only beginning, but I have been on the marriage market for years now. If there was a man for me out there, I would have found him."

"Perhaps you have and just don't know it," Eve retorted.

Her friend rolled her eyes and motioned her toward the door. "Enough of this nonsense. It's time for you to get married to the man *you* love."

Eve smiled, her stomach suddenly fluttering with nerves. She walked out of the room with her friends and around to the side entrance that led into the small chapel. The other three women slipped into the chapel and took their seats. Then Eve stepped in by herself.

It was a beautiful scene that lay before her—the quaint stone chapel, lit by a multitude of flickering white candles, her dearest friends waiting to witness the most important day of her life. And there, at the end of the short aisle, next to the priest, stood Fitz.

He was impossibly handsome in his formal black coat

and breeches, ruffles cascading down the front of his shirt. A ruby stickpin gleamed in the folds of his neckcloth, matching the rubies at his cuffs. But she knew that he would have been equally handsome to her if he had been clad in boots and buckskins.

Fitz smiled at her, and her heart leaped in response. She walked down the short aisle, her eyes fixed on his. The nerves in her stomach disappeared as she joined him and slipped her hand into his.

The priest began to speak. "Dearly beloved, we are gathered together here in the sight of God . . ."

At her first wedding, Eve remembered, she had been so nervous that afterward she could remember nothing that was said. This time was entirely different. She soaked up every word, engraved each vow on her heart as she said it. This was her life. Her love. And after this day nothing would ever be the same again.

When it came time for Fitz's vows he turned to Eve, their hands linked, and gazed down into her face, his eyes glowing with love. "I, Fitzhugh Alan Edward Talbot, take thee, Eve Childe Hawthorne, to be my wedded wife, to have and to hold from this day forward, for better, for worse, for richer, for poorer, in sickness and in health, to love and to cherish, till death us do part, according to God's holy ordinance; and thereto I plight thee my troth."

Eve made her own promise clearly, firmly, her heart pounding madly in her chest. Then, faster than seemed possible, the vicar was pronouncing them man and wife.

Fitz turned up her fragile little veil and bent to kiss her. His mouth was warm and soft on hers, and a tremor of joy shook her.

"I love you, Mrs. Talbot," he whispered. "And I intend to spend the rest of my life making you happy."

Eve let out a breathy little laugh of sheer joy. "I'll hold you to that."

Eve put her hand in his, and he raised it to his mouth, kissing her hand lightly. They turned and began to walk down the aisle into their new life.

Turn the page for a sneak peek
at the final book in the sparkling Willowmere series

AN AFFAIR WITHOUT END

by
New York Times bestselling author
Candace Camp

Coming soon from Pocket Star Books

London was cold, damp, and dirty.

And Lady Vivian Carlyle was delighted to be there.

As she swept into Lady Wilbourne's ballroom, she was relieved to see Lady Charlotte Ludley at the edge of the dance floor. Charlotte had been her friend since they were still in short skirts and had come out the year after Vivian had made her debut. But while Vivian had remained determinedly single all the years since, Charlotte had married Lord Ludley in her second Season and was now the proud mother of a lively brood of boys.

"Charlotte, how wonderful to see you. You are not usually here this early."

"Vivian! I am so happy to see you!" Charlotte squeezed Vivian's hands.

"I could not bear to stay away any longer," Vivian confessed. "'Tis almost five months since I was last in London. I think it's the first Little Season I've missed since I came out."

"I could scarcely believe you stayed at Halstead House with your uncle for so long—especially since there was an outbreak of measles."

"It was ghastly. I had to tend to Sabrina, and you can imagine how much I enjoyed that." Vivian rolled her eyes.

Sabrina was the young woman her uncle had married after his first wife died. She was only a few years older than Vivian herself, and their relationship was rocky, at best. "But I could not leave them in the lurch that way. And I did at least have the satisfaction of seeing Sabrina come all over in spots."

"That would have been worth any price. And there was more excitement at Willowmere, I understand. I don't know why I am never there when these things happen."

Willowmere was the country estate of the Talbot family, to which Charlotte belonged. It was only a few miles from Vivian's uncle's house, and it was on Vivian's frequent summer visits to her aunt and uncle that she and Charlotte had become friends. Willowmere was now the residence of Charlotte's cousin Oliver, the ninth Earl of Stewkesbury—and of his set of American cousins, the Bascombe sisters.

She laughed now, recalling the events of the preceding autumn. "Things do tend to happen wherever the Bascombe girls go. If it isn't kidnappers popping up, it's French balloonists falling from the sky. Indeed, I found Marchester sadly lacking in excitement after being around your cousins for a few months."

"Tell me, which did you miss more—Camellia's and Lily's escapades or your exchanges with Stewkesbury?" Charlotte's eyes twinkled.

"Stewkesbury!" Vivian grimaced. "As if I would miss *his* sniping."

The last thing she intended to admit to her friend was that more than once while she was at her father's house, she had found herself thinking of some particularly clever remark she could make to the earl, only to remember, with a distinct sense of disappointment, that Stewkesbury was not around.

"And here I thought it was usually *you* sniping at *him*."

Vivian let out an inelegant snort. "I would not have to snipe at him if the man didn't insist on being so stiff-necked and self-righteous."

Charlotte shook her head, making a sound that was half laugh, half sigh. "And Oliver is never so stiff-necked as when you are about."

"Then you see what I mean." Vivian shrugged. "The two of us simply cannot get along."

"Yes, but what is odd, I think, is how much the two of you seem to *enjoy* not getting along."

Vivian glanced at her friend, startled, and found Charlotte watching her with a knowing expression. "I haven't the faintest idea what you're talking about."

"Mm. Yet, if I remember correctly, you admitted only a few months ago that you once had a *tendre* for Oliver."

Color bloomed along Vivian's cheekbones. "When I was fourteen! Good heavens, I hope you don't think I am still carrying some sort of . . . of schoolgirl infatuation with the man."

"No. I am sure not. If you were interested in a man, I feel sure you would act upon it."

Vivian tilted her head to the side thoughtfully. "I suppose I would . . . *if* there were such a man."

"And if you were aware how you felt."

"I beg your pardon?" Vivian's eyes widened with surprise. "Are you saying . . . do you think . . . ?"

Charlotte simply waited, her eyebrows faintly raised in interest as she watched her usually articulate friend fumble for words.

"I am not interested in Oliver," Vivian said at last. "And, believe me, I know my own feelings."

"Of course."

"I will admit," Vivian went on candidly, "that Stewkesbury is a handsome man. That much is obvious."

"Of course," her friend agreed soberly.

"There is nothing to mislike in his face or form."

"No, indeed."

"He is intelligent, if often provokingly narrow in his thinking. He rides well. He dances well."

"It goes without saying." Charlotte's eyes danced, though she kept her lips pressed firmly together.

"I am sure that he is as eagerly pursued by marriage-minded young ladies as is my brother."

"Mm."

"But I am not marriage-minded. And I am not foolish enough to think that there is any possibility of romance between Stewkesbury and me."

"Still, I cannot help but notice that you seem . . . happy . . . when you and Cousin Oliver are engaged in one of your clashes."

Vivian's lips curved up faintly. "Sometimes it *is* rather fun."

"Even though you dislike him."

"I don't dislike him," Vivian protested quickly.

"No?" Charlotte cut her eyes toward her slyly.

"Of course not. Why, there is no one I would trust more if I needed help." She paused, then added judiciously, "Though he would, of course, make a perfect nuisance of himself afterward telling me how foolish I had been."

Her friend chuckled. "Indeed he would."

"But the two of us? We are as unlikely as oil and water."

From behind her came a deep male voice. "Lady Vivian. Cousin Charlotte."

Vivian's stomach dropped, and her face went suddenly hot, her hands cold. "Stewkesbury!"

Stewkesbury had seen his cousin and Lady Vivian the moment he stepped into the ballroom. Indeed, he thought, it would have been hard to miss her. She was dressed in rich black satin overlaid with a filmy material of the same color, a stark contrast to the pale white skin of her shoulders and elegantly narrow neck above it. Her flame-red hair burned like a beacon.

It was one of the many annoying things about the woman, he thought. She never blended in, never entered a room quietly. She was always immediately, flamboyantly *there*. He started across the room toward her, wondering as he did so how she managed to make a simple black ball gown look so thoroughly elegant yet also seductive. Vivian Carlyle was never anything but a lady, stylish and tasteful, though there was something about her that made one think of secret, illicit passion. Oliver was not sure if it was the way her lips curved up in a slow smile, her green eyes lighting, as if only the person she looked at shared in her humor, or perhaps it was the way the delicate hairs curled upon the milk-white skin of her slender neck, or maybe the way she carried herself, without stiffness or shyness, her curvaceous body pliant and soft.

Whatever it was, Oliver was certain that only a dead man could look at Vivian and not imagine, at least for an instant, having her in his arms, that soft skin beneath his hands. He had imagined so himself on more than one occasion, and he was more immune to the lady's charms than most. After all, he had known her when she was a gawky girl, all sharp angles and giggles and mischief, that wealth of fiery hair tamed into bright orange braids down her back. She had been the bane of his summers down from Oxford, always up to some trick or other with his cousin. And she still had the ability to annoy him as almost no one else could.

His resolve was tested the moment Vivian turned to greet him and he received the full impact of her dress up close. The heart-shaped neckline was low and wide, skimming the soft tops of her breasts and leaving much of her chest and shoulders bare. The rich satin hugged her breasts, and the jet bugle beads that adorned the neck seemed designed to draw one's eye to the swelling creamy white tops. Desire slammed through him, fierce and immediate, and it was only years-long training that kept his face expressionless.

"Stewkesbury." Vivian smiled at him in that way she did, a way that hinted of secrets and laughter.

Oliver was aware that Vivian considered him a hopelessly dull sort, and he often had the faint suspicion that she was laughing at him, a fact that served to make him even more unbending in her presence. Now, in response to her greeting, he gave her a punctiliously correct bow. Despite his best efforts, his gaze kept returning to Vivian's bosom. *Damn the woman—the way she was dressed was bloody distracting.*

"I am surprised to find you here alone," Vivian said. "I know how infrequently you are wont to visit London."

He wasn't sure why her assumption irritated him, but it did. "On the contrary, my lady, I am often in the city. I don't know why people persist in thinking that I am always stuck away up at Willowmere."

"Because no one ever sees you around."

"I am in London. I simply do not spend my time at parties."

"Ah, I see." A smile twitched at the corner of Vivian's mouth. "No doubt you are occupied in far more useful activities."

Sometimes he thought how delightful it would be to do or say something outrageous, just to see the surprise that would flare on Vivian's face. But, of course, that would be an entirely silly thing to do, so he said only, "I am usually here on business."

His cousin, who had been watching their exchange, spoke up for the first time. "Oh, Oliver, surely that does not take up all your evenings as well. You might at least go to a dinner or to a ball or two."

Vivian glanced at Oliver, her eyes glinting a little. "I suspect, dear Charlotte, that your cousin finds such things as balls or dinners tedious. Isn't that true, Stewkesbury?"

"Not at all," he responded drily, meeting Vivian's glance with something of a challenge in his gray eyes. "I find them much too stimulating for someone of my sedate nature. I might be utterly overcome."

Vivian let out a little laugh. "Now, that is something I should like to see. I have always wondered what it would take to overcome you."

"Ah, Lady Vivian, you should know that 'tis easily done. You have accomplished it on many an occasion."

Vivian hesitated, looking faintly surprised. Then she furled her fan and reached out to tap him lightly on the arm with it, her eyes twinkling, a smile lurking at the corners of her mouth. "A very pretty compliment, my lord. I am shocked."

"You do not think me capable of it?"

"Oh, no, you are capable enough. You forget, I have heard you talk to others. But I would not have thought you willing to hand a compliment to me."

He raised his brows. "What a picture you hold of me, my lady. Do I appear such a boor?"

"Indeed, no, not a boor. But not capable, perhaps, of polite flattery."

It was Oliver's turn to look surprised. Polite flattery? Could Vivian possibly think that he was not aware of her beauty or her powerful effect on men? Did she not realize that even now, as he stood here, chatting, carefully keeping his features composed, his nerves tingled with an awareness of her? That her perfume teased at his senses and his very blood hummed? He presumed that she had chosen her dress and styled her hair, dabbed a scent behind her ears, in the hope of eliciting this exact response. She must know how men reacted to her. The only possible reason for her surprise was that she did not expect him to react as a man.

The idea galled him. Did he appear so sober, so boring to her?

"Dearest Vivian," he said, his tone taking on a sharper edge, "I suspect you would be surprised what I am capable of."

Her eyes rounded a little, and he had the satisfaction of knowing that his words had taken her aback. Ignoring his cousin's indrawn breath of surprise, he went on, extending his hand to Vivian. "Perhaps, my lady, you would favor me with this dance."

What in the world had come over the man? For an instant, Vivian could only stare at Stewkesbury in astonishment. It wasn't as if he had never asked her to dance or even that he had not paid her a compliment. But there was something different about tonight. Something in his eyes, in his tone, when he spoke to her. The compliment he had paid her had not been extravagant, but neither had it been the bland, customary acknowledgment of her looks that one heard at every turn. It had been . . . almost flirtatious. And his words before his invitation to dance had carried a dare. Indeed, his very invitation to her seemed almost a challenge.

Well, a challenge was certainly something Vivian never turned down.

And if you missed the first book
in Camp's delightful series . . .

here's a special look at

A LADY NEVER TELLS

Now available from Pocket Star Books

Mary Bascombe was scared. She had been frightened before—one could not have grown up in a new and dangerous land and not have faced something that set one's heart
to beating double-time. But this wasn't like the time they
had seen the bear nosing around their mother's clothesline.
Or even like the way her heart had leapt into her throat
the day her stepfather had grabbed her arm and pulled her
against him, his breath reeking of alcohol. Then she had
known what to do—how to back slowly and quietly into
the house and load the pistol, or how to stomp down hard
on Cosmo's instep so that he released her with a howl of
pain.

No, this was an entirely new sensation. She was in a
strange city filled with strange people, and she had absolutely no idea what to do next. She felt . . . lost.

Mary took another glance around her at the bustling
docks. She had never seen so much noise and activity or
so many people in one place in her life. She had thought
the docks in Philadelphia were busy, but that was nothing
compared to London. All around them were piles of goods,
with stevedores loading and unloading them, and people

hurried about, all seemingly with someplace to be and little time to get there.

There were no women. The few whom she had seen disembark from ships had been whisked away in carriages with their male companions. Indeed, all the passengers from their own ship were long gone, only she and her sisters still standing here in a forlorn group beside their small pile of luggage. The shadows were beginning to lengthen; it would not be long until night began to fall. And though Mary might be a naïve American cast adrift in London, she was smart enough to know that the London docks at night were no place for four young women alone.

The problem was that Mary didn't know what to do next. She had expected there to be an inn not far from where they left their ship. But as soon as they disembarked, she had realized that the area around these docks would not house an inn where a respectable group of young women could stay. Indeed, she was reluctant for them even to walk through the narrow streets she could see stretching out in front of her. A few hacks had come by and Mary had tried to stop one or two, but the drivers had simply rolled past, ignoring her. No doubt they presumed from the rather ragtag pile of luggage that Mary and her sisters would not be a good fare.

They could not stay here. Unless a carriage happened by soon, they would be forced to pick up their bags and walk into the narrow, dingy streets beyond the docks. Mary glanced uncertainly around her. Several of the men loading the ships had been casting their eyes toward Mary and her sisters for some time. Now, as her gaze fell on one of them, he gave her a bold grin. Mary stiffened, returning her most freezing look, and pivoted away slowly and deliberately.

She studied her three sisters—Rose, the next oldest to Mary and the acknowledged beauty of the family, with her limpid blue eyes and thick black hair; Camellia, whose gray eyes were, as always, no-nonsense and alert, her dark gold hair efficiently braided and wrapped into a knot at the crown of her head; and Lily, the youngest and most like their father, with her light brown, sun-streaked hair and gray-green eyes.

All three girls gazed back at Mary with a steadfast trust that only made the icy knot in her stomach clench tighter. Her sisters were counting on her to take care of them, just as Mama had counted on her to get the girls away from their stepfather's house after their mother's death and across the ocean to London, to the safety and security of their grandfather's home. Mary had managed the first part of it. But all of that, she knew, would be for naught if she failed now. She had to get her sisters someplace safe and proper for the night, and then she had to face a grandfather none of them had ever met—the man who had tossed out his own daughter for defying his wishes—and convince him to take in that same daughter's children. Instinctively, Mary clutched her slender stitched-leather satchel closer to her chest.

At that moment, a figure came hurtling toward them and careened into Mary, sending her sprawling to the ground. For an instant, she was too startled to move or even to think. Then she realized that her hands were empty. *Her satchel!* Frantically, she glanced around her. It wasn't there.

"My case! He stole our papers!" Mary bounded to her feet and swung around, spying the running figure. "Stop! Thief!"

Pausing only long enough to cast a look at Rose and point to the luggage, Mary lifted her skirts and took off running after the man. Rose, interpreting her sister's look with the ease of years of familiarity, went to stand next to their bags, but Lily and Camellia were hot on Mary's heels. Mary ran faster than she had ever run, her heart pounding with terror.

Everything important to them was in that case—everything that could prove their honesty to a disbelieving relative. Without those papers, they had no hope; they would be stranded here in a huge, horrid, completely strange town with nowhere to go and no one to ask for help. She had to get the satchel back!

Her sisters were right behind her; indeed, Camellia, the swiftest of them all, had almost caught up with her. But the wiry thief who had taken her case was faster than any of them. As they rounded a corner, she spied him half a block ahead, and realized, with a wrenching despair, that they could not catch him.

A few yards beyond the thief, two men stood outside a door, chatting. In a last, desperate effort, Mary screamed, "Stop him! Thief!"

The two men turned and looked at her, but they made no move toward the man, and Mary knew with a sinking heart that her sisters' future was disappearing before her eyes.

Sir Royce Winslow strolled out of the gambling hell, giving his gold-headed cane a casual twirl before he set its tip on the ground. A handsome man in his early thirties, with blond hair and green eyes, he was not the sort one expected to see emerging from a dockside gaming establishment. His broad shoulders were encased in a coat of blue superfine so elegantly cut that it could only have been made by Weston, just as the polished Hessians on his feet were clearly the work of Hoby. The fitted fawn trousers and white shirt, the starched and intricately tied cravat, the plain gold watch chain and fobs all bespoke a man of refinement and wealth—and one far too knowing to have been caught in the kind of place frequented, as his brother Fitz would say, by "sharps and flats."

"Well, Gordon, you've led me on another merry chase,"

Sir Royce said, turning to the man who had followed him out the door.

His companion, a man barely out of his teens, looked a trifle abashed at the comment. Unlike Sir Royce's, Gordon's clothes evinced the unmistakable extremes of style and color that branded him a fop. His coat was a yellow reminiscent of an egg yolk, and the patterned satin waistcoat beneath it was lavender, his pantaloons striped with the same shade. The shoulders of the coat were impossibly wide and stuffed with padding, and the waist nipped in tightly. A huge boutonnière was thrust through his lapel, and his watch chain jangled with its load of fobs.

Gordon drew himself up in an exaggeratedly dignified manner, though the picture he hoped to create was somewhat marred by the fact that he could not keep from swaying as he stood there. "I know. I beg your pardon, Cousin Royce. Jeremy should never have told you."

"Don't blame your brother," the other man replied mildly. "He was worried about you—and rightly so. You were being fleeced quite royally back there."

Gordon flushed and started to argue, but the other man stopped him with an adroitly cocked eyebrow and went on, "You'd best be grateful to Jeremy for coming to me instead of going to the earl."

"I should think so!" Gordon admitted in shocked tones. "Cousin Oliver would have prosed on forever about the family dignity and what I owed to my parents."

"With good cause."

"Here, now, don't tell me you and Cousin Fitz never kicked up a lark!" the younger man protested.

A faint smile curved Sir Royce's well-formed lips. "We might have done so, yes—but I would never have gotten myself kicked out of Oxford and then gone to town to throw myself into yet more scrapes." He narrowed his gaze. "And I would never have taken it into my head to wear that yellow coat."

"But it's all the crack!" Gordon exclaimed.

However, his companion was no longer listening to him. Sir Royce's attention had been caught by the sight of a man tearing down the street toward them, clutching a small leather satchel. What was even more arresting was that running after him was a young woman in a blue frock, her dark brown hair loose and streaming out behind her and her gown hiked up almost to her knees, exposing slender stocking-clad legs. Behind her were two more young women, running with equal fervor, bonnets dangling by their ribbons or tumbling off altogether, their faces flushed.

"Stop him!" the woman in the lead shouted. "Thief!"

Royce gazed at the scene in some amazement. Then, as the thief drew almost abreast of him, he casually thrust his cane out, neatly catching the runner's feet and sending him tumbling to the ground. The man landed with a thud and the case went flying from his hands, skidding across the street and coming to a stop against a lamppost.

Cursing, the runner tried to scramble to his feet, but Royce planted a foot on his back and firmly pressed him down.

"Gordon, fetch that leather satchel, will you? There's a good lad."

Gordon was gaping at the thief twisting and flailing around under Sir Royce's booted foot, but at the older man's words, he picked up the case, weaving only slightly.

"Thank you!" The woman at the head of the pack trotted up to them and stopped, panting. The other two pulled up beside her, and for a moment the two men and three women gazed at each other with considerable interest.

They were, Sir Royce thought, a veritable bevy of beauties, even flushed and disheveled as they were, but it was the one in front who intrigued him most. Her hair was a deep chocolate brown and her eyes an entrancing mingling of blue and green that made him long to draw closer to determine the precise color. There was a firm set to her chin that, along with her generous mouth and prominent cheekbones, gave her face an unmistakable strength. Moreover, that mouth had a delectably plump bottom lip with a most alluring little crease down the center of it. It was, he thought, impossible to see those lips and not think of kissing them.

"You are most welcome," Sir Royce replied, pulling his booted foot off the miscreant's back in order to execute a bow.

The thief took advantage of this gesture to spring to his feet and run, but Royce's hand lashed out and caught him by his collar. He glanced inquiringly at the women.

"Do you want to press charges? Should we take him to a magistrate?"

"No." The first woman shook her head. "As long as I have my case back, that is all that matters."

"Very well." Sir Royce looked at the man he held in his grip. "Fortunately, the lady has a kind heart. You may not be so lucky next time."

He released the thief, who scrambled away and vanished around a corner, and turned back to the group of young women. "Pray, allow me to introduce myself—Sir Royce Winslow, at your service. And this young chap is my cousin, Mr. Harrington."

"I am Mary Bascombe," the young woman replied without hesitation. "And these are my sisters Camellia and Lily."

"Appropriately so, for you make a lovely bouquet."

Mary Bascombe responded to this flattery with a roll of

her eyes. "My mother had an exceeding fondness for flowers, I fear."

"Then tell me, Miss Bascombe, how did it happen that you are not named for a flower?"

"Oh, but I am," she responded, smiling, and a charming dimple popped into her cheek. "My name is actually Marigold." She watched him struggle to come up with a polite response, and chuckled. "Don't worry. You need not pretend it isn't horrid. That is why I go by Mary. But . . ." She shrugged. "I suppose it could have been worse. Mother could have named me Mugwort or Delphinium."

Royce chuckled, growing more intrigued by the instant. The girls were all lovely, and Mary, at least, spoke as perfect English as any lady—even though there was a certain odd accent he could not quite place. Looking at their fresh, appealing faces or hearing her speech, he would have presumed that she and her sisters were young gentlewomen. But their clothes were not anything that a young lady would wear, even one just up from the country. The dresses and hairstyles were plain and several years out of date, as though the sisters had never seen a fashion book. But, more than that, the girls behaved with the most astonishing lack of decorum.

There was no sign of an older female chaperoning them. And they had just gone running through the streets with no regard for their appearance or the fact that their bonnets had come off. Then they had stood here, regarding him straightforwardly with never a blush or averted gaze or a giggle, as if it were perfectly ordinary to converse with strange men. Of course, they could hardly be expected to follow the dictum of not speaking to a man without having been properly introduced, given the way they had met. But no well-bred young lady would have casually offered up her name to a stranger even if he had helped her. And she certainly would not have volunteered the girls' first names as Mary Bascombe had just cheerfully done. Nor would she have commented in that unrestrained way regarding her mother's naming them. Most of all—what in the world were they doing down here by the docks?

"Are you—Americans?" he asked abruptly.

Mary laughed. "Yes. How did you know?"

"A lucky guess," he replied with a faint smile.

Mary smiled back, and her face flooded with light. Royce's hand tightened involuntarily on the handle of his cane, and he forgot what he had been about to say.

Mary, too, seemed suddenly at a loss for words, and she glanced away, color rising in her cheeks. Her hands went to her hair, as though she had suddenly realized its tumbled-down state, and she fumbled to repin it.

"I—oh, dear, I seem to have lost my hat." She glanced around.

"If I may be so bold, Miss Bascombe. You and your sisters are—well, this is not a very savory area, I fear. Are you by chance lost?"

"No." Mary straightened her shoulders and returned his gaze. "We aren't lost."

Behind her, one of her sisters let out an inelegant snort. "No, just stranded."

"Stranded?"

"We got off the ship this afternoon," explained the youngest-looking of the Bascombe sisters, turning large gray-green eyes on him. Her voice lowered dramatically. "We are all alone here, and we haven't any idea where to go. You see—"

"Lily!" Mary cut in sharply. "I am sure that Mr. Winslow isn't interested in hearing our tale." She turned to Sir Royce. "Now, if you will be so kind as to hand back our case, we will be on our way."

"Sir Royce," he corrected her gently.

"What?"

"My name. 'Tis Sir Royce, not Mr. Winslow. And I will be happy to return your case." He plucked it from Gordon's clasp and handed it to Mary but kept hold of it, saying, "However, I cannot simply walk away and leave three young ladies alone in this disreputable part of the city."

"It is all right, really," Mary argued.

"I insist. I will escort you to . . ." He paused significantly.

"An inn," Mary said firmly, and tugged the case from his hand. Her chin went up a little. "Indeed, we are most grateful for your help, sir. If you will but direct us toward an appropriate inn, we shall not bother you anymore."

Sir Royce bowed to her, schooling his face to hide his amusement. Her words were a dismissal as much as a thanks, he knew. Well, he thought, Miss Mary Bascombe might find dismissing him was easier said than done.